THE MAIDEN AND HER MONSTER

THE MAIDEN AND HER MONSTER

MADDIE MARTINEZ

TOR

TOR PUBLISHING GROUP

NEW YORK

This is a work of fiction. All of the characters, organizations, and events portrayed in this novel are either products of the author's imagination or are used fictitiously.

THE MAIDEN AND HER MONSTER

Copyright © 2025 by Maddie Martinez

Excerpt from *The Poetry of Kabbalah: Mystical Verse from the Jewish Tradition* © 2012 by Yale University Press, translated and annotated by Peter Cole © 2012. Reprinted by permission of Yale University Press.

All rights reserved.

Map by Rhys Davies

A Tor Book
Published by Tom Doherty Associates / Tor Publishing Group
120 Broadway
New York, NY 10271

www.torpublishinggroup.com

Tor® is a registered trademark of Macmillan Publishing Group, LLC.

EU Representative: Macmillan Publishers Ireland Ltd, 1st Floor, The Liffey Trust Centre, 117–126 Sheriff Street Upper, Dublin 1, DO1 YC43

The Library of Congress Cataloging-in-Publication Data is available upon request.

ISBN 978-1-250-36775-4 (hardcover)
ISBN 978-1-250-36776-1 (ebook)

The publisher of this book does not authorize the use or reproduction of any part of this book in any manner for the purpose of training artificial intelligence technologies or systems. The publisher of this book expressly reserves this book from the Text and Data Mining exception in accordance with Article 4(3) of the European Union Digital Single Market Directive 2019/790.

Our books may be purchased in bulk for specialty retail/wholesale, literacy, corporate/premium, educational, and subscription box use. Please contact MacmillanSpecialMarkets@macmillan.com.

First Edition: 2025

Printed in the United States of America

10 9 8 7 6 5 4 3 2 1

For my grandparents.
What are my words but your words? My story but your story?
May your memories live on through the pages of this book.
I love and miss you both dearly.

Lei
Orzegali Mountains
Naška Slova
KINGDOM of ORDOBAV
VALÓN
VIGARY KINGDOM
Orlon Clock
Yahadi Quarter
MAVETÉH
Leirit River
KINGDOM of AGAMERE
ESKRAVÉ
Jašni River
Cedyz Forest
Vyš
Szaj-Nev
BALKISK KINGDOM
RHAŠKAN EMPIRE

Twenty-two letters to start with.

He engraved, quarried, and weighed,

    exchanged and combined—

and with them formed all of creation

and all that He was destined to fashion.

. . . .

From here on in consider

what a mouth can't utter

and what the ear can't hear . . .

Sefer Yetzirah (Book of Creation)
Circa Third to Sixth Century AD, trans. Peter Cole

PART
One

CHAPTER 1

The forest ate the girls who wandered out after dark.

Once the sun sank below the horizon, the villagers closed their doors and shuttered their windows. The dim, tinted orange glow of tallow candles became the only wash of light spilling onto the streets. Inside the houses lining the dirt roads, families gathered. They told stories in hushed tones, animated by hands making shadow figures in the candlelight. Braided bread cooked slowly in ovens and stoves boiled stock and vegetables for supper.

In one such house, a woman sat on her knees, elbows leaning on the window's edge as she gazed out to the barren street. Over the line of sturdy stone houses, the shektal bell rang. Her skin prickled hard with goose bumps. The bell sounded every night save the Sabbath, and every night its warning melody, signaling curfew, crawled inside her skin.

She focused instead on the cool touch of the window. When she breathed, fog weaved like a spider's web on the glass, crawling up and wide. She drew her finger up the pane, then looped it around and around to paint a flower on the window.

"Malka."

The voice was as warm as the candles puddling light into the room.

"Baby, please get away from the window. I don't like when you linger near it."

"Yes, Imma," Malka said, pushing from the ledge. She fell into her mother's waiting arms and rested her head between the bones of her chest. Malka's hands tightened around Imma's waist, too aware of her mother's sharp ribs and protruding collarbones.

Imma grasped Malka's cheeks between her cold, brittle hands. "It's time to light the yahrzeit candle."

"Without Abba?"

"Your father is on another Rayga hunt. You know how that goes. He'll either join us halfway through supper or stumble in at sunrise stinking of wine."

Imma gently rubbed her calloused thumb along the gash decorating Malka's cheek, half scabbed over but still bruised. The flickering candles made Imma's eyes, normally the bright green of spring leaves, a hollow forest dark. Imma's gaze softened, for she knew what had made the gash in her skin. *Who* had made it. Shame clawed up Malka's throat, but she swallowed it down.

Malka gritted her teeth. "The men should not have a Rayga hunt while the mourner's prayer is being sung in every household in Eskravé."

Imma tucked a curl behind Malka's ear. "To them, vengeance is a mourner's prayer. However unholy you may think it is."

In the kitchen, Malka's two sisters stood against the small, rectangular wooden table decorated with an embroidered cloth and the intricate copper plate meant to catch the dripping candle wax.

Hadar, the youngest of the siblings at only eight years old, grinned at Malka as she and Imma entered the room. Her smile was all crooked teeth, brown eyes doe-like in a way Malka hoped she would never outgrow. When a piece of Hadar's raven black hair fell into her face, she puffed her cheeks to blow it aside.

Malka chuckled, having done the same many times with her unruly curls.

Her other sister Danya, five years younger than Malka at eighteen, held the match in her hand. Where Malka and Hadar's hair was unruly and black like Abba's, Danya had gotten Imma's curly golden locks which fell gracefully around her face.

Danya stretched out her lanky arms. "Would you like to light it?"

Malka gripped the match and stepped close to the candle. As she struck the match against the tinder, she held her breath. This part was always sacred to her—the creation of light as divine, the transition from everyday life to the holy.

She began to sing.

The prayer was soft, familiar. It rolled off her tongue like honey, words shaped by memory and heartbreak. Malka could hardly believe there was a time when she lit the mourner's candle less often. A time before the woods began its haunting, and the monster, its hunger.

A monster which had become so feared, her village had affixed it a name: the Rayga.

With each word sung, Malka remembered the faces of the girls claimed by the woods, and the monster within:

A young girl of five, too caught up in her game of chase with her twin brother to notice the sun's last rays falling through the burly copse of trees.

A woman of twenty, who stole away to the woods with her lover to escape the watchful eye of her parents, and in her lust, did not see the day slip to night.

A grandmother of seventy, who fell asleep by her husband's grave, situated within the forest's grasp.

And Chaia. Taken a year ago. The anniversary of her loss prompting the burning of the mourner's candle tonight.

The prayer turned to ash in her mouth.

⚹

Later that night, Malka sat on the floor of the bedroom she shared with her sisters as they made paper cuttings to decorate their house for *Bayit Ohr*, the upcoming winter festival of lights. It was a quiet night, as they all had become once the curfew bell rang. Only the faint rustle of trees in the wind and the crackling of dim fires broke through the weighty silence.

It was on these still, quiet nights Malka remembered Chaia most. The silk brown of her hair, always brushed into smooth waves, falling to her shoulders. The mischievous glint in her eye as they would escape into the night to tell haunting stories. During the day, they each had their duties; but once the sun set, they were free to talk about anything and everything under the dark cover of the sky and its glimmering stars.

"I know you miss her," Hadar said, bringing Malka out of her reverie. The graphite she had traced onto her paper bled through the page, ruining it.

Malka set her ruined paper cutting aside and swallowed any grief with it. "Everyone misses her, *Achoti*. It's a time of mourning for the village."

"But you miss her most," Hadar responded. She smoothed her thumb on the edge of a cut she had made, perfecting the shape. Her creation was already beautiful, with patterns of stars, moons, and intricately cut block letters lining the paper. Vines of ivy wove around the letters like pillars, shaded by half-sketched lemon trees. Malka imagined what it would look like once it glistened with color, vibrant as the stained-glass windows on Eskravé's shul when the sun peered in through the glass.

Even Danya's paper cutting was beginning to take shape—the sketch of an oak tree with its impressive root system shaped into the letters of the ancient Yahadi holy language.

The beauty made Malka long for the Eskravé of her childhood. Like the Rayga, the villagers also gave the woods a new name when it soured: Mavetéh. *Into death.*

But that was not always what Malka knew it as. Before it was Mavetéh, it was called Kratzka Šujana in her language, named for the forest's elder trees and their thick, gnarled branches.

"It was not always like this, you know," Malka said, remembering Kratzka Šujana. "The curfew and the mourning."

Hadar licked the graphite smeared on her hand. "What was it like?"

Malka patted her leg, beckoning Hadar. Her sister smiled big and settled into Malka's lap. Malka wrapped her hand around Hadar's curls like the vines of ivy on her paper cutting.

Eyes closed, Malka pulled forth the shaded memories of a vibrant Eskravé, known to her only five years before, where birds sang their melodies, and the breeze carried the hum of violins from the shul during evening services. When Imma would take Malka and Danya to a meadow in Kratzka Šujana and teach them about the flowers sprouting there. Danya, only thirteen, would hold the basket in her arms as Malka plucked the flowers. They would pick marigold and foxglove for Imma's medicinal uses, and woad and madder for Chaia's parents to use as fabric dye.

Eskraven villagers took pride in the goods they made—from clothing and furniture to food prepared according to Yahadi law. Families in Eskravé went back generations, and trade specialties carried down through bloodlines.

Chaia had hated the unchanging nature of her village, the clear path it paved for their lives, but it was something Malka cherished.

"I wish I could pick flowers, like you both did."

Malka brushed a kiss on Hadar's forehead. "Hopefully you will soon."

"Do you think Abba will ever find the Rayga?"

"The men have certainly invested enough alcohol into their Rayga hunts. Better be worth something," Danya responded, eyes still fixed on her own craft.

Malka glared at her. "There's no use speaking like that in front of our little sister."

Danya rolled her eyes, still focused on her meticulous brushstrokes. "Malka, you have to be kidding me. Hadar isn't sheltered from the fact that every man comes back drunk from their heroic Rayga hunt. Especially not when one of the men is Abba."

"That doesn't mean—"

The loud bang of the front door slamming shut rattled the wooden beams in their room. A deep, raspy laugh filled the air, which left the argument dead on both sisters' lips.

"Stay here, I'll go see if there's news," Malka said.

She lifted Hadar from her lap, closing the door behind her as she left the room.

In the kitchen, Abba sat defeatedly on a creaky wooden chair. Imma bent over him, wiping at the dirt clinging to his cheeks and around his nose.

In the back corner of the room, their hearth blazed, flames licking a suspended iron pot. The boiling water growled and spilled over the lip, sizzling when it slapped the hot coal beneath.

Malka ran to it, adjusting the trammel hook so the pot hung higher off the heat.

"How was the Rayga hunt, Abba?" Malka asked over her shoulder.

"Nothing," Abba spat, running his hand through his hair. "Not as if we ever get to stay and search long, a bunch of women these men are. One sound and they go running."

"Did you collect any of the herbs I asked for?" Imma asked, squeezing out the dirty rag into the bucket by her side.

"It was dark. I couldn't tell the difference between black perphona and the poisonous plant I brought you last time."

Imma's face fell before frustration tightened her jaw. "I told you, there's a bright white variegation that runs through the black perphona. Devil's alphonsa is completely black."

"*You* try finding the time to wander around *Mavetéh* and stare at plants, No'omi!"

Abba said the forest's name like a slur. Malka shivered, wondering if the woods could hear its name said with vitriol in the darkness.

Imma brushed her wet hands on her apron, decorating the stained white cloth with streaks of muck. "We'll have nothing by the month's end without that herb. Sick people are showing up at our door every day now. I'm going to have to start turning them away."

Eskravé was never a wealthy village, but it wasn't a poor one, either, before Kratzka Šujana became Mavetéh. But the forest's curse brought more than the fear of stolen maidens to Eskravé. In the months before the Rayga took its first maiden half a decade ago, a wickedness had descended upon the forest. Felled trees rotted before woodcarvers could shape them, animals became rabid and inedible, and many plants began to shrivel and die. They had chalked the change up to an unusually long winter—until spring came without its normal growth, and her village could barely make use of Kratzka Šujana at all.

Then, they found the first woman's body.

Abba tapped his fingers on the table. "Then make the trip south to Szaj-Nev with the traders and get more there."

Szaj-Nev might be free of monsters, but it was not an old-growth forest like Kratzka Šujana, and black perphona struggled to grow there. Though Mavetéh had shriveled up many of the plants that had once grown beneath its trees, pockets of black perphona remained. A blessing from Yohev, Imma called it.

"Maybe I should just go into Mavetéh," Imma said. "It would not be so dangerous if the sun has not yet set. I would know what to look for. It would be quick."

Malka's chest seized. She imagined the blackened copse of trees, gouging into Imma's chest and squeezing her heart until it burst like an overripe plum.

"No," Malka said fiercely. "It's not worth the risk."

"Listen to your daughter, No'omi. She speaks sense."

Imma crossed her boney arms. "There's no sense to any of it. We go into Mavetéh, we die. We avoid it but spend all our resources getting materials and food from farther places like Szaj-Nev, only to use them up combatting this strange sickness. And after all that, what is left? Just enough for the Church to collect in tithes."

"Those damn tithes." Abba stood with a huff, the splintering wood groaning under the shift in weight. He knocked into the table, sending the yahrzeit candle they had lit for Chaia tumbling to the ground.

Malka yelped, hands flying to her cheeks as she and Imma danced on the flame to extinguish it. She fell to her knees, collecting the spilled ash in her palms. Cradling it like something precious.

"Oh, quiet, Malka." Abba pinched the space between his brows. "That headstrong girl got what she deserved."

Malka stared at Abba. *You're wrong!* she wanted to retort. *You didn't know her.* But Abba was already red-faced and agitated. She didn't want to worsen his mood. Not with her sisters in the next room. She tried to even her breathing, but tightness still caved in her throat.

Hadar's shriek interrupted the heated silence between them, causing Malka to jolt. The ashes she had cupped in her palms spilled to the ground once more.

Both sisters came into view. Hadar ran to Imma, clinging to her legs and burying her face in Imma's wool skirt. Her words were muffled, but unmistakable.

"The Paja is here."

Danya wrapped her arms around herself, but it didn't hide her full body shudder. "We heard their drums from our window."

Malka's stomach coiled. *Already?*

Imma cursed. She hurried around the room, smothering the fire after using it to light a lantern.

Abba gripped Hadar's arm. "Wait in your room with Danya."

Danya scoffed. "Abba, I am old enough to come—"

"You'll stay with Hadar." His firm tone made Malka flinch.

Danya opened her mouth to speak, but hesitated. With a sigh, she decided against it and nodded instead.

Relief teemed, knowing how rapidly Abba could snap, how his eyes could sharpen like an arrow, setting sight on his target. Malka had felt the pierce of it too many times.

"Malka, get the spices from the back."

Imma's request drew her attention.

At the back of their house, she grabbed the large key hanging on a nail by the door. The icy weather hit her like a fist. It pinched at her skin, which puckered a soft pink across her nose and knuckles.

Snow lightly fell from the swollen clouds above, casting a white film over the treetops in the distance, made even brighter by the glistening moonlight. The fog pulled down into Mavetéh, like even Yohev's own sky was victim to its dangerous draw.

Malka's heartbeat quickened, and she refocused on the locked trunk. It was dark, and in her haste, she had not procured a candle. Only the soft light from the back window and the reflective brightness of the snow guided her hand. The key hit against the lock a few times, made difficult by the lack of light and the chill stiffening her soot-covered fingers. Malka hauled the trunk open, and a few flecks of snow fell lazily to the ground.

The scents overwhelmed her. The rich musk of frankincense, the sickly sweetness of goldenmase. Though they kept the spices for the tithes separate—outside so they would never be tempted to use them—Malka couldn't help but remember how the scent of goldenmase once filled their house. Imma used it for everything. Hot, golden baths which soothed her muscle aches from long days hunched over gardening; a salve of Imma's own conception that helped her inflamed, cracked skin in the winter; and the dried stems of the plant that sweetened their apples as the scents and flavors baked together in the oven.

She filled the sack with jars.

Malka jogged to the road to join her parents, jars clinking inside the sack. They walked in tense silence, interrupted only by the brief greetings of their neighbors as they continued toward the shektal, the village center and marketplace.

"Three months!" a voice admonished behind her. It was Minton, the village metalsmith who made their Shabbos and yahrzeit candle holders. "Do they think we are made of grain and spices? That we don't have our own mouths to feed?"

"Something must be wrong," said Masheva, his wife. Her voice was hoarse, like she had recently woken. Imma had given her a sleeping draught to help with her nightmares, and Malka hoped it had soothed her sleep. The Paja's interruption couldn't have helped.

They drifted ahead and Malka strained to hear Masheva. "Do you think there's trouble within the Church?"

The Order of the Paja was the Ozmini Church's creation, charged with tithe collection across every Ordobavian village. For as long as Malka could remember, the Paja had come to Eskravé. Collections used to be yearly but now were unpredictable and more frequent than their resources allowed. Only three months had passed since the last collection bled her village dry. Malka had had to soothe a crying Hadar to sleep while hunger cramped their bellies for weeks afterward.

On the shektal steps stood an unfamiliar man, at ease despite the firm clasp of his hands behind his back. He was draped in robes the color of stained wine, hair hidden underneath a golden squared cap. Gold prayer beads looped through his belt. There was something sinister about the dip in his smile, the way his lips tugged back enough to catch a glimpse of his yellowing teeth. Malka shoved her trembling hands further into the folds of her skirt to hide them.

Next to him stood Lord Kašpar Chotek, a wealthy Ozmini landlord who owned half of the houses in Eskravé and managed the village's formal municipal business, including the market dealings. He was dressed in his work regalia, but his hair was disheveled. He must have readied in a rush.

Fear bubbled in Malka's chest as her nerves built. She thought of the collection three months ago, when scant resources prevented them from satisfying their tithe requirements and golden Yahadi necklaces were taken to be sold as consequence. A comforting symbol to her—the small flame representing eternal light—melted down to nothing.

What would they take now?

"We are sorry to disturb you at this late hour," Chotek began. "The weather, as you can imagine, has made travel difficult. We offer a warm welcome to the Order of the Paja, led by Father Brożek, after the long journey they have made from Ordobav's western border."

His words sounded rehearsed, curated carefully after years of practice. He spoke like the noble he was, clear and distinguished in his native language of Kražki, no doubt accentuated by the priest's presence at his side. Kražki was the language of nobility and municipality. Over the past few decades, it had even become the language of church administration instead of the ancient Jalgani script.

Malka could speak Kražki, but the smooth vowels were made harsh by her Kraž-Yadi tongue—the language most Yahad in Ordobav spoke. She remembered her first interaction with Chotek, how her mouth felt clotted with honey when she spoke Kražki, how her tongue could not find the right place to rest for her words to take shape.

You'd have a beautiful voice, he had said to her once. *If your people's language wasn't so barbaric.*

To this day, Malka found ways to avoid speaking Kražki.

Cold bit the air. Malka snugged close to Imma for warmth, having forgotten her wool cloak in her haste. She blinked tears from the wind, attention drifting toward the priest's accompaniment—a mix of knights, administrators, and peasants who made up the Order. Her eyes caught on a tall man with bronze hair and golden eyes who held a horse's reins taut.

Unlike Father Brożek, this man was dressed plainly in a white linen tunic and trousers. A sheepskin cloak the color of drenched earth hung around his shoulders, matching his leather boots that were more mud than shoe.

He caught her staring and winked.

Heat prickled up her neck. She glanced away, embarrassed.

The priest continued. "It's a harsh winter and it will be harsher still. It is hard work for your landlords to maintain this village and keep your markets busy. But our Heavenly Father, Triorzay, has given you shelter from the cold through the outstretched hand of the Ozmini Church. He has watched over you despite not leaning to His will. It is time to give back."

Two men rolled out several empty barrels from their wagons. The Ozmini bursar followed them to observe and count the transfer.

The villagers began to form lines, passing down their jars to empty into the bins.

They had enough to fill the first barrel, but not the second.

Brożek's yellow teeth came out again. A predator ready to strike in the shadows. His lips curved up, creases the sharp teeth of a portcullis. "Perhaps there's been a mistake, Chotek."

Despite the chill, the noble wiped a bead of sweat caressing his forehead. "I'll see to it they are punished, Father."

The gathered crowd of Eskraven villagers, hands empty of their herbs and spices, now held only a steeling breath. Punishment to the Ozmini lords meant eviction or criminal convictions, an upending fate for any Yahadi family.

From the silent crowd came a voice—Masheva. "Please," she begged, shuffling closer to the steps. "I know the women and I have some more jewelry we can find. We can make up the amount."

Malka's hand fell to her chest, feeling the cold press of her own pendant necklace. She was grateful for its hiding place under her clothes, chain hidden by her thick, raven curls.

Father Brożek raised his brow, the bushy white as untamed as his wily grin. "So, you admit you have purposefully hidden from the tithe?"

Masheva paled. Her mouth opened, but no words came.

Minton laid his calloused hand on his wife's shoulder. "It's not our fault, Father."

"Fault?" Father Brożek spread his arms, cupping the crowd between his palms. "There is no one else you can blame but yourselves."

Minton worked his jaw. To his side, Masheva gave a timid shake of her head, her fingers digging into the underbelly of Minton's wrist.

"It's the woods."

Masheva closed her eyes. A rush of murmurs from the villagers.

Imma set a protective hand on Malka's arm.

In the Paja's past visits, no one had mentioned Mavetéh. Maybe it had been the fear of not being believed, or the terror of legitimizing the curse with its public incantation. Malka didn't know.

Despite the nervous energy of the crowd, Minton did not relent. "Inside the woods is a monster, evil and bloodthirsty. It has taken our women and corrupted much of the forest. That is why our resources have dwindled."

Tinkling laughter glided its way around the Order.

"A bloodthirsty and evil monster?" the priest mocked, tilting his head.

Through the crowd, Malka sought Chaia's parents. In a moment she found them, huddled together toward the back. The ache in her heart grew every time Mavetéh was mentioned, worsened now that Minton had given voice to it so boldly. She could only guess Chaia's parents were dealing with a similar pain from losing their child to Mavetéh—like a tender scab reopening.

Chaia had always been all sharp teeth when the Paja appeared to collect tithes, especially when their visits became more frequent. One time, a knight had purposefully spilled over a wheat barrel, making a group of Yahadi villagers drop to their knees to pick up the grain. Chaia had berated the knight for his vile behavior and earned twenty lashings as a result. She took them in stride, only gritting her teeth. She did not cry even when the rope split her skin and her dress spoiled deep red.

Her pestering didn't relent after that, only emboldened. She had begun to question how the Paja delivered the tithes—where they went after the knights loaded the barrels into the wagon and whipped their horses into their speedy canter. She gathered more welts before the first were fully healed.

Malka blinked the memory of Chaia away, swallowing the tightness in her throat.

Father Brożek raised his brow at Chotek. "Perhaps we should remind these Yahadi villagers what happens to those who disgrace and mock the Church, Kašpar?"

The priest motioned to one of the knights with a flick of his hand.

The knight seized Minton's shoulders and jostled him forcefully to the steps, tearing him from Masheva's grip. He fell to his knees, tripping on the stone.

"We do not steal from Triorzay. We sacrifice for Him. You live on Church-sanctioned grounds in Ozmini-owned houses and will follow our rules." Father Brożek addressed the crowd. "You all will do well to remember that."

The priest nodded to the knight, who unsheathed a cleaver from his belt. He snatched Minton's hand and splayed it on the ground.

Minton begged in a mix of Kražki and Kraž-Yadi. The two languages fought each other—the push and pull of soft and strong vowels. Tears rolled down his face.

Malka's heart sped, pounding in her ears so loudly Minton's cries dimmed. Imma left her side, moving instead to cover Masheva's sobs and hold her back.

With one swing, the cleaver cut through Minton's hand with a pop. He screamed, loud and guttural. Malka couldn't forget that scream, the way it echoed through the square, shaking even the canopy of leaves in Mavetéh.

It was a dirty cut made with a dull blade and pieces of his fingers lay limp, held only by lingering sinew, the bone bloodied as it stuck out from his fingers. Spots of crimson decorated the ground. The wind blew, carrying the scent through the air—metal and rust.

Bile rose in Malka's throat, and she moved in time to empty herself on the dirtied snow.

CHAPTER 2

The next morning, the sun did not rise.

It hid behind dense clouds and fog, leaden with heavy moisture. The wind rustled through the trees, blowing the front wisps of Malka's hair from her kerchief. She wiped at them with the back of her fist, pulling a piece from her mouth. The bag tugged at her shoulder, and she shifted its weight to the other side for some relief.

Sleep had been fruitless. She tossed and turned throughout the night, eyes stitched open with images of Minton's mutilated hand and his blood splattering over stone. When dawn shone in though her window, she had sighed and finally slipped from bed.

She began her routine early, filling her bag with the medicinal tonics Imma made for the villagers. Imma used to charge extra for delivery, but the strange sickness spreading around their village had left fewer people able to rise from their beds or leave their houses. It was a type of consumption illness which whittled its victims away until nothing of them was left. Cases had begun to crop up a year ago in Eskravé but had worsened in the last six months. They attributed the sickness as another symptom of Mavetéh's curse, since a handful of men from the Rayga hunt were the first to catch it.

So Imma made exceptions to her fee, and Malka delivered them at daybreak.

In the quiet dawn, Malka swore she heard Minton's pleas in the howling wind, brushing thunderously against her ear.

She shook the sound of him away and stepped to the door, knocking on the wood which had gone concave from the heavy winter.

"Peace and light, Malka," the shektal meat carver, Chanoch, greeted her when he opened the door. His daughter Yael, thin and boney, had always been prone to terrible illness, but her condition had worsened severely after developing symptoms from the consumption sickness a week ago.

"Peace and light," Malka responded, digging into her bag. "How is Yael's cough?"

Chanoch frowned, the creases on his forehead deepening. His beard caught a few drops of snow, glistening as they melted into his graying hair. "Getting worse. Yesterday, when she awoke, we found blood on her pillow."

Malka's throat tightened. "I will let my mother know." His broad figure was made small by his grief. "Do not lose hope yet, Chanoch."

He smiled tiredly, the bags under his eyes murky pools. "Thank you, Malka."

She handed him a glass bottle from the bag. "Make sure she takes all of it and follows with some food. I'll be back tomorrow."

The wind howled again, sweeping the tails of her skirt as she headed back to the dirt path. The lingering snow on the ground was caked with mud and crunched under her boots.

Beyond the jagged canopy of houses, Malka could hear the murmurs of her village livening as another day unfurled.

After they threw Minton back into the horror-struck crowd, the Order had declared they would remain in Eskravé until twice the tithe could be procured in full. Faces of sorrow had overtaken the villagers, the lit torches making their tears gleam in the night.

The Paja had erected magnificent tents alongside the shektal, though many forced their way into Yahadi houses when the weather began to slip at night. The villagers could say nothing, for they did not own the houses they occupied. Instead, they crammed together to make space for the members who demanded beds and warm meals, who rummaged through their cabinets for food they did not have. Malka was glad her own house, far on the outskirts of the village, went unnoticed.

"Malka!"

She twisted her neck to see her friend Amnon jogging to meet her.

"Peace and light," he greeted, lips curving into a smile. He was vibrant against the overcast morning: his eyes green like the darkest juniper, hair the color of oiled frankincense glimmering in the sun.

"Peace and light, Amnon."

"You're out early."

He appeared boyish, red from the cold filling his cheeks, nose scrunched as the snow landed like freckles across his skin. It was exactly how he had looked when they were younger, chasing each other through the woods.

The woods. Mavetéh. *Minton*.

She swallowed the taste of copper. "I couldn't sleep."

His eyes lost their glimmer. "I heard about last night. I'm sorry you had to witness that." He raised his hand as if to console her but decided against it.

"I'm glad Danya stayed with Hadar. She's so stubborn I thought she would sneak out anyway. But I'm glad she didn't have to see that. I don't think I will ever forget."

Even though only the eldest child could accompany their parents to each shektal announcement due to crowding, Malka knew Danya would betray the rules without a second thought. She had done so once—snuck out after Malka had left with their parents and hid behind a market cart until the vendor kicked her out. Malka still remembered how loudly Abba had roared, how red his face had bloomed.

"How is Minton?" Amnon asked.

"Resting. But Imma says he will never regain the use of his right hand." A terrible fate for any smith.

"I will pray for his speedy recovery." He eyed her bag. "Do you need help with that? I've finished my morning chores."

Malka opened her mouth to protest but decided against it, knowing Amnon's determination to feel helpful. Instead, she passed over the bag, rubbing at the dull pain in her shoulder.

They continued down the path, weaving through the houses and streets until there were only a handful of tonics clinking in the bag.

"I should've been there," Amnon said, kicking the mud at his feet.

Malka settled her hand on his shoulder. "It is a blessing you were not. Believe me."

"I could have—"

"You could have what, Amnon?" Malka dropped her hand. "Stood up against the Church yourself? Talked back to Father Brożek? That's exactly what Minton did, and you know what happened to him."

Amnon ran his fingers through his hair. "I wish I had been there to cover your eyes. To shield you from the violence."

"Then it would be me consoling you through the nightmares instead. Either way, we do not win."

"I only want to protect you, Malka," he said softer, letting his thumb trace the vestiges of the bruise on her cheek. "Have you given anymore thought to it, at least?"

Malka closed her eyes. Mavetéh's curse had stolen the rest of her youth, leaving her flush against the expectation of marriage and motherhood. But Malka couldn't imagine leaving the house with her sisters yet or leaving Imma to care for patients without her. Not when the Rayga captured lives in the night and illness raged.

"Not yet," Malka responded softly. "But I will. When things get a little better here and I'm not needed as much."

Amnon's smile didn't reach his eyes, but he nodded.

"Is your brother back from Valón?" Malka asked, desperate to change the subject.

"Got in early this morning," Amnon responded. "Abba was happy."

Valón, Ordobav's capital city, existed in her mind as a fantasy, drenched in color by stories from Eskravé's merchant traders like Amnon's oldest brother Micah, who bought wool materials from Valón's renowned spinners and sold them to the southern villagers who traveled to Eskravé's marketplace. Micah had told them stories of grand buildings painted in every color of clay and the shul Bachta—the greatest synagogue in Ordobav—with its stained-glass windows and spiraling tower. It had long been known to the outer Yahadi villages as a place of safety and refuge, its Yahadi Quarter flush with thriving businesses. It had its own municipality, the Qehillah, where Yahadi leaders wrote up laws for the Yahadi Quarter. Some even served in the king's court.

Even Baba, her grandfather, had shared stories of the city before he passed a few years ago. As a prominent healer, he often helped with Valón's brutal sick seasons, bringing back tales to a wide-eyed Malka. A street vendor adorned with many colorful hats juggling his produce; a Fanavi woman's delicious, sweet bread which filled the whole street with its scent; fire-lit torches flying through the air as a parade crossed the sprawling hilltop castle.

She had swallowed the stories like plum juice, her curiosity as constant as its sticky sweetness on the roof of her mouth.

Though, as with most sweet things, rot rode in on its coattails.

Addicted to the saccharin, Malka still dared to ask, "Does he have any new stories?"

Amnon sighed. "It's been months since he shared anything. I don't even bother asking at this point."

Her shoulders sagged, but she could only blame herself. The memory of her mistake gnawed at her again. Micah's last few stories had been a smooth balm over the worsening state of the forest's curse, and she had pushed too hard, asking what she knew she shouldn't.

The Maharal and his magic.

He was more myth than man to Malka, a Valonian rabbi revered and reviled for practicing a contentious Yahadi mysticism known as Kefesh. Whenever Malka asked about the Maharal, Baba unfurled his stories like allegorical, century-old tales, told in the same way the sacred Yahadi scrolls revealed their lessons and commands. They were never grounded the way his other stories had been, and almost never mentioned Kefesh. It was as if Baba did not want to place the Maharal in the present, as someone still existing and practicing a magic her village declared forbidden, even if the city didn't.

Only one of Baba's stories mentioned Kefesh so boldly: the Maharal's creation of his golem, a voiceless creature crafted from mud and stone and animated with prayer. The creature, of course, became as unwieldy as Kefesh itself. It terrorized the Yahadi Quarter and murdered an innocent boy in cold blood. All the while, the Maharal could do nothing to tame the beast he had created. A warning to Malka—not even a rabbi was exempt from the dangers of the mysticism.

Yet, every time Malka attended services or sang her people's ancient prayers, thoughts of Kefesh flittered across her mind, untamable as a bleating sheep adrift from its shepherd. It frightened her, that the holy prayers she chanted with devotion could also evoke such violence. It made her want to know more than Baba was ever willing to tell, to make sure she never fell victim to its ensorcellment.

So, when she asked Micah if he had heard anything about Kefesh, she was not surprised when his lips had thinned in response.

Of course not, Malka. It's forbidden.

There were no stories after that from Micah, and soon the rest of the merchants' stories ceased the same way Kratzka Šujana became Mavetéh: slowly, then all at once.

"Maybe it's on purpose," Amnon considered.

"What is?"

"That our traders are disparaged and forced to cut back their trips to Valón. Maybe the Ozmins are making it hard for them to afford traveling on purpose by increasing the tithes, so we stop coming to the city altogether. It would make sense since they hate us. I mean, *you* saw what they did to Minton."

Malka gritted her teeth. "Yes, I did see."

"I'm sorry, Malka, I didn't mean—"

He sounded like Chaia, brazen and ready to make wine from water; to conjure up a connection when there was none.

It made her spiteful. Made her mad with grief again.

A scream pierced the air, cutting off whatever apology Amnon had begun.

They hurried back toward the main road, breathless. When Malka caught sight of Sid, the bread maker's daughter, struggling against a tall and jaunty Paja knight, her skin ignited in a cold sweat. Sid's cheeks were flushed bright red, and white rings had formed around her wrists where the knight held them firm.

"You have taken as much bread as we have to give, *Ctihodný*," Sid heaved, the knight's honorific heavy on her tongue. "Please, let me go."

"Perhaps you can give me something else I want," he said, leaning close to whisper in her ear. A whisper so dark, it drained the color from her face.

"Pick on someone else, *Ctihodný*," Amnon said, mocking the honorific. "If we could not pay your tithe, it should be no wonder we can't feed your bottomless appetites."

The knight dropped his grip on Sid, his attention, and now his ire, directed toward them instead. "What did you say, *Medvadi*?"

The slur sliced through Amnon and Malka both. One they were not used to hearing in their Yahadi village. It meant *betrayer of God*. Though whose God, Malka had never been certain.

Worse yet, it was the same knight who had raised the cleaver to Minton's hand. He had been emotionless, even as Minton's blood stippled his cheeks like glimmering rubies. Even as he smeared it across his face with his palm, unbothered.

Malka wanted to bottle Amnon's words and make him drink them back, to save him a fate like Minton's.

"Amnon, please," Malka pleaded, tugging on his arm.

Amnon gritted his jaw, pulling away from her. "I said—"

"He said that if you are hungry," Malka interrupted, "he has fish to give." She ignored Amnon's glare. "He told me he deboned a large trout. You won't find fresh trout as delicious as the ones his family catches from the river Jašni. They are the first to go at every market."

The knight raised his brow. "If you say the trout is the best, it seems only fair he prepare one for my supper every evening. You can do that, can't you?"

The infernal taunt lingered in the air.

With Amnon's puffed chest and surly gaze, Malka thought he would defy the knight again. But much to her relief, he sighed and reluctantly murmured his agreement.

"Good." The knight brushed the crest on his tunic, stroking the lion from its head to its tail. "And, boy?" He wrapped his fist into Amnon's tunic. "Don't ever speak to me like that again."

He swung his other fist into Amnon's cheekbone, the force of it hurling Amnon toward the ground. Malka dropped to her knees in an attempt to catch him, and winced as they struck the frozen earth.

"Václav, the priest has summoned us," another knight said as he approached. "If you've had your fill of bullying weak Yahadi men, that is."

When Václav took his leave, Malka turned her attention back to Amnon, tracing her thumb along his swelling cheekbone. Thankfully, it didn't look broken. She wanted to curse him, strike him herself for antagonizing the knight. But relief overshadowed her anger.

"Are you alright?" she then asked Sid, who was rubbing at her wrists. Malka couldn't look away from the bruises flowering on them, similar to the marks banding her own wrists—made not by a knight, but her own father, drunk from a Rayga hunt.

"Yes," Sid said. "Damn them. They touched all the bread for the Sabbath, their hands caked with mud and who knows what else. We'll have to throw it all out!"

Amnon stirred in Malka's arms, grunting as he stood with Malka's support. "I'm sorry about them," he said, wincing. "If it's any help, I could bring my brothers as extra hands. I am not particularly graced with skill in braiding, but I can leave an oven spotless."

"Thank you, but we will manage." Sid rubbed at her wrist again. "You're brave, Amnon."

Amnon's lip curled as his face brightened. Malka sighed, knowing those two words flowed through him like wine. He would not regret his brazen actions after that praise.

"Come," Malka said, grabbing Amnon's arm. "Let Imma check your injury."

CHAPTER 3

A fortnight into the Paja's stay, Malka was certain they would never satisfy the tithe. Every time they came close, a fevered hunger overcame the knights, and they would eat and eat until their bellies ballooned and they left Yahadi cabinets ravaged. Her days assisting Imma grew longer as more Yahad fell ill, often never leaving the cramped room in their house where they treated patients.

Hands slick with thyme oil, Malka fell back against the hard wood of her home's exterior, tucked under the side awning shading her from falling snow. Imma's workspace had been hot and stuffy with sickness, causing her to sweat despite the deep winter. When a soft breeze rustled through the air, she welcomed the sting.

Minton's hand, despite Imma's fastidious care, had become infected.

That morning, he had come to their door with Masheva at his side, the creases of her forehead drawn taut with worry. He was hot with fever, hand swollen red and oozing yellow pus. Asked to prepare a disinfectant oil, Malka had dutifully gone to the kitchen, muddling thyme into paste with a stone, and heating it in oil while Danya put a cool cloth over his forehead. When she began to apply the salve to Minton's hand, she had faltered. The feel of his wound reminded her of the blade splitting his skin, tearing flesh and bone. When Malka swallowed, it had tasted metallic.

"Go, Malka," Imma had said when she noticed Malka's shaking hands. "Danya and I can handle this."

Malka was not new to injury. She had stood by Imma while she treated burns, helped when childbirth required extra hands. She washed blood from her hands like clockwork. But this injury . . .

She breathed deep, the scent of healing herbs and burning fire centering her. She began to walk, something that had always helped her clear her head, despite the cold stiffening her legs.

Hoping to avoid any knights, Malka chose to walk along the edge of the village, closer to her house and farther from the shektal. It was barely past noon, and the sun held at its zenith. Though a block of houses still separated her from the cusp of the forest, the handful of hours until nightfall were a comfort. Her village didn't know how close women had to be before Mavetéh lured them, so they erred on the side of caution, marking the last row of houses as the border for women to venture.

Across the road, Malka caught sight of a group of Paja members lounging against a tree stump, felled in desperation when Mavetéh's trees could no longer provide for them. Malka attempted to shrink herself so they wouldn't notice her, but one of the men caught her gaze anyway. He had bronze hair and bright gold eyes. The same Ozmini man, Malka noted, that had winked at her during Father Brożek's speech.

He called out, and Malka darted her attention anywhere but at the tree shading them. He shouted again, and Malka's stiff legs moved toward them before she could think better of it.

"Peace and light," she said, the traditional Kraž-Yadi greeting rolling off her tongue.

The man smirked. "Peace and light." His Kraž-Yadi was softer than it should've been, words muddling together. He switched to Kražki. "I remember your face in the crowd, that first night."

"Are you going to introduce us to your friend, Aleksi?" The woman sitting next to Aleksi punched him teasingly. She was beautiful. Her eyes river blue, hair like the forest's shade. She had a pale, rounded face, and it fit well around her smirk. Her decorated apron was much more intricate than Malka's, the vermillion embroidery peeking out from her hefty wool cloak.

"I caught her staring at me during Father Brożek's speech."

Malka flushed. "I was not staring."

His smile grew, slightly crooked. "I think your blush says otherwise."

She fought the heat pooling to her cheeks again, but it was fruitless.

"What's your name, girl-who-didn't-stare?"

Malka thought about leaving without another word, but she knew the consequences of disobeying the Paja.

Aleksi's smile exaggerated his rounded, well-fed cheeks.

"It's Malka," she said finally, lengthening the vowels of her name to better suit his mother tongue.

Satisfied, Aleksi leaned back, bottle dangling between his fingers like a loose fruit from a tree. A scar ran up his arm, still pink around the edges. "Malka, this is my little brother, Bori, and our friend Rzepka. Of course, I'm Aleksi."

Bori appeared only a few years younger than Danya, and a copy of his brother, but youth still tugged at him, rounding his cheeks and lightening his voice when he greeted her.

"Pleased to meet you, Malka," Rzepka said. She nabbed the bottle from Aleksi's hand and held it toward her. "Want some?"

Malka shook her head.

"Maybe it's against her religion," Bori said, shrugging.

Aleksi flicked Bori's head but raised his eyebrow. "Is it?"

"No." She regarded Aleksi. "You're drinking at noon, and that does not sound particularly pleasing."

"Then stay until evening," Aleksi said, a grin spreading across his face. "Are you not curious to learn the life of those of us in the Order? We have travel tales that would blow those wool socks off your feet."

"I get my fill of travel tales from our Yahadi merchants." She did once, anyway.

"Ah, yes, your market made for people too lazy to venture to Valón for their goods in the first place. The Yahad, middlemen as always. Tell me, Malka, do they hike the prices as high as they say for those southern travelers? It's all anyone talks about, how the Yahad get rich from usury."

"Perhaps she'd be more interested in stories of Valón, Aleksi," Rzepka suggested. "After all, the Yahadi merchants only know the marketplace. That is, if they ever glance away from their shiny Ordon coin."

Malka gnawed on her lip. She thought of Baba's death, which took his tales of the capital city with him, of the merchants like Micah who no longer shared their stories.

Perhaps it would not be so bad, to hear what they knew. To get a taste of that sweetness again.

"I can't stay long."

Her answer pleased Aleksi. He draped his arm around Rzepka, plucking the bottle from her hands and taking a swig. "What bad company we are!

Come sit, Malka. Enjoy this wonderful view of the forest canopy and watch how the snowflakes dance."

The snow soiled her cloak as she settled on the ground, the thin woven blanket already damp. The umber embroidery on her own apron darkened as it wetted.

"Hard to believe we've been here a fortnight." Aleksi raised the bottle. "Thank Triorzay's Grace for wine to keep the boredom at bay."

Rzepka stole the bottle from Aleksi's grip. "You are always bored, Aleksi, if your throat doesn't burn with alcohol or your mouth isn't on some woman's neck."

Aleksi clutched at his chest. "Rzepka, such insults before noon?"

Rzepka rolled her eyes. "So, Malka, how do you keep yourself entertained around here?"

"Imma and I are healers. As you can imagine, we have enough people to tend to that our days are filled."

"My mother is a healer, as well," Rzepka responded. "In fact, she's now the royal healer."

Malka straightened. "Really?"

"Yes. Have you heard the story of King Valski's son, Evžen, and his miracle birth?"

Malka knew the Ordobavian prince's birth was special, but not why. Only that it warranted a city-wide festival each year. Eskravé's merchants had long given up any trips to Valón the week of the celebration, since most vendors sold out of their goods before Eskravé's traders could purchase them.

"I haven't." It was only half a lie.

"Well," Rzepka began. "When Evžen was born... let's say it was a terrible birth. He came out of the queen with his cord wrapped around his neck. His face was so blue, many thought him already dead. He could not be roused from slumber, even with the most potent herb under his nose. My mother, pregnant with me, was a miracle healer in Naška Slova. People made trips through the northwestern mountains to be healed by her. King Valski had heard of her abilities and brought her to Ordobav's palace. After an hour with my mother, his eyes opened wide."

"What did your mother do to save him?"

"She healed him as she would've anyone else... only, she heard a whispering in the room, and a hand guided her own as she fed herbs to the prince."

"Saint Celine guided her," Bori added. "She wanted Evžen to live. And that's why we have the Léčrey celebration every year on the prince's birthday, to commemorate the miracle of his birth and the blessing of a saint on the continued Valski rule."

"Another blessed day with wine and dancing," Aleksi said, stealing the bottle from Rzepka and taking another swig.

"We live in the New Royal Palace now. It is where I was born, after the king offered my mother employment," said Rzepka.

"I don't understand. If you live in the palace, why are you here with the Paja?"

Rzepka smiled. "It is my duty. Triorzay's guidance of the Ozmini Church has given me so much. When Archbishop Sévren asked for me to join the Order for a few years, it was something I felt called to do."

"You've been away for years?"

"It is not as bad as you think. The road has become a home of its own." She motioned toward Bori. "He has grown up on these missions."

Rzepka lifted her sleeve to scratch at her wrist, revealing a scar along her forearm. Curiously, in the same location as Aleksi's puckering scar.

"And this is my last tour with the Paja before I go back to Valón," Aleksi said proudly.

"What will you do after?" Malka asked.

"I am open to what the world has to offer. Maybe I'll take up the mandolin and entertain. I've always been good with my hands." Aleksi smirked suggestively.

"You are too free willed for your own good," Rzepka admonished.

"I prefer to spread my wings than tie myself down." He raised his brow. "Well, at least in this context."

"Didn't you talk about going to Lei?"

Malka squinted. "Where?"

"*Lei*," Rzepka said again, but slower. "The capital of the Vigary Kingdom?"

Right. Malka didn't know much about the other kingdoms in the Rhaškan Empire. Vigary sat too far northeast for local trade and didn't promise enough specialized materials to warrant the strenuous journey for Eskraven merchants. Malka only knew the northern cities in the Balkisk

Kingdom, including its capital Vyš, as they were closest to Eskravé from the south.

"Maybe I'll go to Vyš instead," Aleksi said. "See what the king's brother is all about. I heard he wears a robe embroidered with human bones. That, I would *love* to see."

"I'm sure in Duke Sigmund's dreams he wears a robe of the king's bones instead," Rzepka teased.

"What do you mean?" Malka asked.

Aleksi quirked a brow. "You don't get out much do you, Malka?"

Malka played with a loose thread on her cloak. "I've never left Eskravé."

In her village, letters addressing political matters went straight to Lord Chotek; any other letters were read to them by a handful of merchants, like Micah, who were literate in the spoken languages. Mostly, though, news traveled by mouth. And rarely did it reach Malka's ears.

"The king and the duke disagree on many things. Sigmund doesn't like that the Church plays an important role in the empire. Valski sees the vitality of keeping God close to the law. But there is a reason Valski is king, and Sigmund is not. If Triorzay wills it, it will be true. And Valski's only son was born a miracle. You'd be hard pressed to find a clearer sign about who's right and who's wrong."

Malka scrunched her brows. Separating the Ozmini Church from the empire felt impossible. They had been entwined for generations. The idea of someone as powerful as a duke—the king's brother, no less—critiquing the Church's role in politics shocked her.

Most of what Malka knew of imperial politics had come from Chaia. She wished her here now to make her less foolish.

Rzepka swatted Aleksi. "Enough about politics, Aleksi. The poor girl is growing paler with each word you say."

"Then let's finish this bottle instead," He stretched out the wine to Malka again. "Drink, Malka. To celebrate new friends."

⚹

Her head buzzed, a lazy smile decorating her face. The wine had relaxed the ache in her bones, her face flushed warm despite the chill. Malka leaned back on her palms, her legs folded on the snow-damp blanket.

"So, Malka," Aleksi prompted, drawing Malka out of her languid haze.

"The things the Yahad say about the forest." He stared beyond her to Mavetéh's impending canopy. "What do you make of them?"

The blood drained from her face, the warm coat of wine fading, causing her to shiver. "Minton spoke the truth." She recited to them the nursery rhyme Eskraven mothers had created to teach their children of the forest's curse:

The forest billowed awake, leaves like teeth and blood for sap, and swallowed its first woman whole. Beware the blanket of darkness, for the forest always demands its toll.

"That's so silly, Malka. A children's rhyme! If the forest was eating women, I'm sure we'd know. Valón borders the same woods, just on its northern side instead of the south."

"It isn't a lie," Malka responded, wine emboldening her. Imma would surely swat her if she were here. But she couldn't help her defensiveness.

She thought of Chaia, her death bruised by these Ozmini travelers who denied Mavetéh's power. Who could not even speak the language of the village from which they demanded payment. Her own people, upended by the tragedy of Mavetéh's souring. The women whose lives were taken by the same forest that had once given them life.

"It's hard to tell with you Yahadi people, I must admit," Aleksi said.

"Why do you say that?" Malka asked.

Aleksi shrugged. "Your Maharal, for example."

"What about the Maharal?" Now the wine less-so emboldened her, as it did make her queasy.

"What came out about him six months ago . . ."

Malka shook her head. If the merchants had brought back news, it never got to Malka.

"Huh." Aleksi kicked around the empty wine bottle with his foot. "Well, a Yahadi woman came to confession with a long-held secret. She had witnessed the Maharal kill an Ozmini bride right before her wedding to use her blood for his spells."

"He claims he played no part at all," continued Bori. "But as we Ozmins say, a witness's eyes tell no lies."

"When they searched the rabbi's house, they found her blood bottled in his basement. He was supposed to have a trial, but he fell ill. They're holding him in Valón Castle while he recovers."

While the Maharal had not escaped Kefesh's corruption in his creation of the golem, he himself was never depicted as murderous, not even by Baba—he didn't steal blood for spells. He was too venerated, too sacred.

But she had learned men could snap like twigs and become something unrecognizable. All it took was a night hunting for the Rayga. Perhaps Mavetéh had lured the Maharal inside its nefarious thickets and changed him like it had Abba.

Only, if what the Order said was true, Mavetéh's curse had not touched Valón in the same way. She began to pick at the skin on her nail, troubled with this new information.

A breeze riffled through the air. Malka crossed her arms to keep her warmth close, but the sun barely held beyond the horizon, making space for the clouds to pull in the night.

The *night*. The Rayga's awakening.

Reality pummeled her.

She stumbled from the ground, palms sinking into the damp earth as she balanced herself, slightly dizzy. "It's almost dark, we have to leave."

The three exchanged an impetuous glance.

"So?" Aleksi asked.

Bori elbowed him, understanding dawning. "Ah, remember, Aleksi, the woods will eat us if we don't!"

"Aleksi, you must understand I am *not* lying," Malka pleaded. "We must go."

He winked again, like he did when she had first caught his eye. "Very forward, Malka."

"You're not listening." She focused on Rzepka. "Please, leave. You have not seen what this monster does to the women it takes. Go back to your tent for the night."

Rzepka was silent for a moment, eyes darting from Mavetéh to Malka, uncertain.

"I appreciate your concern, Malka. But as you said, this . . . *creature* has only taken Yahadi women. We are protected by different Gods, and mine has not let me down yet."

Malka knew the implication of her words—that Yohev was a false God. It was the same story many Ozmini travelers spread when they remarked on their synagogue. When they criticized the shape of their symbolic flame necklaces.

Rzepka could be stubborn, but Malka wouldn't. She ran.

She arrived home out of breath and cramping from the wine. Imma was waiting for her, and pulled her close as soon as she crossed the doorframe. Imma's warm scent of chickweed and spiced honey enveloped her, and a hot tear fell to her shoulder.

"I'm sorry I stayed out so late." Fear crept its way up her neck, and Malka shook in her mother's arms.

CHAPTER 4

Hushed voices woke Malka gradually. With a yawn, she rubbed the sleep from her eyes. It was early still, the sun hanging low and casting a hazy red glow through the window.

Hadar curled further into her. She was a deep sleeper, and when she snored, the gap between her two front teeth peeked out from her parted lips.

Malka kissed her forehead, warm and sticky from sleep, before slipping out of bed.

The creaking floorboards greeted Malka's weight as she tiptoed from the bedroom.

Danya and Abba were hunched close in the kitchen. Their conversation silenced when Malka entered the room.

Her sister's face was pale and drawn with worry. Her coarse brows creased together, arms holding herself. Thin-lipped anger tugged Abba's face as he began to lace his boots tight with white knuckles.

"What's wrong?" Malka asked, then noticed the absence in the room. "Where's Imma?"

"She left." Abba kicked his spare boots off the bench by the door, making Malka wince. "That damnable woman."

Danya added, "We think she went to pick black perphona from Mavetéh. Minton's infection had drained the last of our stock. But, Malka, I didn't think she'd—"

"Only your mother would think she could outwit death." Abba unhooked his dagger from the wall.

Malka's heart pounded, her head spinning like it had from the wine. *She wouldn't have done that,* she wanted to believe. But she knew Imma, how heedlessly she'd risk her life if it meant providing better care for her patients.

Danya removed her cloak from the hook. "We're going to go find her."

Malka realized then Danya was already dressed. She had snuck from their room without waking her, without saying anything.

But Malka was the eldest sister. When Kratzka Šujana became Mavetéh, it was Malka who spent her days with Danya and Hadar when Imma was busy with patients and Abba began to hunt the Rayga with the other village men. It was she who shielded them when Abba returned from the woods and vomited his drinking behind their house. *She* who taught Hadar how to make paper cuttings, how to drag the blade across the paper to avoid jagged lines, how to mix paints to create the colors of the forest's trees.

"You didn't wake me?" she asked meekly.

Danya gave her a pitying look. "Malka, you have not been well since the incident with Minton in the shektal. I'm just—I'm of age, Malka. I can handle this. Take a break from it. Go back to sleep. We'll come back with her. I promise."

"Abba," Malka pleaded.

Abba attached the dagger's sheath to his belt. "Danya is right. You've barely done your chores. Danya says you're stumbling in No'omi's workroom. Your eyes have been as glazed over as a honey cake."

"I'm fine!" she cried out in desperation. When Hadar stirred in the next room, Malka winced.

Abba clutched Malka's chin. She gasped as he yanked her close, until his breath was hot on her face.

"How dare you speak back to me, Malka? You may be of age, but you are unwed and still live in this house. You heed *my* orders."

He let go, but the phantom grasp of his fingers dug into her skin.

She stared at the floor and didn't look up when Danya muttered an apology and the door shut, leaving Malka alone.

Tears stung her eyes, and she pressed herself small into the corner.

The tendrils of light caught on a glass crystal hanging from the ceiling, transforming the deep scarlet of the morning sun into a spectrum of colors across the floorboards. Malka extended her hand, and watched as the colors illuminated her skin.

She thought of a time kinder to Eskravé, when she and Danya would twist the crystals around their fingers, let go, and try to catch the fluttering light in their hands. Abba had laughed, his touches kinder. Before he turned to the bottle to deal with the nightmares Mavetéh gave him on the Rayga hunts. Imma's skin had glowed with youth, pigment blushing her cheeks as she prepared dinner for the Sabbath.

Oh, the smells. If she closed her eyes, she could still imagine the salted fish on her plate, the sweetness of apples with goat cheese, honey, and almonds. Pastries filled with jam, chocolate, and dates. Even the terrible, syrupy red wine Imma would press to Malka's lips on holidays.

Hadar yawned loudly from the other room, and Malka wiped her tears. She would not let Hadar see her like this. Her sister, who was too young to enjoy life before the shadow of Mavetéh. Too young to remember the sound of every household in Eskravé chanting the Sabbath at the same time, like a choir song.

"Malka?" her youngest sister intoned, peeking in from the hallway.

"Good morning, *Achoti*." Malka pushed herself from the wall. "Come here."

She held her sister in her arms, throat tight.

Only a few moments could've passed before the galloping of horses sounded from outside. Through the window, a group of Paja members—all men—sped down the otherwise quiet street. They were a blur of red and purple, their robes stark against the dour dawn.

Her gut tilted. They were headed in the same direction as Danya and Abba.

Abba was already in a foul mood this morning, his anger on the verge of rupturing. One wrong word from him and who knew what the Paja would do to him or Danya.

"Lock the door behind me, *Achoti*," she told Hadar, then put on her cloak.

⋎

Snow crunched under Malka's feet as she trailed behind the Paja. Through the gathering fog, the cluster of Paja members in their bright cloaks began to curve right. They picked up speed, and soon Malka had to run to keep them in sight.

By the time Malka had caught up with them, there had been some kind of commotion. The neighing of horses was silenced by their masters, the scream of swords drawing from their sheaths sliced the air.

Malka slowed, hiding herself behind some shrubbery, and attempted to squint through the pockets of leaves. She could make out Father Brożek, tall on his horse. When his animal spooked at something, the priest tamed it with a kick.

Two knights flanked him; one, Václav, who had antagonized Sid and given Amnon his yellowing bruise. Aleksi was also there, his face pale as the fog which enveloped them.

Across from them, two knights held a woman in iron clutches, golden hair spilling from the hood of her cloak.

Imma.

Malka's hand flew to her mouth.

Every eye was trained behind Imma, to a spot on the ground obscured from Malka's view. Legs shaking, she stood on her toes, shifting to a wider gap in the shrub.

Bile burned her throat.

From this distance, Malka was spared the details of the Rayga's newest victim. Yet even she saw the scrape of teeth separating skin from bone, the blood staining the snow like crushed cherries. The woman's leg fell unnaturally, bent outward at the knee. It took a minute before Malka realized she knew who the victim was—the dark hair and mutilated red robes.

Rzepka.

Malka squeezed her eyes shut. If only Rzepka had listened to her pleas, there wouldn't be another body so soon after the last.

My God has not let me down yet.

Malka didn't know Rzepka's God, but she knew Mavetéh. It had defied the prayers she said each night. She did not know the lengths the Rayga would go to devour its women.

When she opened her eyes, Rzepka's body had been shrouded.

"What have you done, Yahadi woman?" Father Brożek dismounted, pacing toward Imma in measured, confident strides.

"I did nothing," Imma said fiercely. "It was the Rayga, the monster we have warned you about. It's taken another victim."

The knight twisted her arm, and she cried out.

"Did you think you could go unnoticed? That we were not alerted when a Yahadi woman snuck away early in the morning with nothing but her cloak and a bag of Yahadi witch supplies? We were always going to find you."

No, this was wrong. *All* wrong.

Malka pushed through the bush, crying in opposition. She succeeded in garnering their attention, all eyes flicking toward her. Her heart pounded wildly, and her legs had numbed where she stood, shoes heavy as boulders on her feet.

When Imma called her name, a knight shoved cloth into her mouth.

"She's telling the truth, Father. I warned Rzepka yesterday—" Malka pleaded, circling her arms around herself.

"Are you saying you are her accomplice?" Father Brożek raised his hand, motioning for Václav to restrain her. Before the knight reached her, Aleksi stepped forward.

"Malka was with me all night," he said, crossing the gap to stand close to her. "Whatever the witch did, she did alone." He bent down and whispered in Malka's ear. "Stay quiet if you want to live."

Aleksi had given her a cover, a way out. No one would bat an eye at an Ozmini Paja member bedding a Yahadi girl during one of their visits. It had happened before, many times. Too many times. But a cover was nothing if it meant Imma was charged with a crime she did not commit. It meant nothing if Malka had to watch her in pain.

Václav licked his lips. "Father, you know their history with our people as well as I. There's no doubt this was a sacrifice. Look at the blood staining her hands." He splayed Imma's hand wide for all to see. It was stained crimson.

Malka hadn't noticed a crowd gathering around them until the gasps filled the air.

"It seems, once again, an Ozmini woman has been subject to Yahadi cruelty," said Father Brożek.

"She is not cruel at all," Malka sneered. "She is a healer. She was trying to help her!"

Aleksi covered her mouth with his hand. It was salty with sweat.

Father Brożek raised his brow. "And it is exactly a healer witch who would know how to cast your foul curses." He addressed Imma. "Which holiday bread will her blood be used to make this time? Tell me, is her death worth the taste?"

Malka shoved and shoved against Aleksi, but he held her firm. Her tears soaked his palm.

"We've been so accommodating of your religion," the priest continued. "Not only have you failed to meet your tithe, but you have taken an Ozmini woman to sacrifice. May she be with Triorzay now. You'll die a death worthy of your sin and have no one left but the devil to beg for mercy."

The words slapped Malka like needles pressing into her skin, each sharp point drawing blood.

She thought she was screaming, but no sound escaped her lips. Aleksi's fingers dug into her ribs to keep her planted. Malka wondered if his fingers would bruise her skin. If they would remind Malka of this moment, when she watched the knights drag Imma away, her scraped knees tracking blood in the dirt.

No matter how weak Malka felt, her hunger-whittled muscles no match for Aleksi's strong grip, she couldn't lose Imma.

Malka jutted her elbow in Aleksi's side with all her might. He grunted and doubled over, allowing Malka to pull free.

"Wait!"

Father Brożek turned, but it was Imma who found her eyes. They were resolute—the same brave face she had seen many times. She was going to let this happen. Let the Paja kill her and leave Malka and her sisters to light yet another yahrzeit candle.

"What if I can prove she was not the one who killed Rzepka? That we have no use for her blood?"

"And how would you do that?"

"This creature—what we call the Rayga—it is real."

"Must I remind you, girl, of what happened the last time the Ozmini Church was taken for a fool?"

He didn't need to. Malka could still hear the crunch of Minton's fingers. "Let me bring you the Rayga, this monster. I will prove my mother is innocent, that we are not liars."

The words settled in her bones like smoke, suffocating. But she couldn't live in a world where Imma didn't. Couldn't let Hadar grow up without knowing her loving touches or gentle hands braiding her hair for the holy days. Not when their father had swaddled a wine bottle instead of his children.

Father Brożek jumped from his horse and strolled toward Malka until they were a hair's breadth apart. She could see the creases along his mouth, the gentle scar he had across his nose, the raised skin puckering in the cold. He smelled thickly of eucalyptus and the cedar oil the Ozmins used at their churches.

"If you say the Rayga targets women," he eyed her up and down, "what hope should you have of bringing it to me?"

Malka faltered, for it was true. What hope should she have when the Rayga had taken any girl who wandered too close to Mavetéh?

"I will accompany her." Amnon emerged from the amassed crowd; the sleeves of his fisherman's tunic were still coated in fish innards. Malka wanted to kill him and his valor-driven tongue.

"No, you won't," Malka snapped.

"It's the only way you have a chance, Malka," he said gently as he approached. "Let me protect you from the Rayga. Men go on their hunts all the time, and they come back. If this is the deal you will strike, let me help you see it through."

Malka recalled Abba, and the hollow bags under his eyes, how he reeked of the manta plant each night.

Men do not come back from Mavetéh, Malka thought. *Only shadows of them do.*

She didn't want to see sense in Amnon's proposition, but he was right. No women who wandered close when night fell were safe. She couldn't fool herself into thinking Mavetéh wouldn't consume her. That it wouldn't be her body next, chewed and splayed on the ground. Yet the men had not been successful in their hunts, either. What choice did she truly have?

Václav bellowed a laugh behind them. "You know what they say about a man who speaks louder than the force of his punch? He is a dead one."

"I am interested in their plight," Father Brożek said. "After all, if they are willing to risk so much, as they say, does Triorzay not demand we give them the benefit of the doubt?"

"Father—"

"If you bring this . . . *monster* back to me, we will see if it's proof enough to settle our accusation. If you don't show, well, then I'm afraid the witch will pay for her crimes with her life."

Malka shook as disbelief gripped her. Imma was not safe yet, but she could be. And that was all Malka needed to be brave. "I will show you the truth of those woods. And prove my mother's innocence."

"You have until the eve of the Léčrey celebration," Father Brożek instructed. *Three weeks.* "Say it's . . . in *honor* of Saint Celine." His leer evoked a bone-deep shiver.

Malka didn't want to see Imma's sallow face, torn by the deal she had struck. But she could not leave her—couldn't face Mavetéh without seeing her one last time.

Perhaps Imma knew what Malka wanted to see, and granted it, despite her true feeling. A soft smile, eyes shining. *I love you,* her eyes said from across the field.

With the might of every star in the sky, Malka mouthed back, throat so constricted she could hardly swallow.

The knights took Imma away. Malka watched her disappear beyond the clearing, leaving Father Brożek and the rest of his entourage to settle the crowd.

Amnon's father ushered him away to reprimand him. He shot her an apologetic look, but Malka was no longer present. The fog settled dense around her. It was like losing Chaia all over again—the schism when her parents came to say she had not come home, separating the life Malka had known and the life she had to now endure.

But this was different. She would *make* it different.

"Malka," Father Brożek called. Reluctantly, she met his piercing stare. "Remember the grace Triorzay has granted you. And remember what it means to disgrace the Ozmini Church."

Malka forced herself to nod, the priest's words a spider crawling up her neck and tingling the back of her ears.

She didn't know how long she stood there. When everyone was gone, she was still there, staring at the stained, melting snow.

When the villagers had accepted that Chaia's disappearance meant she was dead, Malka had sat in the field they frequented until her feet were numb with mild frostbite and her fingers fattened. She didn't know why she had gone there. To feel the memory of her in the wind or hear her laughter in the flow of the stream. To hear her best friend adorn her with her nickname one more time. *Yedid Nefesh.* Beloved of the soul, it meant. That's what they had been to each other.

Perhaps if Malka stayed in the clearing long enough, she could reverse the moment when Imma had stumbled across Rzepka. She imagined her mother, ever the healer, dropping to her knees to examine the body. Getting blood on her hands attempting to find a pulse. Freezing when time played its cruel joke and the Paja appeared before her.

It was no use, yet she stayed until the cruelty of frostbite began to nip at her hands and feet, forcing her inside.

↯

That night was full of stars spilling across the sky so brightly, Malka could count them from her bedroom. Perched on the windowsill, knees drawn to her chest, she pointed to each one, whispering their names. Those would be the stars to guide her, after all.

Danya called to her as she shuffled from her bed, the darkness silhouetting her lanky frame.

When Danya joined Malka on the window perch, it hit her how grown her sister had become. Her strong nose and deep-set eyes—features they shared but wore so differently—gleamed in the moonlight.

"You're going through with this deal, aren't you?" Danya whispered, careful not to wake Hadar.

News of Rzepka's death had already crawled through Eskravé's streets, Imma's arrest on every whispering tongue. Exactly what had happened when Chaia had gone missing. Those whispers haunted her still.

I must lose a child or a wife, Abba had said about the deal Malka had struck. *Wherever God is, They are not here.*

Yet, he did not stop her. Instead, he slammed the front door behind him. Outside, a glass bottle shattered. He never did have a backbone where it mattered.

She could not help Chaia anymore, but she could save Imma from a similar fate. "I must."

Danya rested her head against the window. "I know you *believe* you must."

Her sister was pragmatic, always balancing options in the furrow of her brow, the purse of her lips. It didn't surprise Malka that Danya weighed her decision to hunt down the Rayga.

Malka reasoned, "If I don't try, Imma will die. Do you think we'll be happy here with Abba? How long do you think it'll be before you're the next victim of his wrath?"

The pale pink of Danya's nightgown glimmered as she sighed. "It's too late for that." She rotated so Malka faced her back, then lifted her dress up to her shoulder blades.

Dread pooled in Malka's gut. Bruises faded to shades of purple lined her back, stark against the milky wash of moonlight illuminating her skin.

Malka touched the bruises softly, as she had traced her own many times. Hot anger pricked her throat. "You know why I must go. The Rayga hunts made him like this. If the Rayga is killed, maybe we can go back to how we were."

Danya shrugged the nightgown back down. "Malka, we can never be like we were. Those people who come into our village demanding payment because we don't believe in the same God? They're not going to disappear. They'll keep collecting payment from us until our resources are dry and we are drained of hope and prayer. Until we are nothing but dust."

"We must replenish our hope," Malka said. "Believe in me, Danya. Please. Let me take this chance to free Imma. To rid Eskravé of this plague of dead women. To give Hadar the chance to grow up unafraid."

Danya's lips wavered. Malka thought she might fight back, unravel her plan with ways Malka could fail. But instead, Danya held her hand, a strangely intimate gesture for her sister. She squeezed it and settled their joined hands on her knee, turning back to stare out the window.

Tomorrow, she didn't know what would come. She wouldn't prepare poultices for Imma or deliver medicines as the sun rose. She wouldn't hear the curfew bell crawl into her skin like a burrowing screwworm or watch the last of Eskravé's villagers scurry into their houses. She wouldn't see the men gather for the Rayga hunt and squint to find Abba among them.

Instead, she would become the Rayga hunt, spending her days searching for a creature in the shadows. If she survived long enough. No other girl had lasted the night.

And finding the creature was only half the battle. Then, she had to bring it to the priest.

She swallowed her fears, her worries, and her doubts. It was a practiced art she had begun the first day Abba came home from the Rayga hunt and passed out drunk. Malka had scooped a toddler Hadar in her arms and played with her while Imma saw patients. She had settled Hadar on her hip and cleaned Abba's sick from the floor.

Malka always did what she needed to do. And she would do the same now.

CHAPTER 5

When he was alive, Baba had nicknamed her Simcha Shachar, meaning the joy of dawn. He had said one night Malka forgot to close her window before she fell asleep. When the dregs of night drifted away and the sun rose beyond the tree brush, it yawned warm rays, spreading far and wide over Eskravé. One such ray fell through Malka's window, illuminating her sleeping form.

"I think the sun speaks to you in the morning," Baba had said. "It likes your company."

Malka had giggled, curls bouncing on her shoulder. "Baba, that doesn't make any sense! Why would the sun want company?"

Baba had smiled, pulling Malka onto his lap. "The stars keep each other company at night. But during the day, the sun is the only light in the sky. Perhaps it gets lonely burning so bright."

"Is the sun magic?" Malka had asked, staring at how the sun made the dust motes dance.

"Some may believe that. But I think there is a danger in assuming the world is made of magic. Men will try to command it."

Today's dawn shone dimly, white-yellow tinted fingers sprawling out from ashy storm clouds. Malka wondered what her grandfather would say now, as little light fell through her bedroom window.

There was certainly no magic now. Not on Malka's side, anyway.

She adjusted her cloak and tightened the sack across her body. At the doorway, she committed to memory the bedroom she shared with her sisters. With two beds crowding the walls and a single window between them, it wasn't much. But it was the room Malka had lived in her entire life. She could still remember sharing this room with her parents when her grandparents were alive, and after, when the room became hers and Danya's to share. They treated it like a castle and played games of suitors and princesses with all their newfound space.

When Hadar moved into their room, she had curled her warm sleeping body into Malka's arms and her heart had been at the edge of bursting.

The three of them had made the room their own, paper cuttings lining a small shelf on the wall. Hadar's were the most beautiful and intricate among them. Malka would have taken one as a reminder of home but could not bear to ruin any of Hadar's creations.

Before Malka left, she unhooked Abba's dagger from the wall and weighed it in her palm. It was heavy and intimidating, the silver smooth and sharp. Once, she had retrieved it for him, and nicked her thumb brushing the blade. Her skin had peeled wide open, blood gushing from the cut. It reminded Malka of the leather workers who flayed the skin from dead sheep, stringy sinew lingering on the carcass.

With unsteady hands, she slid the dagger back into its sheath and attached it to the waistband of her apron. Already in her sack was the snare Abba took on the Rayga hunts.

Tears streamed down her face, freezing against the frigid wind. They pierced her skin, and Malka rubbed them away before burrowing further into her cloak.

The air was fresh—pine and earth not yet tainted by the day. Bakers had not yet slipped their dough into ovens, and the shektal vendors had many hours before they would roll out their carts and fragrance the air with perfumes and dyes. It made sense to start her search early with the full day ahead. It gave her the best chance to find the Rayga before night overtook the woods.

Someone called Malka's name. Amnon stepped through the pathway between houses and onto the street.

Like Malka, he wore his weighty wool cloak and a sack filled to the brim around his shoulders. A sword hung from his hips, so long it nearly dragged in the snow as he walked. The swift schedule Brożek imposed upon them had left little time for preparation.

"Amnon, you should go home," she pleaded.

His smile fell. "What happened to *good morning,* Amnon? *How are the fish today,* Amnon?"

"Are you really teasing me now?"

"Malka, you can fight me on this all you'd like. But I am not leaving you to face Mavetéh alone."

"You have nothing to prove." she said, her last hope at convincing her stubborn friend. "To me, or to anyone."

Malka had always imagined Amnon as the Falag pine trees, which grew faster than any other tree in the Rhaškan Empire. So fast, they say the Balkisk Kingdom's Cedyz Forest grew in a year's time, from nothing to impending canopies. But rising high was not without its consequences. The Falag grew so quick, the sky could not prepare for them in time. Once they brushed the bottom of the clouds, where the cerulean blue faded to the gray white, they began to slope back down until the weight of their down-turned trunks caused them to snap.

Young, with flimsy limbs and wide eyes, Amnon had dreamed of standing taller than his older brothers, whom his father favored. Even if he had to strain his neck so high it began to curve back toward the earth and snap.

"You're doing this for your family, let me do this for mine. We all would feel much better if the Rayga is found. And your Imma . . ." Amnon shuffled a hand through his hair. "Well, you know my youngest brother wouldn't be around if it wasn't for her."

Imma had healed so many over the years, including Amnon's youngest brother, who had developed a cough so fierce during his first year, they did not think he would have made it if not for Imma's consistent healing tonics.

Malka grew more confident in her decision. Eskravé needed Imma. Her family needed Imma.

As they approached the edge of Mavetéh's grasp, two people came into view, their chestnut horses vibrant against the thicket of trees.

"Aleksi?"

"Hi, Malka." Aleksi flashed her his signature smile, though his eyes were glassy.

His horse puttered to the side, revealing the knight behind him. Václav.

Malka spared Amnon a distressing glance, heart sinking. She imagined the knight grabbing her blouse with his fist, the same way he had Amnon, proclaiming that Father Brożek had changed his mind, or perhaps he never intended to let her go at all.

She cleared her throat. "What's happening?"

"Father Brożek has decided we should accompany you in your mission," Aleksi said.

"To make sure you don't do anything suspicious—or conjure any curses with your Yahadi magic," Václav added. "Sent me to lead and Aleksi here since you two already looked so friendly."

Malka almost felt bad for Aleksi. He had defended her and as a result, would face Mavetéh. Even if neither he nor Father Brožek believed the forest a threat, she knew better.

"What exactly do you think we could do? Create a new monster to bring back and claim as the Rayga?" Amnon asked, incredulous.

"Never know with you Yahad," Václav said.

Amnon opened his mouth, but Malka set a placating hand on his arm.

Aleksi and Václav readied their horses, and Amnon used the distraction to lean in close and whisper, "Malka, are you sure this is a good idea?"

"I don't know if it's a *good* idea. But it can't be a bad one, to have two extra swords swinging. Besides, we don't exactly have a choice."

"Let's hope they swing at the Rayga and not at our heads," Amnon grumbled.

With a kick, Václav and Aleksi began their jaunt into Mavetéh, with Malka and Amnon trailing behind on foot.

"So, do you have a plan, Malka?" Aleksi asked. "Or are we wandering around?"

In truth, Malka didn't have a plan. It had all happened so fast—from volunteering, to saying her goodbyes, to making sure she had enough sleep to keep her wits about her today. But like an animal, the monster still fed. It must thirst, too, eventually.

Malka gulped, hand tightening around the shoulder strap of her bag. "We should walk along the bank of the Leirit river."

The monster always found its girls—of that, Malka was sure. She wanted the upper hand, to catch it unawares before it caught her. It was the only way she could imagine a situation where she might win.

It was foolish, she knew, but she did not have the luxury of choice.

Reality chilled her bones, like a clutching cold that made anyone shake long after snuggling close to a warm fire. Her heart pulsed in her ears.

It is only dawn, she reminded herself. *You don't have to worry until nightfall.*

The shadow of the trees swallowed them, sun slipping from view as the opaque canopy overtook the sky. The ground crunched like brittle bones beneath her feet. It had been five years since she last stepped foot in these woods, and nothing rang familiar. The trees now emerged from the ground like unfurling pin curls, trunks twisted unnaturally. The leaves dressing them were as serrated as the dagger at her hip. A fallen berry splattered under her boot, sending specks of red on the surrounding snow. She imagined the berry as fingers, crunched beneath her boot as beneath a blade.

Malka didn't want to think about Minton, so instead she recalled the rhyme she used to sing with Imma to learn how to forage in Kratzka Šujana:

> *Trees with trunks the size of boulders*
> *And berries as small as stars*
> *Will you pick the one that feeds our bellies*
> *Or one that stops the heart?*
> *Black will pucker on the tongue*
> *Eat the blue and be forever undone!*

She never considered placing one of the belladonna berries in her mouth, but it would be a far more favorable death than the Rayga. She made a note to store some if she found a plant.

Trees towered over them, shadowed limbs tangling together in the canopy above. On some oaks, a kind of glowing fruit. It was eerily quiet, the only sounds the crunch of their boots on dead leaves and the horses' steady trot.

The rich scent of earth and rotten flora were stifling, the freshness of the crisp morning long gone. The clouds of Malka's breath swirled languidly, caught in the syrupy air.

The wind howled a wolf cry. "Perhaps we should walk a little faster," she suggested, breath hitching.

Aleksi craned his head to look back, a lazy smile on his face. "You're in quite the rush to die if what you say about these woods is true, Malka. Is my company that bad?"

Some of us have a lot to lose, she would have said if she were braver.

Malka's only indication of time was the increasing ache in her feet and the numbness of her reddened nose.

"The forest was not always like this," Amnon said, breaking the silence. He watched the shimmer of wind brush the blackened leaves, his eyes glazed over by the cold.

Malka knew the phrase well, having uttered it over and over to herself. When the shektal filled with visitors, Eskraven villagers expressed the same sentiment to the southern travelers. *The forest was not always like this,* they would claim. It didn't matter to the southerners, who were happy if they acquired their Valonian furs for a good barter price. Mavetéh didn't take their girls. The Yahad kept the phrase close. Perhaps it kept the memory of the past alive, dragging its existence into the present. Maybe they said the phrase over and over again to make it true. *The forest was not always like this. The forest was not always like this. The forest was not always like this.*

She uttered the phrase now as the wind blew a foul odor through the trees.

"Do you think there are dybbukim here, Malka?" Amnon asked, his voice wavering on the word.

Malka tucked her arms around her waist. The idea of restless spirits did nothing to keep her calm. But with the body count Mavetéh racked up, it was hard to believe there weren't dybbukim waiting for warm bodies to inhabit.

The woods were restless and cold—the same way all stories of dybbukim began. A person walking through the woods only to be met with an untimely end. So untimely, they had not yet made peace with their wrongs. They had not doused themselves in white and atoned, or serviced themselves to make amends for their sins. Thus, a restless spirit was birthed from their death and climbed into the body of another living soul.

Malka had wondered if Chaia became a dybbuk, forced into death too early. But Chaia did not leave her sins to fester; did not hold guilt close as Malka did. She was steadfast in her decisiveness, no matter the consequences. There would be no unforgiven sins to which the dybbuk could cling.

Perhaps Malka's bravery to find the Rayga budded from her friendship with Chaia.

Václav stopped abruptly and jumped off his horse. He handed the reins to Aleksi. "Hold him, will you? Gotta piss."

"It smells like someone did already," Aleksi remarked, scrunching his nose.

Václav disappeared behind the trees.

The wind blew stronger, and Malka recoiled from the rancid odor. She covered her nose with the back of her hand.

Aleksi lifted his cloak above his nose. "What is that smell?"

Malka had an idea, and desperately wanted to be wrong. But the wind further carried the scent, and she couldn't deny it, like rotted meat and the sickly sweetness of fruit.

Decay.

A crash rang through the woods, and Václav grunted from behind the trees.

Aleksi cursed and jumped off the horse, abandoning the reins as he jogged toward Václav.

Malka moved to follow, but Amnon halted her. "Malka, we're not here to protect them, as they sure as hell won't protect us."

Malka shrugged out of his grip. "I don't think the threat is a live one, Amnon."

When he came into sight, Václav was on his knees, his metal armor covered in muck and . . . blood.

Bile pooled in her throat. Dead bodies rose from the ground like half-raked plants. Their limbs twisted in unnatural angles; intestines strewn across the ground like snakes. Dried blood caked their remaining skin, mixed with earth and secretion. On the still intact skin were bite marks near missing limbs, the rough cut of flesh and the white bone visible among the wreckage. There must've been four or five of them, though Malka couldn't be sure.

The putrid scent of their rotting flesh soured the air.

Amnon doubled over and retched. But Malka scanned her eyes over the bodies, looking for any signs of Chaia—her silk brown hair, her round face, the scar on the palm of her hand she had had since birth.

She whispered a soft prayer. *Do not let her be here,* she begged. *Do not let me find her body here.* Her mind fogged with rot and grief. It had been a year since Chaia had disappeared, and the truth was she would be long past recognition by now, just bones pasted with lingering dried tissue.

Despite knowing that, she still searched.

There was no familiarity among the dead women. *I would know her even here.* She said it the same way the villagers talked about the forest. *I would know, I would know, I would know.* If she said it enough, it would be true.

Malka shuddered thinking what the night held in store. If Mavetéh stole girls once the sun set, she did not have much time left before the Rayga would come for her. She needed to come for *it* first.

"There is a man here," Aleksi remarked, crossing himself. "An Ozmini man."

Malka examined the bodies again. He was right. The Rayga had not only killed the women, but a man, too. Ozmini, denoted by the array of prayer beads on the ground. Rzepka was not the first Ozmin the Rayga had taken.

And the attack had been recent; the bodies were still bloated with gas, feasted on by insects. Their intestines recognizable.

"Do you think the Church knows about this yet?"

Václav shrugged, but his jaw tensed. "The Church knows what Triorzay shares. There is no reason to worry, Aleksi, if you have been pious and followed Triorzay's wishes. After all, sinners hide like mice." He locked eyes with Malka. "In the cracks, where they think they won't be found. But they always squeal."

"I don't know if . . ." Aleksi began, rolling on the balls of his feet, fingering his own prayer beads attached to his belt.

"There is no reason to worry, you understand? There is no reason to worry."

Malka wondered if the man had died the same way she worried Amnon would—defending the women and ensnaring himself between the Rayga's teeth.

The Yahad would be blamed for the Ozmini deaths. She couldn't help what Václav and Aleksi reported to Father Brożek, but she would die before letting Amnon end up forgotten in the dirt with only feasting beetles for company.

Václav stomped away, disappearing again through the brush and back on the path they had chosen. With one last regretful glance at the bodies, Malka followed.

⚲

"We should rest here." Václav drew his horse to a stop.

Hours had passed since they stumbled upon the decaying bodies. Malka ached, her sides cramping from a full day of walking. Night had washed over them in a blackness deeper than a devil's alphonsa plant, leeching its poison into skin. When their lanterns died, Malka held her hand in front of her face and stared at nothing.

Malka drew a match from her sack, replacing the candle in her lantern and lighting it. The fresh flame erupted, and Malka blinked to adjust to the light. They were in a clearing.

"Out in the open?" Amnon questioned.

Aleksi tilted his head toward the trickling sound of the stream. "Isn't the point to attract the Rayga, pretty boy? We're by a water source and in plain sight."

Amnon swallowed, face ashen. "Right."

They pulled dry kindling from their pouches and assembled the firewood.

Once the fire was lit, Malka leaned into its warmth, the cold visceral without the heat of the sun. Some dexterity returned to her fingers, but they were still fattened by the cold.

Václav slapped Amnon on the back. "Time for a fisherman's son to shine, boy."

Amnon eyed Aleksi. "I'm not going to leave either of you alone with her."

Václav wrapped his fist into Amnon's cloak and hoisted him back. "You don't have a choice."

"Go," Malka said, heart twinging. "I'll be fine."

Amnon threw up his hands in surrender. "Alright, alright."

Malka watched them until the lanterns they carried grew dim behind the thicket.

"Don't worry," Aleksi said. "Václav's appetite is bigger than his fist."

Malka raised her brow. "How much do the odds of violence increase if Amnon is already acquainted with his fist?"

Aleksi chuckled, his handsome face softening. "If there's one thing you Yahad are, it's sharp-tongued. I guess it's helpful, to slide your way into Ordobav's politicking. Well, not *you*. But your people."

Her mind drifted back to the bodies they had found.

"Do you believe me now?" she asked. "That the Rayga is real. That Imma didn't do anything to Rzepka."

Aleksi sucked his bottom lip between his teeth. "We don't know what happened, Malka. Could've been a bad deer attack. Or a bear. Hell, maybe even a human drugged up on a manta joint who had access to a rake."

He wouldn't meet her eyes. Wouldn't lie to her face.

"Maybe it was that golem your infamous rabbi created. I was there when it happened, you know. When it killed that boy." He considered. "I wouldn't put this past something it could do."

Her gut twisted. Of course, he would find another way to blame her people. But it was not possible. After the tragedy, the Maharal had been desperate to save his reputation. He laid the golem to rest in the attic of the shul Bachta, where it would stay, forever slumbering, unable to do more harm. A constant reminder of the Maharal's mistake and the dangers of Kefesh.

The same holy magic her mind drifted to when she prayed.

"Václav said you were safe if you followed Triorzay's wishes. That He would protect you here," Malka said, pivoting the conversation before her mind knotted on thoughts of Kefesh. "What exactly does your God wish?"

Aleksi leaned back on his palms, more at ease now the conversation had shifted. "Triorzay gives us so much. The earth beneath our feet, the fish our travel companions will catch to satiate us. Protection from harm and the chances we seize during this life. But beyond the everyday blessings, Triorzay prepares us for the life that begins once this one ceases. Our eternal life, in Vasicati."

Vasicati, the Ozmini afterlife for the righteous. She knew of it from the Church's mandated religious lectures all Eskraven children attended, despite the only Ozmins in her village being those who managed local governance and property, like Chotek.

To some, Vasicati was rolling fields of goldenmase which scented the air with a sultry deep dizzying sweetness. Like a high from the manta plant that lasted for eternity as they were free to daze, responsibility no longer clinging to anyone's shoulders. To others, Vasicati was not so much a place as a feeling. Being forever satisfied—an already warmed cloak against cold shoulders, endless meals that did not grow lukewarm.

"What awaits you in Vasicati?" Malka asked.

Aleksi smiled wickedly. "A place where pleasure is never absent. Where I am consumed whole by bliss and unworried by anything else. Do you know that kind of bliss, Malka? God, I want to drown in it."

"Pleasure?"

"The forbidden kind," Aleksi added, eyes drifting to the curve of Malka's neck. "The best kind."

She did know that kind of pleasure, only it wasn't forbidden. Not for her or her people. She didn't often have the chance, but when she did, she didn't feel guilt. Not when she ran her hand over her curves, nor when she dipped her fingers between her thighs. Malka had never been with someone else like that, but it was hard not to imagine it now. Someone else's fingers on her, lips at the contour of her neck where she brushed her thumb.

Malka covered her blush with both hands.

"You know it, then," Aleksi said, lecherous.

"How is your place in Vasicati guaranteed?" Malka asked, wishing the cold didn't exacerbate her ripened cheeks.

Aleksi didn't antagonize her further, much to Malka's relief.

Instead, he said, "We have to be selfless. We must sacrifice."

"Sacrifice what? Lambs or cows?"

Aleksi shook his head. "Sacrifice ourselves."

"Kill yourself, you mean?"

"Saints, Malka. You know so little, don't you? That is a sin itself. We sacrifice parts of ourselves to show Him we are selfless. That we give ourselves as payment for His protection. For our spot in Vasicati."

Malka recalled what Rzepka had said. Triorzay had given her a life in the royal palace, and in return, she left it to join the Paja.

"Your sacrifice is collecting tithes with the priest?"

"One of many. The more you sacrifice, the more you are absolved. But sacrifice is different for everyone. Something to one person might mean nothing to another. So, we sacrifice what is meaningful to us."

Her eyes flickered down to Aleksi's arm, where she had seen a peek of his scar, identical to Rzepka's.

Aleksi caught her stare and began to roll up his sleeve. He smoothed his fingers over the puckering white scar, similar to the pale mark of a tree sliced for sap. "What is meaningful to every Ozmin? Life, carried by the blood flowing through our veins."

"You sacrifice your own blood." Malka did not say this accusingly, but as if the statement was a ragged puzzle piece she had fit into place.

"It is the same as how you Yahad fast for your holy days. We are both giving something vital. You give up food, while we give up blood."

Malka bit her tongue. They did not fast as a sacrifice, to give themselves to Yohev or guarantee their place in an afterlife. They fasted to show their dedication and resilience. To recognize hunger and appreciate fullness when the fast broke.

"Boy might not be so inept after all," Václav said as he and Amnon reappeared, two small trout strung along some twine.

Malka swallowed whatever response she had planned for Aleksi. It was not worth the argument or angering the Ozmin by challenging his beliefs. Malka had learned many years ago silence was the best way to tame a beast. Instead, she ate.

※

Malka leaned into the fire's warmth, grateful as her fingers regained their full range of motion. Her eyelids hung low, blurring the light into hazy shades of orange and white.

She was exhausted, frightened, and still on edge, like a strung-up chicken in the butcher's window. She imagined a noose around her neck, held in

Mavetéh's teeth. When the Rayga wanted her, she would have no choice. It would pull the string taut, and Malka's neck would break.

Except the Rayga did not give a painless death. She knew it from the dead girls in Eskravé. Rzepka's ruined body. The Ozmini peasants whose limbs appeared from the earth, staining the dirt around them like beet juice.

"I will not let anything happen to you tonight," Amnon said beside her, softly so Václav and Aleksi wouldn't hear from their resting spot by a nearby tree. He brushed his knuckle across Malka's cheek. It lingered too long—the intention of a lover not a friend.

Malka thought of the noose around her neck, the prickle of it tightening against her skin. She wrapped his hand in hers. "I know you will try."

Amnon sighed. He was exhausted, too. His under eyes were drawn as loose as a rooster's neck, creases deep and pigmented from the cold.

"Malka, you can't end up like them. The Ozmins we found . . . they were unrecognizable."

Amnon had been spared from seeing the Rayga's other victims, Rzepka's body already covered when he arrived. He had only heard the stories whispered in the night. But it was different, seeing them in these woods—the sharp tang of blood still hanging in the air, decay crawling into their noses and burrowing deep.

But Malka had seen Rzepka. Her flesh torn and bones jutted. Her eyes strewn on the ground like a pair of dice, soft tissue licking hardened snow.

A bone-deep fear sunk into Malka's stomach.

She pictured Imma's loving face. Her calloused fingers that put Malka and her sisters back together again when they had hurt themselves. There was a reason Malka was here in Mavetéh. And it was not to die.

"I will not end up like them, Amnon," she declared. But they were not fools. And the promise soured on her tongue.

But neither Malka nor Amnon wanted to discuss her fate further. Instead, Amnon said to her, "Sleep. I will keep watch."

Malka shook her head. "Only for a bit. You will be exhausted if you don't rest tonight. We'll alternate."

When he perched against the tree closest to Malka, vise grip on his sword, Malka settled on the ground and pulled her cloak tightly around.

She had fallen asleep drenched in cold many times, but without the walls of her home to block out the wind, her teeth chattered painfully. She bit her tongue and tasted blood.

Václav joined her near the fire, leaving Aleksi to keep watch with Amnon.

He sprawled out and yawned, his eyes catching Malka's from across the flame. "We could always cuddle for warmth, you know."

Malka shifted so her back faced both the heat and Václav, grinding her teeth.

Distracted by the weather, Malka had not let herself think of what the night brought with it, wrapped in the darkness like a garden onion. If she peeled back the night, would she find endless layers of its terror?

The wind rustled through the trees again, whipping against her ears as brutal as ice. As the howl pressed close, she swore she heard her name in its wake, intoned like the poisonous berry rhyme, warning her away.

She turned and turned, batting at her ears. No matter which way she laid, she could not escape the sound of her name on the wind's taunting lips.

Malka wondered if this craze tormented Abba. If a wine bottle could dull the sounds. Could the alcohol tear her name away from the wind's mouth and strip her of its haunting?

Hopeless of any sleep, Malka stood. "I'm going to go relieve myself."

Amnon frowned. "Not alone."

Malka crossed her arms, indignant. "Just on the other side of those trees, I'll be in your line of sight."

Amnon tested his lookout. Once he confirmed he could see Malka from the river, he relented. "Have your dagger?"

Malka shifted her cloak, revealing the weapon at her hip.

Guided by her torch lantern, she disappeared behind the trees.

On her way back, she caught her reflection on the water. It was half frozen where the current slowed, speckling the river with hazy white ice.

Her appearance was as wearied as she felt, the bags under her eyes as deep purple as Amnon's bruised face had been.

It was the first night she had slept without Hadar tucked by her side in many years. The ache hurt more than any cold. She could come back from this. She must. Closing her eyes, Malka thought of Hadar's soft breathing and matched hers to the figment.

When at last she settled, Malka opened her eyes and observed her reflection once more. Her ringlets splayed out of her kerchief, the rest of her hair wild against her shoulders. The undulating flow of the river shadowed the angular jut of her nose.

A sharp movement caught her eye from above her reflection, there and gone so quickly it must've been a trick of the torchlight.

Malka blinked hard, and it was there again. A shadow lurking behind her reflection. She spun quick, holding out the lantern to the dark. She met only the bole of a tree, bald branches dipped in snow.

She untensed. It should not have been a surprise Mavetéh made her see imaginary things. The men of the Rayga hunt claimed Mavetéh's curse brought with it hallucinogenic sap, which made men inconsolable whenever it touched their skin. Hallucinations only cured by alcohol burning down their throat.

Malka ran a hand through her hair, feeling for sticky sap. She stared at her palm as it came away dry.

Peering in the water again, she watched the arms of the tree intently. Hot breath caressed her neck.

It's wind, she told herself. But the self-consoling was fruitless.

Through the undulations, the branches began to slither from the tree.

Malka shot around, gasping. The tree loomed over her, roots ripped from the ground, upending the earth into jagged slices that stomped around like feet. The bark had torn away, crafting a rotten mouth in the cavity's swirls.

Pain tore through her side as one of the branches whipped her, sending the torch lantern flying from her hand. She would've fallen from the impact, but the whip-like branch coiled around her instead, squeezing her arms against her chest.

She couldn't breathe and heaved in panic as her feet left the ground.

"Malka!" Amnon cried out, appearing from behind the trees. He swung his sword and it caught in the animated branch holding her captive. He tugged frantically, but the metal held firm.

Malka's vision blurred at the edges as the branch began to constrict around her body, as if she were a mouse ensnared by a snake desperate to feed. She wanted to scream, to shout at Amnon to leave, but she couldn't speak, couldn't do anything but try to stay conscious.

Aleksi and Václav galloped in on their horses, rearing as they regarded the animated tree. They cursed, and watched as the cavity of the tree swelled, the smile on its bark widening until the hole was the length of three grown men. Claws appeared from its depth, slick with black sap, and a creature crawled out of the opening.

The monster was nightmarish, ooze dripping from pustules across its body, hands, and legs like the warts on a tree. Its eyes, the reddish-brown of old blood, glowed in the darkness.

Malka had feared before, but it dwindled compared to the raucous thumping of her heart. She had never seen a creature so unimaginable as this, so monstrous. No doubt in her mind this was the Rayga, here to eat its next girl. Malka was already on its dinner plate, suspended in the air and helpless.

How naive she had been to think she could tame the Rayga. And she would pay for that naivety with her life.

Aleksi swung his sword, but the Rayga was faster. Its wooden hands stole the blade and flung it aside. It launched at him, knocking him from his horse, and his back hit the ground with a terrible crack.

The horse reared and bolted through the trees.

The Rayga towered over Aleksi. It clutched one of the slithering branches, which straightened like a sword in its grasp, and swung it through Aleksi's neck, severing his head. His face, struck with terror, drooped at an unnatural angle as his jugular veins cried out in fits of blood. His head remained attached to his body only by the fierce grip of viscous muscle and sinew, which jutted from his neck like grisly fangs.

Aleksi's eyes darted, and Malka watched, terrified. *He was still alive.*

Václav jumped from his horse, ducking to avoid a swinging branch, and kneeled close to Aleksi.

"Be with Triorzay now, my friend," he said, crossing himself, and cut through his neck until Aleksi grew still. Stiller than Malka had ever seen him. All the light which had gleamed in his eyes as he joked, gone.

The Rayga had loosened its grip on her, distracted by Aleksi. Malka took advantage and squirmed from its hold, dropping clumsily to the ground. Sharp pain radiated up her leg and she sucked in air, ignoring the hot needles of each labored breath.

Amnon sprinted to help her, but Václav, after dodging a blow from the Rayga, halted Amnon by fisting his cloak. He hit Amnon's skull with the hilt of his sword, sending him crumbling to the ground.

"You think you deserve to live when he is dead?" Václav asked Malka, hand pointing toward Aleksi's lifeless body. His face was beaten and bloodied, chain mail no match for the Rayga's sharp teeth. "It wants you, so it'll have you. Filthy *Medvadi*."

Václav seized Malka's injured leg and dragged her toward the Rayga.

Malka shrieked, fighting against Václav's grip. She kicked with all her might, her foot landing on his crotch. Václav gasped, hands flying between his legs. Malka used the distraction and rammed him away with her foot. Already weakened by her kick, he stumbled, slipping on the wet rock near the water. He fell, head sinking onto a jutting stone, catching like a fish to a spear.

Those eyes that had stared at her with such hatred only minutes before, were now empty and lifeless.

"Malka, watch out!" Amnon warned, having returned to consciousness. Malka barely had time to look before one of the branches slammed into her, sending her tumbling into the water. Only, the thin stream of river had yawned into something gargantuan—like the violent sea with a violent current, which hooked her inside and swallowed.

Her vision blurred as she sank, down far enough that Amnon's screams, deafened by the water, silenced entirely. When the daze cleared, Malka began to panic. She attempted to wade to the surface, but the freezing water had stunned her muscles.

Her skin burned as if she had sunk into a boiling pot, limbs rigid and chest constricted, as the icy tendrils enveloped her. She needed to move, to swim and breathe air. But her legs were iron, and she sank, sank, sank, as darkness crept in.

Then, a sound sliced through the water. A scream, or a grunt. Malka, in her faint consciousness, wondered if she had made the sound. But the scream did not sound human. It sounded like the woods when it had howled her name.

It didn't matter. Mavetéh had her now.

The flame necklace she wore drifted in front of her, the chain still around her neck. It glinted, and Malka wished so desperately to grab for it, and press the pendant to her lips.

A hand wrapped around her arm, but that was all she knew when everything went dark.

PART
TWO

CHAPTER 6

Malka awoke with a start. She was promptly greeted by the raucous throbbing of her head, like galloping hoofbeats inside her skull.

She was in a room—the roof woven from thick, rounded wood. In front of her, a fire roared in an open hearth, coating her skin with ash and soot. Its warmth drew Malka closer, and she grasped for the heat like she would an embrace. But her muscles were slow and awkward, movements jerky, and she lost her balance, rolling so close to the fire it burned her cheeks and the tip of her nose, the fierce sting of smoke blurring her eyes with tears. She resisted the urge to cough.

"Was drowning not enough for you? Now you must add burns to your list of ailments?"

The woman's voice was unfamiliar, but deep and warm, like it was made for the dregs of winter. Malka shifted toward it, the wood beneath her croaking.

"I feel terrible," Malka said huskily. The rest of her body throbbed with as much pain as her head. Every muscle screamed in opposition to her movements, every joint swollen and whimpering.

"Drink this." The woman thrust a steaming mug in front of her.

Malka blinked clear her tears until the woman came into focus. Her breath caught in horror. The woman had a body more stone than skin, vines for veins, with eyes the sable color of damp soil and skin a graying brown like the rocks on a riverbed. Thick black hair fell in waves down her back, settling on her tunic. Her face was half stone, and on her forehead, a word carved from the sacred language of Malka's people. Three letters: אמת. *Emet*. Meaning *truth*.

Her unnatural appearance made Malka remember the Rayga, who had crawled out of the belly of a tree and decapitated a grown man. Aleksi's head, separated from his body, tendons and blood decorating the ground. Václav, eyes going vacant as his head hit rock.

The icy needles of the river enveloped her again, the burning pressure in her lungs, her throat, her nose. Losing feeling in her legs. The murky water growing dim until she remembered nothing at all. A river that became a violent sea.

She fought back a dry heave.

Malka eyed the steaming liquid. Even the woman's fingers, wrapped around the mug, were stone.

"Who are you?" Malka demanded, throat burning. "What's in that mug?"

The woman's lips thinned. "Fine, don't drink it." She slammed the mug on a wooden stump of a table, sending liquid splashing. "Be miserable."

The woman crossed her arms and stormed away. In the wake of her steps, roots slithered from the ground like serpents. She busied herself in the small kitchen, crushing some herbs beneath a pebble.

It reminded Malka of Imma, preparing poultices in her workroom. Her throat constricted. "What is your name, monster?"

The woman paused, rock midair, and met Malka's gaze. Her eyes were impossibly dark. "You seem to have given me one already."

Silence lingered as the woman returned to her task. Malka took in her impressively tall frame, and with it, the deep shadow it cast on the wall behind her. Malka flinched at how abruptly it took her back to the river again. The Rayga's shadow, dancing on the ice before it wrapped its arms around her.

She closed her eyes, evened her breathing.

"It's . . . you caught me off guard, I'm sorry." A beat of silence. "May I ask your name again?"

The woman raised her brow. "You may ask."

A snarky response, but Malka could hardly blame her for her hard edges when Malka had already called her a monster. But Malka wasn't convinced she wasn't one, either.

"What is your name?"

The woman funneled the crushed herbs into a small glass and covered the top with a thin piece of animal skin and twine. "You may call me Nimrah."

"And this is your hut?"

Annoyance curled her lips. "You have the same astuteness as your ginger friend. Yes, this is my hut."

Malka's heart leapt. "Amnon? He's here? He's safe?"

"He's asleep," Nimrah said, nodding toward the back of the room where Amnon sat hunched against the wall, his head perched to the side and mouth agape as he breathed evenly. "His only harm is how much he worried over you."

The dirt and soot from the fire was cleaned from his face, though a bruise had discolored his forehead. He had a red mark across his cheek where the branch had slapped him.

"Did he bring me here?" Malka asked, her tensed shoulders relaxing. She hadn't realized they'd been so rigid.

"No, I brought you both here."

Malka waited for her to continue; either to explain how she had found them or how they had managed to survive the Rayga attack in the first place. But Nimrah didn't. She kept at her work in the kitchen as if Malka were not there.

Malka cleared her throat, but Nimrah did not so much as shift her gaze or raise her brow.

She frowned.

"Malka?" Amnon's groggy voice broke through the silence.

Malka's heart clenched. "Amnon?"

Amnon rose from the ground and hurried toward her, bending to his knees to better study her. He beamed, though drowsiness still softened his features. "I'm so glad you're awake. I was so afraid you were in that icy water for too long."

He squeezed her arm.

"How long have I been asleep?" she asked Amnon since Nimrah was not keen to answer her questions.

Amnon's face fell. "A day."

"*A day*?"

"You are lucky to be alive at all," Nimrah interrupted, deeming Malka finally worthy of a response. She threw some more wood into the fireplace. The flames yawned and growled. "These woods are not kind. Especially not to girls like you."

"Girls like me?"

Nimrah quirked her brow, bending to match Malka's gaze. "Yahadi girls. You are a Yahad, are you not?"

Malka fumbled for her necklace and was relieved to find it pressed against her chest. "I am."

This close, Malka could see more letters from the Yahadi ancient alphabet carved into the stone of Nimrah's arm. The skin on her body unmarred, as far as she could tell.

Amnon cleared his throat. "Nimrah saved us, Malka. I don't think we would be alive without her."

Malka remembered a hand around her arm before she went unconscious. She peered at Nimrah. "You pulled me from the water?"

Amnon added, "She subdued the creature, Malka. Without any weapons."

"How—" Malka tried to stand, but her muscles seized, ankle searing with hot pain under her weight. She fell back, running her palm over her swollen joint to soothe it.

"Did you drink Nimrah's tea yet?" Amnon's face paled when he noticed the black-blue decorating her foot.

Malka shook her head, eyes catching on the table where the steaming mug sat untouched.

Amnon held it out to her. "You'll feel better if you drink this."

She hesitated, curling her hand into a fist instead.

Amnon ran his knuckles over Malka's cold cheek. "It's fine, Malka. I drank some earlier. It healed my wounds faster than any of your Imma's poultices."

Malka eyed him suspiciously. Tea was a wonderful treatment, but it could not heal broken bones and fade bruises. But the aches had worsened in the time she had been awake, and the pain clawed at her. Frostbite had provoked grueling and painful blisters on her hands and toes, making any movement laborious.

Relenting, Malka wrapped her stiff hands around the mug and tilted it to her lips.

She would know the bold taste of sage anywhere, earthy like eucalyptus, the bite of pepper and sour lemon on her tongue. But there was something else underneath the herb—a tang she couldn't place.

The tea worked as soon as she swallowed it, warmth spreading inside of her. Her muscles loosened, her foggy mind began to clear, and the aching in her head and body dulled.

Her mind sharpened enough for her to realize she was dressed in a man's tunic.

"Did someone undress me?"

Amnon blushed. "I . . ."

"I did," said Nimrah, a smirk playing on her lips. "Would you rather I had left you to freeze in your soaking clothes?"

Malka flushed.

Nimrah tilted her chin toward the fire where Malka's clothes were strung up with twine. "They'll be dry soon."

"We were as good as dead," Malka emphasized. "How could you possibly have saved the both of us?"

"Eat first, then you may interrogate me. Since you seem so determined to ask every question that crosses your mind," Nimrah said. "Whatever you had in your stomach was emptied on my shoes when I dragged you from the river."

Malka's protest died on her lips when her stomach cramped sharply. Her last meal had been the trout Amnon caught. Inevitably, her thoughts drifted to Václav and Aleksi, whose bodies now lay rotting on the forest floor.

Václav's death was Malka's fault, but she wasn't ashamed for defending herself. Though she wouldn't forget him, either, or the hatred in his eyes as he bruised her leg in his grasp.

And then, there was Aleksi.

She wondered what would become of his body, left without a proper burial. Did the Ozmins have creatures like the dybbukim to worry about? Would Aleksi's soul wander in search of a host to relieve his torment?

Maybe his soul had made it to his expected afterlife in Vasicati. Or maybe the forest took it instead.

Malka shivered at the thought. She distracted herself, accepting Amnon's help as he wrapped Malka's arm around his neck and hauled her from the ground. Her side ached, and she was sure she'd find a sizable bruise under her borrowed tunic.

The world spun and she blinked until the room came into focus.

The hut was much smaller than her house in Eskravé. The wooden walls were braided with twine, greenery peeking through the cracks like the stubborn weeds Malka used to pull from Imma's medicinal garden. Aside from the open hearth, there was a more proper clay oven for baking, the wide tree-stump table, chairs woven from roots, and a couple wheat sacks pressed together. But what stole Malka's breath was the trunk of a giant oak tree, which split the room like the great stone pillars of Eskravé's synagogue. Like the rest of the hut, there was something magical about the tree—the wood groaned when Nimrah walked by, the bark shimmering with sap.

Malka slid into a wobbly chair at the table, where a cauldron sat, steam wafting from the stew. It was mouth-wateringly rich, the salty smell of some kind of meat filling her nose.

Amnon ladled some into a bowl for her.

Malka muttered the prayer for sustenance under her breath, then filled her mouth despite the heat.

When she finished, she drew her hand to her belly, relishing in the discomfort that came with fullness. It was a sensation she had long forgotten.

Amnon refilled her empty mug with tea from the kettle.

"Did you kill the Rayga?" Malka asked Nimrah.

The question felt like a juncture of fate. The monster was not what she expected. What use was her snare in capturing the creature, when it crawled out of a yawning tree and wielded the branches as weapons? How would she prove to Father Brożek she had found the Rayga when she was unsure how to trudge back with the spoils of her hunt?

Though, if Nimrah hadn't killed it, she would have no spoils of which to speak. She had already come face to face with the Rayga and almost died. *Would* have died if Nimrah had not saved them. Their next encounter would surely kill her.

"The Rayga?" Nimrah raised her brow. "Oh, that's right. Your friend here told me that's what you call the creature who attacked you. No, I did not kill it. Cursed creatures are hard to catch when they are made—or remade—by Kefesh."

Malka paled. "The Rayga is a creature of Kefesh?"

Nimrah shrugged, as if the question bored her. "In a sense."

"Are you sure?" Amnon asked, but Malka was no longer present.

She closed her eyes. She thought of every girl the woods had taken. Their bodies disemboweled by a monster created with Kefesh. Chaia, lost to her forever due to that blasphemous magic.

Baba had been right to instill in her a fear of Yahadi mysticism. Any good it could do was rendered obsolete with its capacity for violence.

If Father Brożek discovered the Paja members were killed by a monster of Yahadi magic, it would surely strengthen his ire instead of soothing it. Though, was it truly much different if he already deemed Imma a Yahadi witch who killed Rzepka for her blood? At least with the Rayga caught, the priest's fury would fall upon a guilty target.

When Malka opened her eyes again, she found Nimrah regarding her, her fingers curled against her mouth while her other hand—this one flesh—drew lazy circles on the table.

Such a human act, yet Nimrah did not seem human. Not with the stone eating half her body, green veins discoloring the skin she did have. Her height, unnatural for a woman and many men. Despite her unusual appearance, there was a mystical air about her, too. The way the earth bent with her as she moved, how her voice shimmered like rustling trees.

When Nimrah noticed her stare, she stilled her fingers and curled her hand into a fist.

"You're different than us," Malka remarked.

Nimrah barked a laugh, and a gust of wind howled through the room, disrupting the steam in the fresh cup of tea Amnon had poured for her. "Because I actually have survival instincts?"

"Because the earth reacts to you," Malka said, running her hand through the steam to imitate what Nimrah had done.

"I am different than you both, but not because of that. Any Yahad can provoke a reaction from the earth. That is the purpose of Kefesh, is it not?"

"Is that how you subdued the Rayga?" Malka's throat began to tighten. "You used Kefesh, too?"

"In the way I was made to use it." Nimrah studied them. "You don't know who I am?"

Malka stared again at the letters of the ancient Yahadi holy language on Nimrah's forehead. *Truth.* "You bear the mark of our holy language."

Nimrah traced the finger over the etching on her stone forehead. "Yes."

In the way I was made to use it.

"Made . . ." Amnon trailed off.

Malka paused. "You're a golem?"

"I was made from the clay and stone of this forest a decade ago, twisted into life by the prayer of the Maharal of Valón."

Heat pricked up her neck. "The *Maharal's* golem?"

Impossible. In the stories told, the Maharal's golem was not at all shaped like what—*who*—sat before her now. The tales had deemed the golem a voiceless giant of assembled stone. Not . . . a woman, whose body fought back and forth between stone and life, whose mouth had bite.

The golem's demeanor shifted as she straightened and clenched her jaw. "So, you do know me."

"Are you lying?" Malka asked, clutching her knees. "You do not look like the golem of the stories."

Nimrah bent forward, her shadow crawling across the table until it was consumed entirely. Her stare sent a strike of fear up Malka's spine. "And how exactly does this golem of your stories look?"

She saw it now, the reason her feminine characteristics were omitted from the stories. It must've scared men so profoundly to fear a woman this much.

But she was not like any woman Malka had known.

"We know the Maharal created you to protect the Yahad and in response, you killed an innocent Yahadi boy."

She had imagined it before—the stone giant, soulless and unflinching, murdering a child. It was worse imagining it with the golem before her in its place, more monstrous knowing this golem thought and felt, and killed that boy anyway. More vicious.

"Good to know how far stories travel," Nimrah grumbled.

The groaning fire warmed the room, yet still Malka shivered. "You're a lesson on Kefesh's destructiveness. Even the legendary Maharal couldn't control the Kefesh he possessed. It's dangerous."

Nimrah's face hardened. "Your stories don't get everything right. It is easy to change history when you wish to forget the truth."

"You're right," Malka agreed. "The stories *didn't* get everything right. They say the Maharal laid you to rest in the synagogue attic after what you had done, so you could not harm anyone else. Yet, you are here."

Nimrah's knuckles whitened as she clenched the table, wood crying under her grasp.

Malka imagined those same fists fighting back the Rayga—a creature she had thought impervious when it had squeezed her breathless. Fear crawled up her neck. Those fists could have effortlessly crushed bone.

"The people of Valón wanted me to die after what I had done," Nimrah explained. "I did not blame them. That's the story they shared, after all. The story you heard. But the Maharal was like a father to me, and I suppose I had become like a daughter to him. He brought me here, instead, to the middle of the forest marked by this Great Oak. He prayed and made it so I could only go as far as the roots of this tree spread."

Nimrah pointed to the Great Oak. At her attention, the tree groaned, shaking the wooden beams above them. A cry whistled through the air and the fire flickered. The tree had darkened—its bark a deep brownish-gray, the way wood turns when dampened.

"Lucky for you and your near drowning, that's a decent portion of the forest, as the roots seem to grow at an unnatural pace. So, I've been trapped here ever since. Good as dead if you ask me."

Nimrah hiked up her sleeve and rubbed absently at her arm. Glimpsing her skin, Malka noticed a Yahadi word carved into the stone, but she couldn't make it out.

"We don't want any trouble," Malka said, eyes trailing Nimrah's fingers, imagining them flexing around her own neck.

Nimrah snorted. "Then you better leave the forest before another creature like that finds you."

"It's imperative—" Malka began, then paled when she registered what Nimrah had said. "What do you mean *another* creature like that?"

The golem raised her brow. "You thought there only one?"

It had been her village's assumption since the killings began. A monster who, overnight, began to hunt their girls. They had been killed the same inhumane way, left with wounds no normal creature could create.

Outside, it had begun to hail, sharp raps of ice hitting the wooden hut in waves. A small puddle began to pool near the slit in the door where the intruding ice had melted.

Malka listened to the storm as her head spun. It had been one thing, to think that bringing back one creature would stop the killings and prove to Father Brożek a beast was to blame for Rzepka's death. It was quite another if there were multiple beasts. Even if they managed to capture one, the killings wouldn't stop. Father Brożek would remain unconvinced. Or even worse, he would see it as an attempt at subterfuge.

"You two make a strange choice for a hunting party," Nimrah observed. "Stranger yet with the two dead Ozmins I found you with."

"I made a bargain with an Ozmini priest. To bring him what we thought was a singular creature—the Rayga."

"You thought it smart to bargain with an Ozmini priest?"

"I had no choice," Malka said vehemently. "The Church accused my mother of killing an Ozmini woman. They claim she's a witch who planned to use the Ozmin's blood to conjure curses. But it was the creature who killed the woman. Same as it—or *they*—have killed many girls from my village. We were going to prove it."

Nimrah was silent for a moment. She shifted away from the fire, dousing much of her face in shadow. "Sounds foolish."

"I didn't *ask* for your opinion," Malka rebuked, tightening her hands around her mug.

"I didn't *request* your permission."

Malka's eyes thinned. "I didn't realize you were as rude as you were dangerous. They left that part out of the stories."

Nimrah's lips curved. "Now you understand not every story shares the whole truth."

Malka eyed the puddle. It had grown, now trailing toward them in rivulets. She wanted to rile the golem somehow, wipe the smirk from her face. She thought of Nimrah's creator, and the story Aleksi had shared about him. "If that's the case, what do you think of what's being said about the Maharal?"

"What are they saying now?"

Malka creased her brow. "You don't know?"

Nimrah waved around her hut. "Does it look like I get much communication here?"

Aleksi had been blase in his deliverance of the news, but despite Malka's desire to provoke Nimrah, she could not muster the same nonchalance. "A witness came forward accusing the Maharal of killing an Ozmini woman. They found her blood in his basement when they checked the claims of the accusation. He's been imprisoned in Valón Castle while he receives treatment for some kind of sickness. His trial has been postponed."

The golem's face paled, and she grew rigid. "What witness, exactly?"

"An Ozmin—Valonian... I don't know. I only heard it from a Paja member." One who was now dead.

Malka hadn't questioned the information at the time, hadn't asked more. She had become accustomed to swallowing her dissent. Minton's screams echoed in her head. She knew what happened to those who didn't.

"Liars as always, desperate to frame any powerful Yahad they can." Nimrah ran a hand along her jaw. "You said they're holding him in the castle?" Her eyes focused on a scabbard leaned against the corner of the room. A layer of dust turned the onyx covering gray.

"Yes."

"That's not in accordance with Ordobavian court law. Valonian Yahad accused of crimes but not yet convicted are allowed to roam freely within the Yahadi Quarter. They're not supposed to keep him captive until he's found guilty, illness or not."

Malka felt a stab of grief; the words could've easily been Chaia's.

She said now what she would've said to her best friend. "Even so, it is what it is. We are no power against the Church and crown combined."

Nimrah shook her head. "I won't let it happen. I can't fail him again. My relationship with him aside, the Yahad of Valón rely on him. There is a reason you know stories of him even in your small village—he is a pillar of the Yahadi community in Valón. He is a sign of strength. The Yahad replenish their hope with his sermons. I can't let the Church's beguiling extinguish that."

"Do you truly believe that?" Malka asked. "Perhaps you are not objective when it comes to the Maharal."

"*Please*," Nimrah *tsk*ed. "You have come to save your mother from false accusations of blood cursing, yet you believe what the Church says about the Maharal?"

"My imma has not used Kefesh."

"Tell me, village girl, why would the Maharal keep blood in his basement? If he were using it for spells, wouldn't it be gone by now? Maybe *you* cannot be objective when it comes to a practitioner of Kefesh."

Haughty, this golem was. Malka resisted the urge to scrape her fingers on the wood. She spared a glance at Amnon, who appeared as suspicious of Nimrah as she. "How are you planning to help the Maharal, then?" Malka asked. "You said yourself, he commanded you to stay here, tied to the Great Oak tree."

Nimrah leaned back in her chair and crossed her arms. "I'll find a way."

Amnon scoffed. "You want to disobey the last command the Maharal gave you by leaving?"

"He gave me no choice." She traced the engravings on her arm again, as if they anchored her the same way Malka's flame necklace did.

"Fine. We'll leave you to it." Malka pushed up from her chair, but her ankle cried in opposition. She hissed through the pain, falling ungracefully back into the seat.

Tears began to well in her eyes, and she wiped at them furiously. She had never felt this hopeless. She couldn't walk, couldn't fight. The Rayga was a myth—there were many creatures responsible for the haunting of her village. She had nothing to bring Father Brożek. She had failed Imma, failed her sisters. Failed all the women who lived in fear.

"What are we going to do, Amnon?" Her voice was so small, so disparaged. It made her even more ashamed.

"We'll figure out something, Malka, I promise," Amnon said fiercely, reaching for her. He repeated himself, again and again. As if saying it enough could make it true. *I promise. I promise. I promise.*

She wanted to believe him.

So much so that when Nimrah murmured her proposition, Malka thought, at first, that she had imagined it.

CHAPTER 7

"Stay, if you want," Nimrah repeated tamely, despite Malka's and Amnon's obvious bewilderment. "Until you figure things out."

She had left the table, now attending the sword she had previously eyed. She wiped her hand down the scabbard, clearing the dust. "Believe me, I can't wait to be rid of you both. But I'd prefer not to find you two dead, seeing as I went through so much trouble to save you once already."

Malka doubted that was the reason. She found it hard to believe Nimrah cared about their fate at all. Which left her even more suspicious.

"How do we know you are any less of a threat than what waits out there?" she asked.

Nimrah unsheathed the sword, metal glinting in the firelight. She began to sharpen the blade by running it through the thumb and forefinger of her stone hand. "You don't."

Malka resisted the urge to squirm in her seat.

"We might as well, Malka," Amnon said. "We need to reevaluate what to do."

She couldn't bring herself to argue. He was right. Whatever plan they had had would no longer work.

When she relented, Malka didn't miss the smirk that flickered across Nimrah's face.

⚶

"You'll be safe in here," Nimrah said the next morning, slinging a sack around her shoulder. She donned a man's doublet, but it was not oversized. Instead, the silver brocade lining emphasized her broad shoulders and towering stature. When Nimrah wrapped a cloak around her shoulders, Malka found she missed the way the silver glinted with her movement. "The creatures do not come close to the trunk of the Great Oak tree. I'm not sure why, but I haven't ever been bothered within these walls."

Malka watched her slip out, tall and impending against the carved door.

The golem had left last night, too. Malka had woken from a fitful sleep when it was still dark, only to find Nimrah gone. By the time she woke that morning, Nimrah had already returned, mentioning nothing of her midnight trip.

Malka wondered what Nimrah did when she left, what secrets she held close. Malka didn't trust her. Didn't trust they were saved from the same fate as that poor Yahadi boy years ago.

Amnon joined Malka at the table, where Malka had begun to strain the tea Nimrah had given her with netting found in one of the drawers.

"What are you doing?" he asked.

"The tea—I don't understand it. It should not be healing us like it is."

Amnon ran a hand along the back of his neck. "I saw her make it that first night. What she used . . . you won't find it within that netting."

Malka blinked. "What do you mean?"

He scratched his cheek. It had been days since he shaved, and thin bristles of curly hair were beginning to speckle his jaw. "You know . . . she's a creature of it. Makes sense she'd use it, too."

It.

Malka frowned. "You think she performed Kefesh to make the tea?"

"I highly doubt it could've been anything else."

It took more effort to even her breathing than she would've liked. "I should've known."

Amnon shook his head. "We went from Kefesh being a distant, rotted mysticism to surrounding ourselves with it. Whether we leave or stay here with her, we are at its mercy."

Malka pressed her thumb along the pad of her hand. "I keep thinking about what we were told of her. How one day she became something even the Maharal couldn't recognize. All because of Kefesh and our hubris to control the earth."

"She didn't look at all unsure when she made the tea. She held the leaves tight in her palm and rubbed at one of the etchings on her arm with the other. Like she had done it many times before."

Malka mulled that over, dipping her finger into the old tea, as if she could discover its secrets from touch alone.

When she had first felt the tea's effects, how quickly it soothed her, she had imagined what it would've been like for someone like Yael to sip from this tea—if it would aid her brittle bones or mitigate the symptoms of the sickness which gripped her. A traitorous thought now, yet she couldn't let it go.

"There's a specific story your Baba used to tell . . ." Amnon's eyes drifted toward the roof as he thought. His cheek was still red where he had scratched it. "Ah, yes. The story of Tzvidi the librarian and the holy book he left open, allowing the demons to take advantage of his mistake."

Malka remembered. The tale had kept her awake in the darkest hours of the night. She traced the contour of her throat, remembering the quick work the tea made of her frostbite symptoms.

Baba had first told her the story of Tzvidi when Malka witnessed Kefesh for the first time.

She and Baba had been in the shektal early one morning. A Yahadi merchant from the southern Balkisk Kingdom had come for market day, and much to his dismay, had accidentally overturned his crate of apples, bruising them all. Malka thought he would either sell the fruit for a discounted price or accept his losses and trek back to his kingdom. Instead, he had closed his eyes and whispered a spell, carving a word onto an apple until the bruised fruit lost its purple hue and shone bright green once again.

"You must not tell anyone what you saw," Baba had said. "Kefesh is not always what it appears."

The Balkisk Yahad were more casual toward mysticism. It had been a cultural difference Baba staunchly opposed. To Ordobavian Yahad, Kefesh was highly taboo, and while people accepted the Maharal's practice of Kefesh as being ordained by Yohev, the wave of secularization in the Balkisk Kingdom meant some Balkisk Yahad began to use the holy magic carelessly and without understanding its true portentous weight.

"*Have I told you the story of Tzvidi?*" he had asked.

Malka had shaken her head.

"Ah, well," Baba had said, reclining in his chair. It creaked under his weight. "*Let me tell you a cautionary tale, and as with all stories, you can see why we share it.*"

Malka recalled the story now.

Once, there lived a Yahadi scholar named Tzvidi, who held his position in the Great Library in the highest regard. He cataloged all the scrolls and books like any librarian would. Only, this was not an ordinary library. The Great Library was a holy library filled with holy books written by Yahadi religious scholars since the dawn of time.

There was one book in the Great Library that Tzvidi considered his greatest joy and privilege to catalog and protect. It was the *Seefa Narach*, a holy book written by the holiest man of their time—a scholar named Gabriel who had studied Yahadi mysticism for many years. In the *Seefa Narach*, he wrote of his trials and errors of commanding the mysticism. Some said he succeeded in understanding the magic, others said he could try as much as he'd like, but Yahadi mysticism was a magic that could not be fully understood by anyone.

Regardless, when Gabriel died, his grandson—far less of a holy man but a man who still respected his grandfather as one—inherited the book. But he had no desire to continue his grandfather's studies of Yahadi mysticism, so he donated the book to the Great Library, where it came into Tzvidi's care.

Tzvidi gleamed with excitement. He could not wait to read what Gabriel had discovered. Only, as soon as it came into the library so, too, did it bring a line of scholars desperate to read its pages.

Given the specialty of this book, no one—no matter how powerful—was allowed to take the book home. They could only visit the library and read it there. Day after day, Tzvidi watched with jealousy as his fellow scholars devoured the pages of the *Seefa Narach*.

Until he realized what he could do that no others could.

Tzvidi worked at the library and could study the *Seefa Narach* long after the library closed its doors for the night. After all, no one could take the book home. Only, the library *was* Tzvidi's home.

So, every night after the library closed, he would slip through the side door with his key and pull the *Seefa Narach* from the shelf. He would pore over the text until the sun traced the horizon, and he could no longer keep his eyes open. Gingerly, he would place the book back and rush to his bed to slumber for the next hour until his work began.

Oh, how tired he became. He would work all day and read all night. To him, the chance at studying Gabriel's words was worth all the sleep he lost.

One night, Tzvidi had become so tired he fell asleep on top of the book and woke far after the sun. In his haste to get home and change before coming back to work again, he forgot to put the *Seefa Narach* back in its place, leaving its pages open on the table.

With any other book this would not be a problem. A book is just a book, after all.

Except when a book is holy.

Except when a book has Kefesh pressed between its pages.

Then, it is something far more dangerous. For scholars are not the only ones who lurk in the library. Trembling on the shelves waiting for men like Tzvidi are shalkat—demons who sneak into holy books left open by their readers and corrupt the prayer and magic within them. And as Tzvidi hastily left, so did the shalkat come and crawl into the *Seefa Narach*. They burrowed into the prayers which Gabriel had twisted into magic and turned them into something nefarious. Spells which brought vitality to the earth were manipulated to cause famine. Spells which shared ways to improve health became spells which grew pus-filled pox from the skin. Spells which asked for rain in the dry climate transformed to spells of drought.

The changes were not noticed right away, especially not by Tzvidi. However, as more and more scholars began to take notes from the *Seefa Narach* and attempt to use the spells Gabriel had written, the more and more things began to go terribly wrong. Soon, the shalkat's manipulated words began to plague the city—sick people grew sicker when doctors tried to heal them, storms grew wilder when scholars tried to tame them.

But perhaps worst of all to a scholar like Tzvidi was when, oblivious to the disastrous repercussions of the *Seefa Narach*, he decided to cast his first spell from the book. Late in the night, his light had grown dim—too dim to properly read. So, emboldened by all of his stolen nights studying, he used a spell from the book to brighten the fires of his candelabra.

However, instead of brightening his lights, from his spell grew a fire so large, the flames licked up the walls and, in its mouth, swallowed Tzvidi and the Great Library whole, until there was nothing left but ash and the snickering shalkat.

When he had finished telling Malka the story, Baba had patted her cheek gently. "*Let this be a lesson to you, Simcha Shachar. Power like that cannot be contained. There will always be shalkat in the wings waiting to strike.*"

Frightened by her memory of Tzvidi's story, Malka decidedly lost her taste for the tea, and any potential use of it. Tzvidi, Mavetéh, the golem . . . Nothing good came from Kefesh. If there was one thing Malka was sure of, it was that.

CHAPTER 8

The Great Oak was unruly at night. Malka learned this as she feigned sleep, determined to see if Nimrah would sneak out again. She lay there, focused on breathing deep and even. Every so often, the Great Oak would groan and rile its branches, drumming against the roof of Nimrah's hut. It rattled her, but thankfully did not wake Amnon, who snored lazily at her side.

It could have been minutes or hours of Malka waiting in anticipation when Nimrah finally rose from the ground. Her footsteps creaked around the room. In the kitchen, she rummaged through a drawer and collected several jars. They clinked as she stuffed them in her bag. One was particularly pungent—a sweetness that made Malka's nose twitch in recognition.

The Great Oak wailed again, louder, as if it were in the throes of a violent dream. Malka spared it a glance; a mountain of sap had oozed from its bark and pooled onto the ground. From her sidelong view, it could easily be mistaken as blood.

"Quiet," Nimrah chastised, voice barely above a whisper. The tree, much to Malka's surprise, listened.

The golem began to survey them. Malka shut her eyes, heart pounding, desperate not to betray herself.

It was silent, and for a moment, Malka thought she had been caught. But then Nimrah's footsteps creaked against the floor again, her cloak flapping as she stepped outside into the grueling wind. The door closed with a soft rattle.

Malka waited a beat, then two.

Silently, she got to her feet, and followed Nimrah out the door, sparing one last pleading look at the Great Oak, praying it kept quiet.

Malka had grown too accustomed to the ever-burning hearth in Nimrah's hut. The cold pinched her raw, the sharp bite of its greeting an ominous reminder of how swiftly it could puncture her once again. She hid deeper in her warm cloak.

Malka relied on the dim light from Nimrah's lantern for her navigation, having forgone her own to conceal herself.

Ahead, Nimrah set down her light and bent low to examine the ground. Malka squinted but couldn't see what had her attention. Nimrah withdrew something from her satchel. From the way she balanced it, Malka could only tell it was not much larger than the size of her fist.

There was a scraping sound, then a curse.

Malka tried for a closer look, but she was too far, and the barrier of night too stalwart. No matter how much she blinked, her eyes refused to adjust to the fuzz of blackness, especially with Nimrah's shadow blocking the lantern.

Malka stepped forward cautiously. One foot ahead, then the other. Yet she was no match for the network of roots below her. Her foot snagged on one and she careened forward, yelping as her hands barely caught her fall.

Pain shot up her wrists. They'd develop matching purple bruises to her ankles.

Nimrah whipped around, task forgotten as she whisked the lantern from the ground and held it out at arm's length. "Who's there?"

Malka held her breath, hoping her cloak would camouflage her in the dark.

"I see you there, by the tree. Come out." She did not raise her voice, but the threat was palpable. Almost worsened by her calm demeanor.

Malka could try to stay there, silent and frozen, until Nimrah grew exhausted of waiting. If the golem *did* wait. Something, though, told Malka she was not the patient type, nor was she the type to exhaust.

Slowly, Malka rose from her knees until the light caught her face.

Nimrah's grip on the lantern loosened, her arms relaxing. "It's not safe for you to be here. Go back."

"You're keeping secrets."

"*Secrets*," Nimrah *tsk*ed. "Have you considered that my business is simply not yours to know?"

Malka raised her chin to the expansive, gnarled root of the Great Oak which Nimrah hid behind her person. "What were you doing just now?"

"What part of *not your business* was unclear?"

Malka skirted around Nimrah's attempt at a block, and found a familiar herb scattered over the root. "What are you doing with the devil's alphonsa plant?"

Her veins turned to ice. If Nimrah had healed her with herbs, Malka didn't want to find out what she could do with poison and Kefesh at her fingertips.

Nimrah's forehead creased, mouth slightly agape. "You know what that herb is from this distance?"

Malka shrugged. "It's very distinct."

"It's crushed—it could be any herb. Maybe it's black perphona."

"It's not," Malka said confidently, taking another step forward. "Black perphona has a potent odor, like burning citrus. Unlike its poisonous look-alike, which deceptively smells sweet, like caramel. I smell it now just as I smelled it before you walked out of your hut."

"How do you know that?"

"I'm a village healer's daughter."

Malka was close enough to see Nimrah's face smooth. "With such knowledge of herbs, I'm surprised you've never been keen to use magic to assist with your healing duties."

Malka blinked. Nimrah said it so casually, like she was teasing. "Healing isn't magic."

"And yet you've been drinking a tea made from Kefesh to heal your ankle." She eyed where Malka soothed her wrist with her thumb. "And now most likely your wrists."

Malka resisted the urge to touch the skin at her throat. "I know magic exists, but I refuse to use it. It's forbidden."

"Not all Yahad believe Kefesh is forbidden."

Malka recalled the Balkisk Yahad and the vendor who had unbruised his apples. "Their hubris will catch up to them." It was what Baba had always said.

"You sound naïve." Nimrah crossed her arms. Long gone was the look of surprise Malka had managed to evoke from her with her honed knowledge of herbs.

"Maybe. But I do know one thing. The Maharal used Kefesh to create you, and you betrayed him."

Nimrah's jaw clenched. "You don't know anything."

"I trust what my ancestors say, and the stories that have been passed down to their children as warnings. Kefesh is not something I hold, nor do I want to."

"I'm not so sure about that, village girl. I was made from gathered stones and clay. It was prayer and intention that brought me to life. The Maharal is magical because of his devout prayer and belief. I have seen you whisper prayers over your meals. I know the meaning of the necklace you wear. Do you not also think you could wield prayer into magic?"

Malka clutched the flame necklace against her chest, ignoring the twinge in her wrist, and pressed her thumb into its points. "Prayer is not a weapon to wield."

"Kefesh is not always used as a weapon. The tea, for example. How can you say it's only a weapon when it has healed you even now?"

"Kefesh is not to be trusted, including any creatures made from it."

Nimrah's lips thinned. "You know the monsters made by Kefesh in this forest and you have assumed that is all the magic can do. But it can also be good."

Was that how Nimrah saw herself—a righteous creation of Kefesh? Malka scoffed. "Kefesh is not neutral. Not when it can easily turn into something the commander did not intend. Like the story of Tzvidi and the library. Do you know it?"

"Yes, I do," Nimrah responded. She kicked a rock by her foot. "So, this is truly how you get your information, then. From bedtime stories."

It struck her again, the dissimilarity between the golem of the stories and the half woman, half monster before her. A monster who had turned on her master, cold and unflinching. Maiming and killing a child. It was hard to believe, in that moment, they were one and the same.

But if Malka had learned anything from the traveling Paja and her father, the worst monsters often wore the faces of ordinary men.

An owl screeched, and Malka jumped. She wrapped the cloak tighter around herself, though it had dampened from her fall. "It doesn't matter if Kefesh has the potential to be good. There is always the danger of the shalkat. Of rearranging the letters of the spell to transform it into something worse."

Nimrah scrunched her brow in deep thought. "Say that again."

Malka opened her mouth, then closed it. "What?"

"Say what you just said."

Cautiously, Malka acquiesced. "With Kefesh, there is always the danger of shalkat rearranging the letters from their original intent to become something worse."

"Rearranging the letters," Nimrah said, eyes drifting somewhere left of Malka. "Maybe..."

Malka didn't think she had said anything so thought provoking. Only what was obvious to all who knew Kefesh's infamous legacies. But Nimrah did not seem to agree.

She waited for Nimrah to speak again or dismiss her. But the golem did neither. Instead, she walked away without another word, the cloak enveloping her into the blackness of the woods as she went, the scattered devil's alphonsa on the ground forgotten.

Malka contemplated following her, but the cold had made her ankle stiff with pain and already she was losing sight of Nimrah. She refused to let her curiosity skew her judgment anymore than it already had.

Sighing, Malka returned to the hut, where she settled quietly next to Amnon and tucked her cloak tight around herself as if it were a blanket, hoping the fire would dry it as it would warm her.

It was not long before sleep came.

⚹

By late morning, Nimrah still had not returned.

Amnon wiped breadcrumbs from the corner of his mouth with his thumb and reclined in his chair, finished with his breakfast. "How's your ankle?"

Malka lifted her foot and rolled it around, testing. It ached still but the pain had lessened. She leaned forward, settling it on the ground. She could apply pressure without losing her breath in pain. "Much better."

Her wrists, too, hadn't fared as poorly as she expected. She was loath to admit the tea played any significant role.

"Think you can walk for long periods again?"

Malka nodded.

"Good," Amnon said. "I've been thinking. We should go on as planned—try to find one creature to catch. There's no reason for the priest to know there are multiple monsters. We didn't know until now, and we have dealt with Mavetéh for years."

"And if he finds out we lied?" Malka questioned. "It will not look good if another Ozmin is killed while a monster is in captivity and Imma is free."

The priest would surely have them all killed.

Malka watched the crackling fire. "We were fools, Amnon, to think we could best any monster in this forest. A healer's daughter and a fisherman's son. It's laughable."

Amnon toyed with the leather of his belt loop. "We'll find a way."

The door burst open, wind whipping the flames in the hearth and rustling the loose hair from Malka's kerchief. Nimrah spilled through, not bothering to shake the snow loose from her cloak. It dampened the ground as she tossed it haphazardly on the hook.

"I've found it," Nimrah said, plopping into the chair across the table.

"Found what?" asked Amnon.

"The loophole to the Maharal's order."

"What?" asked Malka, jarred by the golem's rapid return. "His order to root you to the Great Oak?"

"Yes."

A pause.

Malka exchanged a glance with Amnon.

"Loophole..." Malka shook her head. "That sounds sacrilegious."

Nimrah shrugged. "Even the Maharal and his sacred words are fallible to interpretations. It's the price of religion, to be subject to exegesis."

Unnerved, Malka clasped her hand around the ceramic mug of half-drunk tea.

"Besides," Nimrah continued. "I prefer to look at it as another interpretation of his command. A *reinterpretation*, so to speak."

The fire popped, and a log tumbled, char falling away and revealing its raw brown underbelly. It was the same color as Chaia's hair, and Malka's throat tightened.

"What do you mean reinterpretation?" Malka asked.

"Got the idea thanks to you, village girl. What you said last night in the dark."

Malka slid down in her seat, ignoring Amnon's raised brow. If her suggestion was meant to embarrass her, Nimrah had succeeded.

"When the Maharal birthed me, he tied my shadow to his. He said I was a new kind of life, that it would take time, maybe decades, for the earth to adjust to me. Our binding grounded me, kept me from trouble. When he brought me here, he severed our shadows." She rolled up her sleeve more fully this time, revealing the Yahadi word in its entirety: שורש. *Shoresh.*

Root. "I needed to be bound to something, so he rooted me here by carving these letters in my arm and into a root of the Great Oak. Two birds with one stone—confining me, grounding me."

"What are you trying to say with all this?" Amnon urged, crossing his arms.

"Tying shadows together is difficult magic known only to Kefesh's greatest scholars. I had always thought the Maharal would be my only hope at leaving my confines. But then I realized, maybe I didn't need to mess with shadows at all. Maybe the solution was in the command the Maharal made to root me to the Great Oak. Maybe I just need someone to change the letters of the spell carved into the Great Oak to command my freedom instead of my rooting."

Malka shook her head in disbelief. "That story was not supposed to encourage you. It was meant to warn you away from such careless endeavors. You of all people should understand how ruinous messing with Kefesh can be."

Nimrah swallowed, then pivoted her gaze.

"You'd be left without a tether," Amnon added. "A situation in which nothing at all would go wrong, surely."

"If a new rooting spell is initiated shortly after the current one is severed, I could be bound to another life source. A more . . . portable life source, you could say. One that would allow me to travel out of the forest."

Malka shook her head. "It wouldn't work. You'd need someone willing to be rooted to you. Willing to mess with magic."

Nimrah shifted, chair creaking in the silence of Malka's remark. Their eyes met. "I would."

Malka scrutinized her for a long moment, then let out an exasperated laugh. "And why exactly do you think we'd agree to that? After everything we have said. After everything you have done."

Nimrah traced her stone hand with her flesh one. "Because I have something you need. Something no one else can give you."

Amnon narrowed his eyes. "What are you saying?"

Another pause. "I wasn't lying when I said that creature was one of many Kefesh-created monsters here. Even if you hunted them all, you couldn't stop more from emerging. It would be a waste of your time."

A sharp pain rapped Malka's chest. Nimrah had not said anything she didn't already know. But the way the golem voiced it, confident in its impossibility, perturbed her. She gritted her teeth. "Are you getting somewhere with this?"

Nimrah made no rush to continue. She only licked her lips and leaned back in her chair, the corner of her mouth curving up as Malka became more and more tense. "Patience, village girl, ever heard of it?"

Malka was surprised only the stories of her violence had reached Eskravé, and not her petulance.

Only when Malka waved her hands in surrender did Nimrah finally proceed. "*However,* there *is* a reason for the sudden creation of these creatures. A source, so to speak. If this source dies, it's possible the creatures will die, too."

"What?" Amnon sat upright. "Why didn't you say this earlier?"

Nimrah shrugged. Malka was slowly coming to know this movement, always associated with her confessions. As if she wished to distance herself from the truths she offered. "You didn't ask. You thought there was one creature, I told you there are many. Which is true."

"Yet you omitted the most vital truth of all—one that could save Imma." Heat colored Malka's cheeks. She had been on the verge of tears in front of Nimrah, convinced their mission was hopeless. Meanwhile, the golem had kept this revelation hidden. She tightened her fists, resisting the urge to wrap her hands around Nimrah's flesh throat and take a stab at cracking the stone of her face.

"I did not mention it," Nimrah said, interest drifting to a beetle scurrying across the table, "because I knew what question would follow."

"You know where the source is," Malka said slowly, understanding dawning. "And only now that you want something from us, you'll share it?" Oh, how accurate the stories of Nimrah had been. She was just as heartless, just as selfish.

"It's not information shared lightly."

"Why?" Amnon pushed.

Emotion clouded Nimrah's face, a crack in her disinterested facade. But as quickly as it came, Nimrah shook it away, her eyes turning as cold as the stone she was made from. Another shrug of her shoulders. "Because I am that magical source. The curse on the woods—the creation of those monsters—took root when my magic was tied to the Great Oak."

It was not the confession Malka had expected, that is, if she could anticipate anything about the golem. Nimrah's words twisted her on an axis. She could do nothing but grow rigid in her seat.

Next to her, Amnon's face was the color of milk. "Are you saying this to trick us into doing your bidding?" He leaned closer to Malka. It was his instinctive motion every time he sensed trouble, always ready to defend.

"I don't trick."

"When did the Maharal bring you here?" Malka questioned. "When was your magic tied to the Great Oak?"

"The first of spring, five years ago."

The events had happened the same year—the forest taking its first girl and Nimrah killing the Yahadi boy. That Malka already knew. She hadn't known, however, just how closely they had aligned. Malka remembered that season—it had been an unusually late spring, when the forest took its first girl. Winter had stayed far past its welcome. Imma had been mad about the delay of the bloom. A bloom that never came. Malka had never considered the golem the cause. Their village thought she slumbered in the attic of the shul Bachta.

But she had been here.

Her magic, this cursed Kefesh, had turned Kratzka Šujana into Mavetéh, the source of all her nightmares and all her heartache. She was right to have called Nimrah a monster, only she had not known how truly venomous.

When her village had named the Rayga, it was with the thought that one monster was the source of their grief. One monster could be hunted, killed, and then the women would be safe. Though she knew now many creatures hunted their girls, the beasts all came from the same monstrous source. A source that could be killed. And with it, all its creatures.

The true Rayga: Nimrah.

Malka had been lured by a false sense of safety, eating Nimrah's food and sleeping in her fire-warmed quarters. She wanted to spill out the contents of her stomach, cleanse herself of Nimrah's depravity. She would not be fooled again. By this golem, or by Kefesh.

"You lied about who you are, *Rayga*," Malka spat. She felt for Abba's dagger, but she hadn't attached it to her hip that morning. It still lay useless by her cloak. The snare she had was packed deep in her bag.

"Why would I tell you this freely when you're so dead set in your ways?"

Her voice began to raise slightly, building like the first cracks of thunder. Then, the stormy gloss of her words was gone, replaced by that indifferent tone she was so fond of. "When you wish me dead simply because I am the Maharal's golem."

"You think this would make us want to help you?" Amnon's fists were clenched so hard on the table his knuckles were fading to white. "Wrong."

"No." Nimrah rolled her eyes. "But I *am* going to offer you a deal."

Amnon caught Malka's attention, his eyes drifting to his belt. The hilt of Abba's dagger peeked out of the leather at his hips, an ambitious glint in his eye.

Malka swallowed.

There, with the Rayga in front of them, was an opportunity to get everything they wanted. Malka, obtaining Imma's freedom. Amnon, marked a hero for killing a creature not even his father could kill.

But the Rayga was no ordinary creature and had command of the forbidden Yahadi magic. Malka hoped Amnon would not prove himself a Falag pine tree now, and let his desires be the death of him.

Metal glinted as Amnon slid out the dagger and charged toward Nimrah, aiming for her neck.

With a flick of Nimrah's wrist, roots rose from the cracked floorboard and wrapped around Amnon, squeezing until he was red in the face. The dagger clattered on the table.

Nimrah's command of the vines mirrored the creature that had held tree branches as whips, with Amnon's life hanging in the balance.

Malka slammed the clay mug in front of her. Lukewarm tea splattered across the table and a few sharp pieces pricked at her skin, welting bright red. She closed her hand around one of the larger shards and pressed it to Nimrah's neck.

"Let him go!"

"Your friend drew his knife first." Nimrah's gaze steadied on the shard, held in a vise grip in Malka's fist. "I know you want me dead, but I cannot let the Maharal be charged unfairly. I have already failed him once."

Malka pressed the shard deeper, and Nimrah's flesh split open, red soaking into the clay. "Why would you think we'd make a deal with you?"

The golem's eyes were set on her, sharp and dark, like thorns on the most poisonous berry plant. Even the touch of her gaze could irritate skin.

"Perhaps if you remove that shard from my neck, I can tell you how we both get what we want. You want your mother's freedom, don't you?"

Against her better judgment, Malka lowered the shard, and the roots wrapped around Amnon slithered as they receded.

Nimrah wiped the speck of red from her neck. She slipped her blood-covered finger between her lips and sucked. When Nimrah caught her staring, Malka jolted her chin to the ceiling, and the floor, her cheeks hot.

"I'll go back to your village. Give myself up to that Ozmini priest to save your Imma . . ." Her neck was already welting a fresh dot of blood. "*If*, and only if, you help me rescue the Maharal from his unfair imprisonment. To start, by using Kefesh to unroot me from the Great Oak and bind me to one of you instead."

Malka reared back. "You think we'd use Kefesh?"

"I think you'd do anything to save your Imma. Besides, you'd need to perform Kefesh either way—to get me to your village or Valón. I am tied here otherwise, remember? But there is only one option in which I will go to your village willingly." Nimrah spread her arm wide above the ground, and roots began to crawl like spiders across the floor. Malka shivered as they scurried across her feet. "And trust me, you don't want to find out just how unwilling I can be."

Malka gnawed on her lip, resisting the urge to kick at the roots. Nimrah's threat had hit its target. She was right, and Malka hated her for it. Hated her for being the source of her problem, and the solution.

Amnon still wheezed beside her from Nimrah's attack.

Malka took her necklace in her fist.

Nimrah crossed her arms, jaw tightening. "Do we have a deal or not?"

We were fools, Amnon, to think we could best any monster in this forest. This was what she had said, hopeless and disparaged. Now, a chance. Now, a way to achieve the impossible. It didn't feel real. Did she have any clue what freeing the Maharal would entail, if she were even capable of what Nimrah would ask of her? No. But Nimrah was right about Malka's commitment to the promises she had made to her family.

"What exactly would it be like to be rooted with you?"

Amnon began to object, but Malka held up her free hand. She could not lose herself to fear now.

"I don't know," Nimrah responded mildly, as if she did not take Malka's curiosity as any indication of the answer she would give. "With Kefesh, the commands never result in clear answers. You ask the earth to bend for you and it interprets that as it wishes. I have never been rooted with someone like this. But it would bond us in some way—physically, mentally."

"And you will sever that bond after?"

"There will be no need for it once I am dead," Nimrah said plainly. "Will there?"

Malka studied her. She spoke so plainly of her own death, as if it were nothing but another measured task. Like Amnon spoke of descaling a fish, or Imma of stripping herbs for medicine. "How can we trust your word that you will come back with us? You are fond of *omitting* truths."

"Do you have another choice?" Nimrah drawled. "Besides, I can't exactly escape if I am rooted to one of you."

Amnon shook his head. "Malka, this is Kefesh we're talking about."

"But the stakes are different now," Nimrah said, the corner of her mouth upturned as she eyed Malka. "Aren't they?"

She was hot under Nimrah's knowing look, her breathing fast and heartbeat untethered. Unconsciously, her choice had been made, and her body knew it. Even if her mind refused it still.

Perhaps she did not hide her thoughts well, for Amnon stood abruptly. "I need to speak with Malka. *Alone.*"

Nimrah huffed, running a hand through her hair. For a moment, Malka thought she would deny him, punish him for demanding anything of her. But she relented, throwing her hands up.

"Fine," she said. "Just know, if you forgo my offer, you're on your own. Unless, of course, your friend here decides to try *that* again." She pointed to Abba's dagger on the floor. "Then the woods will be the least of your problems."

With a sweep of her cloak, she stormed out of the hut again, wood rattling as the door slammed behind her.

Malka and Amnon did not speak for many minutes after she left. Malka shook despite her attempt to keep her resolve. Amnon dropped to his knees in front of her, resting his head on her lap. Malka threaded a hand through his hair. It was gritty with dried blood and dirt.

"We could find a way to kill her," he said, voice muffled by her skirts. "Catch her off guard or something, I don't know. We don't have to agree to this."

Malka shook her head. "Didn't you just see what she was capable of? The way she almost killed you . . ."

"Of course, I did, Malka." She felt the pulse of his uneven breaths. "You truly think this is the best option?"

Malka sighed. "I think this is our only option. I didn't even think I would survive one night in Mavetéh. It is a miracle we are both still alive." Her voice dropped low, words catching in her throat. "Imma does not have much time."

"Making a deal with the Rayga, Malka . . . I don't know."

"I understand. And using Kefesh? Just the idea of it makes my stomach turn. But I'm worried we're out of chances. Maybe this is the only way we could actually save Imma. The only way we can have a chance at the life we once knew."

Amnon stared up at her, his long eyelashes accentuated by his low angle. "If this is it, then I will be the one to use Kefesh. I'll be rooted to her. I don't mind taking that burden from you."

She untensed her shoulders, ignoring the twinge in her chest.

He cradled Malka's hand in his. "But if we agree to this . . . will you consider it? After everything?"

"Consider what?" she asked, but she already knew.

Longing softened his eyes, his mouth parting where his lips bowed. "Marrying me."

Malka tried to draw back her hand, but Amnon held her tight, like a lifeline. He sweated, even against the chill of her hand. His sharp nose was shadowed by the firelight, his jaw and cheekbones highlighted and warmed. His curly hair tickled his forehead and complemented his eyes. Even now, bruised and afraid, he was beautiful.

But Malka didn't know if she could love him the way he desired to be loved. If she could be happy being married to someone yet. But it was her duty as eldest daughter, and if she did have to marry, she supposed she would want it to be him. The man who followed her into Mavetéh with his chin held high.

"I'll consider it."

CHAPTER 9

"Pack up," was Nimrah's only response when they agreed to her deal. As soon as a new dawn appeared on the horizon, they headed north to the capital city.

Upon their arrival, they would find an old Ozmini laundress who owed the Maharal a favor. Nimrah seemed confident she would help shape their plan on how to rescue him from the dungeons, having insider knowledge from her years of service.

Malka supposed it wasn't a bad plan, with what little information they had. Chaia used to hear all kinds of gossip while mending clothing as a seamstress. Perhaps this was also the experience of the palace workers.

Strange, that Malka would soon be in Valón. She had consumed knowledge of the fantastical city like the merchants' stories were sugar pastries and drunk with the Paja just to know even more. And yet, it mattered little now. With the famous city nearly at her fingertips, all she could think of was Imma.

Five days had passed since they left Eskravé, each one a gut punch of lost time. She did not feel completely back to herself after her injuries, was not sure if she ever would. Nerves for the journey ahead began to sicken her worse than any frostbite.

Above, the sun pulled like a taut arrow in the sky, rays slipping through trees and onto plants like painted targets. But it was just clear enough to track the sun's position. The ground was slick with blood, and it stuck to the bottom of Malka's shoes like a stubborn stain. The air was drenched in a foul odor, like blooming corpse weed, and suffocating like wood smoke. Some part of her was glad there hadn't been enough food for breakfast, for her stomach soured at the stench.

Through the gaps in the tangled branches clouding the sky, Malka could pretend she was somewhere safer, where crisping dough fragranced the air, and the wood was soft beneath her feet, warped over generations and creaking when she danced with her sisters.

Nimrah explained that no spell would be required until the end of the Great Oak's reach, for the Maharal had written the command on a tip of the tree's roots instead of its bole, intending for it to disappear into the earth over time, hiding it from anyone who wished Nimrah harm. It did not matter to the Maharal that Nimrah could trace the path of the command on its root, for she could not change the spell on her own.

"How far have you attempted to venture this way?" Amnon asked Nimrah.

The Maharal had purposefully written the command on a root facing north, so that it would stretch toward Valón as a safeguard, in case he ever needed to reach Nimrah quickly. The golem could meet him at the end of the root if summoned through a command already written into her stone.

It was useful to them now, as they didn't have to add much time to their journey for the diversion.

"It's been a couple years since I last tried," Nimrah answered. "A day, then. But it will be longer now that the roots have spread."

Amnon nodded, though his lip quivered.

"What do you know of Kefesh already?" Nimrah asked, ducking under a particularly low branch.

"I know it's performed using commands written in the Yahadi holy language," Amnon responded, face ashen.

"Yes," Nimrah replied. "But do you know why?"

Amnon shrugged, then looked to Malka. But she didn't know much more than him. It was as unknown to her as the stars or moon.

Nimrah huffed. "You two have strong opinions of a mysticism you know nothing about."

"And you have strong opinions of us, yet know why we were raised this way," Malka jeered.

Nimrah ignored her. "Yohev first created the holy language to achieve the creation of the earth. They sculpted the first section of letters to represent water, the next fire, and the last wind and earth until They finished the alphabet."

She ran her hand along her arm below her sleeve. "It is a similar concept to how the holy magic is used now. As Yohev combined the letters representing those elements to create different facets of the earth, we, too, combine letters in a way that creates new meaning. As you've seen, the letters on my arm—*shoresh*, root. The same command is scratched onto the Great Oak, rooting us together." Nimrah pointed to her forehead. "The word here—*emet*. It means truth, and it made my existence so that the carved words did not lie. Just as the holy language brought me to life, it can change other aspects of the world."

Malka thought of Tzvidi and how men had tried to use Kefesh to heal, but since the shalkat had changed the letters around, the spells had become something different. Something they were not meant to be.

Nimrah, created to protect the Yahad, killing one instead.

"You will frighten the people of Valón with your return. They think you were laid to rest," Malka said.

Nimrah was in front of her now, so Malka could not see her face, only the slight hunch of her shoulders. "You'd be surprised how easy it is to stay hidden in a trading city with a good cloak."

As they walked, more glowing fruit began to appear low on the trees, pulsing in various shades of red, blue, and purple. The wind howled, loosening a pack of snow from one of the branches and scattering the flakes. One of the fruits began to wobble.

Nimrah flung her arm out, stopping them short.

The glowing fruit fell from the tree and splattered in front of them, sizzling as the glow faded into the charred ground beneath. A few more steps and the charred ground would've been Malka's head.

"What was that?"

"Waral fruit," Nimrah said. "Highly acidic fruit that began to grow on the Great Oak soon after I was rooted to it. It's germinated to most of the forest now. Some colors are more poisonous than others, but many can burn straight through skin and bone."

Malka took a shaky breath. During a Rayga hunt, one of the village men had lost his arm from a serious burn. She wondered if this was the culprit they wouldn't mention. The men did not like to speak about their hunts.

"You could practice on one of the fruits, if you'd like," Nimrah said to Amnon. "Little commands, like getting them to shine again or change color. To get a handle on Kefesh. They are not as dangerous once they have ruptured."

Amnon's face greened where the cold hadn't already reddened. "I'll take my chances."

"Fools," Nimrah whispered under her breath. "Absolute fools."

⇘

They paused their trek while Amnon disappeared to relieve himself.

A glimpse of black caught Malka's eye, and she bent to pull the plant up by its roots, stuffing it into her satchel pocket.

"You keep collecting black perphona. Why?"

Nimrah's breath plumed against the frigid air like chimney smoke. She looked like a myth, half earth and half human, her black hair the mane of a wild animal. The smoke around her mouth reminded Malka of the Yahadi myth of Tannin, the dreaded water dragon with scales as green as moss and a body like a serpent.

"To bring back. Eskravé has been in short supply, seeing that every maiden who walks into the forest comes out dead. Let alone the sickness which has begun to spread." Malka's spite seeped into her response, and it was fueled by Nimrah's tight-lipped reaction. She couldn't help herself. "It's not the only way you've made Eskravé suffer. Without that herb, many are dying of infection. Innocent people who had the misfortune of getting a nasty cut."

If Malka had garnered a reaction from Nimrah, it was gone now, replaced with indifference. Nimrah began to rock her leg on a nearby log.

Malka bit back the twinge in her throat. Plants made her think of Imma, of the hours they had spent side by side treating ailments. She breathed in the harsh odor of black perphona and closed her eyes, picturing Imma. Her broad nose and twisted golden curls, risking her life to find this exact plant in the woods.

Nimrah watched the movement of the log underneath her foot. Back and forth. "I did not make the conscious choice to terrorize your village. I didn't demand for every plant to die or for hungry creatures to arise with my presence."

Her green veins pulsed under her skin. Malka was reminded how quickly she had commanded the vines from the earth, which squeezed Amnon the same way the tree creature had squeezed her.

"I don't believe you."

Nimrah kicked the log away. It flew into a tree, shaking loose the compacted snow on its branches. Malka watched the white fall to the ground and join the dirt-caked snow below.

"Fine. Make me into the monster you want." Nimrah stared at her, jaw clicking. "But if you wish to speak of monsters, then answer me this. You walked into these woods, knowing it craves women like you, yet you know neither sword nor magic. How exactly did you plan to survive?"

She hadn't thought she would. Entering Mavetéh had been choiceless for her. A necessity. But Nimrah did not deserve to know that.

So, instead, Malka brushed Abba's dagger at her side. "What makes you say I don't know the sword?"

Nimrah lifted an imperious brow.

Malka straightened, ignoring the unfamiliar curl in her stomach evoked by Nimrah's expression. She was not used to the intensity the sharp angles of Nimrah's face awarded her. Human and not, at the same time. Each emboldening the other.

When Amnon appeared, Nimrah grinned. "Amnon, toss me your sword, will you?"

Amnon gave her an incredulous look. "Over my dead body."

"Is that a promise, lover boy?" With the stretch of her arm, a root erupted from the ground at Amnon's feet. It wrapped around the hilt of his sword and pulled it from the sheath. The root receded, releasing the sword into Nimrah's grip.

"Hey!" Amnon started toward her, but Nimrah held up her hand.

"Relax." Nimrah offered the sword to Malka. "It's for her anyway."

Malka's eyes traveled warily to the weapon. "What are you doing?"

"You said you know how to use a sword. So, prove it."

Malka did not like the prickle of satisfaction gleaming in her eyes.

"If you hurt her, I'll kill you." Amnon said the threat full heartedly, despite how effortlessly Nimrah had disarmed him of Abba's knife back in her hut.

But Nimrah's eyes were on Malka, unstirred by Amnon's threat. Malka hated being the focus of her gaze, those darkened eyes flaring heat inside of her. It was like taking a bite from the waral fruit, letting its poison seep inside of her until there was nothing left but the burning.

"If I wanted her dead," Nimrah intoned, "I would have left her in the river. As you have said."

"It's okay, Amnon," Malka said, fending off the flame in the pit of her stomach. "Let her."

Malka gripped the sword at its hilt. When Nimrah released her hold, and Malka bore its full weight, the tip wobbled downward. She struggled to keep it level, shifting it in her hands until she adjusted to the unnatural feel of it.

She was in over her head. Amnon knew it, too, from the way he stood ready to pounce at Nimrah if she so much as moved the wrong way.

Across from her, Nimrah unsheathed her sword. "Hit me here," she said, motioning to her chest. "Should be easy if you truly know the sword."

Nimrah didn't wait for her to ready. She swung out her own weapon. Malka lifted the sword to block her. Metal clanked against metal. Malka's heart beat out of her chest at how narrowly Nimrah had missed slicing her skin.

"I will not kill you." Malka's labored breathing made her voice rough, deep. "Yohev forbids it."

"Isn't that what you're doing, though?" Nimrah smirked. "Bringing me to my death?"

"Last I recall, you *proposed* the deal. You're going willingly."

Malka swung high but didn't come close to hitting her.

"You will not be the one who kills me when I am brought to your village," Nimrah conceded. "But the Ozmini God also forbids murder. So, in the end, who will disobey their God for vengeance?"

Malka's lips thinned. "It's not like that." She swung her sword again, ignoring the burning sensation in her arms. But Nimrah parried, elegant footwork following the way Nimrah moved her upper body to dodge the blow. "The Ozmini Church is not happy."

"The Ozmini Church will never be happy when their only goal is power." Nimrah slashed her sword low, and Malka yelped as she jumped.

Her cloak caught on her weapon, and she tripped onto her back. Nimrah kicked Malka's sword from her hand, pointing the tip of her blade to Malka's chest.

Amnon moved toward them, but Malka lifted her hand.

During her fall, her sack had spilled out, revealing the snare trap.

Nimrah smirked, eyeing the rope. "Was that for me?"

Her tone, which did not entirely read as displeasure, made Malka blush from her neck to her ears.

"I don't know the details of your fate, Rayga," Malka said, her breaths still laborious.

"It often seems like those who decide the fate of others never do know or care about the details."

She lifted her weapon from Malka's chest and offered her a hand.

"You are a liar, village girl." Nimrah sheathed her sword. "You hold the sword like you are afraid of it, yet you did not hesitate to use it. What makes Kefesh so different?"

"Why do you care? We have agreed to your bargain. What difference do my feelings on Kefesh make?"

The wind swept through Nimrah's hair, wrapping her in a black shroud. "You really don't understand, do you?"

But it was the golem who didn't understand. Malka had not been raised on stories which cautioned her away from using weapons. Only magic. Weapons were how Abba and the rest of the village men defended themselves during their Rayga hunts. Weapons were what killed the animals who gave their lives to fill achingly hungry bellies.

Weapons were predictable. Metal could not bend, could not think for itself. Shalkat could not scramble their way into the metalworking and rearrange it to make it something vicious. A sword could not destroy an entire library with one blow.

Kefesh could.

"All my life, I have been taught to fear Kefesh. That the magic teeters too close to Yohev's domain. That it has the power to make man a betrayal of his Creator."

Nimrah's lips thinned, but Malka was not sorry. The Maharal had created Nimrah using Kefesh, and Malka's people suffered the consequences. Mavetéh. The Rayga. The sickness.

"Others will argue those who practice Kefesh are closest to Yohev. They are guided by Their hand in the process of creation. It is a practice birthed from the power of language: letters have the power to be shaped into words and those words take on meanings."

Malka shrugged. "Such is the nature of any language."

"Yes, but it is different in a holy language. One that is called forth by prayer and scripture alone."

Malka's eyes fell to the back of Nimrah's hand, where the engravings of a Yahadi holy word peeked out from her sleeve. Then to her forehead, and the carving of *emet*.

Nimrah caught her stare. "The recitations of these words brought me to life. The engraved letters command me. Just as you could use words to control the plants around you to heal. The letters of the Yahadi holy script were created by Yohev and used to speak the world into existence. It's something Yohev created for Their people. That is what the Maharal says."

Malka let out an exasperated laugh. "And where exactly did that get him?"

Nimrah's mouth set in a hard line. "Watch your mouth, village girl."

"Or what?"

A pulse of silence coursed between them, heavy and blazing.

Nimrah's eyes narrowed to slits, but it was not only anger in their black depths. Something else, too, unbidden. "My loyalty lies with the Maharal," she said finally, "and it would befit you to remember *just* what I'm capable of."

Malka didn't need the reminder; she knew Nimrah's capabilities. Knew what power corrupted her. And that was exactly why Malka feared Kefesh. She would not hold that power in her hands. Would not corrupt herself in the same way. She couldn't bear it.

CHAPTER 10

Malka thought of the Maharal.

Tzvidi's was not the only tale Malka had been told of Kefesh. Nor was the story of the golem. She had been raised on fables of the earth's magic, of men who cradled it in their palms and whispered commands to shape the world, and the hubris which damned them.

After the golem incident, more had come to light about the Maharal's use of magic. The Eskraven merchants said the Maharal had grown careless with the holy magic long before Nimrah was created. They said he used Kefesh to make the stained-glass windows of the shul Bachta glimmer even when no sun shined through. That he relied on magic instead of scribes to craft his letters. So, it should've been no surprise when the golem turned on him. Baba had felt vindicated, long suspicious of the Maharal's true intentions. Ever dark, corrupted by power.

Now, a breeze curled through the air and tickled Malka's neck. She suppressed a shiver.

"The sun will set soon." Nimrah pressed her hand to a strip of bark. The waral fruit hung dangerously low on the tree's branches. Already, Malka had knocked Amnon out of the way of another falling fruit, which split open on the ground and ate through the soil, hissing as it consumed a protruding root.

"Lucky for your head," Nimrah had said. Amnon had grumbled in response but ran a hand through his hair when he thought no one was looking.

The memory of that first night in Mavetéh enveloped her. Tight, coiling branches, shadows singing her name as a taunt. Václav's vacant eyes and Aleksi's decapitation.

Bile threatened to rise in her throat.

Nimrah had saved her from drowning, and tamed what Malka had thought then was the dreaded Rayga. She knew better now. The most dangerous threat stood in front of her, with eyes like spoiled olives and lips as plush as oleander flower.

But looking at the golem now, she appeared more worried than dangerous. Her taut lips and souring cheeks reminded Malka of Danya's when the coin Imma had given her could not buy enough fish to feed all five of them, even with the discounted price Amnon had whispered in her ear so his father didn't hear.

"We should find a place to rest. I'm going to scope out the clearing to see if the water has attracted any . . . unwanted guests," Nimrah said. She unsheathed her sword, handing it out to Malka with a smirk curling her lip. "For the sword girl."

Malka didn't bother hiding the foul look which crossed her face as she reluctantly accepted the sword. Once Nimrah disappeared through the trees, she frowned. "She's not what I expected." Malka didn't know if she meant to speak it aloud, but Amnon was already shrugging.

"I still don't trust her."

"Neither do I, of course," Malka responded. "I just . . . keep thinking about how Mavetéh would change our men."

"Yes," Amnon said. "The sap holding hallucinogens that drove them mad, they suspected. My abba never was the same after the hunts began. Wouldn't let me take his place, even though I begged him."

They had always bonded over this, the need to protect the ones they loved. Malka was the eldest, but Amnon's older brothers were merchants, and were largely off selling at other markets, leaving him to look out for his younger siblings. Leaving him for his father's expectations, too.

"Do you notice a difference?" she asked. "In me? In yourself?"

She watched the quick movement of his eyes as he examined her, the increasing furrow of his brow. "No. But we should be wary still."

She swallowed hard. "Of course."

⚹

Malka's eyelids were growing heavy, but Nimrah still had not returned. The sky was awash in dusty blue. Soon they would lose the last drop of light.

"We should find her," Malka said, pausing her pacing. "She's been gone too long."

Nimrah would not leave them; Malka was sure of that. They needed each other. An uneasy feeling coiled in her chest. She had considered Nimrah to be as indomitable as the earth itself. It had never occurred to her that something could happen to the golem. That she could be harmed by something in this forest, driving a wedge in their bargain.

They began to search through the brush. Amnon trailed behind her, his footsteps steadily crunching on the old snow until they stopped abruptly. She did not hear Amnon frantically whispering her name, drowned out by the rush of river water, nor notice his attempts to reach her through the brush. She was razor focused on a different sound, something in the undertone of the water rush, like the brush of wind, or a grumble—

A hand pressed against her mouth, flattening her back against something broad and hard. *Someone* broad and hard.

Malka lashed out, but the grip only tightened. Then, another hand moved to jolt her chin back so she could see her attacker's face.

Nimrah. Her eyes pointed to the place where Malka had almost stepped.

On the edge of the river lazed a giant reptile, scaly with brownish green skin, chest under its fleshy wings rising and falling. *A Tannin?* It couldn't be. The water dragon she had once compared to Nimrah, the water dragon of myths.

Malka gasped, but Nimrah's hand swallowed the sound.

Nimrah raised her eyebrows, willing Malka to remain quiet as she lifted her palm.

The Tannin's hot breath brushed her skirt against her ankles. It plumed in the air, humid and sticking to the cold so that it lingered far after the dragon had snored again. It was as big as the river was wide, camouflaged to the blue-gray of the water.

It snored again, this time loosening its jaw to reveal its sharp, claw-shaped teeth.

Panic seized her, but she swallowed any movement or sound that could agitate the Tannin's sleep. She did not need the golem to tell her what would happen if the creature awoke and fixed its sight on Malka. She had heard the myths of the water serpent who swallowed people whole, whose presence foretold a much worse ending for those who sighted it.

She held Nimrah's sword flaccidly. Even if Malka had a semblance of skill with the blade, her chances did not bode well. She could see the toughness of the Tannin's skin and its flinty scales.

Nimrah motioned, instructing her to follow back through the brush.

Malka began to walk on her toes, each crunch of snow-covered leaves under her feet shooting dread inside of her. When she stepped again and a twig broke under her weight, Malka cursed.

The Tannin shifted in its sleep. Malka held her breath, desperate not to make another sound. When the Tannin's snores began again, her shoulders sank in relief.

Once the three of them were safely out of the brush, Nimrah poked her finger at Malka's chest. "What happened to *stay here*?"

"You were gone so long!"

"How sweet, you have suddenly started to care for me."

"I *care* about keeping you in sight. Alive. We are both invested in this bargain."

Nimrah huffed a laugh. "You are worried about me surviving? Look at yourself, village girl. What exactly would you have done if that dragon awoke?"

Malka opened her mouth, then closed it. What would she have done? No mortal sword could have pierced those scales, of that she was certain. Greater men had died trying.

"You know that Kefesh has changed the stakes of traveling through this forest. Yet you refuse to do what you must to survive."

"It's not worth it," Malka pushed, though she still shook with fear. It was too easy to picture the water dragon's teeth still, imprinted behind her eyes. The shape of them like scythe blades.

"You'd not say such a thing if Kefesh were any other tool. You wouldn't fight against a sword without a shield strong enough to capture the cuts of the blade. Nor would you defend against a cannon blow without a fortress capable of withstanding its force."

At Malka's silence, Nimrah rolled her eyes. But it lacked her usual impudence. It was something much worse. Total disappointment. Resignation. "You forget, village girl. If you both die here, there is no bargain left."

Then, she was gone through the trees.

When Malka met Amnon's eyes, she was not expecting to see the fear that glossed them, though it should not have surprised her. They had both seen it, the mythic water dragon.

Malka cupped her hand along her side, feeling a twinge between her ribs.

The Tannin's presence was an inexorable sign of devastation. In the holy scrolls, the Tannin was described as a primordial force of chaos, appearing in bodies of water to foretell ruinous events. It had lazed on the long river of the ancient city before the collapse of its temples, waded in the Anaya Sea before the toppling of the Jalgani Empire. Now, it was here.

A revelation sunk deep in her belly:

Destruction was coming.

Chapter 11

That night, Malka curled into herself on the snow-covered ground, shivering as wetness seeped through her cloak. They didn't dare light a fire, for fear they'd attract more unwanted attention. Malka dreaded what other mythic creatures lurked in these woods. The lack of light made it impossibly cold, and she shivered against the frozen ground as she attempted sleep.

"I can hear your teeth chattering from here," Nimrah remarked, voice barely above a whisper. She sat propped against a tree a few feet away from them, hand curled around the sword's hilt. The only light around them a lantern at Nimrah's side. She had agreed to keep watch while Malka and Amnon rested.

"Are you not freezing?"

"No," Nimrah admitted. "The benefit of being half stone."

Malka watched in the dim light of the lantern as Nimrah traced the hilt of her sword with her thumb.

Half stone, yes, but half flesh, as well. Fidgeting now, as a human would when on edge. She had been wrong to compare Nimrah to the Tannin. They were much different beasts.

She thought of the water dragon. How one misplaced step could've wiped away all the progress they had made.

"The Tannin," Malka started, gnawing nervously on her lip. "It was only ever supposed to be a myth."

Nimrah shrugged. "There are many real things we make into myths. And many myths we make real."

Could Kefesh do that? Create monsters from myths? Maybe the Tannin had always been real, waiting for its time to emerge from the Leirit river and warn Ordobav of its doom.

No. It couldn't be. It had to be another way Kefesh cursed. Another way it ruined.

"You speak like my grandfather. He always talked in riddles." She wasn't sure what made her say it, only that Nimrah's words had evoked in her a pang of grief for him. For his stories and how he had made her feel bigger than the world.

A smile brushed Nimrah's lips before disappearing again. So slight, Malka could barely perceive it in the dim halo of light across her face. "They aren't my words. They're the Maharal's."

Yet with thoughts of Baba always came his warnings—his staunch belief in right and wrong, which had guided her all her life. "My grandfather warned me how corrupt Kefesh could be, just as his grandfather had warned him. If he could see what this forest has become, I'm sure he'd bow his head in disgrace."

"I'm not surprised."

Malka scrunched her brow. "What do you mean by that?"

"I see why he would warn you away from Kefesh. You are strongly committed to your faith, and dedicated to your beliefs in ways most men could only dream of. It is always hungry men who gorge themselves, never content ones."

"I don't want to know everything," she responded. "I am not like Tzvidi."

Nimrah paused the movement of her thumb. "I never said that."

You are strongly committed to your faith, and dedicated to your beliefs in ways most men could only dream of. "Are you saying my beliefs are strong like the Maharal's?"

"You are nothing like him or his beliefs," Nimrah said vehemently. "He's leagues more than anything you can ever be."

"He's a cautionary tale," Malka countered, cheeks heating. "After all, he created you, and look what you have done."

Nimrah barked out an exasperated laugh. "You don't know anything about me or the Maharal."

"I do—"

"All you know are *stories*."

"Are stories not retellings of the truth? Do we not pass stories down generations to keep history alive?"

"Versions of history," Nimrah corrected. "Changed through the eyes of each teller."

Malka shrugged, aware too late Nimrah could not see her movement in the dark. "I have heard no stories of your versions of history."

"Then let me tell you one."

Malka stilled. "I—what?"

Nimrah was quiet for a while. "Is it so hard to believe I am capable of telling a story?"

Why would I want to hear a story from you? It was what she should've said. But she was curious, and tasted that sweetness on the back of her tongue again at the promise of a new story. She did not have to believe it, she reminded herself. But she could hear it.

"Tell it," Malka said, shocking herself with the softness of her voice. She blamed her drowsiness, taking away all the bite from her tongue.

Nimrah began.

"Many legends are old, but some are new. New as the painted buildings in Valón's Yahadi Quarter. Or new as the strong wagons which do not sag as they carry goods between shektal markets. No, it does not matter the age of a legend, for a legend becomes a legend when a story is told and not forgotten. That is what Anya said as she spread her legs and screamed and pushed, giving birth to a perfect baby boy. All parents think their child is special, but Anya knew right away something was different about her boy, whose cries enchanted even the most curmudgeonly nurse.

"'You will be a legend,' she said to him, letting his hand encircle her thumb. 'I do not know much but I know that.'"

Nimrah's voice was not her own, but the same melodious voice storytellers used to enrapture their audience. The same voice Baba had used years ago.

"So, the boy grew," Nimrah continued, "the weight of his destiny upon him like a snug doublet. Many boys would tug at the tight neckline, sweat beading on their neck. To be a legend is to carry the weight of your story. This is impossible for many. But not this boy, who worked his muscles until he could capably hold the weight of it.

"One day, his rabbi asked him after prayer service, 'You are special, for you came out of the womb already knowing Yohev's true name. The name They do not tell many Yahad at all. They have blessed you and the life you will lead. Does it ever feel too much for such a small boy?'

"The boy shook his head. 'I hold it comfortably.'

"That is what he always said, you see, when people asked if his destiny felt too great. He held it comfortably, the way parents ease into the love of their child, or children ease into loving their family animals.

"As the boy grew into a man, his answer did not change. However, the question did. Instead of asking if his destiny felt too great, people now asked *when* he would fulfill his destiny, for time passes quickly for mortals. And despite being blessed, this boy-now-man was only that—a mortal.

"(This part is contested. Some say he was not mortal at all, or he was mortal how the ancients were—destined to stay alive for as long as they needed to fulfill their destiny, even if that meant hundreds and hundreds of years. When I tell this story, however, I choose to say he was mortal. He would like it to be told that way.)

"The truth was, it took the man until his middle age to see his true purpose. In the dead of night, the city began to wake to the clacking of horse heels and violent screams. Yahadi men were torn from their houses and accused of killing Ozmini boys, who began to die off in droves. Most likely these boys had died of the outbreak of an infection brought to Valón by the northeastern traders in the Orzegali mountains, but it did not matter. Logic never did. Instead, they told stories of Yahad who sucked the blood from these boys and used it for their holy bread. That is why, they claim, so many of the boys had facial deformities—from the touch of Yahadi lips.

"The chosen man knew what he must do. One night he stole away under the twilight cover of the stars bent close to the Leirit river—the largest part before it clogged into streams. Guided by all of his studies and all of his beliefs, he looked toward the sky, toward the trees, toward the ground, and toward himself—all the places where he knew Yohev lived.

"'This is why I know Your name,' he said to Yohev, and began to dig into the riverbed, not stopping until his fingernails were embedded with dirt and blood from jagged, tiny rocks. He collected all the stones he could find, and kissed each one, before stacking them into a human shape. He did not let anyone see what happened next—not even the storytellers who passed on the tale—for what he did was sacred. Sacred, not secret, let me clarify. He did not share his methods because they were only for his eyes. He did not share it like one does not flippantly say Yohev's true name. Sacred things are not supposed to be spoken. They are supposed to be lived.

"And so, from stone and mud, he created what many would call a monster. And that's what the monster would come to think of itself as, sometimes. But as it was created, the murdering of Yahadi men ceased, for the

Ozmini knights began to fear the creature's aptitude. They only knew how to stick their metal into flesh and bone, not mud and stone. So, they left the Yahad alone, and soon the accusations became murmurs.

"When the chosen man was done with his creation, he appeared to have aged many decades, for that is what happens when a man performs a miracle. It is the way of Yohev's world. But he did not miss the years he lost. For him, it was not a sacrifice. It was an honor. For he created something that protected his people and would protect them long after he was gone."

Malka imagined the Maharal carving his command into Nimrah's forehead. *Emet*. Truth. It made sense of how the Maharal's other commands worked. All he had to do was take a knife to Nimrah's body and write his desires on her skin.

"How did it feel to be created?" Malka asked.

Nimrah was silent for a moment, save for the rustle of her cloak as she readjusted herself against the tree. When she did speak, it was soft, relenting. "That's not part of the story, village girl. I only meant to share that perhaps it is more damaging to fear Kefesh than to learn how to command it."

But Malka knew that was not completely true. Nimrah did not have to tell her story or make it personal. There were many fables made for morals. Nimrah had chosen her own. This affected Nimrah—that much was obvious by the way she told the story, emotion deepening her voice. Malka knew the kind of torment only family could create.

When Malka fell asleep, she dreamed of Abba carving orders into her skin with his dagger until he left her to bleed out.

※

It could only have been a few hours since Nimrah had whispered her creation story—how the Maharal had used Kefesh to create and command her. Life, from nothing.

Kefesh.

The magic that had saved Malka. The magic that landed her here in the first place.

Dawn crusted the sky, though it was still nearly dark through the dense crown of the trees. Nimrah had fallen asleep against the trunk, face scowling despite the peace of sleep.

Malka's mind drifted to Imma. The days since their last embrace felt like a lifetime. But each hour, each minute Malka stayed alive gave her hope.

Quietly, she stole Nimrah's dwindling lantern and began to walk.

She arrived at a waral tree several paces from their camp. The fruit was a dulled blue—a less potent variety, Nimrah had said. Many had fallen; some were crushed, the ground charred from acidity. But others were still intact, only bruised like the apples Malka had seen the merchant transform. Baba had instilled in her great fear, but she never could forget what she saw. Never could forget the word the merchant drew into the apple, so clear in the holy language she had been taught: חדש. *Chodesh*. Renew.

And he commanded it to be true.

Malka hovered her finger above the dirt, tracing the letters she had seen before, as if she were the disgruntled vendor and the waral fruit the apple.

She closed her eyes. Breathed. Opened them again.

Of course, nothing had happened. She didn't want anything to happen. She didn't trace the words into the fruit, did not make them real. She did not speak the prayer to will the command into existence.

Malka didn't know how to pray that way—for power, for control. She never had. She wouldn't start now.

Still, she closed her eyes again, breathing deep the moment of quiet, alone with the prayers she did know. A prayer of peace, of righteousness, for Amnon's bravery taking this tumultuous magic in his hands to save Imma. Prayers that comforted her in the bitter cold and howling woods.

When she opened them again, her gaze caught on a glint of light. The waral fruit shimmered. Thinking it was a trick of the lantern, Malka cast her hand over the flame, descending a shadow over the fruit. Still, it glimmered, the brown-yellow of the bruise diminished.

Malka startled to her feet, kicking over the lantern. The light went out, leaving her enveloped in the night. She heaved, stepping back from the fruit like she had done the Tannin, heart pounding and limbs shaking, worried about what the creature could do. She backed away until the glimmering fruit was nothing but a speck in the darkness.

Her fingers buzzed where she had traced the word in the air, like the pins and needles from sleeping. She slapped her hands on her thighs, desperate to be rid of the sensation.

The waral fruit was playing tricks on her.

But somewhere deep, a shift occurred. A sensation wholly new to her, heart buzzing and head spinning. A satiation that required no meal. She didn't like how it felt. *She wanted to feel it again.*

When Tzvidi attempted to light a candle using Kefesh, he set the library ablaze.

Malka did not want to be Tzvidi. She had done nothing. *Nothing.*

She lay on the ground once more and drew her knees up to her chest, heart pounding.

She was not Tzvidi.

She was not.

CHAPTER 12

The Great Oak's roots had spread.

They had ventured past Nimrah's previous boundary, marked by slashes she had carved into one of trees. A small miracle, though it was just delaying the inevitable. But Malka's interaction with the waral fruit had gnawed at her, instilling more anxiety about the deal she had struck, even if she herself wouldn't be rooted to Nimrah.

It would be worth the cost, though. She thought of Imma every moment, but particularly as the nights drew near. The jail in Eskravé was damp and decrepit, riddled with critters which thrived in the wet dark. At best, Imma would be freezing. At worst, disease would crawl inside her like flesh beetles. That is, if the Paja did not find other ways to torture her.

She shut her eyes. Inhaled.

The encounter with the Tannin had been a brush with death; a chasm of fear for her life and failure in her promise to Imma. It couldn't happen again.

As the last of the sun dripped from the sky, the woods grew quiet.

Until the sound of something rolling in the snow paused Malka in her tracks.

"Sorry," Amnon said. "That was me. I kicked something."

They shone their lights onto the head of a fox carcass. Maggots had scattered when Amnon had jostled it, some lingering in the eye socket and mouth. They had eaten well, almost nothing left but bone, residual tissue, and stained blood.

"I'm gonna vomit," Amnon said, face paling.

Malka was just grateful it wasn't a human corpse.

She thought of Chaia here and hoped her death had been a quick one. It was the last kindness this world could've given her.

"Have you come across anyone here before us?"

She had been chewing on the question since they first met, letting it roll around her tongue until she could swallow whatever truth revealed itself in the answer. If Nimrah had ever come across someone fitting Chaia's description, any stubborn hope Malka held on to would be snuffed out. She did not know if she was ready to change the shape of her grief, to feel it raw again.

But the days in Mavetéh were not guaranteed. She had swiftly learned that. One wrong step and she would have woken the Tannin, could have charred her face on an ill-timed falling waral fruit.

So, she asked. Ready for whatever answer Nimrah had to give her.

The golem shook her head. "When people venture this far into the forest, they tend to be dead by the time I find them."

Malka bit her lower lip as a hot rush of tears threatened to fall.

"Well, actually," Nimrah amended, "weeks ago, a group did pass through. I did not engage with them, but I did overhear they were headed toward Vyš. Anyway, next time I encountered them further south, they were dead. Torn limb from limb."

Could it have been the same group they had come across that first day in Mavetéh?

"You didn't try to warn them?" Amnon asked, disapproval lacing his voice.

"I'm supposed to be dead," Nimrah responded dryly. "Remember that?"

Amnon crossed his arms. "You saved us."

Nimrah shrugged noncommittally. "Perhaps if they had been actively dying when I found them, I would've saved them. Starting to think they would've have been more palatable companions."

Malka ignored their bickering, her interest instead snagging on the mention of Vyš. It was the second time Balkisk's capital city had come up recently—the first when Aleksi reflected on the duke's robe of human bones.

The duke who also thought the papacy could fail, according to Aleksi. Malka had never considered it before, a life not run by the Church, but the idea had rooted inside her since he said it.

"What do you know of the Duke of Vyš?" She racked her brain to think of his name.

If Nimrah was thrown by the shift in subject, she did not show it. "Everything I know is five years out of date."

Malka stared at the fox's jaw, its sharp teeth slicing the shadows of its mouth. His name came to her. "I've heard that Duke Sigmund hates King Valski."

Nimrah laughed, gazing at the skull. "There's not much of the king to hate. If you hate the king, you hate his puppeteers."

There was a scattering in the brush.

Amnon unsheathed his sword. Malka held tight to Abba's dagger, fox and conversation forgotten. Nimrah raised her finger to her lips.

Malka tried to regulate her labored breathing. They waited in silence, long after the scattering had ceased.

"Maybe it went the other way?" Amnon whispered.

Nimrah shot him an annoyed look, but Malka's eyes caught on something behind Nimrah's hair, moving so subtly between the trees Malka questioned her sight. She squinted against the twilight, but only the low tangle of branches came into focus.

Nimrah followed her gaze between the trees.

The roots from the ground hissed as Nimrah commanded them, rising as vipers.

"Run, now!" Nimrah ordered, but Malka was frozen. The lantern illuminated the creature's form as it approached from the shadows—branches and bone tangled together by sinew to form the creature's mass, like a resurrected deer. Horns jutted from its skull, a tangle of vines dripping from its mouth like saliva. But most stark, and deceptively animalistic, were its feet, scaly like a rooster's, which dug muddy prints into the snow. Fear clawed up her throat, its talons like acid.

Throughout their childhood, Chaia had told Malka many haunting stories of gruesome animals, tales she had coaxed out of older Eskraven boys, who were always desperate to impress her with their knowledge. But this creature was unlike any of the monsters she had known. Worse than anything her mind could conjure.

The air stilled as the creature stalked forward, all murmuring of the forest's creatures quieting like frightened babes. Nimrah's warning echoed again, ordering her to flee, but the creature had a mystifying hold on her. The same hold the Tannin had as she held her breath, anticipating its waking. Maybe this was how it would end. How the creatures had drawn in the other women. Her luck had run out.

It charged toward her. Malka wrapped her hands around its antlers to keep them from pressing into her chest. The creature was much stronger than her, though, and the force of its charge knocked her to the cold, hard ground. Under the creature's weight, she gasped for breath.

Then, the pressure lifted. Vines had wrapped around the antlers like rope, and the deer had fallen to its side. *Nimrah's magic did that.* Malka scrambled to her knees as Nimrah hauled the creature up with her hands.

If Malka had questioned the golem's monstrosity before, she didn't now. She looked cousin to the deer, green veins protruding against her skin as her muscles flexed to keep the deer at bay. The stone across her face and arms shone in the moonlight.

"Malka!" Amnon screamed, clutching her arm.

But the golem could not hold back the deer any longer. It rammed into Nimrah, sending her flying back. The deer set its sights on Malka once again, like a lion to a lamb. A fox to a rabbit.

Amnon swung his sword hard against the deer, metal tangling in its branches. It growled low and feral before jumping and sinking its teeth into Amnon's shoulder.

Malka screeched as Amnon was thrown from his feet, falling hard against the ground.

A root burst from the soil, impaling the creature through its skull. The growls, one fierce, became whimpers as it crumbled to the ground.

Malka stared in shock before her wits came to her. She ran to Amnon on wobbly legs, falling to her knees to cradle his head in her hands.

"It's only subdued," Nimrah warned, coming closer to Malka. She still panted, voice strained. "We need to get away from here."

"Help him," Malka pleaded. "Please, I can't lift him."

Nimrah sighed, and hoisted Amnon on her back with a grunt.

They found a clearing far enough away that the deer could lose Malka's scent, and Nimrah transferred Amnon carefully to the ground.

"Malka?" he called, voice barely a whisper.

"I'm here."

He convulsed in pain. The deer's teeth had ripped away his cloak and the layers of his travel kroj, exposing his bloody shoulder and the stark white of his bone through the muscle.

She needed to stop the bleeding. Clean the wound. Prevent infection.

Malka knew how to do this. She knew how to heal.

Malka tore from the fabric of her petticoat—what she hoped was the cleanest part.

"Help me raise his arm."

Much to her shock, Nimrah obeyed, helping to slip Amnon's arm from the bulky cloak.

With a practiced hand, Malka formed a tourniquet from the linen. She bit back despair when the cloth immediately soiled deep red.

Amnon's eyes drooped back, and his body slacked as he fell unconscious.

Malka dug into her satchel, hand searching its depth for the black perphona. Its thorns pricked her skin. She cursed but didn't stop.

"I . . . I need a stone, some sort of flat surface. I need to make a poultice."

"I don't know if—"

"A stone," Malka pressed, unwilling to hear what Nimrah had to say. "A flat surface."

Nimrah's lips thinned. She saw the sweep of Nimrah's cloak in the corner of her eye as she disappeared.

When she reemerged, Nimrah dropped a handful of stones to the ground. Some rounded, some flat.

She let her healer instincts take over as she prepared a poultice, grinding the leaves rhythmically until they were powder. She didn't have hot water to make the plant pliant and ready for use, nor did she have all the ingredients she would have liked. She didn't have her sewing needles to stitch Amnon's gaping wound.

So, when Nimrah said to her, "I don't think it's enough," Malka couldn't bite back with anything, because she agreed. It wasn't going to be enough.

Underneath her, Amnon began to convulse, sweat soaking his face.

Malka threw her hands up. They were covered in the black perphona paste and blood. This wasn't right.

"He shouldn't be reacting like this," Malka said, voice threadbare and desperate, hands trying to quell Amnon's violent shivers. "Infection wouldn't have kicked in this fast. I—I don't know what's wrong with him."

"He's dying." It was the softest Malka had heard the golem speak. She hated it. Not now. Not for this.

Malka caressed Amnon's burning forehead. "He has a fever. How does he have a fever already?"

"It isn't just any beastly bite. It's a bite from the mouth of a Kefesh-cursed creature. He's not long for this world."

Every horrible death she had seen Mavetéh give. Every sickness that had come from it. Yael's terrible cough and her skin as pale as stretched animal hide. Rzepka's body. The Ozmins raked in the snow.

"He cannot die. The forest is not allowed to claim him, too." Malka curled her hands into fists. "This is your fault. He's dying because of *you*."

"That's fine," Nimrah responded, no vitriol in her voice. "But you can save him. I can help you save him."

A warmth ran down her face from where the deer had scratched her. It curved into her mouth, tasting like copper. "How?"

"It was not a jest, earlier, when I said you could be powerful." Nimrah's voice was close to her ear, and softer than she had ever heard it. Malka wanted to yell at her, have her be flippant and uncaring. It was worse, this way. It was real this way. Amnon was going to die. "You can try to heal him with Kefesh."

Malka shook her head. "If he can be healed with magic, why can't you do it? I have seen how you command the earth. Just like the Maharal."

Nimrah's face twisted, hand cupping her side. She had not been left unscathed from the deer attack, either. "It doesn't work like that. I can only do what I'm commanded to do." She pointed to the words which decorated the stone along her face and her body. "The Maharal gave me the ability to make basic healing tonics, since I used to make them so frequently for him when his experiments went awry." She tugged on the collar of her brocade doublet, revealing more words sliced into her chest. "Just like I can only command the vines because the Maharal gave me the command to do so. I can't . . . I can't do anything for Amnon. I'm sorry."

Nimrah scrubbed a hand over her face. Hers, too, was covered in blood. "I'm a command. Not the commander." She paused. "But you can be."

"I don't want this," Malka whispered, digging the heels of her palms into the earth. It was cool underneath her touch, and a stroke of fear seized her at the idea of commanding Kefesh. Who was she to demand things of the earth?

She thought of the bruised waral fruit. But that was not real magic. She had traced letters into the air. She knew it didn't work like that.

She curled her hand into a fist.

"*What* don't you want, village girl?" Nimrah pressed. "To save Amnon? To hold a God-granted power in your hands?"

Malka sighed, and sharp pain jolted through her where the deer had rammed its antlers. "All I ever wanted was to have Eskravé return to the village I once loved. One not plagued by famine or violence. I want to heal alongside my mother and make paper cuts for the holidays with my sisters."

"That's not your life right now. This is, with your dying friend against the trunk of this tree and his blood stained on your neck." Nimrah tilted a water pouch against his lips. "Decide if your fear of magic is worth the price of his life."

Amnon was so pale. Sweat gleamed across his skin. He shifted, beginning to rouse.

"Malka." It was more breath than voice. The two syllables of her name slipped through his lips like a prayer.

She couldn't deny him like this. When he was laid bare; when his lips trembled in pain and sweat stained the hollow of his neck.

"The fear isn't worth losing him." Her declaration shocked even herself. She felt the words on her tongue, what weight they carried.

"Is it not?" Nimrah asked, and Malka realized she was being genuine. Was the fear of Kefesh's dangers worth the price of Amnon's life?

"The fear isn't worth his life," Malka repeated again, like if she said it enough it would be true. It would be real.

She heard Baba's warnings, but she also imagined Amnon dead when he didn't have to be. When Malka could do something to save him.

He was sick and Malka was a healer. He was her friend and needed her.

Amnon had offered to use Kefesh without a second thought to spare her. He deserved for her to do the same for him.

Malka closed her eyes, her blood-stained hand wrapping around the flame pendant at her neck. The phantom scent of bitter thyme and the acrid odor of celandine juice from Imma's workroom filled her nose.

Imma would do the same, Malka thought. Even if there was a chance of failure. Even if it was forbidden. She moved through life with a grace that for anyone else would become easily muddled. She had braved Mavetéh to pick black perphona, after all. Malka owed it to Imma's teachings, to Amnon, to try.

"What will I need to do?" Malka asked, her knees digging into the damp soil. He could not die. She was willing to bend the world to save him.

"Take the herbs leftover from your poultice and hold them tight."

Malka followed Nimrah's instructions, the black perphona crumbling in her fists. The thorns cut into her skin, but she barely registered the pain as she scattered the herb around a small patch of snowy dirt. Instructions were something she could do well. She had years of practice following Imma's hurried guidance and requests that sent her scurrying around her workroom. She knew this. She knew how to be told to heal another.

"It'll never work if you keep on like that."

Malka jerked her head up at Nimrah's disapproval. Though she was not all human, red tinted the puckering skin on her neck and her cheek. Malka was pleased to know the cold bit her, too. "I am doing everything you say!"

"It's not possible to perform Kefesh mechanically. It's a prayer deeper than most will experience in their lifetime. You cannot sit with God while your head is empty!"

"For someone who cannot perform Kefesh at all, you sure hold your criticisms like scripture."

Nimrah huffed, and fog swirled by her mouth. "I may not be a believer, but I know how your religion works. You pray in synagogue. With others. That's what Yahadism is all about. But this is something alongside that. Kefesh are the prayers you utter to yourself when you think no one is looking. Kefesh is the way you talk to Yohev when you are desperate, sad, joyful, in pain. It is the company you allow yourself in your bleakest moments. It is the love you share in your greatest joys. Think of those moments and let them console you."

Malka closed her eyes. Mavetéh was unnervingly quiet, like even the woods had stilled in anticipation of what magic might unfurl. Malka wondered how the woods had reacted when magic tied Nimrah to the Great Oak. Whether the limbs of the trees shook violently as it happened; if the wind became sick and pungent with poisonous odor as she slept; if the animals grew feral, their eyes as red as blood when she traced the Great Oak tree's roots.

Malka questioned how the magic which gave Mavetéh its name could have the same power to heal Amnon. But Malka was desperate. She tightened her grip around Amnon's clammy hand.

Malka thought of her first prayer after Chaia had disappeared into Mavetéh. How the fear shaped her voiceless laments, becoming something else entirely. They were no longer words, but a place where Malka lived. It was a place where Chaia was not missing, where the bell tower never rang curfew, and Hadar could play without worry. In the quietness of her room in Eskravé, the moon washing its glow across the floorboards, Malka remembered how her prayer opened in a way it had not before.

She had been desperate for Chaia's safety, and she was desperate for Amnon's health now. She let her mind shape the holy words. They were laced with the same fear of loss she felt for Chaia. The same fear of being at Mavetéh's knees again. She chanted the familiar words, letting them coat her tongue like goldenmase. She thought of the comfort prayer brought her, how her words alone could have Yohev's ear. The God who gave her life, who gave her Danya and Hadar as sisters. Who gave her Chaia's and Amnon's friendship. The God who brought joy and light, pain and suffering.

And that pain racked her chest.

But like the thickest beam in the shul, Yohev also gave her the strength to overcome.

Fill me with strength, she said, unsure if her words were Kraž-Yadi or her ancient holy language or both. *Like the grandest oak tree, the most torrented river. Give me a strength as ancient as the earth itself.*

Something within her broke. She was no longer in Mavetéh, no longer stung with cold or her skin torn with cuts. She was somewhere no one could follow, where she existed with Yohev alone.

Holding tight to this feeling, Malka dragged her finger along the scattered herb, letting the earth guide her hand. She drew out the block letters: רפא. *Rapha.* Heal. Ancient words from her holy language running across her tongue.

When she was done, she held her breath.

The earth was silent, and then it was not.

She felt it, warm and heady. There were no words to describe how it felt to command the earth, only an understanding that it heeded her. And Malka churned with power. She opened her eyes, blinking away the white spots clouding her vision. Careful not to smudge the letters, she collected the crumbled black perphona plant and shoved it into Amnon's mouth.

She held his head in her palm and helped him chase down the herb with water. He coughed, but Malka held his mouth closed until he swallowed.

He fell still.

Malka, dizzy with power, leaned over him, hand tracking the pulse at his wrist. It beat slow, but steady.

Nimrah stared at her wildly, eyebrows knit together and mouth hung open. Malka wondered what she looked like, cheeks flushed and pupils blown wide. The look the golem gave her sent a chill up her spine, despite the heat of magic flowing through her. She was unbarred, and Malka swore the golem's lips trembled.

⤴

Her hands were still slick with magic as she fled from Nimrah and Amnon. Her body was stiff from the creature's attack, back in sharp swaths of pain from being thrown on the ground. She bled where she had landed on jagged rock, soiling the right sleeve of her blouse. Adrenaline coursed through her, numbing the pain that would worsen later. She needed to be alone, to subdue the power that ached in her bones. The sickly-sweet scent trailed behind her like smoke. When she hid herself behind the tight-knit trees, she faced the direction of the ancient holy city and pressed her forehead to the tree in front of her. The bark was cool, rough edges digging into her skin. She inhaled, and the tree breathed with her, undulating like the movement of her chest.

It was like the whisper of those holy words, the letters of Yohev's language wrapped in her mouth like cinnamon and myrrh, made her something dangerous. For a moment, when the words awoke the herbs in her hand, she felt a power long lost to her. There was no tithe collection, no knights or bishops with their iron threats. There was no sickness, no Mavetéh. There was only her and the words she had spoken since childhood, since her mouth was able to form a prayer.

Eternal One, Malka prayed. *Is this what it means to be held close? To walk with You without fear of falling?*

A warmth flowed through her cheeks, the erratic beat of her heart loud in her ears. *God of My Ancestors, give me the strength to hold prayer in my mouth like magic.*

The tree rumbled in response, sending shivers down her neck. She stayed there, against the fluttering woods, until she could no longer hold her trembling body upright; until the cold whipped her down to her knees and the roots cracked against her bone.

CHAPTER 13

The woodland had not eased its haunting, as another day bled into night. The waral fruit hung in shades of indigo blue and midnight purple, the most poisonous they had come by thus far. Frenzied vultures danced through trees with roots bubbling from the ground like acidic healing potions. Their sickly scaled feet caught Malka's eye and soured her stomach.

She had commanded the earth like the shalkat Baba had warned her against. Stories of taboo magic, grown even more sinister since Mavetéh's power clawed, awake and deadly. But the same magic bent to her will, filled her soul. And because of it, Amnon was alive.

If she closed her eyes, Malka could still feel the magic on her skin. Kefesh, she was learning, was not so easily forgotten. It lingered like a blood stain, memorialized like a puckering scar tainting smooth skin.

"We should rest," Nimrah said, bending until Malka could help settle Amnon on the ground. She had been carrying him on her back for hours, yet signaled no tiredness, no aches.

The fog was dense, and it slithered through the trees like snakes, reminding Malka she was not the only one to command the earth.

Nimrah had used vines like whips and tree roots as spears. She was dangerous, and Malka could not forget that. But now that her fear from the deer creature's attack had settled, she realized something else, as well. The creature had hurt Nimrah, too. She didn't know what to make of that.

She recalled what Nimrah had said about Kefesh being unpredictable, the earth interpreting commands as it wished. Maybe this had been an unintended consequence. Though her magic had created the creatures, she was not safe from them, either.

Malka's stomach growled loudly.

"Start building a fire," Nimrah instructed. "I'll find dinner."

When Nimrah came back through the thicket with a rabbit slung over her shoulder, its feet bunched in her hand, Malka was still struggling to ignite a flame. Snow had dampened the rest of her matches, which she had regrettably left unprotected and forgotten, distracted with Amnon's injury.

Her palms burned again as she rolled the wood between them, failing to catch a spark.

"You can start it with magic, you know," Nimrah said. She had already begun to skin and gut the rabbit with Abba's dagger. The air filled with the tangy scent of fresh blood.

"I can start it with my hands, too," Malka retorted.

"The only thing your hands will start is bleeding the way you're rubbing them raw."

Malka continued to work the stick between her palms to no avail. When she pulled them away, her hands were covered in angry red abrasions.

"I shouldn't be surprised anymore," Nimrah said between her teeth, "that you'd rather bleed than listen to me."

Malka lifted her gaze and steadied it on Nimrah's stone-cut face. "You once told me not to forget what you're capable of. I never *have*. I'm reminded every time we come across a vile thing in this forest, every time I look at Amnon's wound. So, no, you should not be surprised if I'd rather bleed."

Nimrah clenched her jaw, and the same unfettered look crossed her face as when she had seen Malka command Kefesh. She peered at Amnon, who slept huddled against Malka's bag. "You both fear me. That, I understand. But Amnon does not hate me with such fervor as you. No, your hate for me is personal. Your cheeks redden when you look at me, and your fists tighten until your knuckles turn white. What is it that makes your hate for me run so deep?"

Malka fought the heat that crept to her cheeks. They always betrayed her. When she was young, Imma could always tell when Malka lied, for her cheeks would flush like ripe cherries. Chaia was always better at fibs and saying the right thing to get her way. She resisted the urge to turn her face as tears threatened. Chaia was in the deepest part of her heart, and her grief weakened her. She did not want to be weak now.

The sky croaked, and rain began to fall in spatters. Malka relinquished the stick and flung the wet tinder away from her.

Nimrah wiped the guts on her trousers. The rabbit wasn't getting cooked any time soon.

The rain turned to hail, the pellets thrashing down on them as ferocious as swarming wasps. Nimrah settled back into a nearby larch tree's cavity for shelter. Malka tugged her cloak around herself and Amnon, despite the cold fabric making her teeth rattle, but it was a meager protection against the turbulent shards of ice.

"I've got you," Malka told Amnon, even though his eyes were rolled back in his head, caught in the deepest part of his delirious sleep. The hail had left scrapes across his face, some beginning to welt blood.

"There is room in here for all of us," Nimrah said, motioning to the cavity concealing her from the elements. "Come."

Malka hesitated, but Amnon was already hurt from the storm. She swallowed her opposition and wrapped her hands around Amnon's shoulders, dragging him until she pressed against the back of the tree hollow. She settled herself next to Amnon, putting as much space between her and the golem as possible. The space was already tight and suffocating. As she pressed her body further into the cavity, she caught Nimrah staring. She was grateful for the shadows that cloaked them, hiding her face.

Until a spark eclipsed the dark air, and light filled the cavity.

Malka's mouth fell agape. "Did you do that with magic?"

Nimrah's lip quirked. "No. Unlike you, I'm adept with wood and tinder."

"You couldn't have done that before our dinner spoiled?"

Nimrah shrugged. "I was trying to prove a point."

"You'll find my hatred grows when I am hungry."

Nimrah's smirk fell. "Someone you knew fell victim to Mavetéh, didn't they?"

In the hollow of the tree, Malka could hear her own shaky breathing. She swallowed hard and drew her necklace between her fingers.

"Tell me."

It wasn't said as a command, but a lament. Nimrah's eyes were no longer on her. She had hiked up her sleeve and was tracing the word carved into her stone forearm.

"Chaia."

She gave her name time to breathe, let it fill the small space between them.

"My best friend. Unlike the others taken by Mavetéh, we never found her body. Still, they declared her dead. After seeing these woods and what they did to Amnon . . . I don't have much hope she survived." Malka expected to cry, but numbness pierced her instead. "It is indescribable. To lose someone you couldn't imagine life without." She faced Nimrah, cheeks heating. "And then stare her killer in the face."

"I'm sorry."

Malka had heard those words so many times since Chaia's disappearance, they had become shallow to her ears. "Sorry doesn't bring her back."

Amnon coughed, and Malka brushed her hand across his forehead to soothe him.

"Let me say this: I will be glad to die. For Chaia. For your mother. For all the Yahad I was supposed to protect and have let down." Nimrah shifted her attention to the woods, looking past the hail which fogged the air hazy white. She held her chin high, like a soldier from the Rhaškan Empire's military would. Resolute. Unyielding. "After I atone for yet another of my piled sins."

The air held silence like the fog held water. Malka recalled something she had not processed earlier, mind too occupied with thoughts of saving Amnon.

I may not be a believer, but I know how your religion works, Nimrah had said.

"Earlier, you said you were not a believer of the Yahadi faith. But you were created by a rabbi using holy magic to protect the Yahadi people. How can you brush against Yohev so closely and still not believe?"

The golem sighed. "It's complicated. I was made to protect the Yahad, that's all. There was no room for anything else. I couldn't have my own belief. Couldn't forge my own path. I was not born young and nurtured. One day, I appeared, ready to do the Maharal's bidding."

Facing Nimrah's stone side, she could not read her well, expressions dimmed by the carving of her face. It bothered her more than she wanted to admit, how her eyes could trace the sharp edges of Nimrah's chin, her nose, the deep chisels of her cheeks, and have so little grasp on the truth of her. A permanent veil.

It reminded her of the Feast of Lots mask she had worn when she was younger. Wood carved to the shape of her face, berries dyed a pigmented flush on the cheeks, and charcoal-painted eyebrows. All to match the appearance of the Shabhe Queen—the heroine of the Feast of Lots story.

She thought of pressing the mask to her face. Hiding behind the costume, becoming someone else for the night.

"Your thoughts are very loud," Nimrah said, lips curling in the shadow light.

"I was thinking of the Feast of Lots story. Do you know it?"

"It is told every year at the festival."

A *yes* would've sufficed.

"The Shabhe King hated the Yahad. So much so that even his own wife had to keep her Yahadi identity a secret."

Nimrah raised her brow, willing her to continue.

"We've learned to keep Kefesh at arm's length the way the Shabhe Queen learned to hide her identity. It wasn't until the crown threatened slaughter of her people that she cast aside her safely hidden identity for a desperate attempt at saving them."

"You think the Shabhe Queen desperate for revealing her identity?"

Malka shrugged. "What else could you call it?"

Nimrah steepled her hands. "Bravery, some may say. In fact, I believe those are the exact words from the song made for her. *Shabhe Queen, brave and true, who spoke to her king, breaking all the rules.*"

Though Nimrah didn't sing the song, she recited it like poetry, intonations drawn out in her smoky voice.

Heat prickled up Malka's neck. "To me, desperation and bravery are one and the same. She was desperate enough to come forward, and brave enough to deal with the consequences that would come if the Shabhe King did not accept her."

Nimrah hummed. It was hard to tell if she disagreed, expression never changing, eyes cast upon the falling hail outside their shelter. "In the end, she did not have to worry, for the Shabhe King treasured her more than anything and reversed the dreaded decree. She saved her people and was revered by them for it."

Nimrah's palm traced the wood's bark, eerily similar to what Malka had done when she fled after healing Amnon with Kefesh.

"You say your sole duty is to protect the Yahad. Like the Shabhe Queen."

Nimrah's expression soured, but she didn't remark on Malka's comparison. Instead, she said, "If I'm not protecting the Yahad, I have no purpose. I know no other purpose. I don't expect forgiveness, nor do I want it. From you, or from the Yahadi people. All I want is to right my wrongs and stay true to the one responsibility Yohev has granted me—protecting the Yahad."

But she hadn't protected the Yahad. Not like the Shabhe Queen. Once, they could've both been revered. But Nimrah had not become a hero. She had become something that left the dead leaves of winter rugged with gooseflesh and gave life to jewel-eyed creatures lurking in the shadows. A path that had taken Chaia from Malka. That would take Imma if Malka could not deliver on her promise to the priest.

Malka traced her hand through Amnon's hair. He was much cooler now. "Then why did you kill that poor Yahadi boy?" she asked.

Nimrah hardened, whatever vulnerability she had displayed gone. "You don't know what happened. You weren't there."

"Baba told me—"

Nimrah barked a laugh. "Starting to feel like your Baba told you more gossip than truth in those stories of his."

Malka reared at the coldness in her voice, how dangerous it felt angering her. Yet Malka couldn't stop. She had no one else to blame. To fight.

"You have caused so much pain for so many," Malka said. "It's hard to look at you."

"And yet, your eyes betray you. Do you think I don't see you staring?" Her words echoed on the wood, sending her voice around them like the timbrels which rang in the monthly Eskraven market, gruff and sepulchral.

The blush threatened her again, crawling from her neck to her cheeks faster than Malka could tame it. "You were created with a power I don't understand yet have commanded. You were made from the earth itself and brought the woods of my childhood to life with a vengeance. It is only natural to try and make sense of you."

Nimrah's jaw clicked. "Is that what I should prepare for in Eskravé? Tell me, am I to be gawked at before they kill me? Will a more gruesome death bring more or fewer people to my funeral pyre? Will their curiosity get the best of them?"

"We have a deal—"

"Oh, we have a deal, village girl," Nimrah said, her voice dropping low. "One I promise not to forget."

The ground below Malka's knees grumbled, and Malka wondered if Nimrah's anger had caused it. But the golem did not seem to notice. *How much she is like stone*, Malka thought. And how much she envied her contempt.

Malka had always dreamed of seeing Valón, but never thought she'd see it like this, aiding a golem in her pursuit of justice, rescuing the beloved

Maharal from his unfair fate. Was she a criminal now? Was this where her sins began?

Václav's lifeless eyes crossed her mind. She had shoved him, and he had fallen to his death, head cracking on the slick rock. Would she instead collect sins like tokens? Maybe she would become a dybbuk, her uneasy soul drifting as it searched desperately for a body to inhabit.

Malka wanted to flee—claustrophobic in this tree cave with her. Yet the hail still came down hard. Instead, she shoved her hand in her pocket and toyed with the rest of the black perphona she had collected earlier. What she hadn't scattered on the earth and traced holy words on to heal Amnon with Kefesh.

Malka frowned, recalling another herb she had seen scattered on the ground.

"When I followed you from your hut that night, you had scattered devil's alphonsa on the ground. What for?"

Nimrah raised her brow. "Observant *and* nosy, a horrid combination."

The herbs began to crumble under Malka's tight grip. "Well?"

Nimrah's smirk faded. "I was trying to poison the tree. I thought that, maybe, if the Great Oak died, so would its hold on me. Only, as you know, it failed, because I cannot perform Kefesh the way you can. I didn't even care it would've left me bondless. All I thought about was getting to the Maharal."

Malka shook her head. "You knew you could not command Kefesh, but you attempted it, anyway."

Nimrah shrugged tighter into her cloak. "Are we any different? Both seeking impossibilities out of desperation to save those we love. I try to poison the Great Oak; you leave your village in search of a monster who has spared no maiden before?"

"One maiden," Malka responded, so faintly her voice was almost carried away with the wind.

"What?"

She swallowed. "You've spared one maiden."

Nimrah stared at her through the dark.

You've spared one maiden and doomed the rest.

It would be so easy for Malka to add. Another accusation Nimrah deserved. Yet something held her back. Maybe she was too tired to fight; too exhausted to feed her anger.

Maybe she understood Nimrah's desperation. Saw the wretched look in her deep-set eyes.

So, she said nothing more.

When Nimrah closed her eyes and rested her head on the wood, the sharp jut of her chin caught the shadow. Yet Malka could still make out the slight bob of her throat.

"I suppose."

CHAPTER 14

Dawn brought swollen clouds and snow which dusted the trees like powdered sugar. The sight of them made Malka hunger for Imma's sufganiyot, filled to the brim with strawberry preserves that stuck to her fingers. She craved them now, as she gnawed on a rabbit bone, the marrow staining her lips a brownish red.

At last, Nimrah had begun to feel the pull of the Great Oak's thinning roots. The veins in her neck had bulged, but she otherwise cloaked how the strain began to affect her.

"We'll have to do the rooting spell soon," she had said, setting Amnon down. "Early tomorrow, I imagine, with our . . . speed."

Unspoken between them, the knowledge that Malka would take Amnon's place performing the rooting spell. He was too sick.

And though Malka had used Kefesh to save Amnon from the brink of death, it nauseated her to imagine herself bonded with Nimrah. *The Rayga.*

"You've been quiet," Nimrah remarked, the bones of her meal already discarded on the ground.

Malka wiped her greasy fingers on her already ruined apron. "I have nothing to say."

Nimrah threw a bone across her shoulder with more force than necessary. "It will be a long day, in silence."

"I find Amnon's deep snores rather calming, actually."

"You're a terrible liar."

"It was a sweet lie," Malka corrected. "One I offered so you did not have to hear how I truly feel about you."

Nimrah sighed and a breath caressed the nape of Malka's neck. Until, she realized, it was the dim whirling of the wind. Unbidden heat crawled up her ears.

"We should enter Valón on Trader's Day," Nimrah said, thankfully unaware of Malka's distress. Her attention was cast somewhere between the tangle of branches, as if she could see the city lying somewhere beyond them. "Foreign merchants and vendors will fill the streets. There's no better day to blend in."

The day after tomorrow. Ten days from the priest's deadline, Malka mentally tallied. "Good."

Nimrah ground her teeth. Malka's clipped answers had been bothering her all morning, at which Malka took great satisfaction.

Malka began to strip the cloth from Amnon's shoulder. He jostled, waking slowly as she rubbed more salve into his wound. It had coagulated, and its redness had lessened.

Deep bags hung under his eyes, but his skin had become less sallow.

"Start slow," she ordered. "A couple of steps and we will rest again."

He nodded, then raised his hand as if to say *I know, I know*. But he gripped her hard as he stood. Malka stumbled under the press of his weight but found her footing as his arm draped across her shoulder.

"I'm a dead weight." Amnon closed his eyes, drooping his head.

"You're alive," Malka corrected. "And that means everything."

"Only because of you."

Malka swore magic sparked in the palms of her hands. "I could not watch you die."

"And I'm grateful." He glanced at Nimrah as he took a timid step forward. "My injury has messed with my sense of time. When do I have to perform the rooting spell?"

"You're not performing it at all," Malka said.

His eyes darted between them, then he shook his head. "Malka, you don't have to do this."

"I do."

"Let me take the burden of Kefesh, like I promised," he pleaded. His breathing had become labored again, his chest rising and falling in sharp puffs. She helped settle him on the ground, back leaned against a fallen trunk.

Malka felt Nimrah's eyes on her. She resisted the urge to cradle her palm. "I have already used Kefesh, to save you."

"What?" He paled even whiter. "You shouldn't have done that, Malka. You didn't have to do that for me." There was no judgment in his voice, only guilt.

"I did, Amnon, and I don't regret it."

It was what he needed to hear, to absolve himself. And Malka mostly believed it, too.

Amnon's eyes searched hers. "What was it like?"

"It . . . it was nothing like I have ever experienced." Malka sat next to him, looping her arm through his.

It was one thing for her to perform magic, another to speak of it. As if voicing the experience would tear down whatever lasting barriers she had placed between herself and Kefesh.

Instead, she recalled a story she had been told in her childhood, one that spoke the words she dared not say aloud.

"Do you remember the story of Abayda the Mystic?"

Amnon leaned his head back against the trunk, casting his eyes toward the canopy above them, as if willing the memory of the story to him.

"A little. Will you tell it again? Like you told those stories all those years ago, when I fell from that wretched tree, and you whispered the tales to me as your mother threaded stitches in my leg?"

Malka nodded, warmed by the memory.

"Abayda the Mystic was not always Abayda, nor was he always a mystic. For, sometimes, our names are given to us long after we are around to turn ears at them. Abayda, before he was Abayda, was called Yosef. He was not yet a mystic, but a farmer, who lived at the edge of the only forest Yohev had yet created."

Nimrah settled herself on the ground. She nodded to Malka to continue her story.

"It was a simple job, to tend to the sheep and cows. Yosef would wake at the first red touch of dawn, say his morning prayers, shear the sheep, milk the cows, and herd the animals into their pen once night spilled blue across the land, sand whipping into stars and constellations above.

"Yosef wanted to be content with his life, he truly did. For he went to sleep each night with his belly full and his livestock happy. But he would toss and turn in his cot, feeling an absence he could not describe. A cavity he could not fill. But Yosef had all he needed to be happy. So, he closed his eyes and believed the feeling would disperse in the daylight.

"But the next morning, the sadness did not cease. If anything, it grew. Grew until it clenched his heart like a taloned claw. He prayed, sheared the sheep, milked the cows, and herded the animals into their pens once night had fallen, but he was still not content. Again, he tossed and turned in his cot, the creaking of the wooden bed loud in the drowsy air.

"Soon, Yosef would forgo herding the animals back into their pens. He would no longer milk the cows or shear the sheep. He pulled himself out of bed only to pray and then slipped back under his tattered blanket to sleep even when the sun still hung high in the heavens.

"One day, he woke to a shattering wind which blew through his open window like a wildfire. He prepared for the chill, as it was dead winter. But the chill did not come. Instead: warmth. Yosef leaned into it.

"*Yosef,* the wind spoke to him. *You are troubled. I see the cows are not milked and the sheep are not sheared. What is preventing you from doing so?*

"Yosef had no doubt it was Yohev, the God of His Ancestors, speaking to him.

"'Eternal one,' Yosef spoke back in reverence. 'I am sorry I have forsaken my duties. But I am heavy with the weight of a sadness I cannot elude.'

"*Ah,* Yohev said through another gust of wind. *I know the sadness which you name. You are aching for a wife. You desire children to fill your farm with laughter and singing.*

"'Yes!' Yosef shouted. 'It is a wife and children I am missing! I feel their absence like a hole in my heart. Like the sting of a bee that grows with each throb.'

"*You shall have a wife, Yosef, but you must do one thing.*

"'Anything!'

"*There is a book held in a cobblestone tower just east of this forest. You must bring it to me.*

"'Yes!'

"*But caution, Yosef, for you must not open the book. If you disobey me, I cannot grant you what you desire.*

"Yosef promised not to open the book.

"*I will be here tomorrow at midnight to collect the book,* Yohev said, and left with another breeze.

"So, Yosef set off the next morning, eager to please Yohev and get a wife. When he arrived at the tower, he began the climb to the top. The stairs wound around and around and by the time he reached the top of the tower, he was sweating and aching for breath.

"But there, in the middle of the room, was a brown leather book made from the finest sheepskin. A golden clasp hugged the book, with a jagged lock at its center. Next to the book was a key with the same jagged pattern. Yosef peered back and forth, from the book to the key, and decided to take both in case Yohev had need of it.

"On his walk home, Yosef's heart grew heavy once again. He was so close to having a wife, but the promise of one did not subdue the ache he felt now, as he walked alone on the dirt path.

"When he arrived back at his farm, Yosef returned to his cot. It was early still—the sun hung low, streaming light through his window. Dust motes danced in the light, and Yosef watched them tenderly from his cot.

"The bed creaked and creaked as he tossed and turned, waiting for Yohev to come. He grew impatient, and in his boredom, he eyed his bag, shrugged up against his wall. The leather book peeking out the rim.

"Yosef wondered if he should check on the book to make sure he had the right one. One peek inside and he would be able to confirm. And, oh!, how he wondered what knowledge the book held. Maybe the book revealed how Yosef's wife would come to him. He reared at that thought and scrambled out of the bed. Surely, Yohev would not mind if he caught a glimpse of what was to come.

"Gingerly, he removed the book from the bag and held it above him, running his fingers over the smooth leather. Holding his breath, he put the key in the lock.

"What would he see in the pages, he wondered? Would they tell of his wife's beauty, or perhaps of his children's likeness to him? Would they have his bushy eyebrows, or his rounded nose?

"The key clicked, and the pages fell open.

"For hours, Yosef read. Inside the book were stories of the universe, how language made the stars, the moon, and the sky; how letters built mountains, rivers, and plains. The sounds he shaped into prayers were the same sounds used to make the rain, the snow, and the clouds.

"So engrossed was he in the book, Yosef did not see the sun set behind the mountains. A breeze blew through the room, fluttering a few pages of the book in its wake.

"*You disobeyed me,* the breeze said.

"'Forgive me,' Yosef said, still reeling from the words he had read. 'But I had to see. Is this how You created the universe, Eternal One?'

"*Yes,* the wind answered. *But it was not for you to know. You broke our agreement, Yosef, and thus, I can no longer give you a wife.*

"With another whip of wind across Yosef's face, Yohev was gone.

"Yosef cried as Yohev left him. He still felt broken, still craved a wife. He wanted desperately to hear the laughter of children in his home. His head filled with the mystical knowledge he had learned from the book, Yosef spent the rest of his days trying to conjure a wife for himself. He attempted day in and day out, until he was too old to move from his rickety cot.

"But word had spread of Yosef's knowledge, and people began to visit his home in hopes of learning what Yosef had read from Yohev's secret book. Time after time, Yosef turned them away, his only desire to create a wife. Even as he grew old and frail, lingering on his deathbed, he did not stop whispering the words he had read in that book long ago.

"So, the people gave Yosef a new name. Abayda, meaning the hoarder of knowledge. And with that name, Abayda spent his last moments tossing and turning on his bed, until the creaking of his cot stopped, and the incessant prayer he whispered day after day died on his lips."

Malka swallowed, her voice dry from narration.

"You feel like Abayda reading from Yohev's secret book?" Amnon asked.

Malka nodded. "I feel like I know something I shouldn't. Something forbidden. Something that will drive me into a craze if I don't anchor myself."

"The Maharal says there is another story told of Abayda the Mystic," Nimrah said. "Where Yohev had Yosef study the book to better understand and command the universe. Where Yosef's ability to perform magic was a way of getting closer to Them. Where Yosef lost his desire for a wife and took knowledge as a lover instead."

Malka gritted her teeth but did not respond. She hated how Nimrah twisted her stories.

"Did you, Malka? Feel closer to Yohev?" Amnon asked.

Malka wrapped the flame pendant in her hand, the metal cold against her fingers as she pressed her thumb along its points. *Yes,* she thought. *And I will never be the same.* But she dared not speak those words aloud.

CHAPTER 15

"We've reached the end of the Great Oak's roots."

Nimrah's face strained, the veins on her forehead pressing tautly against her skin. They were rigid and murky, like pine needles. She closed her eyes and rolled her shoulders before dipping low. She began to trace her hands along the jagged ground, like one would feel for an object in the dark.

"Here," she said, her hand finishing its search. "Stand back."

The deep green veins bulged through her skin as the ground began to shake. With a crack, the earth split like the scoring line of cooked bread. Underneath, the petering end of a woody root revealed itself. And written on its surface, the Maharal's carving: *shoresh*.

Every use of Nimrah's magic made Malka uneasy. Terrified of the power the golem could wield with the slightest raise of her fingers, the barest clench of her hand.

Nimrah motioned to Malka expectantly. She hardly appeared strained from her exertion. The only sign she had raised the root was the dirt still caked to her palm. "Come."

Malka took a hesitant step forward, peering closer at the etching.

"Your dagger."

Malka blinked. "What?"

Nimrah raised her brow. "Your part of the deal, remember?"

Of course, Malka remembered. Only now that the time had come, fear seized her. She brushed her hand against the hilt of Abba's dagger.

"You are free to walk away." Nimrah tossed her arm away in a flourish. "Our deal is not a blood bond. But if you do, I cannot guarantee your mother's fate."

Malka had already called Kefesh, commanding it in the palm of her hands. She should have less to fear, yet it still struck her. Using Kefesh and being rooted to Nimrah. Two unknowns. Two chances to become Tzvidi or Abayda.

But she was so close to fulfilling her bargain. So close to leaving the forest she had thought she'd die in. She took Abba's dagger from her hip and tightened her sweaty palm around the hilt, dropping to her knees beside the exposed root.

"Remember, exactly what you did when you healed Amnon," said Nimrah. "That same mindset. Change the command: *root* to *rootless*."

Malka nodded, imagining the holy words. She lifted the dagger and around the command, she began to carve a new one.

When she was done, she was breathing heavily. The heady glimmer of Kefesh sparkling in front of her, like the dancing spots when she stared too close to the sun.

"Now hand it to me."

Nimrah's command tore her from her daze, grounding her once again. Gratitude was certainly a foreign concept to this golem.

Flat-lipped, Malka stretched out the dagger, but Nimrah clasped her wrist instead, yanking her forward.

Malka gasped as they brushed close. Shock passed through Nimrah's eyes, like she had forgotten her own strength. And now they were close, too close. Malka watched the slight bob of Nimrah's neck.

Nimrah cleared her throat and jacked up Malka's sleeve. She pressed the flat side of the blade to Malka's arm.

"Now on your skin," Nimrah said, slowly moving the dagger across her skin in the shape of the same word that occupied her own arm. "You'll trace it like this."

Nimrah's hold on the weapon resting coolly on her skin should have scared Malka, but she couldn't look away as the silver of Abba's blade dragged softly across her arm, gooseflesh appearing where the metal touched.

Malka found herself breathless again. "We'll undo it the same way I just freed you from the Great Oak?" She did not expect her voice to be as groggy as it was, as if Kefesh was a powder she had swallowed dry.

Nimrah's face was neutral as she nodded and let go of her grip on the knife. Then, with a softness that surprised her, Nimrah asked, "Are you ready?"

With a swallow, Malka tightened her fist on the hilt. She twisted the blade, setting the tip onto the thin skin of the inside of her forearm. A drop of blood welled.

She had to do it fast to keep ahead of the pain.

She began.

It was a searing sting—the kind that made it hard to think, hard to breathe. She resisted the urge to tighten her hand into a fist and lose more blood. When Malka had helped Imma sew sutures into skin, they would rub clove oil onto the skin to help reduce the pain. Malka wished she had some now, as the blade shaped the word.

The first letter, then the second.

She gritted her teeth, and tasted metal. Malka stared at the gaping wound she self-inflicted on her arm, bleeding like the larch tree's putrid sap, which trailed down the bark, following the rivulets like a maze.

"Your prayer!" Malka heard through the haze of pain.

Malka evened her breathing. This injury couldn't be for nothing. She closed her eyes, trusting herself to know the lettering of her holy language. She had already severed the command to the Great Oak; she could do this.

She went back to the safe space she had found when she healed Amnon. Where prayer was the only thought on her mind. Where no harm could find her. Where Hadar sat waiting for Malka to crawl into bed and hold her snug. Where Imma kissed her forehead and smoothed her hair around her ear. Where Chaia had walked back out from the forest, not a bruise coloring her skin.

She got lost in it, this holy place where miracles became real.

"It's done."

Malka opened her eyes, dizzy from her escape. Her arm throbbed. Thick heartbeats racked through her as blood trickled from the wound. She was faint from the pain and stumbled. Nimrah's hand steadied her.

"How do you feel?" Amnon asked.

A sudden brightness and heat, as if she had jumped into flames. A heady fullness and a sharp saturation of feeling. No matter how she described the sense of it, Nimrah was always at its center. Malka was keenly aware of her, of every touch of her fingers as she wrapped the poultice around her arm.

"Do you feel it, too?" The question slipped out; so small, so breathless.

Nimrah only twitched her jaw in response. "Let's go," she said, before she collected her bag and left them in the clearing.

Malka closed her eyes, soothing the hot rush of anger. Into her own skin she had carved the letters that freed Nimrah. She'd always have the scar, no matter how many salves she applied. And Nimrah didn't even have the decency to care.

Imma's face came to mind. Her deepest contours, thin mouth, and the kindest eyes Malka knew a mother to have. Anything was worth it, for her. Anything was worth it, to Malka, for the chance to return to her life how it once had been. A life she recalled in the quiet when darkness most haunted her.

Malka wiped the side of her mouth with her thumb. It came away a dirty red from where she had bitten her lip and bled.

Later that night, she would dream of the Rayga.

Nimrah, standing in the snow, wind waving her hair into a halo around her face. Smiling devilishly at Malka before curling into herself, becoming the mangled deer which had torn skin from Amnon's shoulder, her legs sprouting into chicken's feet. Returning to her normal form, her teeth saturated with Amnon's blood, his flesh sinewy between her canines. Stalking toward Malka, doublet shining with blood, and pressing their lips together, tangling her hands in Malka's curls. Malka opening her mouth, gasping or moaning, or a mix of both, and tasting Amnon's flesh, his blood.

She'd awake and vomit, dry heaving until her nausea settled.

"Alright?" Amnon would ask, but her eyes would be on Nimrah, falling to the same lips which had been stained with Amnon's blood in her dream. The lips that had pressed to hers. Heat would pool in her stomach and shame would color her cheeks.

She would not go back to sleep.

CHAPTER 16

At Mavetéh's end, the trees split open like a shell, revealing the glimmering pearl of Valón doused in a cloudy midday haze.

Malka bit nervously at her nails. She had expected to die in Mavetéh, just as it had been a death sentence to all the women before her. Ten days she had spent under its ominous shade. Ten days elapsed from her deadline. She pressed her hand against the cobblestone wall, the stone cool under her palm. Moss crept between her fingers, damp from melting snow. It made her choke up to see the sky again, unobstructed by the tree crowns.

Amnon smiled at her and pressed his makeshift cane back into the ground. They had plucked it from a branch and shaped it with Abba's dagger to fit Amnon's height. It wasn't perfect, but it enabled Amnon to walk on his own without pressing his weight onto Malka or Nimrah. It warmed her to see him up and moving again. Malka had feared he would sleep forever, waking only for Malka to feed him and to relieve himself before falling back into a tumultuous slumber.

The southern entrance was an imposing tower made of stone so stark, it resembled brass against the gloom. Giant spires rose from the structure's head, in the same shape as the spiral staircases which trailed up both sides of the tower. Rounded patterns were carved into stone and molded with the crest of Ordobav above each window. She recognized the crest as the same one the Ozmini knights donned—the lion with its teeth and claws unfurled.

A sharpened arch had been carved out of the stone, where the metal gate doors were swung out, and people streamed between them.

Valón came into vivid focus as they flowed through the gate. Streets lined with multi-story buildings spread from city squares like tree roots. The buildings piled on top of each other, each capped with a red pitched roof.

The buildings in Eskravé were simple and earth colored. But these buildings were every color she could think of, standing out of the snowy fog in shades of green, orange, and blue.

Most overwhelming was the odor; cloying potions of boiled cabbage, urine, and woodsmoke. She almost choked on its potency.

A blend of languages swirled around her—some she could recognize: Kražki, Kraž-Yadi, of course, and the Alga-Bak language of the Balkisk Kingdom, which she didn't speak, but knew its sounds from the Balkisk merchants who came to Eskravé's marketplace. Others she couldn't place.

Someone knocked into Malka's side, sending her stumbling. She regained her footing and rubbed her shoulder, unbothered as she watched the waves of people making their way up and down the streets. The clatter of horse hooves against cobblestone, animated conversations, and the faint ringing of a tambourine filled her ears. Her heart pounded wildly, and she brought a hand to her chest as if to tame it. In Eskravé, midday settled the rush of the morning into calm as it brought the village back inside for mealtime. Not here, it seemed.

Thinking of lunch made Malka's stomach whine.

"I don't know where Eliška lives," Nimrah said. "But I know someone who does."

As they walked, Malka stared at Nimrah's cloaked form. She had been right—no one spared her a second glance in the crowd.

But Malka noticed her, felt her presence. She blamed the spell, the command still a fresh wound on her arm. It was not how she had imagined it would be. *Root,* as if the bond between them would be as hard and unmalleable as wood, chaining them together like metal. It was something much worse. This constant awareness, the maddening heat when she felt their tether. What would happen if they stretched their connection too thin? If she dared to test the limits? The thought almost brought a blush to her cheeks. Saving Amnon had been life or death. This was reckless temptation; it should not have crossed her mind at all. Yet curiosity had embedded itself there, reignited by this new connection.

Nimrah stopped short outside of an unassuming stone building, wooden doors hooked open by iron slats. Scrawled above the arch of the entrance, Malka guessed, was the name of the place. Like most Eskraven villagers, the only language she could read was the ancient Yahadi script.

She was about to ask Nimrah when a heady waft of braised meat came from the entrance, followed by the loud roar of conversation when the door at the bottom of the stairs opened and two drunk men stumbled out.

Ah. A tavern.

"The owner is a friend of the Maharal's," Nimrah explained, resituating her cloak.

"Another Yahad?" Amnon asked.

Nimrah shook her head. "An Ozmin, like Eliška."

Before they descended the stairs, Malka's eyes caught on a sign painted near the entrance. A crow slashed through with blood red. A warning of some sort, but Malka couldn't linger on it any longer as she was motioned down.

The tavern was packed, the heat from bodies and torch lanterns bouncing off the curved stone of the underground room. Men filled the wooden benches spread around the small space, the tables cluttered with half-drunk glasses of ale, sucked-clean bones of pork ribs, and plates of knedlíky stuffed with meat. On the far side of the room, a large cauldron bubbled some kind of stew, which a barmaid ladled into bowls in exchange for coins.

"I'm going to find him," Nimrah said to them. "I'll be back."

Malka gripped her forearm before she could leave. It was the first time they had touched since their rooting spell, when Nimrah had drawn her close enough to trace the command onto her arm. Nimrah's gaze cut sharply to hers.

"How do I know you won't leave now that you're here?" Malka questioned, swallowing hard.

Nimrah glanced at Malka's arm, where the command was traced under her layers of clothing.

"You're not free of me yet, village girl," Nimrah said, then disappeared into the back of the tavern, leaving Malka and Amnon on their own.

It was odd, this tether. Even as Nimrah left from view, Malka could feel her closeness, the ebb and flow of it dancing with the distance set between them. She hated it but recognized its utility. Nimrah truly could not run from her.

Another unfortunate truth: Malka could not run from Nimrah, either.

Amnon pressed his hand to Malka's shoulder.

He was already sweating from the heat of the room, his strength most likely dwindling from the walk here. She searched around the room, but there were no open seats.

She leaned in close. "I'm going to get you some water, okay?"

Shuffling through the crowd, she scanned for a barkeep.

An eruption of bellowing laughs caught Malka's attention instead. In the back corner, a group of Valonian knights sat around one of the larger tables, decorated with piles of discarded bones, plates of picked-over dumplings, scattered crumbs of bread, and stacked ale glasses. They had stuffed themselves, now drunk and rowdy.

Self-consciously, Malka began to play with her necklace.

"It's disgusting, isn't it?" a woman next to her said, tilting her head toward the knights. "Paying for their gluttony."

Malka's brows furrowed. "What do you mean?"

The woman eyed Malka's necklace, then threw back the rest of her drink. "We pay the Church's tithes. The knights trade the tithe collections for Ordon coins. They use those coins to pay for barrels of alcohol. So, therefore, every drink of theirs is technically on us."

Malka stared at the knights again, at how even since she last looked more food had appeared on the table.

Her stomach growled again, fierce and painful.

Malka recalled Chaia's curiosity about the tithes the last few years before she had disappeared. Maybe Malka should've questioned it, too.

"They have competitions sometimes, on who can spend the most at once, whether on jewels or alcohol," the woman said, the smile on her lips deeply unsettling. She stared at the knights with hatred gleaming in her eyes. With the anger loosening her tongue, Malka noticed her Kražki was accented. But it was not pronounced enough for Malka to place.

"Does the Church know the knights do this?"

The woman laughed. "Do they know? They are doing the same thing. The clergy is as bad as the knights. Perhaps even worse, using money to buy political favors. But you won't catch them doing business in a seedy place like this."

Surely it was blasphemous to say such a thing, especially to a stranger. Yet the woman didn't seem to care.

Malka appraised her intently. She was by no means tall, but took up all the space she wanted, elbow leaned on the free end of the table next to them, legs crossed. She was a soft beauty, round cheeks and piercing blue eyes. Around her neck, a necklace that disappeared into the cusp of her vest.

"What brings you to a place so seedy, then?" Malka asked, still mulling over what she had said about the misuse of the tithes.

"Best beer in town." The woman winked, then took in the shape of Malka's clothing. "What's got you all roughed up and dirty?"

Behind her, someone cleared their throat.

Nimrah's impending figure was still hidden by her cloak. She tilted her head up, a slice of light piercing her cold glare at the woman Malka had been speaking with. She made sure it was her flesh side. "Let's go."

Before Malka could say anything else to the woman, Nimrah was carting her to the entrance. As they approached the door, Nimrah wrapped her hands around Amnon's cloak, dragging him away from what appeared to be an uncomfortable interaction with the men at the table nearest him.

※

"What was that about?" Malka demanded, the cold air hitting them as they spilled back onto the street.

Nimrah shrugged. "Don't trust everyone you meet, village girl. Even if they've got a pretty face."

"I thought the Paja brutish, but some of these people are just as bad." Amnon shivered. "I'm *not* going back in there."

Nimrah smirked. "If you think the regulars there are bad now, wait until you see one of them lose at darts. It's better entertainment than any theater."

"Did you find who you were looking for?" Malka asked, unable to keep out the bite in her voice.

If Nimrah noticed, she didn't show it. "Eliška's house isn't far. Stay close."

That request was harder than anticipated, as the afternoon had brought with it even more crowded streets than when they had first arrived. Men towered over her with their wooden carts, similar to those wheeled in for Eskravé's market day. A woman carrying a bulky basket of bread dashed around her, holding it above her head to avoid clashing with one of the traders on his horse.

She jumped out of the way of a trotting horse and the wheat-laden wagon it pulled. Everywhere she stepped, she was in someone's way.

Soon, she could no longer see Nimrah and Amnon.

Unexpectedly, a pang racked her chest. She felt dizzy, unmoored from her body. It struck her so suddenly, her legs trembled.

When someone shoved into her again, she was unable to catch herself. She stumbled into a mass behind her, toppling them both to the ground.

The clank of metal against cobblestone stunned the busy crowd into silence.

Malka climbed to her knees, legs still shaky. "Forgive me," she said, distress misshaping the Kražki words. "Let me help you."

She froze, eyes catching on the sweep of a familiar wine-stained robe. *Father Brożek.*

But the man shifted in her direction, and he was not Father Brożek at all. This man was older, with stark blue eyes and a peppered mustache hanging above his lips.

"The monstrance!" the priest wailed. Anger flushed his face like a ripe peach.

"The host, Father, is it still intact?" A man offered his arm to the priest, and he hobbled to his feet.

Malka paled. She had knocked a priest to the ground. An Ozmini priest. She knew what became of Yahad who fell in the way of Ozmini priests. She clenched her hand against the cold cobblestones, remembering the mangled chop of Minton's fingers.

The sense of erring still plagued her—this wrongness tight in her ribs. But her mind had cleared from the shock enough to realize what she no longer felt: the cloying reminder of Nimrah's nearness.

The priest's gaze softened as he collected the golden box that had tumbled from his hands. It was beautiful. Golden lines sprouted from the dome top and curved around the base of the box in intricate patterns.

Malka was hoisted up by the back of her cloak, the clasp digging into her neck and choking. She tried to pry away the hand that held her, but it was no use. The man's fingers were twice her size, and they wouldn't budge.

"It was an accident!" she cried.

The man who had helped the priest to his feet stared at her, his expression hardening. He had sandy blond hair and a deep blue circle cap. His wool habit was the same jeweled blue, and his long neck peeked out of his stiff-hooded scapular. "You're a Yahadi girl."

Her accent—it was always her cursed accent.

"Father," the sandy-haired man continued. "This might not have been an innocent mistake."

The priest frowned and examined the golden box. "The wafer is still intact. Maybe it was an honest mistake. Or she failed at whatever she attempted." He eyed Malka's scraped hands and the cut along her cheek from her fall.

"You may be right," the man continued. "But leaving her unpunished will show the other Yahad there is not a price to be paid for disobedience. Don't you think that's needed at a time like this?"

"This will show an enticement for peace, Brother Asak."

Brother Asak opened his mouth in objection but closed it obediently. "Of course, Father."

"Let her go, *Ctihodný*," the priest instructed the man holding Malka tight.

As his grip loosened, Malka sucked in a deep breath and fell to the ground. Her throat burned; the impression of the clasp was embedded into the skin of her neck. The sensation reminded her too much of almost drowning in the Leirit. She dug her hands into the cracks of the cobblestone, feeling it rough against her knees.

"It would be mindful," the priest said, his tone even, "to walk more attentively." He motioned for the crowd around them to disperse and continued forward.

Brother Asak trailed behind the priest, but stopped as he crossed Malka, still on her knees. He bent to meet her eyes. He smelled like perfumed flora and smoke and Malka's skin tingled as he leaned close to her ear. "Where is your rota?"

"My what?"

"Don't play dumb."

"I'm not from here, Brother, I have no idea what you're talking about."

Pain ruptured in Malka's middle as Brother Asak kicked her. "You may have the Kraž-Yadi accent, but don't think I'm a fool. Was this a planned act of defiance? Are you another Balkisk puppet?"

Malka shook her head. "I don't know what you mean."

"Do you think we are fools—that Archbishop Sévren is a fool?"

Another hard kick.

Malka's breathing trembled as she wrapped an arm around herself. "Is violence what Triorzay demands of you, Brother? To kick a woman already on her knees because she is ignorant?"

"How dare you—"

"Brother, good morning!"

A man only a few years Malka's elder appeared beside them, with a curly golden beard which gave him all his age. His hair was a shade lighter and fell messily around his frame, cascading from his black hat. He nudged his small, wiry glasses up his nose, which sat round on his angular face.

"Good morning, *Odborný*," Brother Asak responded, annoyed. "Now is not a good time."

"Actually, it's a great time. You see, this woman is my betrothed's cousin. We were supposed to meet at the square, but . . . well, you know how it is trying to get anywhere on Trader's Day!"

Brother Asak crossed his arms. "Your betrothed's cousin, you say?"

He nodded, pointing a thumb in Malka's direction. "Yes. Coming from out of town. That's why she's ignorant of Valonian rules. We planned to sew a badge for her as soon as she arrived, but we couldn't find her in the crowd. You'll have to forgive us for our slip up."

"And why exactly are you here, girl?"

Malka opened her mouth to speak, but the curly-haired man interrupted.

"How could you ask that, Brother, when you know my wedding is around the corner!" He said it teasingly, and Malka wondered how familiar they were to each other. Brother Asak did not look convinced.

"Yes, Brother," Malka added, playing along. "I'm from the countryside. I'm unaccustomed to the fast-paced nature of the city. I don't know anything about the Balkisk, I swear."

Brother Asak's lips thinned. "Get her a badge, immediately." He made a face. "And a bath."

"Of course, Brother. May Triorzay bless you."

"May Triorzay bless you, *Odborný*. I will see you at church."

When Brother Asak disappeared into the crowd, Malka sighed in relief. She regarded the man who had saved her—a scholar she gathered, from the honorific Brother Asak gave him.

"Thank you, *Odborný*, you did not need to do that," Malka said, picking herself up from the ground.

"Of course, I did." He handed her sack to her, which she had dropped in the collision.

His smile fell as he regarded her, eyes darting from the cuts on her cheek to the blood and dirt spattered on her clothing. "My, you look like you have been through it and back again. Do you have somewhere to go?"

"I was separated from my group in the crowd."

The thought of Amnon alone with Nimrah made her already unsettled stomach churn. Out of imminent danger, Malka allowed herself to process the unease which struck her. She could only imagine it as one thing: a symptom of the rooting spell. It was strange, how Malka could sense Nimrah's distance. When they were near, it was cloying, distracting in its potency. As space between them grew, a queasy malaise took over. As if she were caught between a battle of waves in a stormy sea, her reaching hands able to grasp nothing but the slithering water.

She recently dared to think about testing the limits of their rooting. Now they'd truly find out. And Malka was beginning to fear she might not survive it.

She swallowed hard. "I have to find them as soon as possible."

"Of course," the man said, though his forehead creased. "It's only, well—I mean you no harm, but others might, if you continue to walk around Valón without a badge."

Malka's hand dropped to her side. She winced in pain.

"I live around the corner. Please, my betrothed will be home soon. She'll be able to sew a badge onto your cloak. Have some tea in the meanwhile."

Malka bit her lip. Her instinct was to reject his offer and find Nimrah and Amnon as soon as possible. But what good would it be if she kept having run-ins like the one with Brother Asak?

"Only to re-dress my wound and get this rota," Malka agreed. "Thank you for your generosity, *Odborný*."

"Please, call me Vilém." He extended his hand.

She shook it. "Malka."

"Peace and light, Malka," he said in Kraž-Yadi.

A smile curled her lips as the familiar greeting put her at ease. "Peace and light. Are you Yahadi, as well?"

"No, but my betrothed is. I have studied the Yahadi language for many years but find the best practice with the language is her witty quips."

Malka chuckled. "I imagine those are endless. My grandmother used to say Yahadi languages are made for complaining."

Vilém beamed. "Ha! She will like you."

Malka had ached to have a normal conversation, to joke and be jovial. A temporary escape from the pressure of Imma's fate, which rested delicately in the palm of her hand.

Malka examined the crowd around them—the women carrying baskets, the men towing along their market stalls. She did not see a badge among their clothing. Vilém did not wear one, either.

"This badge," Malka questioned, "must all citizens of Valón wear them? I don't see yours."

Vilém cleared his throat and wiped at his brow with a kerchief. "No, not everyone. Just the Yahad. It's a new mandate that Archbishop Sévren proposed to King Valski. It's . . . it's to distinguish the Yahad from their Ozmini counterparts."

The mention of the archbishop stirred a memory. He had asked Rzepka to join the Paja. And now she was dead.

"Why do they want to distinguish us?"

Vilém cast an anxious inspection around them and ducked his head low. "It might be best if we have this conversation in private. You never know who catches wind of things nowadays."

Vilém guided them down another street as lively as the last, this one evoking a spark of familiarity. Just as Amnon's brother had described it, the Yahadi Quarter smelled of black bread, braised meat, and boiled cabbage. Wax candles flickered in windows, fragranced with myrrh resin oil. They fogged the windows, glowing orange. Past the roofs of the multi-colored buildings sat the steepling top of the shul Bachta. There was no doubt it was the synagogue. The stained-glass windows glimmered despite the dense clouds, the warm glow tinting the multi-colored glass in the orange-yellow shades of juicy citrus. A tower spun from its side, brushing the clouds.

Magic warmed her hands. She shoved them into the pockets of her cloak, desperate to ignore how they ached.

"We're here," Vilém announced, unlocking an unassuming door to a tan-colored home. It was not much compared to the houses surrounding it, but it beat any of Eskravé's homes in size and structure.

Malka stepped through the doorway and paused as she noticed the decorative prayer box at eye level. Malka had touched her own mezuzah every time she entered her home in Eskravé for as long as she could remember, until she left for Mavetéh. She pressed her fingers to the box and then to her lips.

She followed Vilém into a modest kitchen where he motioned for her to sit at the table affixed with a couple of unlit tallow candles, melted wax decorating the saucers like paint splatters.

Malka hissed as she slid into one of the rickety wooden chairs, rubbing her hand on her abdomen. She wasn't sure which distressed her more—this injury or the affliction from the rooting spell.

"How is your side? A good kick can feel like iron, I know."

"It'll be a nasty bruise, but nothing I can't handle."

Vilém fussed about, setting a pot of water to boil and handing Malka a wet cloth. She pressed it to her face. It came away a ruddy brown.

"You're brave. Though, I shouldn't be surprised. In my experience, Yahadi women are the bravest of them all."

Malka unclasped her cloak and let it sag to her lap, happy to rid herself of the reminder of how severely it had choked her. She resisted the urge to trace its imprint on her neck.

"Why is that?" she asked Vilém.

"Not only do you face oppression from the Ozmins, but from men, as well. No matter if they are Ozmins or Yahad."

Malka chucked. "Another quote from your illustrious betrothed?"

Vilém grinned, brown eyes beaming. "You've caught me."

"Is she here?"

"No." Vilém extinguished the fire and added a thin cloth bag of tea leaves to the boiling water. As it steeped, the room filled with an earthy scent, malty and sweet. *Black tea.* "But she should be home soon. We, like many, are taking advantage of Trader's Day. She went out to buy some fresh vegetables and salted fish for supper. When she returns, she can sew a rota patch onto your cloak."

He handed her a steaming cup of tea.

"If I may ask, what brought you to Valón?"

Malka rubbed her thumb along the glazing of the mug. She thought of Imma again, cold and alone. She had not lost her yet, but grief began to chew at her regardless, a muscle well practiced.

"I am here to help a friend," she said. Another unmooring wave seized her, and she tightened her hands around the mug, desperate to settle herself. This connection would give her no peace while she and Nimrah remained apart. She couldn't wait to be rid of it.

Vilém pattered his fingers on his thigh, seemingly unaware of Malka's distress. He cleared his throat. "I overheard Brother Asak's accusation."

"I truly don't know what he meant."

Balkisk puppet, the priest had said. A puppet for what?

Perhaps Vilém was more suspicious of her than Malka thought, if he had sharpened in on this claim.

But he gave a brief smile that put her at ease. "Ah, I see. Don't worry about it. Valón is rather on edge these days."

She thought about asking why, but indulging in her curiosity never did end well. Instead, she said, "Vilém, I'm looking for someone. A woman called Eliška? She was once a laundress for the king but has since retired."

"I know her." His face contorted. "I did not think she had many visitors, honestly."

"Why?"

He sipped his tea. "It's said that when she left King Valski's service, she also left her manners behind. Worsened now with her old age."

"I see." Malka wondered if they would knock on her door only to have it slammed in their faces. "Do you know where she lives?"

"As a matter of fact, I do. I will walk you there myself."

"Thank you, Vilém."

As they waited for his betrothed, Malka took in the room.

A stack of books sat crowded against the corner of the room, and trinkets decorated the wall like paintings. "*Odborný*. That is the title given to magisters, right? What is your research?"

Vilém knuckled his glasses up the bridge of his nose. "Yes! I work at the University of Valón and teach philosophy. It's a small area of study, snubbed by logic and theology. But it's home to the finest scholars of this day and age, if I do say so myself."

The university. Malka's head spun. The city she had only heard stories about was becoming real before her eyes. A scholar at one of the finest universities in the Rhaškan Empire had made her tea.

"I must admit, I'm overwhelmed with Valón. It's both nothing and everything like I had imagined."

"I never did ask where you were from, Malka."

Eskravé felt far away. A memory diluted in stormy water, like the medicinal eucalyptus she would boil until its color washed away in the heat.

The front door creaked open, swelling the chatter of the street.

"Ah, that must be her!" Vilém exclaimed.

Malka fiddled with her mug as the woman approached.

A flash of silky brown hair appeared in the doorway.

"Malka?"

The voice was so familiar, it stopped her heart. A voice she had thought she would only ever hear again during her quietest moments of prayer, sitting cross-legged in the crook of her room, staring out at the stars. A voice that visited her in grief-ridden nightmares.

Framed by the doorway with her eyes widened in shock, cloth bags hanging from the crooks of her elbows, was Chaia.

CHAPTER 17

The room stilled.

Bewildered, Malka stared at Chaia, or someone who couldn't possibly be Chaia. Maybe the strange plague had finally come for her, wrapping her in its thorny vines. Maybe the hallucinogens in Mavetéh's sap had corrupted her mind as it had so many others'. The same way it had come for Eskravé's men, paranoia seeping into their skin and hollowing their eyes. It had been foolish to think Malka could leave Mavetéh unscathed.

She was so unmistakably similar to Chaia, honeyed hair tied back under her kerchief, eyes the color of light resin.

"Malka!" The bags fell from her shoulders as Chaia moved to wrap her in a hug. The scent of her overwhelming and familiar.

"Chaia," Malka choked, words as difficult to shape as the roaring river which had swallowed her. "I thought you were dead."

Chaia jolted back. "What?"

"Taken by . . ." She was scared to say it—as if voicing the truth would make the dream in front of her shatter. "You were gone one day and did not come back. We thought you were the next maiden taken by the Rayga."

Chaia covered her mouth. "I . . . you never got my letter?"

"You sent . . . ?" Malka choked on her words and shook her head instead.

Chaia cursed, her face paling. "Does this mean everyone—my *family*—thinks I've been dead this whole time?" Her voice tightened. "God, I'm so sorry, Malka."

"Is it really you?" Malka's voice was small.

She grasped Malka's hand. "It is me, *Yedid Nefesh*."

Malka flipped Chaia's palm over and ran her thumb along the familiar scar there. A sob rattled through her. "How are you alive?"

Chaia frowned at Malka's arm. Blood had soiled the fabric and trickled down her wrist. The wound had become hot and tender under the puffy sleeves of her blouse.

"Are you okay?" Chaia tugged up her sleeve in fervent alarm. "What happened?"

"It's nothing," Malka responded, resisting the urge to pull away. "Please, Chaia, what's going on? How are you alive?"

Chaia sighed. "I will tell you everything. Sit, please."

Vilém stepped forward, placing his hand on Chaia's back.

Malka had forgotten about him. She slid into the wooden seat once again.

He whispered something into Chaia's ear. She nodded and moved a curl out of his eye. He kissed her on the forehead. As he left, he shot Malka a sad smile.

Chaia rummaged in a drawer before reappearing with her hands full of jars and a fresh piece of gauze. Malka took note of her collection: a tincture of yarrow, applied topically to the infection, garlic as an antibiotic, and . . . goldenmase?

"What is the goldenmase for?"

"A little sweetness, to help wash down the garlic."

"You'd waste goldenmase on me like that?"

Chaia shrugged. "Vilém makes a decent wage at the university. We don't need to ration it as harshly as we did in Eskravé."

Malka clenched. Something about Chaia's lackluster reaction irked her. She said it so casually, but she had no idea how much worse conditions had become in Eskravé since she disappeared. She had not had to mourn herself like Malka did.

"How did you end up here, Chaia? With Vilém, in Valón." Her voice dropped low. "And why did you not come back?"

"I needed to see for myself," she said slowly, "what the Church was doing with our tithes."

Malka closed her eyes, fingers clamping the bridge of her nose. "Of course, you did."

"Nobody knew or would tell me anything, Malka. I had to find answers."

Malka's mind drifted to the knights in the tavern.

"And did you?" The question held a brutal heat.

"Yes." She guided the garlic toward her with her knuckle, mouth thinning. "Thanks to the Maharal."

Malka wasn't sure her stomach could settle anything, but she took the jar and popped a clove of raw garlic in her mouth. She did not wash it down with the goldenmase.

"You left us thinking you were dead." Chaia wasn't taken by Mavetéh, mauled to death by one of its creatures. She wasn't lost and unable to find her own way back. She had gone on purpose.

Malka gritted her teeth. Hurt pierced her worse than any boot ever could.

Chaia sighed in frustration. "I left to go find answers, but I didn't intend to disappear. When I stole away in the back of a marketer's cart, I had no idea I wouldn't be returning. But what I found here . . . it's bigger than me, Malka."

A hot tear burned the raw skin of Malka's cheek.

"But involving myself was not without its sacrifices," Chaia admitted with a deep-set hollowness in her eyes.

Malka was livid, but relief threatened to wipe away any other emotion she felt. Chaia was here. Real. She had wished for this. Prayed. And Yohev had listened. They had responded.

The magic nipped at her palms again.

Malka remembered the nights she and Chaia had spent under the sky during Ordobav's balmy summers, tracing their dreams in the stars. She also remembered the unrelenting fear when Chaia's parents had knocked at her door late at night. They had spoken with Imma in hushed tones. *Chaia hasn't come home tonight.* And then, *Has another body been found?* Their village had sent search party after search party, stopping when the men drank through half their wheat rations in beer to deal with their fear.

"I said the mourner's prayer for you, Chaia. I said it until my lips were dry and cracked, until my throat closed up. I said it almost a month ago to mark the year of the loss of you."

"I did not mean for it to happen like this." Chaia buried her face in her hands. "They told me to cut contact with home, but I allowed myself one letter. To explain. But when no one from home ever sent a reply, I thought . . . well, it doesn't matter what I thought, does it?" She slouched in her chair. "They are watching closer than I realized."

"What exactly have you gotten yourself into?" The need to hide and cut contact. Being watched. Worry crawled across Malka's skin. "And exactly who is advising you?"

"*Yedid Nefesh,* I want to tell you everything, I swear. May I at least treat your wound first?" Chaia's throat wavered.

It was so unlike the Chaia Malka had known that doubt curled its tendrils inside her.

So many questions. So much hurt and betrayal. But she had never been good at saying no to Chaia. So, she relented.

Chaia set a hot cloth on Malka's arm, loosening the caked poultice. As Chaia cleaned the old medicine, she gasped at the word carved into her skin.

It wasn't just concern etched into Chaia's face, but understanding. "I know what that mark means, Malka. What did you do?"

Malka shook her head.

"I don't mean it accusingly," Chaia rushed to add. "Being here has enlightened me on many things, including Kefesh. The Maharal had begun to teach me just before..."

"You've commanded Kefesh?" Any other time, this revelation would've shocked her. But Chaia was back from the dead, a defter magic than any Kefesh spell.

"I'm only a beginner." Chaia's thumb traced tenderly at the skin around the command. She stared at it, almost wistful. "How did you get this?"

Malka swallowed, then told Chaia everything across the burning flame, from the severing of Minton's fingers to her encounter with Rzepka and the other Paja members. She recounted how Imma had come across Rzepka dead, leading to the Church accusing her of using Rzepka's blood for dirty magic. How she made a deal with the priest and stole away into Mavetéh with Amnon, only to find the Maharal's golem at the center of it all.

Chaia's face grew wretched and pale. "I cannot believe you survived, *Yedid Nefesh*."

"I only survived because of the golem," she admitted, though it pained her. "I can hardly think of what would've become of me otherwise."

In Malka's recounting, she explained the word carved into her arm, how it allowed Nimrah to leave Mavetéh. She shared the deal they had made in detail and how it would free Imma from the Church's unfounded accusations. Malka omitted Amnon's injury and the magic she had used to save him. She couldn't speak of it, not while she still did not understand the power she held.

"You think the Maharal's golem is responsible for Mavetéh's deadly turn?"

"It was her life being tied to the Great Oak tree that led to the corruption of the woods."

Chaia mulled over Malka's words. Outside, the sun evaded the shield of clouds, skidding its light through the window, casting Chaia's face in a golden glow.

Another day was slipping through her fingers, and another night awaited Imma in confinement. Chaia had not yet answered her questions. Malka wanted to push for them, to draw her heels into the ground and refuse to move until Chaia explained everything. But it would be selfish, getting answers for herself, when she had much more important bargains to fulfill. "I need to find them, Chaia," Malka said, regrettably. "I think they'll be at Eliška's home. She's a retired laundress. Vilém says he knows her, do you?"

Chaia nodded, forehead creasing. "I do, but it will be safer for Vilém to escort you. They don't love it when the Yahadi women stay out late. I will go and get him."

When Chaia appeared with Vilém, he smiled. "I don't know why I did not put two and two together! Chaia talks about you so much. I feel as if I'm meeting a legend herself."

Chaia shrugged as if to say, *Of course I talk about you.* A year had passed, but the connection between them was as easy as breathing.

Malka's chest tightened.

Vilém took Malka's arm in his. Before they walked out the door, Malka turned back. "Chaia . . . can I come back here, after I find them? There's so much more to say, I . . ."

"Of course, *Yedid Nefesh.*" Chaia responded with such tenderness that it made Malka ache. For all the time they had lost, for the ease at which they could fall back into each other. But most of all, for the fissure her grief had created between them.

"Before you go, take this." Chaia unclasped the cloak from her shoulders with the sewn rota patch and held it out to her.

Malka wrapped it around herself, grateful to leave her fetid, sullied cloak behind. She relished in the soft scent of it, like rosewater, more familiar to her than any herb. It smelled like Chaia, and that made her throat go tight. Chaia was here, alive.

With one last look back at her best friend, Malka followed Vilém out the door.

CHAPTER 18

It was a short walk out of the Yahadi Quarter to Eliška's residence. They returned to the square where Malka had first arrived. The bustle of the day had tamed into a tranquil evening, the last of the merchants having packed up their unsold goods and wheeled their carts back to their inns.

The ache in her chest continued to set her adrift. One moment she'd think it was improving, the dizziness fading to a dull nausea. But the next, it would seize her again. Maybe she and Nimrah were circling each other, like the sides of a coin turning between two fingers, stuck on a constant loop.

"Valón is so large," Malka remarked, needing to get out of her own head. "I've never seen so many people at once."

Vilém chuckled. "Yes, it certainly is. Some days it feels like we are sheep being herded through the streets!"

Malka regarded the expanse of red pitched roofs worn by the line of houses and shops, windows aglow with the dusty light of torches as the sun began to dwindle. Curiously, on every third doorway or so, was the same sign she had seen outside of the tavern—the black crow slashed in red.

"Vilém," she pointed to the crow, "what does that sign mean?"

He scratched the back of his head, knocking his hat off-kilter, smile wavering. "Valón has been the victim of a terrible plague. In desperation, shop owners have put up those signs to try and keep sick people out."

Malka stopped short. "A plague?"

"Consumption." Vilém nodded. "We've given it a name: the Mázág sickness, since the first cases appeared after some woodcutters came back from the Mázág forest and fell ill. It's worsened ever since."

Mázág was the Kražki name for Mavetéh. Could this Mázág sickness be what was afflicting her village, too?

"When did this plague start?"

Vilém squinted, causing his glasses to slide down the bridge of his nose. "A couple of years ago now, it must be."

Years? Valón had been experiencing a plague for years—longer than Eskravé—and the news had never reached her village? Malka didn't know how it was possible. Dread coated her throat. "We didn't know Valón was experiencing a plague."

"That doesn't surprise me." Vilém sighed deeply. "The kingdom has done its best to shield Trader's Day from the disease, so they don't scare away foreign merchants. We are forbidden to speak of the plague in the marketplace."

It didn't make sense. The Order had acted as if they knew nothing of a strange, spreading illness, when Valón, the center of the parish, had already been in the throes of one.

Malka's head spun.

"To be frank, Malka, the Church believes the sickness doesn't come from the forest at all. They consider it a punishment from Triorzay for those who have not properly atoned, or for those who do not believe. Archbishop Sévren has assured devout Ozmins that their faith will keep them healthy. You can barely close the church doors now, with the amount of people stuffed inside to pray."

Malka pondered Father Brożek's own convictions—if he was unaware of the Mázág sickness, or if he believed his peoples' immunity. Both would explain his nonchalance.

"We're here," Vilém announced, drawing Malka from her thoughts.

She scrunched her nose. Something putrid and sour wafted through the small cracks in the warped, wooden door.

"Thank you, Vilém."

Malka knocked.

They barely had to wait before the door whooshed open, causing her to stumble back.

The woman was old, wrinkles overtaking her pale skin. Her hair, white with age, was tied loosely into a knot at the top of her head. She wore a simple dress with delicate floral embroidery and a matching jacket fastened up stiffly to the neck.

The smell worsened. Malka resisted the urge to cover her nose.

"What do you want?" The woman's eyes traveled to Vilém. She crossed her arms. "Not today, Vilém! For the last time, I do not want to take one of your wretched surveys. To think they let you waltz around like you have the right to know about the entire city of Valón—"

"Actually, Eliška, I am only here to escort," Vilém interrupted, blushing. "This is Malka, she's looking for her friends."

Eliška bent to get a closer look at her.

"Malka?"

Amnon.

She heard the creak of his cane on the floorboard before he appeared in the doorway. Relief coursed through her.

Eliška stepped aside so Malka could wrap Amnon in a tight hug. She leaned into his warmth and tried not to flinch when Amnon wrapped his hand around her bruised torso.

"Thank Yohev," he said. "I was so nervous when we lost you in that crowd."

"So, you are the woman these two have been waiting for. Well, get in before you let out all the warmth," Eliška said.

Malka stepped through the doorway.

Eliška thinned her eyes at Vilém. "Not you."

Vilém raised his hands in surrender. "Of course. Malka, I'll see you back at our house soon?"

Malka nodded and thanked him again.

"Eliška, if you do change your mind about the survey, there is compensation available, and it would greatly help out the Philosophy—"

Eliška threw a variety of curses at Vilém in Kražki. Malka could only pick out a few, but her eyes widened with the old laundress's creativity in stringing the curses together. The door slammed in his face.

Amnon's eyes fell from the door to her unfamiliar cloak in a silent question.

Later, she mouthed. She hadn't the strength to share her discoveries just yet.

Eliška's house was relatively plain, save for the intricately carved wooden seats, with a patterned wool rug underneath. A portable altar sat in the corner. It was gilded in copper and wood, with small relics scattered around it—some bone, others hidden beneath their silk wrappings. Three wooden symbols hung above the altar, which Malka assumed were Ozmini. Smoke twirled lazily through the air from incense, though it did little to cover the putrid smell in the house.

"Sit, girl. I'm cooking soup to help your friend grow stronger." Eliška evaluated Malka and whistled. "Heaven knows this soup could do you good, too, with those hollow cheeks and flourishing bruises."

She sat with Amnon on the sofa. He rested his cane against the arm. "Are you hurt, Malka?"

"It's nothing." The lie soured her tongue. She ached, the wound beneath her ribs pulsing and sore, the incisions tender on her forearm. She was hungry and exhausted, drained from the revelation that Chaia was alive.

It was difficult not to think of the obvious absence in the room—the way their distance still clawed at her, detached her from herself. She had hoped this feeling would settle once she arrived at Eliška's. That Nimrah's presence would ease her aching.

What a treacherous thought.

It didn't matter, though. She wasn't here.

"She's out looking for you," Amnon said. Noticing Malka's shock, he shrugged. "Your eyes kept searching the room. I figured you were wondering."

Malka fidgeted. "What happened after we were separated?"

"We tried to find you for a while, weaving in and out of the streets. When my legs started bothering me, Nimrah brought me here and went back out to search for you." His eyes darted to Eliška. He lowered his voice. "Though, I'm beginning to think I would have preferred to suffer on my legs."

"What's that smell?" Malka whispered back. She had unconsciously brought up her sleeve to cover her nose.

Amnon scrunched his face. "It's her soup. But I am so hungry, I would eat anything warm."

Malka began to laugh, but it caught in her throat when the unmooring of the rooting spell began to finally ease, replaced by a building sense of repletion. The potent, cloying presence of . . . *her.*

The door flew open, flickering the candles and fluttering the ribbons of incense smoke. Nimrah stood tall in the doorframe, her inky waves thick around her face, arms spread wide on either side of the doorway.

"Would it kill you to knock like the rest of 'em?" Eliška shouted from the stove. "She thinks she's a damn prophet the way she lets herself in."

Nimrah's eyes met hers. Something stilled between them. When her gaze lowered to Malka's neck, she became acutely aware of the clasp-shaped bruise forming there. She resisted the urge to cover it with her hand.

"You're here," Nimrah said, as if there wasn't this invisible bond which secured their cooperation. The pitting sensation of their separation may have been gone, but Malka did not forget its unique kind of pain. She wondered if Nimrah had felt the change, too. Abrupt and disorienting. Though, Nimrah had yet to reveal how the rooting spell affected her. If it at all did. Maybe only the spellcaster was plagued with these side effects. It would be just her luck. Regardless, they were stuck together until this was through.

"Our deal," Malka answered.

Whatever strange emotion flickered across Nimrah's face disappeared, her face returning to its stoic, emotionless state. Malka could parse out no vestiges of nausea or discomfort imparted by the rooting spell, which only bolstered her vexation.

"Of course," Nimrah replied, lips thin. As she stepped inside, her nose turned up. "Good heavens, Eliška, what foul thing have you let die in your home?"

Eliška *tsk*ed. "You're lucky I'm making him anything at all, the way you waltz in here unannounced after so many years. Expect me to welcome you back with open arms, after what has become of you and the Maharal!"

She ladled the soup into bowls and passed them around. Despite her objection, Nimrah retrieved a bowl and settled into a rickety chair across from Malka.

The soup was earthy and medicinal, similar to the tea Nimrah had made for her as she healed from nearly drowning. It wasn't tasty, but it warmed her, and staved off her gnawing hunger.

"While I inquired about you, Eliška, I also asked Bogumir about the Maharal. But he warned me against uttering his name in public."

Bogumir must've been the owner of the tavern.

"The accusation against the Maharal was a warning to the Yahad," Eliška responded. "The rabbi is now perceived as a traitor to Valón. A murderer. The Yahad know that if the Ozmins can arrest the Maharal, they could come for anyone."

"I need to know if the information they heard is true." Nimrah motioned to Malka and Amnon. "What happened to the Maharal?"

"I'm not a newsboy, Nimrah."

Nimrah let out a frustrated grunt. "Come on, Eliška."

Eliška huffed, then focused on Malka and Amnon. "Alright then, what exactly did you hear?"

Amnon's eyes shifted to Malka. With a clearing of her throat, she shared the recounting.

When Malka concluded, Eliška put her hands on her hips and mumbled a curse. "It's true that an Ozmini woman went missing years ago. And that a woman—Miriam—reported seeing the Maharal kill her and drain her blood. She was a Yahad, but converted to Ozminism before she shared her story at confession, a special honor bestowed upon her by Archbishop Sévren. Whatever fair trial Valski promised him is never coming. And they have not let him go."

"Sévren set him up, I know it." Nimrah unclasped her cloak and threw it on the seat. She began to pace. "He always had his eye on the Maharal. What happened to this woman—Miriam?"

Eliška rolled her eyes. "She died. Just after her baptism, conveniently."

The similarities between Imma and the Maharal left Malka light-headed. Two Yahad accused of using Ozmini blood for curses that did not exist.

"Sévren... he's the same person who asked Rzepka to join the Paja," Malka remarked, fingers rubbing circles at her temples.

"That doesn't surprise me," Eliška said. "Along with being Ordobav's archbishop, he is also the king's most trusted spiritual advisor. He claims Triorzay sends visions to him, of whom to appoint and who commits crimes against King Valski. A load of horse shit."

Malka peered back to the Ozmini altar in the corner of her room. "Do you not believe in the Ozmini faith?"

Eliška's face twisted, as if Malka had asked a ridiculous question. "Of course, I do. But that is not faith. It's power, and the lust for it."

"We're going to break him out," Nimrah said, then smiled. "How lucky we are to be in the presence of someone with such intimate knowledge of the layout of Valón Castle and the New Royal Palace. Do you know how to get to the dungeon, Eliška?"

"Say you do manage to free him. What happens then?" Eliška pressed, ignoring Nimrah. "He'll be as good as dead, a wanted criminal. Maybe he truly is sick as a dog. The Maharal is not a young man anymore."

"The Maharal does not get sick. He hasn't, for as long as I've known him. He ingests Kefesh-laced tonics to keep sicknesses away. I used to make them for him. They must've lied to keep him close. So, we break him out. Get him far away from here."

Eliška quirked her brow. "What is the Maharal without his people, Nimrah? Do you think he would survive away from the shul Bachta for long?"

Nimrah opened her mouth defensively but faltered. There must've been more truth to Eliška's reasoning than Nimrah cared to admit.

"If what you say is true, Nimrah, the public needs to see the Maharal's health. If he is well, the Valonians will look to King Valski's judges to be fair. Demand they reinstate his trial. He'll be free as long as a trial date is set, until the verdict is reached."

"Are you sure about that?" Amnon asked. "If Sévren and the court are willing to break the rules now, what stops them from breaking them again?"

Eliška smoothed her hands down her kandus. "Do you know why the Yahad are allowed to roam the Yahadi Quarter in between their accusations and trials, boy? Many of the Valonian Yahad are moneylenders. It's a job that Ozmins, for religious reasons, are forbidden from occupying. So, the court enacted a law allowing accused Yahad to keep working in the Yahadi Quarter until they are acquitted or charged. They need that law in place to keep the city functioning. They won't break it, not even for the Maharal."

"And the judges, you think they will sway to the public's will? Isn't that against what they are put in place to do?" Malka asked.

Eliška laughed abrasively. "That's a good one. The judges are loyal to Sévren. King Valski has a nickname in back alleys and underground taverns. *The Dull King.* He is losing popularity among all of Ordobav, but especially here in Valón as the sickness worsens and the people grow poorer."

At the mention of a sickness, Amnon's eyebrows shot up, surprise growing when Malka did not echo his shock. She rested her hand on his arm, another promise to explain later.

"All that," Eliška continued, "has allowed Sévren to pull the important strings for Ordobav instead. If the public looks favorably to something, Sévren might listen, and call the idea his own to draw favor to him."

Malka scrunched her face. "You know a lot about politics for a laundress."

"Yes," Eliška responded. "It is my business to eavesdrop. After all, gossip can be sold for a very high price."

"So, we break him out. Get him in the public eye and show his sickness has gone and there's no reason he cannot remain in the Yahadi Quarter until his trial," Nimrah said confidently.

"Nimrah, do you truly think you could break him out with these two? If I poked them too hard, they would crumble like a stale biscuit."

Eliška had a point. When Malka agreed to this deal, she didn't truly process what it entailed. Her mind whirled. It felt like the first time Imma had called her into her workroom, placing a needle and thread in her small hand. Imma had taken a knife to a slab of sheep skin, cutting a sizable gash into its center, and told Malka to stich it closed.

Malka's hands had shaken badly, her sutures too far apart, leaving gaps in the skin which peeled open again and again. She had poked and prodded too many times. If the sheep were alive, she would've caused it pain.

She was eight again, with a needle in her hand for the first time.

"Amnon will have to help in other ways, I'm sorry." Nimrah attempted an expression that landed somewhere between discomfort and pity. Neither of which, Malka thought, her friend would appreciate.

Amnon swallowed, trying to hide the shame from his face. But he was never good at masking his feelings. He desired to be needed, to be helpful. And he *was* needed, just not in the way he had grown accustomed. Malka needed him to rest, to be safe. She needed him there at the end of all this.

Nimrah's attention darted to Malka. "But her . . ."

Unbidden heat. Nimrah's penetrating gaze made her want to tear at her skin, the intensity of it hitching her breath. "You'd be surprised what she is willing to endure in her hatred for me, and her desire for my death."

Malka recalled what she had said to Nimrah in the belly of the tree, hiding from the pelting hail.

It is indescribable. To lose someone you couldn't imagine life without. And then stare her killer in the face.

It had been easy to hate Nimrah when Malka blamed her for Chaia's death. Easy to hand her over to Father Brożek. A monster. A murderer.

But Chaia was not dead.

Though Nimrah was by no means innocent, Malka reasoned. She remained the cause of Mavetéh's curse. Remained a murderer, a monster.

So why did her gut still stir?

"I see," Eliška said, breaking the tension between them.

"So, I once again ask, Eliška. Do you know where the dungeon is?"

With a dramatic sigh, the laundress shuffled to the edge of the rug and flipped it over, revealing the dense network of warp threads on its underbelly. In the newly uncovered floorboard, she began to dig her fingernails into one of the grooves until a panel popped out of place and revealed a secret compartment. From it, she retrieved an ornate chest, no bigger than a wicker bread basket.

As Eliška set down the chest, plumes of dust began to dance in the air, as if to celebrate their newfound freedom. The laundress, having none of it, waved her hand to disperse the motes before untucking a necklace from her bosom. On the thin chain was a key that she pressed into the lock.

"If this information comes back to me, I will deny it," Eliška warned.

Nimrah bent around Eliška to examine the chest's contents. She reached in, but Eliška slapped her wrist.

"Not all of this is for your eyes, Nimrah."

Malka placed her bowl on the table and came near the chest, though she kept far enough away to avoid getting swatted. It was filled with scrolls and loose pieces of parchment, objects of all shapes, and samples of intricate fabrics.

"What is all this?" Malka asked.

"It's a collection from my time as a laundress."

"You were given these things?" Amnon asked.

"No, boy, I took them. As you must with anything in life. I knew my time as a laundress would only last so long. I needed something to guarantee my livelihood after that time ended. So, I took things here and there. A scroll lying around untouched for years, fabric the seamstresses had discarded. Things no one would miss but would fetch a decent coin if I needed to sell them."

"Ah, here it is." Eliška unrolled a piece of parchment, stretching it flat on the ground. It was a map of some kind, labeled in the Jalgani script.

"Is this a map of the New Royal Palace?" Malka inquired.

"More or less. It's a floorplan made when the late King Manek wanted to extend the chapel to encourage more devotion within the royal laity."

"And they didn't notice its absence?" Amnon asked.

Eliška shrugged. "You'd be surprised how the details get lost when there is political turmoil. At the time, there were trade disputes between Ordobav and Vigary. Once the new chapel was built, I think the papers were forgotten, especially seeing as the architect who planned the chapel had family in Vigary. He was dismissed soon after he drew up these plans."

"That's unfair," Malka voiced.

"Such is the way of politics, girl."

Nimrah reached over Malka's shoulder, plucking the map from the floor. "Do you think it's still accurate? A lot can change in forty years."

"Accurate enough. King Valski might resent his father, but not enough to waste the time and resources to break new ground, especially when the chapel had been proved a success. No, the staff were the ones to feel his petty wrath."

Amnon shook his head. "This is a map of the royal chapel in the palace, not the dungeons. How will it be useful?"

"Ozmins always build tunnels from their royal palace chapels to the castle dungeons. Not only does it allow direct access for the priests to perform a prisoner's last rites, but this closeness fosters a more watchful eye of Triorzay, the desired outcome being either salvation of the dying, or a punishing reminder of their sin."

"That leaves one question," Amnon said slowly. "How exactly will you get inside of the palace to get to this so-called chapel?"

"You have anything else in that hiding place of yours that might be able to help us answer that?" Nimrah asked Eliška.

"You are too accustomed to the Maharal and his endless wisdom," Eliška said, a little sadly. "I don't have every solution for you. I'm sorry."

Nimrah cursed, putting a fist to her mouth.

Malka's brows pressed together, thinking of Vilém. If he worked at the university, he might have connections to the palace, or at least advice. The thought of dragging Chaia into this unsettled her, but their rescue had to be meticulous.

"I might know a man to ask."

CHAPTER 19

Though Malka had warned Amnon of the Mázág sickness, and more crucially of Chaia's survival, she couldn't help but wonder if the same shock in his eyes had suffused hers only hours ago. It was dreamlike to see her there. The year between them had changed them both into something unknown to each other.

Chaia had sliced through their reality when she left without telling Malka. She had thought them closer than anything. *Beloved of the Soul,* her nickname, a declaration. Yet still, Chaia went without a word. Maybe Malka had been wrong.

Now, Malka took Chaia in at a distance. She had braided her hair around her head like a thickly laid diadem. She looked sophisticated and beautiful, but it did not hide the puffiness in her eyes and the sag of her cheeks. Had she cried after their conversation when Malka left to find Eliška?

She had only seen Chaia cry a handful of times, mostly when they were younger, and it was always to get her way. Malka envied her for it, as her own eyes pricked with tears at the slightest provocation. But she would not cry now. She would be strong, just as she had promised to Danya that last night in Eskravé. If she started to cry, she did not know if she would be able to stop.

"Should've known we couldn't have gotten rid of you that easily," Amnon said after he recovered from shock, drawing Chaia into a hug. Her shoulders sagged in relief as she hugged him back. Amnon had not been as close to Chaia, and Malka envied the way Amnon could forgive her—could move on from the mourning.

"It's good to see you, Amnon." Chaia turned a sly eye to Nimrah. "And you are the legendary golem I have heard so much about. The one who took a knife to my best friend's arm, if I heard correctly?"

Nimrah's fixed stare on Malka made her squirm, like the golem was attempting to dissect her emotions. Malka had, after all, foolishly told her about Chaia as they waited out the hailstorm in the belly of a tree.

"It was a dagger," Nimrah responded, her eyes still on Malka. "And she technically did it to herself."

"Ah, yes, of course. Much better," Chaia responded, but there was amusement in her eyes. "Come, we are cooking up a spread for supper."

"We ate," Nimrah said, finally looking away from Malka.

"Speak for yourself!" Amnon knocked past Nimrah. "I would do anything to get the taste of Eliška's soup off my tongue."

Malka crossed her arms and whispered low, so only Nimrah could hear. "Do you want their help or not?"

With a sigh, Nimrah relented. "Fine."

They crammed around the table as Chaia passed down bowls of the stew from the cauldron above the hearth.

Together, they prayed, the intonation of their voices in the holy language as bright as a flame. Hearing Amnon's and Chaia's voices blend with hers, it almost made her feel normal again. Then one look at Vilém and Nimrah when they finished their recitation wiped that away.

Malka pressed the bowl of stew to her lips. It was delicious—mushrooms, carrots, cabbage, and fish in a savory broth. It had been so long since Malka had anything this hearty.

By now, the sun had set, bathing Chaia's home in a chalky winter moonlight.

"Feel free to say no to what we will ask," Malka prefaced to Chaia and Vilém, who had shared a chair to make room for them.

Chaia clasped her hands together, expression brightening. "You want our help to free the Maharal."

"How did you know that's what—"

"Malka, please. You tell me you have made a deal to free the Maharal in exchange for your mother's life, but you come to Valón with no knowledge of the city, with Amnon, who is in no condition to physically rescue anyone, and with Nimrah, who was banned from Valón years ago. I know you could use the extra help."

Nimrah cut in. "I needed her to—"

"Carve your freedom into her arm, yes," Chaia finished.

Nimrah huffed. "She agreed to the deal."

Malka added, "When we visited Eliška, she made a good point. People need to see that the Maharal is no longer sick, and there is no longer a reason for him to be kept isolated, as Sévren has demanded to avoid Ordobavian court laws. We know there's a passage into the castle dungeons from the palace chapel, but we need help finding out a way into the New Royal Palace itself." Malka shifted toward Vilém. "I thought as a magister you could give us insight. Though it seems you've deduced that already."

"That's easy, Malka. You can come with me. I work as a scullery maid in the kitchens," Chaia answered. "Vilém can help Nimrah sneak in through the library. Scholars flow in and out all day to use the materials. With her height, she can pass as a man if we disguise her well enough."

Malka bit her nail. Chaia had so readily agreed to help, guilt threaded inside of her. Guilt that she had asked; guilt that she had known Chaia would agree.

"It would put you both at risk," Nimrah warned.

"We are already at risk," said Chaia. "Me, because I am a Yahadi woman. Vilém, because he is a progressive thinker and chose to take a Yahadi wife. Besides, you have not been the only ones interested in the Maharal's release."

"There are many of us who understand the Ozmini Church's motive. With the Maharal imprisoned, the Yahad are vulnerable. And the Ozmini Church will certainly take advantage of that." Vilém dabbed a cloth at the side of his mouth.

"Our wedding is only days away. Half the Yahadi Quarter will be there," Chaia began.

Malka's heart twinged. *Days* away. The nearness of their union somehow solidifying the reality of Chaia's second life. The one which hadn't included her.

Malka tried to hamper her despondent thoughts as Chaia continued. "If we could free him by then, it would give the Yahadi Quarter great hope to see the Maharal perform his role as rabbi after the Church tried to snuff him."

"This does not sound like a new idea to you," Nimrah said. "Or a new plan. What exactly are you involved in?"

The couple eyed each other in silent conversation.

There was no doubt Chaia's involvement in Valón extended far past discovering what happened to the tithes. It made the stew sit uneasy.

"There are some last-minute wedding preparations I could use your help with tomorrow," Chaia said to them. "If you three are amenable," she added slyly, her grin as bright as the moonlight slices which curved along Mavetéh's trees.

Malka spared a glance at Nimrah and Amnon, who mirrored her suspicious look.

"Of course," Malka said, eyebrows furrowed.

An ever wider smile. "Great. Now that that's settled, I've heated up a bath. Take turns in there, you are all disgusting."

⟆

Behind the closed door of the washroom, Malka pressed her head against the wall. Alone now, it hit her at once. She was in Chaia's washroom, in the home she shared with Vilém, her betrothed. She was alive. Mavetéh had not taken her.

Growing up, Malka had always wondered if Chaia would marry. She had always been what Malka wasn't—independent, with dreams too big for tradition. But it seemed right that her betrothed would be someone like Vilém, a man who fit her so well. A man who didn't overshadow her, and wasn't jealous of her aptitude, but cherished it.

Malka stripped, discarding the stained, torn pieces of her kroj on the floor and freeing the top half of her hair from the kerchief. She bathed herself in the wooden tub, relishing in the soft scented soap Chaia had left for her. She was careful to wash around the poultice on her arm, scrubbing instead at her dirt-caked skin and legs. She soaked her hair and massaged in the oils and herbs Chaia had, running her fingers through her curls to detangle them.

When she finished, she wrapped herself in a linen cloth, realizing she had no clean clothes to change into. She cursed and headed to the door, still sopping wet.

Malka was stunned to find Nimrah on the other side of the door when she opened it, bent down in front of her. When their eyes met, Malka's cheeks grew torturously hot. The towel around her felt like nothing, clinging to her body as it absorbed the water.

"What are you doing here?" Malka demanded, her voice frayed at the edges.

Nimrah cleared her throat. "Chaia asked me to bring you these." She motioned to the folded clothes on the floor near the door.

With aching slowness, Nimrah stood, and Malka noticed every inch of the golem's height as she did. It took forever for her to stand straight.

A droplet of water dripped from Malka's hair and curved its way to the corner of her mouth. Nimrah's eyes fell to its path. Without thinking, Malka darted her tongue across her lips, capturing the droplet.

Nimrah recovered from her trance and discomfort turned her cheek rosy. She stared at everything but Malka, from the slits in the wooden door to the cobwebs on the ceiling.

Do you like me better like this—Malka would have asked if she were braver—*clean and smelling of roses? Or like I was, slick with blood from the wound you gave me?*

But Malka was not brave.

The wound on her forearm pulsed, reminding Malka of the bond between them. Even when Nimrah hastily left, leaving Malka disarmed of her usual ripostes, her presence continued to linger.

CHAPTER 20

That night, sleep evaded her, stealthy in its escape. Malka tossed and turned near the hearth in Chaia's home, wishing Hadar were curled into her. She would have used her sister's even breaths to lull herself to sleep as she had done so many times before. Malka had not slept well since she had left home. Even the warmth of a fire and a roof above her once more did not ease the racing of her mind.

Soundlessly, as to not wake Amnon who slept nearby, she slipped from her blanket and stole away outside, near enough to maintain the steady connection with Nimrah. The stars were dim in the city, but still, she sought comfort in them. She imagined Danya and Hadar peering out at the same night sky through their bedroom window, wondering what had become of her. If she was dead, like all the girls before her who entered Mavetéh.

Her heart clenched. She wished she could send them a message, but if Father Brożek discovered she was in Valón, he might think she'd gone back on their deal. Imma's fate would be sealed.

Malka wondered how Danya fared alone in their house with Hadar and Abba. Danya's bruised skin was a scar on her mind; she would never forget the flowering of purple and blue covering Danya's back. Malka swallowed a wave of guilt. She had left them. But she had to follow this deal through. Without her family, Malka was nothing.

Now, she sank close to the earth, soiling her knees in the dirt. The ground was cool on her palm. It was hard to deny her want, which echoed through her, clawing inside the skin of her hand like a screwworm. Cloaked by the night, Malka leaned into the hum. She closed her eyes and called forth the same feelings she had when she healed Amnon. She had been desperate to save him and had commanded the earth to shape her desires. Even when she had tied herself to Nimrah, desperation had cloaked her wishes. Desperation for the deal to work, for Nimrah to keep her promises. Now, under the stars, her wishes weren't desperate. Weren't life or death. Her desire to bend the earth was instead assured, where she prayed until she felt the earth in the deepest parts of her and demanded from the earth a growth which had not been there before. She thrust her hand deeper into the dirt, feeling specks of pebble dig into her skin as the word was drawn: צמח. *Tsemach*. Sprout. Her mouth moved in a soft prayer. One she did not know she could speak until the words became something else entirely.

The earth shifted. She opened her eyes.

Peeking from the ground was a stem of black perphona.

A slight smile drew at the corners of her lips as she ran her hand along its innocuous thorns.

"You need to be careful," Nimrah said, appearing behind her. "You never know who's watching."

Malka picked the herb between her fingers and inspected it. "Do you know what it would mean for my family, for Eskravé, to mumble a prayer and have these grow from the cracks of our cobblestone streets?"

"To think you feared Kefesh so intensely, until you held the power in your palm."

"I still fear it," Malka admitted, the warning of shalkat always at the edge of her mind. How her want made her fear it all the more.

"But you crave it." Nimrah frowned. "I can see it in the fervor of your gaze."

Malka stood. She stared at the golem, though the hood cloaked her face in shadow. "Isn't that what you wanted? You did nothing but encourage me to use this holy magic. To command it."

"Yes," Nimrah answered.

"Now you are disappointed I see what the holy magic is capable of? What it can mean for the future of Eskravé and my people?"

"You must understand why Kefesh does not solve all the world's problems, though it sounds like a blessing."

Malka slit her eyes. "That is *rich* coming from you."

"I know I encouraged you. I don't regret teaching you how to command Kefesh. Only I wish to remind you to be cautious how powerful you show yourself to be in front of the Ozmins. You know what they do to powerful Yahad."

Malka sighed, irritated by the truth of Nimrah's warning. Why should she have to hide herself?

"People fear what they don't understand," Nimrah continued, as if hearing her thoughts. "Kefesh is controversial enough within Yahadism. If Eskravé starts to thrive, if everyone is miraculously healed from the Mázág sickness, the Ozmins will start to raise their brows."

"Yet they didn't question it when the Maharal created you?"

"Oh, they did. I was a sinful abomination, according to them. Made by a wicked sorcerer. But they were afraid of me and what I could do. So, they took their fear out on others who could not defend themselves."

Malka's throat tightened. "The Maharal taught Chaia how to command Kefesh. He took her under his tutelage when she arrived. She said the Maharal would teach any Yahad how to command the magic of our people if they were determined to learn."

"That doesn't surprise me." Nimrah had the ghost of a smile on her lips. "The Maharal spent many years studying Kefesh. He strained himself physically and mentally to truly understand the command of it. He would whisper recipes and spells to himself until his voice was raw. Even after he had stretched Kefesh to its limits in his creation of me, he continued to learn, to see what Kefesh could become. Even someone as contained as the Maharal would be desperate to share that knowledge with someone."

Kefesh could not solve Malka's problems. That, she knew. She had seen its failure in the tragedy that led to Nimrah's banishment; how the deer, a creation of Kefesh, had attacked and injured Amnon. Still, Malka dreamed of the perfect solution she could command in the palm of her hands.

"You remind me of the Maharal in many ways," Nimrah said.

Malka scrunched her brows. "You said I was nothing like him when we were in Mavetéh."

Nimrah was silent for a moment, then shrugged. "You once told me a sweet lie to save my feelings. Perhaps I returned a sour lie to rile you."

She couldn't curb the crimson flush of her cheeks. "How am I like him? Because we are both deeply religious?"

"Yes, but it runs deeper than that. It's how your faith gives you strength, motivates you to be brave, and lights a fire in your heart."

The lamplight flickered across Nimrah's face. She looked painfully innocuous in Vilém's resting clothes which sagged around her arms yet fell short around her hips underneath her cloak. In front of her now, Nimrah did not look like the Rayga, only a woman in sleep clothes conversing with Malka under the stars.

"Careful, Rayga," Malka warned, her voice sweet as wine. "One might start to think you like me with talk like that."

Nimrah huffed. "Don't worry, village girl. It is hard to like someone who wants you dead."

The reminder drew Malka away from whatever trance she had been under. A flurry of emotions plagued her then, hard and fast like Ordobav's summer thunderstorms. The uneasy flip of her belly, the blood rushing through her ears. She knew them intimately. Doubt, guilt.

She did her best to shake them. Nimrah was the Rayga. Her death would mean Imma's freedom and an end to the curse on Mavetéh.

"Best you hate me," Malka said hotly, repeating the words in her head like a mantra. *Monster. Murderer. Monster. Murderer.*

Nimrah stepped into Malka's space. She bent, lips brushing the fold of Malka's ear. "Then hate you, I will. I will hate you as much as the Shabhe King hated his deceptive Shabhe Queen when she revealed her Yahadi identity."

Nimrah walked away, leaving the space between them cool. Malka held her breath until she heard the soft click of the front door signaling Nimrah's returned inside.

Malka brought a hand to her ear and brushed it unconsciously. She recalled the story they had debated in the woods, how the Shabhe Queen had risked her life to save her people from annihilation. The king had been so besotted with his wife from the moment his eyes first laid upon her, he had cherished her bravery as she revealed her secret identity and called off the destruction of the Yahad.

The Shabhe King had never hated his Shabhe wife. He had only ever been besotted with her and loved her more fiercely each day than the last.

CHAPTER

21

The merchants outfitted the streets with the vibrant colors of their goods. Wood trinkets painted with every color dye, silk scarves glistening in the rare glimpse of sun. Piles of fruits and vegetables balanced precariously in wooden baskets, shaded by a marketer swatting flies away and grumbling.

Malka's eyes caught on a wood-framed portrait. It was a detailed rendering of a man striding confidently on his horse, garbed in slate-colored armor, holding a string of gilded prayer beads. On this merchant's cart were several depictions of the same man.

"Who's this?" she asked.

"That's King Manek," Nimrah whispered close to her ear, face barely visible beneath her cloak. Her skin heated where Nimrah's breath touched. "King Valski's father and the Holy Imperial Leader."

"Is it common to have a painting of a king in your home?"

Nimrah chuckled. "He's romanticized. When he ruled, Ordobav became more powerful than it had been for centuries. More people could afford to travel to the southern silk market and buy finery. He founded the University of Valón—the first in the kingdom. Elders miss that time, and have taught their children to miss it, too, even though they didn't experience it."

Malka considered that. How it slotted into her own stories of Valón's greatness.

They passed another vendor, their cart draped with furs. It reminded Malka of the Eskraven traders who would buy them in bulk for Eskravé's shektal market. She scrunched her brows. "Chaia, how did no Eskraven merchants see you at all the past year?"

Chaia's mouth dipped into a weak frown. "I was encouraged to purposefully hide from them, so I stayed home the days the Eskraven merchants came. Their visits had become so infrequent, I should've known something was wrong. I didn't—"

The full-bodied roar of a horn pierced the air, drawing the attention of the street.

Malka expected to see a knight or an announcer, but it was just a man standing on an empty cart, forehead gleaming with sweat, instrument held to his mouth.

"Hajek is dead!" he proclaimed. "They've killed him!"

In the space of a breath, the man was knocked to the ground by a guard, then hounded by another. As more people ran to him, the less Malka could see.

A hand wrapped around her arm. "Come on," Chaia said, her previous thoughts forgotten. "We need to hurry."

In one last look back at the brawl, she saw red.

"What was that?" Amnon asked once they spilled into the shop Chaia carted them into. "Who is Hajek?"

"He's a reformer. A preacher. He used to teach with Vilém at the university before he was expelled for his critique of the Church's collection of indulgences."

"And now he's dead?"

"It would seem that way."

"You don't seem surprised," Nimrah added.

"I can't say that I am." She motioned to them. "Come, I'll explain."

The dress shop was filled with layers and layers of fabric covering every wall. Protruding from the corner, a roaring hearth with bubbling cauldrons. Tinctures of berries and flowers littered a worktable, most likely used for dyes. Clasps and needles were thrown haphazardly around the tinctures.

"You don't have to hide yourself here, Nimrah," Chaia said.

With a short nod, Nimrah lifted the hood of her cloak, her hair streaming out like a gush of spilled ink.

"Hello?" a voice called, appearing from behind a curtain. To Malka's surprise, it was the same blonde woman she had spoken with at the tavern.

"Well, isn't this a surprise," she said, taking in the four of them.

"Katarina, these are my friends—Malka, Amnon, and Nimrah. Katarina is Balkisk, but she has lived here the last four years. Her family runs this shop. She's a tailor."

The woman—Katarina—smiled. "We've met." Now that Malka knew she was Balkisk, the lilt of her Alga-Bak accent felt obvious.

Chaia raised her brow.

"At Bogumir's tavern," Katarina explained. "Merely a coincidence."

She pivoted toward Nimrah. "I had a suspicion about you, *golem*. Though I was not here before your banishment, so I was not sure." Katarina did not seem at all frightened or distressed by Nimrah's presence, merely enthused.

"Did you hear about Hajek?" Chaia interrupted.

Katarina nodded grimly. "Some of the messengers came in early this morning to fix the tears in their trousers. Apparently, he was burned at the stake by the Council of Cussot in Agamere."

Agamere was not part of the Rhaškan Empire, but King Valski had married an Agamerian Queen, cementing the relations between the bordering territories.

"The Council of Cussot?" asked Amnon. "Why does that sound familiar?"

"They are the same religious council that helped to settle the papal schism a decade ago by electing a single pope." Chaia motioned behind the same curtain from which Katarina had appeared. "Come, we have more to show you."

"The Church has never quite recovered from the schism," Chaia said, sparing them a glance as she led them down a narrow hallway, Katarina in front. "After a hundred years of multiple popes vying for the position and denouncing each other in the process, Church rule has lost legitimacy."

They approached the end of the hallway, marked by an antiquated wooden door with a lock system stuck in the past. "Are you sure, Chaia?" asked Katarina.

"I trust them with my life."

"Okay then," Katarina slipped a key from her pocket and opened the door.

The room was shockingly large given the narrowness of the hallway. A small slit of a window lined the back wall, ensconcing them from view to anyone ambling the streets and providing the barest strip of light. The lanterns were already ablaze when they entered. Katarina must've been here when she heard them arrive.

In the center of the room stood a long wooden table as cluttered as the one in the shop. Only this one with papers and books, not tinctures and needles.

"What is this place?" Malka asked.

"It's an old meeting room for the Qehillah, but it was left abandoned under King Manek's rule when they moved to the current municipal building," answered Katarina.

"Feel free to sit, Amnon," she said, motioning to the table. He nodded, resting his cane against the back of the chair. As he sat, his attention drew to one of the open letters. His brow dipped and he scowled. Like Malka, Amnon couldn't read any language but the ancient Yahadi script.

"Does the Maharal know about this?" Nimrah asked, taking in the room. She bent close to a substantial piece of parchment affixed to the wall. Whatever she read made her lips thin.

"Who do you think kept it up all these years?" Katarina said with a wicked smile. "The rabbi knows better than most that Ordobav is on a precipice of change. The last decade or so, he spent a lot of time traveling around the empire and throughout the border cities of Agamere talking with religious leaders and feudal lords to understand the shifting opinions of Church rulership." She seized a book from the table and flipped through some pages, tipping it toward them so they could see the scribble of the Maharal's handwriting. "He documented everything."

"You didn't know about this?" Malka asked Nimrah.

"I knew he travelled," Nimrah responded with a scowl. "But he did not confide in me with this."

Malka had a strange desire to wipe away the crease between Nimrah's brows with her thumb.

Chaia pointed to a map nailed to the wall, decorated with many ink circles that resembled the spots on dairy cattle. "We've kept track of Hajek's movements. Where he preaches, to whom. He's had a lot of success in Vigary and Balkisk."

"Is that because of Duke Sigmund?" Malka recalled his robe of bones and the strife between him and King Valski.

"The duke is not a radical," Katarina answered, "but he does see the disfunction of the Church as a practical issue. He doesn't care how the Church oppresses, only that the lack of legitimacy the schism has garnered devalues the power and wealth of the empire."

"What's the purpose of all this, Chaia?" Amnon asked, fingers tapping anxiously on the table. "Not all of us have a scholar husband to teach us the ways of politics."

Chaia's gaze drifted toward the rota embedded into her cloak. "How ugly is this patch?" She disrobed, throwing it with disgust onto the back of a chair. "I'd rather a bullseye painted on my back. At least then I'd know the arrow would always strike true."

She cut across the room and picked up a scroll from the far end of the table. "Each new ordinance, each demarcation or rule the Yahad have to follow. That's how you know they're afraid. When we hold sway, we become threats. Something other than human, like a stain to be scrubbed clean. The Maharal is not the first prisoner they have taken unfairly. It's been happening for years. We've been keeping track." She unrolled the parchment, revealing a grid of lines filled with words. Names, most likely. "Everyone who advocates for the Yahad, or holds any sway with Valski, ends up a target. They suddenly become thieves or corrupt patrons."

"Sévren orchestrated the Maharal's arrest," Nimrah said, studying the paper intently. "I'm sure of that."

Malka stared at each scroll, each book, each feather dripping ink onto the table. The stories had always illustrated Valón as a sanctuary, somewhere the Yahad could go to escape persecution. These papers chronicled a much different tale.

"Manek's rule left Ordobav strong, and Valón a prominent actor in the empire. But Ordobav remains the papacy's strongest connection. If Ordobav begins to sway away, the Church will have no stronghold left in Rhaška. There's an opportunity for real change here."

Chaia pointed to the door. "That outcry we saw? That isn't new. People are losing faith in the Ozmini Church. No one is happy in Valón, especially with the Mázág sickness worsening. The Church cannot save them from the disease. It cares about no faith."

"You saw for yourself where the indulgences are going," Katarina said to Malka. "They are not subtle."

"Who exactly is involved in all this?" Nimrah asked.

"There are many of us, from many places," Katarina said. "You've stepped outside. Ordobav has become quite diverse. Many of us want a future where that is embraced, not feared."

"Why is this so important to you?" Amnon pushed, slitting his eyes. "You can leave if you wish. Back to Balkisk, where the Church is already losing power."

She did not seem to take the slight to heart. Instead, she quirked her lips. "I see why you would think that, given where you're from."

Amnon opened his mouth defensively, but Katarina lifted her hand. "I *just* mean you did not grow up in a city, nor in the thick of imperial politics. But I did." Her eyes drifted to the map pinned to the wall. "It's true the Balkisk Kingdom has secularized over the years, largely due to the duke's influence. But it is still bound to the Rhaškan Empire, and therefore, the Church. You can say a place is not ruled by the word of God, but it's an empty claim if prayers are still etched into the law."

Chaia brushed a loose piece of hair behind her ear. "Duke Sigmund has expressed interest in becoming the Ordobavian King. He believes Valski has driven their father's legacy into the ground with his reliance on Sévren for political counsel."

"But Valski has an heir," Malka countered.

"Evžen won't be better than his father," Chaia sneered. "Sévren is well aware where the kingdom will go once Valski is gone, and how to make sure the prince keeps his counsel."

"So, you think the duke would be a better ruler?"

"He can ride the winds of change, unlike Sévren and his puppet royals. We share an interest in a future devoid of the Church's presence in politics and academia. It's the first step to a fairer empire for all religions, and all people," Chaia added. "He has prominent connections. Even Ozmini priests who view the Church's corruption as a wart on the religion's true purpose support a kingdom under Sigmund's rule. He's willing to engage with us."

Malka considered mentioning his robe of human bones but bit her tongue. Maybe the story Aleksi had shared was more fiction than truth. She rubbed her eyes instead.

Her entire life had become unfamiliar. Once, she had had her routine: plucking herbs from the garden bed, waking her sisters, helping Imma. It was what she loved. Now, she stood in a secret meeting chamber in Valón, the mark of holy magic embedded in her skin. Now, she was privy to Ordobav's politicking and the plot to steal a prisoner away under royal guard. This plot was so much bigger than Malka.

At the end of the day, though, the result was the same. As long as Imma was free and she could return to the life she treasured in Eskravé, Malka would play any role, do any magic necessary. She had already proved it.

"We should go tomorrow," Chaia said. "We don't know what state the

Maharal will be in when we find him. Evaluate his recovery to see if he'll be able to officiate our wedding."

The sooner they freed the Maharal, the sooner they could head back.

"Speaking of our wedding," Chaia spoke shyly, a stark contrast from her confidence seconds ago, when she spoke of politics and upheavals. "It would mean the world if you three came."

Malka gnawed on her lip, thinking of the long travel home on foot along the eastern road. Of Amnon's injury slowing their pace already. "I don't know, Chaia."

Chaia's face fell before she pursed her lips. In only took a minute before her smile reemerged. "One of Vilém's university friends is heading to Vyš after the wedding. He could . . . take you in his carriage? It wouldn't be that much additional time on his journey, and he owes Vilém a favor," Chaia said, staring straight ahead, though a slight blush caressed the tip of her ears. "You'd make up any time lost with the speed of horse travel. In fact, you may even return faster."

Malka considered this. It was a logical solution, efficient even. And despite herself, love swelled in her chest. She had grieved Chaia and their lost moments together. And now, she was here. Was it wrong if she stole some joy for herself on this journey? Guilt still pierced her, even if waiting for a carriage made more sense. Even if the guarantee of their deal was still subject to the whims of the Maharal's rescue.

"Tell the magister thank you," she said, the corner of her lips ticking up.

Before Chaia could respond, Amnon cleared his throat. "Malka, I need to speak with you alone." He was already reaching for his cane.

His abruptness caught her off guard. She stuttered out, "Of course."

"You can use the shop," Katarina said, unperturbed. "We rarely get customers this time of day."

⚹

"This is spiraling out of control, Malka," Amnon said, after they emerged from the curtain. "The golem was one thing," he continued, "but getting involved with *this*?"

"We aren't," Malka promised. "We're just freeing the Maharal, then bringing the Rayga back to Father Brożek. Anything else that happens because of that is not our doing."

"If they—*we*—are caught, that is not how we'll be viewed when they try us at court! I cannot protect you if we are behind bars."

Malka absently played with a piece of silk hanging off a table. "She's changed so much, hasn't she?" Her voice was low, sheepish.

Amnon sighed, his anger dissipating. "Has she, Malka? I think Chaia's always been like this, only hampered by her circumstances."

Malka chewed on the inside of her mouth. Maybe that was true, but Malka didn't want to admit it. If she did, whatever normalcy Malka had convinced herself she'd have would shatter. Maybe it already had, feet seconds away from stepping on the shards.

"We both left Eskravé to prove something," she said finally. "So did she. We owe each other open ears. That's all."

She spoke in a language Amnon understood—desirous for vindication, teetering on the edge of recklessness to get it.

The whoosh of the curtain revealed Chaia and Nimrah.

"Ready to go?" Chaia asked. "You'll both need your rest for tomorrow."

They nodded.

Amnon and Chaia walked ahead, but Nimrah grabbed Malka's arm before she could move. Their eyes locked. Malka's breath hitched, as if the touch between them heightened the heady weight of their connection.

Nimrah opened her mouth, closed it.

"What?" Malka asked, a little breathless. She chalked it up to shock.

So many flitters of emotion in the golem's eyes, too quick for Malka to grasp, but strong enough to notice. It turned out even a permanent mask could slip.

Her gaze drifted to Malka's arm, her hand wrapped loosely above where the command was etched on Malka's skin and glowered. Malka had yet to decipher how their connection affected Nimrah—if it was as violent; overwhelming when they were close, the distance making her sick and disoriented. But Nimrah's eyes had widened at their touch, her body stiffened. It made her feel something. Of that, Malka was sure.

Nimrah swallowed. "Don't forget to re-dress it tonight."

"I am a healer's daughter," Malka said, still flustered. "I know when to re-dress my wounds."

"Of course, village girl," Nimrah responded, mask slipping back into place. "How could I possibly forget?"

CHAPTER 22

Dawn tumbled in like spilled oil, drenching the sky in the pastel colors of blooming peonies. The yellows and pinks swirled together, casting light onto the cobblestone streets as Malka and Chaia walked to Valón Castle, and the New Royal Palace within its complex. Amnon had stayed behind, instructed to keep watch for anything suspicious.

This would be the farthest Nimrah and Malka would venture from each other. She had done her best to mentally prepare for their separation—to anticipate the unmooring. Yet as they ventured apart, it hit her just as fiercely. A wave of nausea that had her keeling over.

"Are you alright?" Chaia asked, resting her hand on Malka's back.

Malka nodded, but her eyes were screwed shut. "An unfortunate side effect of the rooting spell," she explained. "Distract me?"

They began to walk again once Malka collected herself.

"Do you remember those long walks we would go on when we were kids, where we'd stay out so late our parents would yell a storm of worries at us when we finally returned?" Chaia asked lightly, though she still held a cautious eye on Malka.

The memory warmed her. "If I did not convince you to return, I swear you would've had us stay out all night long."

Chaia smiled, readjusting her work bag on her shoulder. "I felt so free. Like I could do anything in the world."

"You were always like that to me. Like you would shout a command to the universe, and it would bend to your will."

"With Kefesh, it feels like that is true sometimes. Though, I'm hardly naive enough to believe I am free anymore. Not while the Ozmini Church rules Ordobav, and the Yahad have so little protection."

Malka blew at an unruly curl that had escaped the confines of her kerchief. "What was the Maharal like as a teacher?"

"When the Maharal offered to teach me the Yahadi magic, I think he believed it would help to ground me after I made the decision to stay. I felt adrift for a while. Kefesh . . . it reminded me of the fire within myself, even when the Ozmini Church tried to extinguish it. It brought me closer to the Yahadi faith and cemented my desire to defend it."

"Do you . . . use it often?" She felt awkward asking. As if they were discussing a sewing needle and not forbidden magic.

Chaia smiled. "For me, it isn't about casting. It's about holding the ancient knowledge inside myself. A weapon that no Ozmin can steal."

"And you don't fear it? Even though we've heard stories of its unpredictability?"

Chaia chuckled. "What in life is predictable, Malka? We don't know the outcome of anything we do or say. I could hardly have known that stealing away to Valón would result in everyone thinking me dead, and Kefesh wasn't involved in that at all."

"Do you regret it?" Malka asked, though unsure if she wanted the answer.

Chaia squeezed her hand. "I regret that it left you thinking I was dead. I regret leaving you. But I don't regret wanting to help the Yahad in any way I could. I don't regret that coming here led me to Vilém."

It was true that Chaia's decision to leave had unintended consequences, like the warnings told of Kefesh. But as Malka had experienced, with those risks also came the possibility for something great—like healing Amnon, or the delicate black perphona plant she had created from nothing.

They veered into a giant square. It wasn't yet crowded, and Malka had an unobstructed view of a protruding tower, the ochre-tinted limestone stark against the morning light. The center of the tower held two clock rings pressing inside of each other like a rippling pool of water. It was stunningly intricate with golden circles marking the time. Symbols were etched into the clock. Malka squinted, but still could not make them out.

"What is that, on the tower?" Malka asked.

"That's the Orlon clock," Chaia answered. "It's one of the most advanced astronomical clocks in the Rhaškan Empire, though it no longer works. The hands move too rapidly. It's under construction right now. Prince Evžen mandated its restoration as part of an initiative to revive the golden age of his grandfather's rule. Every day they're felling what's left of usable trees in Mavetéh and digging up ore to forge into the most intricate metal for it."

When Malka arrived in Valón, she had believed the Yahadi Quarter to be its most beautiful part, with the shul Bachta's glimmering stained glass and colorful winding streets, but the Orlon clock stunned her. The colors of the clock shifted when the sun hit and reflected onto the painted buildings, making them iridescent.

"Don't be too impressed, Malka," Chaia warned. "Do you see the figures flanking the clock?"

Malka made them out—four men carved into stone ledges, two on each side. "I see them."

"Each figure represents what the Ordobav Kingdom despises. The first figure holds a mirror—they call him vanity. The skeletal man holding an hourglass is named death. Across from it, the dark-skinned man playing the mandolin, represents lust. And next to him, the man with an aquiline nose holding a bag of Ordon coin, is greed. Look first at lust. What rings familiar?"

The stereotypes were easy to see—as much as the Ozmins hated the Yahad, they also hated the Fanavi people, who came from a powerful empire along the southern trade route. They called them idolaters, interested in thievery and polygamy. It was drawn from hateful stories the same way the Yahad were accused of hoarding money, of using gold as a way to control politicking because they were forced into moneylending roles. It was dangerous to have beliefs different from the Ozmins. The Church would do all it could to shame those beliefs into destitution.

"The figures are Fanavi and Yahadi men," Malka said.

"And there you see, what Ordobav hates: vanity, death, the Fanavi, and the Yahad."

What Malka had first seen as beautiful, she now recognized as horror. Its shimmering colors, which glistened in the sun, gilded the hate beneath.

It was not always like this, Malka wanted to believe. But the truth was, she did not know. She had never been to Valón. She had lived solely through stories, which were always painted differently by each storyteller who carried them to Eskravé.

"Things will get better," Malka said, unsure who she was trying to convince, Chaia or herself. "Once I return to Eskravé with the Rayga, and the curse is lifted."

"Are you sure that will happen, Malka? That killing Nimrah will lift all of our ails?"

From here, Malka could not see any glimpse of Mavetéh, yet its memory was vivid. It was true, Nimrah was not the Rayga she expected to find. A golem, disgraced.

I'm a command, not the commander, she had said. Even if she did not control the monsters who took their girls, Nimrah was still responsible for their creation.

"She evoked Mavetéh's cursed creatures," Malka said. "I have to believe her death will destroy them, too."

The promise of Eskravé's return to normalcy was the only way Malka knew to move forward. She held Imma's fate in her palms as she held Kefesh's power. She couldn't fathom an alternative where Nimrah's death did not free them. She had killed. Watched Amnon on the brink of death. Woodland monsters now clawed terror into her dreams each night. She had survived what no other Yahadi woman had. That had to mean something.

"If the Maharal has taught me anything, it's that things are rarely as they seem. Magic and its mysteries are not always something we can understand. We are meant to feel close to it, and be comforted by it, but not always to hold the knowledge of it in our hands."

Malka thought of Abayda the Mystic and the forbidden knowledge that destroyed him.

The castle gates stood resolute, stones pummeled together and connected by vaulted iron, melded into spires that resembled plumes of golden smoke. Each side of the open iron gate held the Valski Insignia, two fighting lions with sharp canines. Malka stared at them as they passed through.

They entered into the castle complex, affixed with several looming cathedrals, the courthouses, great halls, and impending military towers which hid the expansive green of the royal gardens. She had thought Trader's Day busy, but preparations for the Léčrey celebration had set the entire castle grounds abuzz.

"We're approaching the palace," Chaia said, drawing her attention. "I'll talk, but don't be afraid to speak if you are asked a question. Skittish behavior will alarm them."

Up close, the New Royal Palace brushed the low-hanging storm clouds, illuminating the pale-yellow stone walls. Bright red broach spires jutted, coming to a point so sharp Malka imagined them piercing the clouds like a dagger would cut skin, rain falling in streams like trickling blood.

Chaia led them to the servant's entrance on the side of the building—an undecorated set of solid swing doors. A knight stood guard.

He eyed Chaia. "You usually arrive alone."

"This is my cousin, Hanna. She is one of the new scullery maids Cook Irenka hired to help prepare for the Léčrey celebration."

Malka attempted a blank face but worry wavered her bottom lip. The day prior, Chaia had eavesdropped on the cook as she had given the names of the new scullery maids to the Seneschal. Vilém and Nimrah had gone to bribe the real Hanna, who agreed to miss work in exchange for the hefty sum of Ordon coins Vilém offered her instead. Though, Malka had a feeling even if the woman had not been tempted by the money, Nimrah's tall, threatening presence had made it impossible to refuse.

The guard clicked his tongue and unrolled his scroll. After a moment of examination, he sighed, rolling up the scroll again and shoving it into the crook of his arm. "See to it she gets an apron and a proper bonnet."

"Of course. Thank you," Chaia said.

Malka slumped her shoulders in relief. Chaia wrapped her hand around Malka's arm and ushered her through the door as the guard stepped aside.

When they arrived, the kitchen was a flurry of activity. Women in aprons danced around each other, holding plates, cutlery, and towels above their heads as breakfast was prepared. It was hot and stuffy, oven fires billowing high, hungry for bread to bake. Flour settled in the air like dust motes as dough was tossed and rolled into loaves. Links of beer sausage and salted duck hung above a roiling fire, browning with the lick of each flame.

"You're late!" shrilled a woman who must have been Cook Irenka, hitting Chaia on her shoulder with a towel. Sweat beaded down her forehead and into the crooks of her crow's feet. "Get to work!"

"Is she not wondering who I am?" Malka whispered to Chaia.

She shrugged. "She rarely keeps track of temporary hires. That, and you are not a food she can bake or cook."

Chaia handed Malka an apron, and they went to work. Malka helped Chaia score dough for the day's bread loaves, and after, Cook Irenka ordered Malka to pluck fowl. The work was demanding, but Malka almost enjoyed it. She had missed the routine of assisting Imma—delivering early morning medicine to patients and preparing tonics from Imma's herb garden.

Homesickness stabbed her like a honed blade.

"Hanna." Chaia approached with a breakfast platter. Malka had almost forgotten her disguise. "Will you take these to Prince Evžen's head servant? The prince should be finishing his morning prayers in the royal chapel."

As Malka nodded and received the platter, Chaia gripped her hands. "Be safe, *Yedid Nefesh*," she whispered low in Kraž-Yadi, so only Malka could hear. "Good luck."

⚹

Malka wandered through the palace halls, amazed at its grandeur. The servant entrance they had funneled through to get to the kitchens paled in comparison to the splendor of the main halls. Caramel beams caressed the walls, crowning together on the ceiling in thick, even arches like the bones of a ribcage. Thin, stone panels with old Jalgani writing engraved on them—the writing of Ozmini prayers—sat fitted between each rib. Imposing lancet windows lined the hall. Through them, light gushed in and pooled along the floor like melted candle wax.

Though Chaia had given her instructions on finding the chapel, Malka wandered, mouth agape at the expansive rooms which fell into each other seamlessly. She ambled into another hall, this one smaller than the rest. It was empty and quiet, only the flaming lanterns on the wall brushing sound against her ears.

She kept her head down as two knights passed by her, ignoring the painful twists of her stomach caused by the rooting spell. Soon, she and Nimrah would reunite, and this sickness would ease.

"Can't we just close the city gates if they're so worried about who's coming through?" one asked.

The other answered, voice a little more distant. "We don't question orders, we follow them."

The clink of their heavy shoes stopped in tandem. "Your Highness."

Malka tensed and stole a glance behind her.

The crown prince was garbed in magnificent dress, his golden collar stiff and glimmering, and a red and white sash crossing his broad shoulders. The same gold crossed his waist, embroidered with indigo crescents, which stood out against the yellow like the moon in a starless sky. His sand-colored hair was combed back to his shoulders and a tight smile lined his face. Another man walked alongside him. While he was also finely dressed, he was nowhere near as opulent as the prince.

Evžen nodded to the knights but kept his pace, passing Malka, who had taken up residence against the wall, as if she could blend herself into it.

He was speaking in low tones to the man next to him in rushed Kražki Malka strained to understand. She didn't catch much, only a few words. But each one made her heart leap.

Eskravé. Paja.

Her breathing grew shallow and fast. It could be innocuous, simply updating the prince on why the Order's movement was delayed. Why they were held up in Eskravé. But there was a potential, however small, that Imma's name could fall from their lips.

Malka wouldn't miss the opportunity to find out.

Her eyes darted toward the chapel where Nimrah waited. But already the prince was disappearing around the corner.

She peeled herself from the wall and followed the prince on light feet.

They approached a door, where the prince gave some parting words to his companion. Evžen watched him leave before stepping inside of the room.

Before she could second-guess herself, Malka stepped one foot on the woven rug and slid it toward the room. It bunched up, catching the door before it closed all the way. A sliver of orange light caressed the heels of the tassels.

She approached cautiously, pressing herself back to the wall and holding her breath as she peered inside.

From the sliver she could see, the room was as opulent as the halls, though more furnished. A grand desk sat in the middle of the room, its legs curved like wobbling knees.

"You are not the young boy you used to be, though you might dream it."

Malka could not see the man who spoke to the prince, though his voice was gritty and threadbare, and his words pummeled out like stones. It was the voice of a graying man.

She could see Evžen more clearly as he ran his hand along his stubbled jaw. He leaned against the desk and crossed his legs. "I am not longing for the past, Sévren. I'm only unsure of the future."

Malka tensed hearing the archbishop's name.

"I don't blame you for dithering." Sévren placed his hand on the prince's shoulder, revealing the silk brocade liturgical cuffs around his wrist, threaded with gold.

"You've been timid in your actions as prince. And the court has allowed it . . . for now. But they will not always. Your father is aging, and he has strayed further and further away from his duties. His long tenure has made him . . . simple-minded, worsened by the prolonged absence of your mother in Agamere."

Prince Evžen raised his brow. "Your Grace, I don't think my father, *your king*, would appreciate those claims. Some would say they are borderline treason."

Malka expected Sévren would grow haughty at the prince's accusation, but he chuckled instead.

"Only you know me too well to accuse me of treason. If anything, it is my love for this kingdom that prompts my free speech. It has depressed me, Evžen, to see the Ordobav Kingdom loosen from your father's grasp. I only fear what would happen if . . . well, if it were to slip completely."

Malka tensed. How much did Sévren know of the duke's plans?

The prince folded his arms, the red and white sash wrinkling. "Have you heard something, Sévren? Is there a coup in the works?"

The prince did not always address Sévren with his honorific, nor did the archbishop always use the prince's title. It could confirm the rumors of their supposed closeness, that neither was particularly fazed by the familiarity of their address.

"Nothing like that, my prince. I only fear your father's legacy will leave the people of Ordobav less than satisfied with your rise to kingship."

The prince reared. "I have done nothing to my people. They have not even come to see my reign yet, or the type of king I will be."

Sévren stepped closer to the prince, finally revealing himself in the slim crack of the door. He was younger than Malka had anticipated and wore a tall burgundy miter.

"Your birth was a delicate thing, Evžen." The archbishop spoke tenderly. "I remember that day you know. I even remember the fog-dusted sky. It had been so gray for the days your mother was in labor. Clouds remained, foretelling rain that wouldn't come. They taunted us and clotted the air, so it was hard to breathe. It was dark, even during the day. Like the sun wouldn't rise until you came."

Sévren drew his knuckles against Evžen's cheek. The prince leaned into the touch.

"You were so small wrapped in your chrisom robe after your baptism. But even then, holding you, I felt the presence of God."

"And I have prayed every day to Triorzay and Saint Celine for saving my life. I have lived in sanctity according to Ozmini law. Is that not how we grew so close, Sévren? From childhood, I have consumed every teaching you have given and confessed to every sin I could think of."

"I don't doubt your holiness, my boy. It's my belief in your piety that led me to speak with you now, candidly."

"Then tell me, *candidly*, Sévren. What fear do you have of the Valski rule?"

Sévren smiled. "You look so much like your grandfather, you know. I admired him very much. He embodied everything a Holy Imperial Leader should: strength, resolve. Brutality, if necessary. But there is a reason the papacy did not bestow the same title over your father."

"You disapprove of his choice in counsel because of his Yahadi advisors." The prince said this tiredly, like it had been a discussion between them before.

"It's not because they are Yahadi, of course. It's because they are a threat to your rule. Valski rule. And you must . . ."

Malka could no longer make out Sévren's words as he disappeared from view. But Evžen's jaw clicked, and he sighed to the heavens. Whatever Sévren said, Evžen was not pleased.

"At the end of it all, Prince Evžen, it's up to you if you decide to give the orders or let another king-making decision pass you by. If Saint Celine made the right choice, or if she will be disappointed again."

A wave of nausea seized Malka, teetering her off balance. She kicked the golden platter and its clattering echoed through the hall. She was *sure* the rooting spell existed solely to betray her.

Footsteps from inside the room were getting louder, closer. She had to go. *Now.* Yet she still dizzied when she attempted to grab the platter from the ground. She swayed and it slipped from her grip once. Then twice.

"Who's out there?" Sévren called. His voice was closer now. In seconds she would be caught.

Malka closed her eyes, tried to ground herself. Breathed deep. Finally, she took hold of the platter. As the crack in the door widened, Malka was already skirting the corner, running toward the chapel.

CHAPTER 23

Malka smelled the chapel first. Musty and drenched in frankincense and the stale, warm scent of burning flora and smoke.

The chapel dwarfed her, spanning upward so high she strained her neck to follow the beams which crisscrossed the domed ceiling adorned with frescoes. Gems glittered in gold dots along the wall, the images surrounding them coming to life as the light flickered across the paint. The murals depicted Saint Wenaska's life—the Ozmini patron saint of Ordobav. In one scene, he appeared honorable. A sword and a cross folded into his hands, crown gleaming across the crest of his head. In another, the scene of his assassination, where his hated brother killed him for his role in uniting the Rhaškan Empire.

The story of the patron saint had always been mysterious to Malka. She had never considered herself Ordobavian because the Order had never treated her as such. They were Yahad only, and that was fine with Malka. Though now she questioned why Ordobav was only for the Ozmins, deemed by their beloved martyr and patron saint. The king commanded her, yet abandoned her people.

Light filtered in from the stained-glass window in shades of purple, blue, green, and yellow. They shone onto the altar, turning it into something otherworldly.

Outside, the wind blew, and the pews creaked, the high-pitch whistle of a singing choir. Malka suppressed a shiver and ran her hand along the back of a wooden pew. She felt out of place as a Yahad, to be somewhere so sacred to others that held no meaning to her. Saint Wenaska's eyes followed her as she crossed the chapel and Malka wondered if the saint could see through to her deceit.

"I didn't think you were coming."

Nimrah leaned against the back of a pew, hood drawn heavy across her face.

Malka had known she was here—had sensed it as she neared the chapel. Her mind steadying with each step, the nausea settling, replaced with the burdensome waxing heat of their nearness.

"There was a hiccup," Malka said, breathy.

Malka untucked the folded map from her pocket, smoothing the paper beneath her fingers. "The map shows that the entrance to the dungeons should be somewhere along this back wall." She squinted at the ornate wooden Ozmini symbols which decorated the wall. In front of them, the wooden confessional booths, covered by purple curtains, obscured any entrance there might have been.

"They must have concealed the entrance with these booths."

Nimrah sighed in frustration. "I don't—"

Conversation cracked through the silence of the chapel and the shadows of two men danced on the walls before they entered the room.

Nimrah yanked Malka hard and fast into one of the confessional booths to hide them, the curtain blanketing them in darkness. Only a faint shard of light fell through, cutting across Nimrah's face like a scythe. Nimrah swallowed Malka's gasp with her hand, just as she had done when Malka nearly woke the water dragon.

The map fluttered to the ground.

In a space only meant for one, the booth pressed them close. Nimrah's unnatural height forced her to hunch, bringing her chin a hair's breadth from Malka's forehead. Each labored breath pressed their bodies together, each hot tendril of Nimrah's exhale against Malka's skin feeding the insatiable, delirious hunger she had painstakingly buried.

When Nimrah lifted her palm from Malka's lips, it was a slow and laborious movement. She dragged the pads of her fingers across Malka's cheek, her chin, the crest of her jaw, until Nimrah's hands settled against the wall, ensnaring Malka between them.

Malka told herself Nimrah caged her for balance, to prevent the booth from creaking with their shifting weight. Yet the vestiges of Nimrah's calloused fingers heated her skin still.

The scythe of light betrayed the bob of Nimrah's neck and the waver of her lips. What a monster she was, her face half stone, veins forest green. And how wretched it was that the monstrous parts of Nimrah made Malka want to step closer, like Abayda the Mystic to the forbidden book.

Her wanting would be the death of her.

"*I will set out more incense for the afternoon service,*" one of the men said, voice muffled by the curtain.

Malka could hardly focus. Nimrah's heated gaze fell to her in the dark. When Nimrah's mouth parted, Malka's attention drew to her lips. They were as plush as the velvet curtain that hid them. She wanted to caress her thumb across Nimrah's bottom lip, see what she would do if Malka slipped her finger inside of her mouth.

Nimrah must have sensed her desire, for the box creaked as Nimrah pressed her leg harder between Malka's thighs. Malka choked on a gasp.

"*Did you hear something?*"

"*It's the wind. You know how it blows through the wooden pews.*"

In their haste to hide, Nimrah's hood had flown off and her hair fell in messy waves around her shoulders—a dark and wild mane to match the monster.

Even as the threat enveloped her, Malka lifted her hand and gently coiled some of the inky strands around her finger.

Nimrah tensed, staring at Malka's pale finger in the abyss of her hair. Frowned at it.

Good. She should hate it. Hate her the way Malka hated in return.

Nimrah's hand left the wall and dropped to Malka's hip, her thumb caressing the opening of Malka's apron pocket.

This was something worse than hate.

Nimrah's face held pain tightly—so subtle one could not decipher it if not for a betrayal of her eyes, wavering like storm clouds. They betrayed the lust that hid there, confirmed by the dart of her tongue across her lips.

"Malka." Her whisper was soft. Wanting. Warning.

Malka swallowed. Hearing her name, said like *that,* made her almost forget what brought them there in the first place.

Nimrah's fate was to die in exchange for Imma's life. It was the deal they had made from the beginning and Malka wouldn't fail Imma again. She would not fail Hadar or Danya and the promise she had made to them both.

This was nothing but the intensity of the rooting spell. It clouded her mind like a manta joint—loosened her thoughts like wine. Betraying her again.

Monster. Murderer. Monster. Murderer.

Malka stepped back, desperate to put space between them, between her and the monster she was meant to hate. But her foot caught on a small hitch in the wood. A click echoed through the small space, and the wooden paneling on the back of the box swung open.

The door to the tunnel. It was hidden inside the confessional.

Nimrah's gaze was on her, but Malka did not look back. Instead, she rushed through the entrance.

Small and dingy, the tunnel stank of mildew and grime. It curved around them so tight it was hardly a reprieve from the confessional booth. Though, Malka was grateful Nimrah couldn't see the pink biting the top of her ears.

Nimrah unhooked a wooden torch from its sconce, then handed it to Malka. "You can light it with Kefesh if you write in the tallow." Her voice was still rough, and Malka pretended not to notice.

Instead, Malka took the torch. She began to mold the word for light into the tallow with her finger: אור. *Ohr.* A flame ignited on the torch, warming the space around them in golden firelight. Malka shocked herself with the ease of her command. She teetered the glowing torch around, marveling.

The passageway was musty with disuse. With each step, small pebbles peeled from the rock and fell around them.

Malka stole a glance at Nimrah over her shoulder and was met only with Nimrah's steely gaze. Gone were the unguarded expressions of pain and lust which had plagued the golem only minutes ago.

Good. It was better that way.

They walked trepidatiously, only their gait and the slow drops of moisture interrupting the hollow silence. Until men's voices carried through the tunnel.

"Extinguish the flame," Nimrah whispered, and Malka suffocated the flame in the dirt.

Trailing her hand against the wall to guide her, she turned a corner. Light skidded across the stone walls from iron torches.

A set of guardsmen came into view, mirror images of each other as they stood stoic at both sides of the locked gate. The guard closest to them looked around Abba's age with a dusting of ginger hair. The other was much younger and had a sizeable scar across his cheek.

"Stay here," Nimrah ordered, so low, Malka barely heard her.

Nimrah flattened her palm to the ground. A vine sprouted between her fingers, studded with thorns. It traveled like a snake and slithered up to meet the younger guard's full height.

The guard bared his sword and shouted to his counterpart before swinging his blade through the vine. It hit the ground with a *thump*. But that snake was only a distraction, as Nimrah already had another one slithering toward them, twisting itself around the older guard's neck before he fell, blue-faced.

The younger guard shouted, hands tight around his sword. "Show yourself!"

While Nimrah sent another snake-like vine, Malka cowered behind the corner of the wall. She didn't know how to fight, nor did she have Abba's dagger. She was too afraid it would've foiled her cover as scullery maid if someone discovered it.

Something sharp poked her back. She flinched, the shadow of a man appearing behind her.

"Who are you?" he demanded, digging the sword further into her skin. She cried out as the blade pierced through the back of her vest, hot blood welling under her blouse.

"I wouldn't do that if I were you." Nimrah appeared in front of the guard, tall and menacing. Vines circled her arms and slithered around her hands.

Malka felt for the wall beside her.

"The golem!" the younger guard exclaimed. Bewilderment had shaken his resolve, but he collected himself swiftly. He slit his eyes and raised his sword again.

"Is she your accomplice?" demanded the guard who held the sword at Malka's back.

Nimrah smirked. "Much to her frustration."

The sword clattered to the ground as the guard behind Malka tripped on vines Nimrah had raised from under his feet.

Malka picked up his sword, and powered by ferocious adrenaline, cracked the hilt against the guard's head. He dropped unconscious.

The younger guard advanced, sword catching on Nimrah's vine. Nimrah clutched the vine's other end, cording it around her wrists to trap the guard. But the guard, instead of attempting to untangle himself or his blade, yanked his sword back with all his might. Nimrah jerked forward and fell.

Before she could get up, the guard kicked her side, then yanked her up by her cloak and threw her against the wall.

She pummeled against the stone with a sickening crack, moaning as she crumpled to the ground.

Something uncomfortable tightened in Malka at the sight.

She didn't have the time to analyze it. The guard turned on her, backing her into the wall. "You know what we do to betrayers?" He licked the sweat from his upper lip. "We lower them into the ground, into a space so small, you can feel your own breath bounce off the walls."

Malka splayed her hand against the wall, an idea sprouting. She didn't know if it could work; if it would be enough. But she had to try. She began to dig her fingernails into the stone, hoping it was hard enough to scuff the surface. *Nun. Kaph.* She bit her lip as blood began to well under her nails, but she did not relent.

"It's not with the other prisoners. Oh, no. It's somewhere where souls are laid bare. The others are here at ground level, but those who need to be taught a lesson . . . they get sent below. But maybe I'll have some fun with you first." He drew his hand along Malka's cheek, and she tried not to vomit. "Get on your knees."

Malka was tired of men intimidating her, tired of their teeth-bared threats. She was tired of being at the end of their swords because of her religion, because she was a woman. She thought of Brother Asak and the threat he had hissed sinisterly into her ear, of Václav's disgusting jabs as she turned to sleep.

One more letter: *Hey.* And the word was written: נכה. *Nakhah.* Strike. The magic flowed through her. As commanded, the stone wall began to pelt shards toward the guard. They all struck true, each shard digging into his skin. He stumbled back but couldn't escape them. When a shard pierced an artery in his neck, blood lashed the air like the violent whip of a rope. Eyes bulging, he cupped his neck, yet still blood seeped through his fingers. Malka watched as he grew paler and paler before his eyes rolled back and he dropped to the ground. He would be dead in minutes.

She wore his blood in a sash across her vest. She could taste the tang of it in her mouth. It sent Malka back to Mavetéh, where Aleksi had been decapitated by the creature who crawled out of the tree cavity and used its branches as weapons.

And Malka had killed someone else, using the same magic.

It was different now, just as it had been different when she had shoved Václav, and the rock had pierced his temple. Malka shivered, thinking of her fate if she had not commanded Kefesh to save her now. She imagined a screwworm burrowing between her thighs and breasts. Her insides writhed. She chose instead to imagine the screwworm under her knife.

Nimrah roused.

Malka ran to her, dropping to her knees.

"You killed him," Nimrah said, eyeing the now dead guard.

Malka swallowed, shame heating her face. "I—"

Nimrah shook her head. "I didn't mean it like that. You defended yourself. I meant, you managed to overtake a trained guard with only Kefesh to help you."

"Yes," Malka responded. She knew Nimrah desired more from her, but it was all she could say. She surprised herself.

An unbridled smile teased at Nimrah's mouth. So sincere, Malka realized she had not seen the golem truly smile until now.

"We don't have long," Malka said finally, breaking whatever lingered between them.

Nimrah groaned as she picked herself up from the ground. "His belt," she said, motioning toward the older guard. "The gate key should be on there."

Malka nodded and unclasped the key from the ring at the guard's belt, heaving open the gate.

※

The dungeon odor was foul—feces and urine tangled in dank air. Malka's stomach twisted. For once, she was glad she had not eaten since dawn.

The cells were built into uniform pockets of the wall, a hive-like formation stretching down the length of the corridor. A rusted metal gate at each cell served to trap its inhabitant. As they walked, dull moans echoed across the hall, reminiscent of the groans from overworked cattle. Raucous sobs came from one of the shaded cells.

"Here!" Nimrah shouted.

Malka's blood pounded through her veins as she approached the Maharal.

So many of the stories she had been told portrayed him as a great man touched by Yohev. The commander of Yahadi magic and forbidden wisdom.

She had seen no portraits of the rabbi, only heard descriptions. Each person had shaped him in a different way...

"*His skin glistens when he uses his magic, his hands made permanently silver by their holy work.*"

"*He appears either as an old man, or a young one. With wrinkles that sag his skin, or the deepest raven hair that looks purple in the sun.*"

"*He has a beard that brushes the floor. Some say it can perform its own magic...*"

Now, he was nothing like what the stories had conjured up in her mind. Behind the iron bars, so small Malka could almost miss him if the torchlight didn't illuminate his pallid skin, he curled into himself. Wilted.

He was pitifully thin. His sleeves were hiked up to his elbows, revealing skin and bone splotched with pale, ugly bruises. His mouth held ajar, yellow crooked teeth hiding behind his cracked, bloody lips drained of any color.

Malka wondered if they had made a mistake—if the Maharal was truly sick. But Sévren's claims of his care were obviously false. If he was sickened, it was the result of Sévren's abusive orders.

Though, the stories did get one thing right about the Maharal. Even in his sallow, starved form, there was something magical about him. Magic prickled her palms and she craved to command the earth once more. Malka thought of the boy-turned-man in Nimrah's story, how he was always destined for greatness.

She couldn't confirm the Maharal's silver hands, for both of them were missing. Instead, his skin had been clumsily stitched at his wrists.

"Rav," Nimrah broke the lock with her fist and dropped to her knees inside the gate. "What did they do to you?"

"Nimrah?"

His voice was scratchy from disuse, so threadbare Malka could hardly imagine him with the commanding voice from the stories that preceded him.

"I am here," Nimrah said, encircling the Maharal in her arms and running her thumb along his frail arm.

His eyes finally opened, and Malka's breath hitched.

They were bloodshot, hardly any color seeping behind the red. When they landed on Malka, her neck prickled.

Shouts echoed down the tunnel, approaching rapidly.

If they were caught now, they'd be rounded up and thrown in here with him, and Imma would be as good as dead.

"I'll stay," Nimrah said. "You get him out of here."

But there was no way Malka could carry the Maharal. She was not strong enough. And they'd be too slow if she tried to shoulder his weight. Nimrah had taken a serious beating and swayed on her feet despite her declaration. She would not last long, even with her powers. Blood trickled down the flesh side of her face, tinting the skin red.

"No," Malka said, before she could think better of it. "I'm not strong enough to carry the Maharal out of here alone. You take him. I'll buy you some time. It's the only way we can free him."

Nimrah's wide eyes found hers, the crease between her forehead deepening. "You don't have to do this."

Malka stared back, eyes tracing Nimrah's stone cheek, which had split like the veins of cracked glass from her fall. "Go. Our bargain, remember?"

Nimrah was silent for a moment, peering to the door where shadows clipped onto the walls, then back to the Maharal's pale face. "Alright," she said, but her voice lacked its usual prickly bite. "But take this." From her cloak, she withdrew Abba's dagger.

Malka nodded, soothed to be reunited with the blade, and wrapped the dagger in her hand.

Nimrah lifted the Maharal's arm around her shoulder and hoisted him into her arms. She opened her mouth, closed it. At war with herself over her words.

But the voices of the guards drew ever closer, forcing Nimrah to forgo any last words. She jogged back into the tunnel with the Maharal in her arms, veering away from the entrance where the guards would soon appear.

Once she was gone, Malka paced.

Alone, the hilarity of her situation hit all at once. Who was she, to think she could defend herself? That she could stand up to trained guards with only a dagger and her hands, calloused not from battle, but delicate suturing.

She wasn't like the brave women from her people's stories. She wasn't the Shabhe Queen, who would save the fate of her people with her cunning words. And that was fine with her. She admired those, like Chaia, who sought adventure. Who let defiance and rebellion simmer in their bones. She was not one of them. All Malka longed for were leisurely cold walks in Eskravé at dawn, and shaping paper cuts with Hadar and Danya on the floor of their bedroom.

But now, she had no choice.

Kefesh made her feel different, powerful for the first time. It was impossible to want. A magical thing, twisted from religion and morphed into something abashedly human. But she wanted it all the same.

Malka slipped the dagger into the band of her apron. It would be her last resort, as she at least showed some skill with Kefesh. As Nimrah retreated, the rooting spell began its rebellion. Her world began to tilt as the unmooring sensation yanked her from her body. Nausea made a home in the pit of Malka's belly, twisting her insides with pain.

Malka breathed, gritted her teeth, desperate to push through the sensation.

Four men reared around the corner, hands gripped tight on their swords. Their armor gleamed in the torchlight and clanked against their bodies as they jogged closer.

The guards stopped short and took in Malka's appearance. She still wore the scullery maid apron. They had not expected the intruder to be someone like her.

Taking advantage of their shock, Malka gathered close to the wall. Her heart pounded hard against her ribcage as she began to shakily scrape the same word—*nakhah*—into the stone, dried blood already caked under what was left of her nails. They'd grown weak, and a nail split off in her effort. She grunted from the pain but continued on. When she finished, she waited, expecting the shards to heed her command as they had before.

They did not come.

A sword sliced through the air, and she tumbled back, barely evading the blade.

It didn't work. Her attempts to use Kefesh had never failed before, not since she had tried to heal Amnon and Nimrah had shouted at her to focus.

It was too late to try again. A knight hoisted her up by her hair and pressed a sword between her shoulders. It irritated the wound already carved down her back, and Malka stifled a scream.

"The Maharal is gone," one of the guards alerted the rest.

The man who held her up like a rag doll sneered. "Who helped you, girl? Tell us now, and you might be spared."

Malka, blessedly, remembered the dagger. She retrieved it from her waistband and stabbed the blade into the meat of the guard's thigh. He howled but did not release his hold on Malka's hair. He only yanked tighter, causing Malka's eyes to water. She was a fool. Such a fool.

The golem now had what she wanted: the Maharal. All Malka had was a promise. She had played all her cards. Would she be imprisoned or killed? What would become of Imma? How long until the Maharal could undo their rooting spell? How long until Nimrah was not beholden to Malka at all? So many questions. Answers to none.

A second guard kicked the dagger from her hand, tearing her back to the present. Pain erupted from her wrist. The knight raised his foot again, the sole as black as an eclipsing sun. The blow to her head was so fierce, she saw stars, and could do nothing as the guards bound her arms and dragged her knees across the stone floor to her fate.

CHAPTER 24

A finger drew across her cheek. For a moment, Malka thought it was Imma rousing her as she had done so many times before. But the finger was too soft, lacking her thick callouses from a lifetime of hard work.

Memories flooded back. The sordid dungeon, the Maharal's shriveled figure like winter's deadened leaves. The guards and the blow to her head. She must've lost consciousness as they transported her.

Her eyelids fluttered, but she kept them closed and tried to even her breathing. Her face was stiff and hot. The swelling from her cheek pulsed with pain.

"Has this convinced you, my prince?" It was Sévren's scaly voice. "Your lineage's legitimacy has quaked so that even a peasant girl feels comfortable breaking into your fort."

"How do you know it won't make more martyrs of them?" came Evžen's response. "We have already tried to jail their Maharal. It didn't stop their disobedience."

"Let them have the Maharal. Better we get the upper hand now and say we have let him go so the Yahad don't start asking their invasive questions. There is still the trial, after all. And no witnesses to take the stand. Meanwhile, you have the loyalty of your fellow Ozmins, your uncle doesn't. He has betrayed his religion. You have embraced it. The saints are on your side . . . for now."

The soft finger slid down her cheek again, this time, not as gentle. A knuckle pressed into the swelling. Malka cried out.

"Prince Evžen, it seems our guest is awake."

When she opened her eyes, she stiffened. They were in the same room where Malka had earlier eavesdropped. She was sprawled on the velvet sofa. The prince leaned against his wooden desk, facing her. Malka blinked against the brightness of the chandelier above them. The flames danced across her vision and nausea climbed up her throat. From the rooting spell or the guard's kick, she didn't know. Didn't make a difference.

"If she gets sick on my carpet, Sévren, I will personally put her head on a spike."

"Settle, my boy. Let me speak with her." Sévren inched toward her, the way one would approach a wild dog. "This is Prince Evžen, son of Valski, and I am Archbishop Sévren, though something tells me you know us already."

He smiled like a long-haired mazik cat, a creature from one of Imma's stories. At night, they crawled out from the woods into the village. They jumped from house to house, scratching at doors until finally a family lamented and tossed them a chicken bone. They settled the meat between their teeth and grizzled it down before swallowing the bone whole. When they were full, their mouths curved up in a human-like smile and their cheeks puffed in a gloat. For once you fed a mazik cat, it could slip inside your home and gorge itself to its heart's content.

What would Sévren gorge on if she opened the door and answered his questions? Nothing good. She stayed quiet.

"Do you know what we do to those who betray the Ordobav Kingdom?" Prince Evžen chimed in. "We behead them, mostly. Or tear them limb from limb and feed them to our cannons, so that their ashes may light the night sky with their disgrace."

What was another threat to add to her pile? Malka scoffed.

The prince raised his brow. "Please, speak your mind."

"Why?" Malka responded. "So you can feed me to the cannons?"

With the flash of his red robe, gold glinting from his rounded cuffs, Sévren slipped behind Prince Evžen, resting his jeweled hand on Evžen's shoulder. It was almost a loving act, if his thumb hadn't whitened as it pressed into the divot between bone.

Malka had been on the receiving end of that stern grip too many times not to notice the way Evžen straightened under it, tilting his chin high. But he could not hide his tension. It bared itself in the bulging veins at his neck and in the clench of his jaw.

Sévren spoke. "I see the guard's kick didn't break your sense of humor. Perhaps we should have him give it another try and see what breaks next."

Her face throbbed, and she involuntarily lifted her hand to trace the inflamed skin of her cheek. "I didn't betray Ordobav. It was you, Your Grace, who spread the lie of the Maharal's illness to keep him imprisoned and suffering against Ordobavian law. I saw his hands. I know what that means for a man like him."

"Ah, yes, the magic your people hold so near and dear. Tell me, is that how you freed the Maharal? Did you bring those treasonous words to life? Perhaps you can see why we made such a . . . precaution. A legal one, I assure you, once Valski's lords see the true cost of your magic."

Malka's failure to call Kefesh forth tugged at her chest. She clenched her teeth, desperate to bury the feeling before it overcame her. "A precaution for what?"

"You're a curious scullery maid," Evžen's lips twitched in a sly smile.

"Too curious, some would say," Sévren agreed. "Take a walk with me, child, for there is something you might wish to see."

The prince exchanged a look with the archbishop, though Malka could not read what passed between them.

Sévren headed to the door, clasped hands curling behind his back. "Well, come on."

Malka feared what game the archbishop wished to play with her.

"I can't walk," Malka said, and it was hardly a lie. Her leg vibrated with pain from the guard's kick.

Sévren raised his brow. "Find a way, or you will lose both your legs the way your venerable rabbi lost his hands."

Fear constricted Malka's throat. Gently, she swung her legs off the couch, wincing as the blood rushed back to them.

"Don't forget your place," Evžen intoned, straightening to emphasize the full breadth of his grandeur. "Bow to your prince."

The prince's cheeks were rosy, his golden eyes foxlike as he stared. When he crossed his arms, the jewels adorning him glinted in a radiant flurry. Malka wondered what he would be like stripped out of his gems and dress, like any other man hunting for more power than he already held.

His eyes flickered to Sévren, and Malka knew he would not ask again. The command was a threat to her, but a show of power to Sévren. *For Sévren.* Malka recalled what the archbishop had said earlier in this same room, about Ordobav's opinion of Evžen, and how it would dwindle each day unless . . . but Malka had not heard what followed.

Malka bowed dramatically, the way Chaia would if she were in Malka's place. The skirts of her scullery maid uniform brushed the floor, puddling around her as she exaggerated her bow.

When she caught Evžen's eyes again, they had darkened and whatever smile he had worn was gone.

Sévren led her down the hallway, guards in tow. They hovered behind, but their shadows swallowed her on the stone floor.

Each step was an exercise in placating the angry whirl of her stomach; of grasping onto anything that would help her stay grounded. The violent nature of the rooting spell made Malka wonder: if the guard's iron foot had caved in her skull and she had died, would Nimrah be freed from this unmooring sickness, or would it forever haunt her? That is, if this connection plagued Nimrah the way it did Malka. The golem had yet to admit any effect it had on her.

Sévren's guards opened the doors to the palace's main entrance, which led out to the castle courtyard. As the overcast day spilled gray into the foyer, Malka blinked rapidly to adjust to the light. The cold struck her, her cloak still hung up on one of the kitchen's hooks. Ahead, there were dozens of people circled around something Malka couldn't see. As she and Sévren descended the steps, the crowd parted, revealing the spectacle.

She brought a hand to her mouth. In the center of the courtyard, a man was splayed naked on a table. He was bound by his hands and feet but did not try to free himself. He was still, save for his rapid breathing that betrayed him. Naked, there was no hiding the way his chest rose and deflated in visceral heaves.

His body was flushed an angry red, swollen, and marred by painful blisters, some oozing white-yellow pus. It was then that Malka noticed a large cauldron off to the side, steam wafting from it in ferocious waves, positioned under a hook and pulley system.

A trail of water led from the cauldron to the table. They had boiled him alive yet spared him death. What did that mean for him now?

"Come, girl. Let's see the consequences of your actions."

Powerless. Just as she was when Kefesh did not come to her beckoning. She had no choice but to follow.

Up close, Malka recognized the man as the knight who had allowed her and Chaia into the royal palace. A new wave of nausea seized her, one not due to the rooting spell.

Sévren nodded in greeting to a brawny, balding man with a barely-there nose—it had been flattened into his face, his nostrils opaque with old blood. A scar from bad stitchwork crawled up the bridge of his nose. Malka wondered where he had obtained such an injury. He was dressed in nothing special, only a plain colored tunic and trousers which anonymized him. He held in his hand a curved knife. Malka's heart pounded as she watched him fix his grasp on the hilt.

"Does she look familiar to you?" Sévren asked the guard disdainfully.

She would never forget the fierce hatred in his eyes as the knight stared at her. She was the sole cause of his strife; it did not matter if the command for his punishment was given by someone else, if another pair of hands bound him. To him, his humiliation was Malka's fault alone. "She lied to me," he spat. More a lament than an excuse. He had been deceived by a maid, and now the Maharal was free.

What a dishonorable end for an Ozmini knight.

"You may begin," Sévren said to the bald man.

The man grinned, revealing his golden teeth, slick with saliva. It clicked, then, who he was. Amnon's brother had told her about them. Revaç. A group of people who traded assassinations for golden teeth and wore them as a symbol of their pride and status. To join the Revaç, a person was beaten close to death, until every one of their teeth had fallen out. If they survived, they were trained as highly skilled torturers. It was every Revaç's goal to fill their mouth with as many golden teeth as their gums would allow. Older and highly revered Revaç had two or three layers of teeth cresting their gums. Malka recalled a particular story Amnon's brother had mentioned, of a Revaç who underpaid for a golden tooth stitching, and the next day it fell from his gum and choked him to death.

Malka counted this man's golden teeth. A full set, which he gladly showed off when he noticed Malka's interest.

The Revaç seized the guard's naked thigh in his hand, and glided the blade along his skin, pressing deep with his thumb until the skin peeled back in a single layer, revealing the pink of the guard's muscle, slick with blood and fat. The knife slid easily through the flesh, softened from the boiling.

Malka tried to turn away, but Sévren's hands gripped her head hard, keeping her eyes spread open wide with a tug of his fingers. She watched as the guard's skin stripped away, first on his legs, then his abdomen, until they flipped him over and flayed the skin from his buttocks and back.

His screams were so loud, Malka desperately wished to put her hands to her ears, but they were blocked by Sévren's arms. Her eyes burned as Sévren held them open, tears jerking their way down her cheeks and into her mouth. Their salty taste in the blood-soaked air made her stomach beg release.

Malka had thought Mavetéh's terrors surpassed anything man could conjure, but they paled in comparison to this. Now, the guard was more monster than man as his throat swelled from overuse and his heart gave out in shock. He lolled in unconsciousness, yet the Revaç continued.

When the gatekeeper's body was all angry blood-soaked muscle and fatty tissue, the Revaç handed his discarded skin to a guard who attached it to the courtyard flagpole and raised it until the wind stretched out his body like a bearskin rug. Blood dripped from it, splattering onto the stone, and decorating the ground in flecks of red.

Sévren faced the crowd, whose faces paled from the spectacle.

"Great people of Ordobav," he began. "Beware those who wish our great kingdom harm and take solace knowing how we treat those who betray us."

When he finished his speech, Sévren shifted his focus upward, where Evžen watched from a balcony, his hands white around the railings. As much as this was a punishment for Malka, it was a taunt for Evžen, too. *Command your power,* he was saying. *Or I will.*

"What a show," said a familiar smoky voice.

From the back of the crowd, a tall, cloaked figure emerged. But Malka needed no confirmation of who it was—her dizziness had subsided, the cloying heat returned.

One stone hand lifted the hood of the cloak.

Whispers trickled through the crowd as they stared at Nimrah, some in horror, some in shock. Some stepped backward, tripping each other as they scrambled away from her.

There was no hiding her return to Valón now.

Sévren released his hands from Malka's face, and she blinked until the burning in her eyes subsided. She wiped at her tears and snot with her sleeve.

He inclined his chin, though surprise flickered in his eyes. "Back from the dead?"

"Turns out, I'm not so easily killed, Your Grace." Nimrah dug inside her cloak pocket, revealing a pale piece of folded parchment between her fingers. "I have a note for you. I wrote it at the request of the Maharal, who would have written it himself had he not lost his hands under your . . .

delicate care. He is healing well, and requests that King Valski give permission to the courts to reinstate his trial while he recovers at home, as per Ordobavian law."

Sévren studied the crowd, who watched him expectantly. The Maharal was a legend to the Yahad, but he was also well-known to the Ozmins. Some feared him, some respected him, some hated him. But all were witnesses now to what the archbishop would do.

"Of course," Sévren said, but his lips thinned.

As Nimrah approached, she did not acknowledge Malka, eyes trained only on the archbishop.

"Your Grace," Nimrah began as Sévren snatched the letter from her.

Sévren examined it closely. "Are you sure the Maharal is well enough to begin his trial again? If he is not even able to deliver his request to me himself, perhaps he is a liar. Perhaps we should add that to his list of crimes, as well."

"He's only following the law, Your Grace, as he is confined to the Yahadi Quarter until his trial."

Sévren's jaw tightened.

Nimrah shrugged. "If you do not believe in the state of his health, you are more than welcome to come to the Yahadi Quarter for the wedding he will officiate tomorrow."

"A wedding," Sévren raised his hand and placed it on Malka's shoulder, the same way he had done with Evžen before. She resisted the urge to turn and see if the prince still lingered on the balustrade. "How lovely."

"Yes," Nimrah said, and her eyes betrayed her, slipping to the injury on Malka's cheek. She could only imagine how horrible it appeared, swollen and flushed like the bleeding woolflower plant Chaia's mother squeezed for dye.

Knowing flickered across Sévren's face. "Ah, I understand now, what you truly want. What you left behind."

Nimrah had revealed herself to Sévren and Valón for Malka's sake. Anyone could've brought that letter, but it was Nimrah who stood there. Nimrah who stared at the archbishop, unflinching despite her lapse of vulnerability.

Nimrah motioned to the crowd. "You are well-known for your generosity."

Sévren's grip on Malka tightened. The tense smile he wore left deep folds around his mouth. Though his face held neutrality well, Malka knew his control was fading. Abba's abuse had always intensified when control slipped through his fingers. It worsened when Mavetéh became a haunted place, sweeping away his ability to hunt and making their income more reliant on the money Imma made from healing. When he could no longer make his nightly trips to the river to suck on a manta joint until the high lulled him to sleep, he became rough with Malka, tossing her around to show he had control of one thing left—his daughters.

Sévren had not expected Nimrah to come back from the dead and rescue the Maharal. He had not expected someone to rescue Malka, either. Witnessing the flaying was not the archbishop's only intended punishment for her.

Malka swallowed hard.

"Unless there is a reason why she cannot return with me?" Nimrah asked innocently.

It was a smart play. In front of the crowd, Sévren could not address Malka's crimes without admitting the condition in which he had kept the Maharal. But Sévren could still pin another crime on her, like he had done with the Maharal in the first place. He could claim he had found a bottle of Ozmini blood in her pocket, or something close to the truth, that she had killed an Ordobavian knight. Nimrah must have known it was a risk, yet played it anyway.

To her shock, Sévren accused her of nothing. Instead, he gave Malka's shoulders a firm squeeze, digging his nails in deep enough to clip her skin. When she winced, his grip only tightened, until at last, small welts of blood began to stain her white blouse. She bit back a cry, the sting of the cuts fierce against her already bruised skin. She wanted to shrug him off, wanted to yell at him to stop. But one look into Sévren's cold eyes kept her mouth screwed shut.

Malka marveled at how well he could school his features, twist them each into different puppets to master. His eyes for Malka, sharp as Abba's dagger, and just as dangerous. His smile for the crowd, warm and charismatic.

In Malka's peripheral vision, Nimrah was completely rigid, save for the sharp rise and fall of her chest.

Only when Malka bit down so hard that her lips split open and gushed red, too, did Sévren finally release his hold on her.

He would not forget this. And he made sure she wouldn't, either. Each time she stared at the red cuts on her shoulder, each time she stared at the scabs which would take their place.

"There is no reason," he said finally. "Of course."

In an instant, Nimrah was by her side, wrapping a defensive arm around her before Sévren could change his mind.

It took forever to exit the courtyard and spill back onto the street outside of the castle complex, the eyes of the crowd like darts on her back. Her shoulder pulsed, blood already coagulating and sticky under her blouse. The air was tense, and the sickening tang of the guard's flayed body still deluged her senses. Or maybe it was now the scent of her own blood.

In her mind flashed an image of the Tannin. Its bladed scales had been replaced with the sharp ovals of Sévren's fingernails. Its slit pupils with Sévren's stern knife points. Destruction was indeed coming, and Malka feared its advent.

CHAPTER 25

Cupping Malka's face between his hands, Amnon examined the gash on her cheek. His thumb traced lightly on Malka's eyelid, and her skin cried in pain. Sévren must have also scratched his fingernail there while he held her eyes open. Thinking of the guard's skinless body made her heave, but there was nothing left inside her to purge.

"Curse your bravery, Malka," he said tightly.

Malka opened her eyes. Amnon's jaw was clenched, eyebrows firmly creased.

"What happened back there?" Nimrah demanded, anger glazing her eyes. But Malka knew by now it was not anger with Malka, but herself. "You killed a man minutes before we left. I shouldn't have . . . I should have stayed. It was naive of me to leave you."

A similarity between Amnon and Nimrah she had never noticed before, this self-inflicted hate when they failed to protect.

Chaia returned with her medicinal bag then, dropping into the chair across from her. Amnon shuffled to the side so Chaia could begin her work.

"You didn't know I'd lose my ability to perform Kefesh," Malka countered.

On their way back, Malka had crowded into an empty alley and tried to command a small plant from the earth as she had done with the sprig of black perphona outside of Chaia's house, but to no avail. The tingling power no longer spread through her hands. Hours ago, she had killed a man with Kefesh. She had become so powerful, only to become powerless again. She didn't understand, for she did no motion differently. She drew the word into the ground and guided her mind to the same place of silent prayer.

At least, so she had thought.

"We'll take the Maharal's counsel once he's recovered." Nimrah began to pace, glancing back and forth, from the door to the bedroom to Malka and back again. "I . . . I need to check on him, are you alright?"

Malka stared at her. She wasn't sure if Nimrah was actually concerned, or if the pounding of her concussed head conjured up the tenderness in her voice.

"I'm fine," Malka promised. "Go."

Nimrah nodded and disappeared into the hall.

"The plan wasn't well-thought-out," Amnon said, shaking his head. "We should've . . . done more. *I* should've done more."

It was Chaia who scoffed. "Amnon, please. You know nothing about the palace. If anyone should take the blame, it is me."

"No one is to blame but Sévren and his guards," Malka said.

"I wanted to go with her to save you, Malka, but Nimrah threatened Vilém to hold me back if I tried to come."

Malka stared at Vilém's wiry frame from across the room. "What a threat."

Chaia cracked a smile. "The Maharal, he . . . needed immediate care. Though I am not as talented of a healer as you, I have done my best to clean his wounds and revive him."

"I'll take a look at him, as well," Malka agreed.

"Yes, but first, your wounds. Tell us everything we should know."

As Chaia began to clean the blood from her face, Malka recounted all that had happened.

"God, Malka." Chaia ran her hand through her hair. It jostled her soft waves. "Sévren is even more vile than I imagined he could be."

Chaia dipped a cloth into the pot of water and pressed it to Malka's inflamed skin.

Malka winced. "When Nimrah came, she brought a letter from the Maharal. Was that your idea?"

Chaia's lips upturned. "It was Amnon's, actually."

Malka raised her eyebrow in Amnon's direction. "And you said you didn't do enough when your idea saved me?"

"I'm just glad it worked," he said, cheeks flushed. "We wanted to give the archbishop as little breathing room as possible."

"It couldn't have worked better that he had already drawn a crowd," Chaia added.

Malka thought of her easy escape. "I think he may have something worse up his sleeve, and that scares me."

The admission hung between the three of them, as if it were a fawn and any slight movement would send it scurrying.

"All that matters right now is that you're safe," Amnon said finally.

After Chaia applied a salve to her wounds, Malka began a poultice for the Maharal's infection. She set a pot to boil on the stove before throwing a handful of thyme sprigs in to soften.

Kefesh had aided her healing abilities, but she wasn't nothing without the magic. She was a healer's daughter and would knead herbs into ointments and suture wounds the way she had been taught—without magic. But Malka would be lying to herself if she didn't admit how much she missed the buzz of Kefesh on her fingertips, how it cleared her head and filled her heart with its power.

She collected the dampened thyme sprigs in a bowl and a cloth for the wrapping and walked toward Chaia's room, where the Maharal rested. Through the door, so rickety it didn't close completely, Nimrah spoke in fierce whispers.

The Maharal's low grumble, voice strained from disuse, responded. His words already more coherent than they had been in the dungeon.

"You shouldn't have come back, Nimrah."

Through the door, Nimrah placed her head in her hands. "I could not live knowing they kept you like that, Rav."

He ran his shaky arms across Nimrah's hands, nudging them away from her face. "And I am grateful, but it is not safe for you here." There was such tenderness in his voice, it made Malka ache for the father she had once loved, not feared.

She stared between them—father and daughter—and understood why the Maharal had spared Nimrah when the Valonians wanted her dead.

"It will be safer now that you are free, that I am the one who helped free you. I will right my wrongs with the people of Valón," said Nimrah.

"You misunderstand, Nimrah—"

"I know you are disappointed in me." Her voice was tinged with sorrow. "You made me for one purpose, and I have failed in that. But I will not fail again. I promise you, Rav."

The Maharal slit his eyes. "What have you done, Nimrah?"

"I've made a promise, one I must keep no matter the consequences."

Malka rapped her knuckle against the door, garnering their attention. "I've brought a poultice. If you wish to apply it to him yourself, you can."

She had intended to be the one to apply the poultice, but the Maharal looked at Nimrah with so much love in his eyes that Nimrah could not see—did not wish to see. Malka was taking Nimrah from him forever and guilt stung her chest.

For Imma, she reminded herself. *For Hadar and Danya and the life they deserve.*

Nimrah clutched the bowl. "Thank you."

She said it so sincerely, Malka almost didn't believe the words were Nimrah's.

"You're welcome," Malka replied gingerly, and closed the door behind her.

⤳

In all the stories Malka had been told of Kefesh souring, none were of someone who lost their ability to perform the magic. It had always been shalkat rearranging the letters of a prayer, or rogue golems turning against their people. Weeks ago, she would've said it was for the best—that it was better the mysticism was taken from her before it could swallow her whole.

She wished she believed it still. It would make the loss satisfying, rather than bitter. Rather than feeling the strike of power at her helm and losing it when she needed it most.

She had been helpless as Sévren peeled open her eyes and forced her to watch the vile punishment; when his nails dug into her shoulder and she had to bite down her scream.

"Trouble sleeping again?" Nimrah appeared in the doorway of the kitchen, where Malka sat with a blanket wrapped around her and her knees drawn to her chest.

Malka nodded but didn't turn her stare away from the dim glow of the oven.

The chair creaked as Nimrah joined her at the table.

They sat in silence for a while, until Malka admitted, "I fear I won't ever forget the sight of that guard being flayed alive. It will be another horror that haunts me."

"I'm sorry you had to see it," Nimrah responded, and Malka finally turned to her.

It was once again strange to see the golem without her doublet and cloak. She wore one of Vilém's white linen tunics, which fit her snug around the shoulders. The front was untied, revealing Nimrah's prominent collarbones—one stone, the other flesh. Malka hated how human it made her look. How normal, like she was not a monster.

Monster. Murderer. Monster. Murderer.

Yet even the chant had grown weak in her mind, like a flickering flame clutching to the last sip of oil.

She had seen true monstrosity. It was the ease in which Sévren had a man tortured by a Revaç. The condition in which he had kept the Maharal. The lines he had carved into her skin as a threat.

And now she, too, was a murderer. She had killed that guard in the dungeon. Had caused another's torture and death. It was her deceit which had led to his punishment. Malka recalled what Chaia had said—how all actions are unpredictable, not just those made by Kefesh. In both ways, immense guilt consumed her.

"How do you live with it?" Malka asked, chin dipped low.

"With what?"

"The guilt. Of the Yahadi boy. Of all the victims Mavetéh has claimed because of your magic."

Nimrah straightened. "By making things right."

"Can you? Make things right?"

"I have to believe that I can," she responded, casting her eyes to a divot in the table. "Even if it means giving up what is most precious to me. Especially if it means that."

Her life. Traded to save Imma. To save the Maharal.

"Your last punishment."

Nimrah hummed. "May I tell you another story, Malka?"

When Malka looked up, Nimrah's eyes were on her bandaged shoulder. "What kind of story?"

"Mine. One you may have heard a version of. I prefer this one."

Malka nodded, picking at the dry flakes of skin around her fingers.

Nimrah steepled her hands. "Before I do, you must remember this: I was not made to be without the Maharal."

She began her story, the same way she had told the Maharal's in the dark.

"As you've come to learn, not all is as peaceful between the religions in Valón as the stories might say. Years ago, as Valón grew more popular with the Yahad fleeing from persecution in other kingdoms, the Yahadi Quarter began to grow and thrive. Even Ozmins settled here, able to own their own houses, as well as their neighbor's. But with Yahadi prosperity came Ozmini fear, and tensions thickened. Desperate to remove their competition, they began to contrive ways to beat the Yahad down. Ozmini peasants would dig up their own children from graves and hide them in the attics of Yahadi households. There was no trial with evidence as clear as that, and the Yahad were jailed.

"It is for this reason I was created. The Maharal birthed me from stone and clay to be a protector—to fight injustice with just violence. The Ozmini peasants began to fear me and the magic I wielded, how I would shape the earth together to fight against oppression. I would patrol the streets at night in his shadow, and together we would look out for the Yahad in Valón."

"It sounds like you were a force for good," Malka said. It was what she had surmised from Nimrah's last story, how her existence brought a lull to Yahadi blood curse accusations. "Until Kefesh corrupted you."

Nimrah shook her head. "You still don't understand. I *was* a force for good. Until the Maharal left. He was called away to consult with the religious council in Lei for some issues related to the papacy. He untied my shadow for the first time cautiously, said I should keep to myself while he was gone.

"And I did, for a while. He knew that tensions in the Yahadi Quarter were high, and misuse of me would end in trouble. I lived in the attic of the shul Bachta, and I stayed there. I watched the sun rise and fall from the hazy window and paced across the floor with the low rumble of services down below.

"One night, I heard a grueling scream from the street outside. I paced, counting the creaking panels under my feet. It was the first time I debated disobeying the Maharal's orders. You don't understand what it was like, to teeter on the edge of betraying your master to fulfill the sole duty for which you were created—to break the faith of the one who granted you life. But this need to help... it tore at my skin. Made me dig my nails into the wooden beams until they bled. I was not made to be a bystander."

Nimrah's voice was as jagged as belladonna leaves, and Malka gripped the pendant around her neck, turning each point into her thumb.

"Heart ruling over my head, I rushed out through the window, breaking the glass. I used the ivy wrapped around the stone as a ladder. It was the day before the Sabbath, and the streets were busy with preparations.

"Even among the busy streets, I was noticed. Stares would heat my back, eyes would dart when I looked, children would gape and hide behind their parent's legs. I was a weapon—something both used for protection and violence.

"A small group of people were huddled by a house in the center of the Yahadi Quarter. As I approached, I recognized the home as Basám's, one of the Yahadi economic advisors to King Valski, where he lived with his small family.

"'What is happening here?' I asked.

"It was a small girl who answered, no more than eight or nine. She said, 'Three knights stormed in.'

"'Rode their horses down the path with enough fervor for battle,' the girl's mother continued. 'They said Basám has stolen from the treasury! Can you believe such a claim? That man would not keep a penny more than was his due.'

"I bent down to the girl, whose eyes widened. 'Was it you who screamed?'

"The little girl blushed. 'I could not help it. Their horses were so frightening, and they were yelling.'

"I pinched her cheek. 'Do not worry, I will do as I am made to do.'

"That was my saying, how I would drench fears until they sizzled out, how I would be the light in a dark room for them to follow. It only took saying those words, and people would relax.

"And as I said those words, the woman's clenched shoulders eased, and relief softened the girl's face. A fat raindrop had fallen, landing like a tear on her cheek. She wiped it away with the back of her fist.

"The clouds had flushed deep. Rain was coming.

"'Stay beneath the awning,' I said to them. 'It is about to pour.'

"With that, I went into the house. As you know, they're small and cramped in the Yahadi Quarter, like the gap between piled stones. Two or more families live in each building, dividing the space by floors. I knew Basám had lived on the top floor, for he played the flute terribly from the second story window facing the street.

"The ceiling creaked above me, and I leaned near the stairs to catch the sound of their voices.

"'Count them again,' I had heard, the voice strong and resolute.

"'I have counted them three times, *Ctihodný*.' It was Basám who spoke, voice wobbly.

"'And you will count them four.'

"I crept up the stairs, my hand trailing against the wall. The clay stretched and sighed, awakening under my touch.

"'This matter does not concern my children,' Basám said. 'I will count the coins again for you, but I implore you to let them return to their room.'

"'Ah, Basám, I think it's a good lesson for them to see what happens when you embezzle from the king.'

"'Perhaps it is an even more thoughtful lesson to learn when a man is innocent,' I said, finally entering the room.

"Basám sat at a small table, a knight leaning close. His wife and kids huddled against a corner on the opposite side of the room by the front window, guarded by another knight.

"'So, the golem appears,' the knight closest to Basám said, 'just as the songs say.' His eyes were soaked with repulsive scrutiny. 'The stories we tell in the barracks do not do you justice. You are truly more of an abomination than I could have imagined.'

"'What is your business here, *Ctihodný*?'

"'The king paid for new textiles from the Balkisk Kingdom to celebrate Prince Evžen's coming of age celebration. He had only discussed the trade among his advisors, given the delicacy of Valón and Balkisk's relations.' The knight turned toward Basám. 'So, you can imagine the shock when the Balkisk King sent back half-finished tapestries to Valón, citing that if his kingdom is only being paid for half the work, Valón should be happy with half the product.'

"'And you are questioning all of King Valski's advisors?' I stepped closer. 'Tell me, *Ctihodný*, will you question the runner boys who carried their correspondence, as well? How about the treasurers who counted out the coin? Or perhaps the noble who carried the payment in his pouch on the journey there?'

"'We will question who needs to be questioned, and that is up for the king to decide.'

"'So, the king is aware you're questioning his trusted advisors? Or tell me, is Basám the only advisor you are questioning? And it is only coincidence, of course, that he is the king's only Yahadi advisor.'

"The knight clenched his fists. 'Remember your place, golem. Leave now with your insubordinate tongue and let us carry on with our business.'

"They always underestimated me. The Maharal had once said he created me to look like a woman because he knew men would misjudge what I could do, and I'd always have the upper hand.

"'I will leave when you admit your bias,' I said to him.

"'Enough,' the knight said.

"'Yes, enough of this, *Ctihodný*.' I bent down, holding my hand against the floor paneling. The wood creaked as it stretched, bending to my touch. At my command, the wood undulated toward the knight, rattling him from his feet. The knight's trained footwork was not enough to keep him upright, and he landed hard against the ground, metal hitting wood in a clanking thud. But *planks* of wood . . . they are not as effortlessly controlled as vines or branches straight from the earth. They are bulky, unbending."

Nimrah traced her finger along her stone cheek. Her eyes were far away. She was lost in the story.

"The wood also shook the chair on which Basám sat, and the ground under which his children and wife stood. They, too, fell to the ground. Basám hit his head hard against the wood, and his children fell in a heap on top of each other.

"I could not risk commanding the wood any longer, so instead I called a vine from outside to cut the children loose from their rope bindings. It burst through the window, and shards of glass flew through the air like snowflakes. The vines sliced through the rope and freed all his children, except for the youngest. He was merely six and swatted at the vine as it came toward him, and as hard as I tried, I could not pull it loose. It had caught on the rope around his wrists, and he had tangled it around his neck in an attempt to escape.

"He stumbled back, until he tipped himself through the broken window. Dragged down by his weight, the vine became a noose. Gasps and screams echoed outside, and I knew I had killed him.

"He mimicked a rag doll, hanging there. A child. A Yahadi child. I was meant to protect them and instead I . . ." she drifted off, clenching her fists. "I will never forget the looks the Yahadi people gave me that night. Dread, horror, and disgust. The last thing I saw before I turned away was Basám falling to his knees in front of the house, hands covering his eyes. Through the same window he had played his flute, I made him see his child hanged.

"I did not leave the temple attic for days after that. Not until the Maharal returned. He could not look at me, and I couldn't blame him. That's when he brought me into the woods and told me my job was done."

Nimrah's throat bobbed as her story finished. She cast down her eyes until the shadow of the lantern swallowed the stone of her face into darkness, and she looked distinctly and invariably human.

Malka trembled.

Nimrah's story was not the same as the ones she had been told. In them, Basám's son did not die on accident. Nimrah did not go to the house to save anyone. She went to kill.

"Why would you tell me this?"

"I know I will always be the monster you hate. But if you're going to hate me, you might as well hate me knowing the truth. Choose to believe it, or not, it doesn't matter. Now you know."

She waited for the chant in her head to come. *Monster. Murderer. Monster. Murderer.*

But her mind was cursedly, undeniably silent.

CHAPTER 26

News of the Maharal's temporary freedom traveled around Valón like a flame on linseed oil. The excitement had heightened now that the Maharal was to make his public appearance during today's wedding ceremony. Last-minute preparations were in full swing, house abuzz with excitement as dozens of people busied themselves with their tasks.

Malka fanned herself with a damp cloth. Though a chill doused the air, the packed house and burning stove made it warm. The cholent, a rich stew with fatty beef, beans, potatoes, and onions, had been cooking all day. It simmered low and filled the room with a salty and hearty scent.

Malka danced her way outside, dodging people until the crisp air hit her face and she breathed in smoke from overworked chimneys, as the whole Yahadi Quarter prepared for the day's wedding.

Tomorrow, they'd head back to Eskravé. It felt unreal to say, as if the possibility had only been in her dreams. It had been two weeks since she left. Two weeks could break many in captivity, but not Imma.

Soon, I'll be home, she said to Imma, as if her thoughts could reach her mother. *Just a little longer.*

Malka pressed her back against the wall. It briefly stung as the stone aggravated her wound, but the coolness it offered was a balm. She thought of Nimrah's story last night, how different it had been from the version of events Malka knew. It was hard not to think of the similarities between them now. Malka, doing what she thought was best and freeing the Maharal from imprisonment, only to watch an innocent man tortured and killed because of her deceit. Nimrah, attempting to protect the Yahad, and killing one instead.

It didn't matter. It couldn't. Not when she was so close. She had done the impossible, but success didn't relieve her as much as she had expected.

Something gnawed at her, but she chalked it up to the anxiety about the journey home. The magister had promised them passage, and Chaia trusted him. That was enough.

"Quite different from the preparation for your wedding ceremonies in Eskravé, I'd imagine."

The Maharal appeared in front of her, cradling a book in the crook of his elbow.

"Peace and light, Rav, I didn't expect to see you here." Malka realized how little she and the Maharal had spoken directly since his rescue. Even as he recovered, the Maharal was a busy man.

The rabbi chuckled. "Peace and light, Malka."

He appeared every bit the legend now. His robes, blue as winter dusk, swept the ground. The white, rectangular woolen mantle of his tallit rested across his shoulders, tassels dangling at each corner. His tall hat matched his robes, and stood out impressively against the pale blue sky, made even paler by the press of gray clouds. Malka hardly recognized him as the man they had rescued from the dungeon. Nimrah must've aided him with the Kefesh-laced healing tonics.

"It's time to bring Vilém and his entourage to the shul for the service. It's a bit untraditional for me to escort him, I will admit, but it would be an honor."

"It's kind of you to officiate their wedding."

"As I would for any Yahad getting married. Plus, Chaia has been a gift to the Qehillah. I only regret my absence the last six months."

Malka bit her lip. If she let herself, she could get lost thinking of the entire other life Chaia had made while Malka mourned her.

Chaia may have been alive, but Malka would still lose her if Chaia stayed in Valón. Malka's life belonged to Eskravé; she couldn't leave it.

A new grief to replace the old.

"She spoke of you, Malka. Endlessly," said the Maharal, raising his bushy eyebrows softly. "I know it's not the same, but she mourned the loss of you, too. And at the same time, had to deal with her anger. Mostly at herself, for leaving you and her family behind."

"You taught her Kefesh." It came out accusingly, though Malka hadn't meant it to sound as such.

"I told her there was a way she could hold prayer in her hands, and helped her shape the words, yes."

"Before I stepped into Mavetéh, Kefesh was mythic, performed in secret—something I only heard about in stories, in folklore that told us we would tangle too close with Yohev if we tried to command it. We had only been told of its destruction." She peered through the window into the house, and caught Nimrah's back in the crowd of people, her doublet glinting in the dim light. "And she encouraged me to use it for myself."

The Maharal followed her gaze. "And you healed Amnon with Kefesh."

"Did she tell you?"

"No, but I know the power of Mavetéh's creatures. I know the taste of Kefesh, like copper and spice, and feel it on my tongue whenever I'm around him. Nimrah has not been commanded to heal like that, so it must've been you."

"I did my best, but he may never return to his full health. Your golem said that the sickness might have seeped too deep into his bones to reverse by magic."

"Such is the curse of men, to be able to create life, but not always save it." The rabbi's eyes grew distant.

"Just as you created the golem."

He blinked hard, and the smile returned to his face. "Yes."

Nimrah's interpretation of her story flickered in her mind, then the memory of the Maharal's soft touch on Nimrah's cheek.

"You love her," she said. "In a way you had not expected."

The Maharal gave her a sad smile. "Deeply."

"That's why you didn't kill her, isn't it?"

"That is part of the reason." He tilted his chin up and sighed. "May I share something with you, Malka?"

"Of course."

"There is an immutable rule of Kefesh. Anyone who kills life made with holy magic will be destroyed with it."

Malka's mind began to race. This new knowledge, altering her perceptions.

She could say that for so many things since she left. Since she met Nimrah. What would the consequences be if an Ozmini executioner died alongside Nimrah?

Malka's gut clenched, bothered both by the implications of another way the Church could blame the Yahad for an Ozmini death and something else she couldn't place. Something that would frighten her if she gave voice to it.

Her mind drifted to the confessional. It had become akin to the rooting, an ever present, biting heat that wouldn't leave her.

She wondered what the Maharal had thought of their deal. *I've made a promise, one I must keep no matter the consequences.* She had not stayed to hear his response after handing Nimrah the poultice.

"Does she know this?"

The Maharal shook his head. "I didn't want her to carry the burden of this knowledge. And I'd prefer to keep it that way, you understand."

"Why tell me now?"

"It is good for someone else close to her to know, in case something happens to me again."

She didn't know what to make of any of this as silence passed between them.

"Nimrah tells me you wished to speak with me about something," he said.

Malka appreciated the change in subject. She dug her shoe into the dirt, recalling how she had commanded Kefesh from this spot, sprouting black perphona like it was nothing. Knowing she could not draw the same life from the earth anymore made her throat tight. How quickly she had become used to Kefesh and holding its magic between her fingertips.

"My ability to command Kefesh was there one minute and gone the next. By the dungeon gate, I killed a man with pelting rocks. When the golem left with you, I could no longer draw power from the earth."

The Maharal considered this. "Kefesh is a tricky thing. It's not a science, nor is it something that can be fully understood by anyone but Yohev. If you choose to return to Valón at any point, I'd be more than happy to work with you and try to call the magic back."

Malka gave a half-hearted smile, knowing she wouldn't.

"Speaking of Nimrah, I've noticed you refuse to speak her given name," the Maharal said. "May I ask why?"

Monster. Murderer. Rayga. Golem. She had dredged up other names as a shield. Names which befit Nimrah's looming fate and would ease her guilt.

She swallowed thickly. "It's for the best we keep a distance between us."

"I see." His mind was far away again. "Do you know the Game of the Foxwit, Malka?"

Malka scrunched her brows. The Game of the Foxwit was a child's game she used to play, where all but one of the players would hide in the woods, behind bulky tree trunks and in the bunchy growth of the underbrush, scattered on the edge of Kratzka Šujana in the best hiding places they could find. The chosen child, who was last to run into the woods, was given the name of the Foxwit, and would search for their hiding friends. They would listen to the wind, focus on flashes of shadow, until they found one of the hiding spots. If the found player wanted, they could whisper in the Foxwit's ear, and reveal where the other players hid. After, the Foxwit would decide to take the player's word or scatter their advice in the wind. For if the Foxwit searched in the places the player whispered and it was deception, the Foxwit would lose the game.

"I know it," Malka said, a question lingering on the upturn of her response.

"And did you ever play?"

"Yes, as all children in Eskravé once did." Malka had vivid memories of Amnon and Chaia, who would race so quickly into Kratzka Šujana that Malka never had a chance to be anything else but the Foxwit. Only when Amnon sprained his ankle and could not sprint as fast did she finally get to hide. But she did not have much practice hiding in the woods, and Amnon soon discovered her. She had tried her hand at deception, pointing to a nearby tree and whispering Chaia's hiding spot within the tangle of branches. Amnon had blushed and searched the tree for Chaia. Of course, she was not there, and he had lost.

"It's a fine game," said the Maharal. "Made even finer by the lessons it teaches us. Of whom to believe, and who gains the most from deceit."

So, Nimrah had told the Maharal about their deal. She understood his warning, of the dangers of trusting someone like Father Brożek. But it hadn't mattered. Any alternative to the deal they had struck was inconceivable. It mattered not how cunning the priest, or how she would fare in the Foxwit's shoes, guessing at who to believe, and who held trickery in their eyes. She would do anything to keep her family safe, even if it meant letting the golem's fate lie with the priest. Even if it meant turning away whenever Nimrah's eyes met hers and forgetting all about that moment in the confessional box.

"Malka," Amnon called, peering out the door. "Chaia is asking for you."

"Go," the Maharal agreed. "It's time for me to return with Vilém anyhow. Come and see me before you leave, will you? Even if you choose to leave Valón. There is a gift I would like to give you."

Weeks ago, she couldn't have fathomed this—the Maharal before her, Chaia alive and nearly wedded. She nodded to the rabbi, though somewhat distractedly, and followed Amnon back into the house.

"Amnon?"

He leaned on his cane. "Yes, Malka?"

"Do you remember the game we used to play, the Game of the Foxwit?"

He chuckled. "Of course."

Malka tugged her arms across her chest. "Was I easy to deceive as the Foxwit?"

Amnon hesitated and ruffled a hand through his curls. He always did that when the truth was hard for him to divulge. It was the same motion he had made when Malka asked for more time to think about his proposal. When she asked if he thought his father was proud of him and the man he had become.

Malka had her answer.

⁂

Chaia was more beautiful than Malka had ever seen her. More grown up, too. A year had changed so much, and Chaia in her traditional Yahadi wedding attire—an ornate white sargenes—revealed the leap of time in ways that words could not.

"You look lovely," Malka said as she entered into the private room. Chaia stopped fussing with her headdress and broke into a smile.

"Peace and light, Malka. So do you."

Malka had borrowed one of Chaia's more ornate kroje for the occasion: a crimson embroidered apron wrapped delicately across her layers of ruffled petticoats. Atop her blouse, a brocade vest fastened with bright ribbon.

"Can you believe this? Me, getting married. To an Ozmini man, no less!"

"Always leave it to you to break tradition." Malka bundled the bottom of the headdress in her hands, readjusting it to cascade around Chaia's face.

Chaia bit her lip and glimpsed out the window. "I miss my parents, Malka. Here I am getting married, and they think I am dead."

"They love you, Chaia. That I can promise."

"I will come home to visit," Chaia assured her. "Once it's safer. Once the duke sits on the throne. Vilém has always wanted to see Eskravé."

Malka shook her head in disbelief. "You speak so casually of having to distance yourself from those you love for fear of the Church's retribution. Doesn't it scare you?"

"They wish." Chaia tugged fervently at Malka's hand. "They don't want us to feel powerful, Malka. They want us scared, like they are. They want to have the upper hand. Do you know what it means that the Maharal's trial will be reinstated, and days after he reappeared in the Yahadi Quarter from Valón Castle, he's officiating a wedding between a Yahad and an Ozmin?"

"So, you and Vilém are marrying as what, a political statement?"

"Malka, I truly love Vilém. But we aren't naive. We know what this marriage means, what the union between us represents."

Malka released her hand. "So, you plan to sleep with one eye open, forever watching your back in case, what, Sévren has another vision sent from Triorzay that your marriage must be dissolved at all costs? They planted a vial filled with a woman's blood in the Maharal's basement. What do you think they will do to you?"

Chaia straightened. "I will live with Vilém in our happy marriage. I'll continue to help with the Qehillah until . . ." Her voice trailed off.

"Until what, Chaia?" She lowered her voice. "Until Duke Sigmund is able to take control?"

"It's more than that, Malka," Chaia replied. "You know how influential Sévren has been in Ordobav, even outside the main roles of the Church. He is a trusted confidante. Even if people are losing trust with King Valski, they still see the archbishop as a beacon of strength. Like Vilém said, Duke Sigmund's dislike of the papal role in the state is more practical than it is political. If someone like Sévren were to start whispering ideas in his ear, there's no way to know which way the duke will eventually sway. Something has to be done to prevent that future."

The realization hit Malka hard. "You plan to kill Sévren?"

"It's been in the works for some time—before the Maharal was imprisoned. The duke has promised to divert any investigation into the archbishop's death if it means he can finally become King of Ordobav and oust his brother from power."

"He could become a martyr."

"Not if he doesn't die for a cause. If he is killed quietly, his death will be viewed as natural. He is an aging man."

"And how exactly do you plan to do this?"

Chaia picked at her nails, shifting her weight between her feet.

A woman bustled through the door before Malka could press for answers.

"It's time!" she shouted. "We must make our way to the synagogue!"

Chaia sagged in relief, but she shot Malka an apologetic look.

This conversation wasn't over, but Malka would set it aside for now. A marriage was no small thing. To see her best friend married to a kind man was to celebrate a moment of intense joy in a life full of suffering and hardship.

She squeezed Chaia's hand and did something Malka thought long lost to her—followed by an entourage of the guests, she led her best friend from her house and through the streets of the Yahadi Quarter, where people cheered and clanged metal pots together in celebration, to the doors of the shul Bachta, which stood imposing in front of them.

Malka stepped inside the synagogue for the first time, her arm wrapped in Amnon's. It made her eyes glassy to be in a building of faith again. *Her* faith. She breathed in the patchouli and frankincense and stared at the transverse arches which hung over them like a second sky. The stone walls tossed around the chattering of the audience like a melody over the lofty ceilings. Chandeliers hung low, pressing their light into even the tightest corners. It was so warm, and Chaia gleamed under their orange glow.

Malka's heart ached at the sight, and everything else fell away. She focused on this moment of joy, on the glimmering sunlight that fell through the windows and sparkled on the glass around them. She focused on Chaia's soft eyes, and the way Vilém smiled dotingly at his bride.

The guests took their places as Chaia and Vilém gathered under the chuppah, adorned with an embroidered cloth, and decorated with vivid green oak leaf and reddened smoke bush. The Maharal stood behind them, and Malka let his prayers seep into her bones, like the warmest sheepskin in the coldest winter.

In an unwilling moment, Malka broke her attention from Chaia and Vilém's union to find Nimrah in the crowd. She was easy to spot, her hair unwrapped and sprawling, her stature tall and imposing. Nimrah's eyes were already on her. They stood on opposite sides of the synagogue, but the distance between them felt negligible when their connection persisted in this heady awareness. She had blamed this hunger on the rooting spell back in the confessional box. But she knew better. The spell wasn't like this when they were near—longing, desperate to be sated. It was already full. Gorged. This was something wholly different.

The Maharal was free, the rooting no longer necessary. But neither of them had mentioned it since their return. She'd been distracted, she reasoned. Maybe a bit afraid, too.

It was easier to blame her feelings on a spell of Kefesh.

Her legs were heavy, and heat crawled up Malka's neck as Nimrah's mouth parted. She remembered the warmth of Nimrah's breath on her cheek, sweet like salted dates and plum wine. The touch of Nimrah's hand on her hip so intoxicating, it lingered there still.

Slowly, without thinking, Malka dragged her hand to her side, and traced the spot where Nimrah had caressed. Nimrah's eyes followed the motion. She swallowed hard, tightening her jaw with a sturdy clench.

It was too easy to think of Nimrah differently after hearing her side of the story.

There's no space for desire between us, Malka reminded herself. Whatever they felt, it had to sour like underripe fruit. Malka couldn't stand to think of what would become of Nimrah after Father Brożek punished her, how insurmountable her own guilt would become if anything but hate budded between them.

Malka tore her gaze away, focusing instead on the ring that Vilém held out. It glittered, the gold shining in its triangular shape. Yahadi rings were not made of gems, but of copper or gold welded into the shape of something familiar to the couple—a house, a place, or even an object. This ring was shaped like their house, and decorated intricately with red pigment, which wove around the shapes of their names in gold like leaves on a vine. It was beautiful, yet simple as far as Yahadi wedding rings went. It suited them.

Her skin prickled, and Malka sensed Nimrah's eyes on her again. She didn't dare confirm it. She only watched as Vilém slipped the ring onto Chaia's finger, and smiled as they solidified their union in this beautiful synagogue with a legendary rabbi, with stars twinkling in their eyes and blushes warming their cheeks. Vilém shattered the glass bottle beneath his feet, and the congregation sang.

CHAPTER 27

The hearty scent of braised beef and smoke blanketed the air as torches lit the square where Vilém and Chaia held their celebration. Musicians gathered on the middle platform and tapped their feet to the melody of songs Malka knew by heart. The vibrato of violins and soft timbre of the drums echoed vibrantly. People gathered around the musicians and swayed to the beat. Plates filled with salted fish and tzimmes, and the savory scent of chicken soup, heavy with fat and salt, made Malka's mouth water. The koilitch was twice the normal size for the celebration, and it was passed around, each person tearing a piece from the bread.

The sweet fragrance of apple pirushkes, honey cakes, and baked lokshen kugels danced together. Malka drifted toward the tables spilling over with food and piled her plate with the sweet treats.

Malka had never attended a wedding outside of Eskravé, and none so extravagant. Dim lanterns lined the square, flickering like fireflies amidst the hum of celebration. Hadar would love the lights and the dancing. Her eyes would widen at every delicacy laid out in front of her, having rarely experienced sweets due to the rationing of sugar since her toddler years. Malka nabbed an extra pirushke in her sister's honor. When she tore a portion from the braided bread handed to her, she thought of Imma. How she'd always make sure Malka had a big piece from the bread passed around at shul services. These small acts made her feel less alone. Like her family was there, guiding her.

She didn't have Imma's bravery, Danya's stubbornness, or Hadar's optimism. But she was not helpless, either. She had rescued the Maharal and stood up to the archbishop, all while learning the magic of her people and holding its power in the palm of her hand.

"You always did love those honey cakes."

Mouth full of cake, Malka blushed. Amnon sat beside her on the bench, leaning his cane between the divots in the wood. It was a beautiful cane Vilém had bought from a local wood carver. The hilt curved like a talon, patterns of stars and quills carved throughout. It reminded Malka strongly of a paper cutting Hadar had made for the Feast of Lots.

"Not as much as Danya, though she'd be loath to admit her affection for sweets."

Amnon laughed heartily, and she smiled at him. It hit her how much she loved Amnon, and she truly wondered if that love could turn romantic. If a life with him as her husband made sense.

Amnon must've thought the same, for he grew serious. "I want to give you everything, Malka. As many pirushkes as you could eat. A beautiful ring. The rarest herbs for your medicinal garden. I've always wanted it, but . . ." His face twisted, and he drew his hands over his cheeks. "When you left to find the Maharal without me, and went somewhere I could not follow, I couldn't stop worrying. Every moment, I worried whether you would be hurt or killed."

"You're a dear friend to me, Amnon."

"Malka, it's more than that. Some things may have changed—I might not be as able to protect you physically as I once could, but I'll protect you with everything I am. I promise to do my best to give you the life you deserve."

He cradled her hand in his and leaned close. His warmth was normally a comfort, but his implication made her grow rigid.

"You promised this conversation would wait until we returned to Eskravé, and Imma was free."

His lips brushed her cheek. "I won't ask you until we are back. But I can't hide my feelings anymore. Not after almost losing you."

Malka opened her mouth to respond, but the music swelled, and Chaia shouted her name.

She ran toward them, glowing from sweat and joy. "Malka, it's our favorite dance! Come!"

Malka shot Amnon an apologetic glance, though her body relaxed after the interruption. She couldn't give Amnon the love he deserved, nor could he protect her as he so wished.

Chaia tugged her close to the circle forming around the musicians, taking her hand as they sank in line with everyone else. They danced together, a song her people knew the steps to like a second language. Laughter brightened her,

her face stretching into a smile as everyone raised their hands in the air and swooshed them down again. Their circle tightened and released, and Malka twirled. When the circle reconnected, the hand she grabbed was far less clammy than Chaia's. She jerked her head and found the golem's hand in hers.

"I didn't think you danced," Malka said, ignoring the shiver passing through her.

Nimrah shrugged, stumbling on her footing as the circle moved. "I don't, but Chaia makes it difficult to say no."

Malka tittered. "She has that effect." Her mood lightened, perhaps due to the wine in her veins or the sweetness on her tongue from the honey-fried cakes. She leaned in close to be heard over the music. "It's second nature to any Yahad. Come, I will show you."

Malka led Nimrah through the movements, encouraging her to sway and shout as the song demanded. At first, Nimrah was tentative, her eyes darting around the circle. It made sense. The Maharal had implored the Yahad to embrace Nimrah once again. While it made Nimrah less fearful to walk the streets without the shade of her hood, the Yahadi people were timid to accept her. Distrust lingered. But now, among the smiles, flushed cheeks, laughter, and dancing, it didn't matter who she was.

It emboldened Nimrah, and soon she mastered the footing. As the dance sped up, their movements quickened.

The song ended and another began, and the crowd roared as Chaia was hoisted high into the air on a wide wooden chair. Four men held the chair's legs, and everyone broke the circle to dance around her, their hands waving in the air.

Malka was breathless from the thrill. Chaia beamed at her, and Malka blew her a kiss.

Nimrah cleared her throat, and Malka realized their hands were still entangled. She stared at them. Nimrah's forest green veins contrasted Malka's pale skin, chapped from the winter. Malka traced her thumb along one of Nimrah's veins, smooth and cold beneath her touch. As sense came, Malka dropped Nimrah's hand, the music dulling in her ears as heat flooded her cheeks. How stupid she was to let the moment linger. To turn something joyful into a complication. She turned away, but not quickly enough to miss Nimrah's hand, reddened from her hold, twitch at her side.

Malka resisted the urge to flee. Even if she wanted to, the crowd bundled them together.

"So, you'll be up on that chair soon, I imagine," Nimrah taunted, breaking the awkward silence between them.

"What do you mean?"

Nimrah nodded toward Amnon, whose eyes were set on them warily. "I saw you two. You were close. He kissed you."

"On the cheek," Malka clarified. Then defeatedly added, "He wants to be married."

"But you don't?"

"I'm not sure what I want."

Nimrah huffed. "Why does that not surprise me. Want another drink?"

She disappeared briefly and returned with two glasses of plum wine.

"Fine." Malka accepted the glass. "What about you? Has a man ever caught your eye? Gotten you on your knees?"

"Not a man."

The oily lamplight illuminated the slight bob of her neck before absconding it back into shadow. Malka drew in a quick, desirous breath.

"Not anyone—" Nimrah added hastily, casting her eyes somewhere left of Malka. "The Maharal made me with one purpose. Anything else would be a betrayal of his creation."

It wasn't new for Nimrah to give explanations of duty and the promises she owed the Maharal. It had been enough for Malka once. But now, with wine flushing her skin and the heady feeling of Nimrah's closeness, she wanted more. She wanted the dark underbelly of Nimrah's thoughts. Her desires.

Malka pressed the wine glass to her mouth and watched as Nimrah's eyes drew to her lips.

She smirked around the rim. "I think you have already betrayed him."

Nimrah's jaw tightened. She threw back the rest of her wine and held the empty glass close, rolling the stem between her fingertips. Now the glass reflected the light, sending golden slits across Nimrah's face.

She was beautiful. Not in the way Malka would find Chaia or Amnon beautiful, but like the moon brushing its glow across a thicket in the blackened night. Like evening sunlight as it slipped through stained glass and washed hazy colors on the floorboards. It hit her so suddenly, it blinded her.

Each day with Nimrah made it harder to hate her. In Mavetéh, they had passed each other stories like the celebration koilitch on Malka's plate, sharing pieces of themselves with one another. Nimrah had come back for

Malka in the castle when she could have easily betrayed her. Nimrah had told her the truth of her story, not even demanding forgiveness.

"You should go easy on the wine, village girl. You're red as a cherry."

The slight went through as easily as the wine. "Why did you come back for me? In Valón Castle. You could have left me in Sévren's hands and forsaken our bargain. Rooted yourself back to the Maharal instead of me."

Nimrah shrugged, though the side of her mouth twitched. "The Maharal's recovery needed a public declaration."

"You could have done that and left me. Sévren was not so pleased to see you demand my return."

"I was created to protect the Yahad. I did what I was made to do."

"And that has gone so well for you, hasn't it?" The surge of regret came after the retort had left her lips, leaving the words to sour the air between them.

Nimrah's eyes flashed. She stepped closer, bending so that Malka barely had to tilt her head to meet her gaze. "Would you prefer that I saved you out of spite? That perhaps I could not bear to think of your head on a spike unless it were I who put it there? Or would you prefer that I say I saved you because the idea of you dying before me became unbearable?"

She was not so monstrous like this, eyes wide and cheeks flushed. Or perhaps, only monstrous in the way anyone was when they were wretched with desire.

Maybe Malka looked just as monstrous—drunk and desperate to know how Nimrah's lips would feel on hers. It was a traitorous thought, wanting. But Malka did not mind the feel of it. She wanted to feel it again, and again, and again.

She grabbed the empty wine glass from Nimrah's hand and set it with hers on a nearby ledge. She trailed her hand down Nimrah's arm, the stone cool beneath her sleeve, until she wrapped her hand around Nimrah's wrist.

Nimrah shivered beneath the trace of Malka's fingers.

So rarely did Malka feel in control. From Mavetéh, Abba, and the constant tithes from the Ozmini Church to the trade she had made for Imma's life, Malka always had to react to the situations she had been dealt.

Not now. Now, she wanted this.

Malka led Nimrah into a narrow alleyway, away from the crowding and noise of the celebration.

"What are you—"

"You admit it," Malka said, voice coarse. "You didn't save me out of duty or service. You saved me because you wanted to. Because you couldn't bear it if I died."

Nimrah's fist curled against the wall near Malka's ear, like she had done in the confessional. This time, vines sprouted from the stone, hissing as they unfurled. "Don't taunt me, Malka."

Her name spoken in Nimrah's rasping voice shot a strike of heat through her. This close, the cloy of their connection was fierce, suffocating.

"I need to know," Malka spoke slowly. "You must feel it, too."

Nimrah did not speak, but Malka knew she understood. The blaze of her eyes and the twitch of her jaw exposed her. It was a relief to finally know that Nimrah, despite her taciturn disposition, was not exempt from the effects of the rooting spell. It frustrated Malka, too, that she had not said a word.

"Why say nothing?"

From the square, a new dance had begun. Laughter, clapping, the echo of shoes tapping on the ground.

"I didn't think I could stand it," Nimrah's voice was so threadbare, Malka could barely hear it above the music. "If the spell only plagued me like this. If its strength came from . . . my own feelings. I'd rather have lived in ignorance."

The admission dissolved Malka's last inhibition. She wanted to fight Nimrah, drag her close. She wanted to press her lips to the soft part of her throat, eclipse her jaw with the brush of her palm.

Malka reached for her, only to be hauled back by the vines crawling across her chest and trapping her against the wall.

"You don't want this." Nimrah's throat bobbed. "You will hate me."

Malka wrapped the vine in her fist. "Is that why you've tied me up? So I don't do anything I'll regret?"

"Go back out there. Dance with your friends. Eat more pirushkes. I'll go home." The vines around her receded, slithering out of her grasp. But the ghost of them lingered, a phantom of Nimrah's attempt to maintain her asceticism.

"Tell me you don't want me. Then I'll go."

Nimrah swallowed hard, her face scrunched in pain. Her eyebrows wavered, as if she were testing each answer before giving one. She was quiet for so long, Malka thought she had misread her. Misread her desire, her want.

Then she said, raspy, "I can't tell you that."

Slowly, as if not to shatter the moment of vulnerability between them, Malka traced her finger along the hollow of Nimrah's neck. She was warm under her fingertips.

Nimrah seized her wrist, holding it away in warning. "Malka, please."

"Take something for yourself for once. Be more than what the Maharal made you to be."

Malka leaned in slowly, allowing Nimrah time to stop her, to cease crossing the boundary they had so laboriously mortared.

Then, she kissed her.

Nimrah's lips were soft, plush like she had imagined them. Every word spoken in this alley had been carefully picked, every action a delicate step along a precipice. But there was no constraint now, as Malka curled her hands through Nimrah's hair and Nimrah pushed her against the wall.

The wound between her shoulders lit with pain, but Malka didn't care. Her hands on Nimrah's waist, her hips, her cheeks—it was everything Malka needed, to feel Nimrah all at once and everywhere.

The desire that shaded her cheeks and riled her stomach mirrored the feeling of performing Kefesh—power flooding through her. She was beginning to learn how similar lust was to prayer.

Nimrah sucked at her bottom lip and want pulsed between Malka's legs. A moan slipped from her, eliciting a wanton growl from Nimrah. She gripped Malka's thigh and hoisted it around her hip.

Groaning, Malka pressed her lips to Nimrah's throat. It was salty and damp, different from the cool stone on her cheek which Malka had traced.

"I'm a fool for wanting you," Nimrah whispered, voice low and husky in Malka's ear. "My death bringer."

Malka didn't want to think about that right now. She didn't want to think about anything save the feel of Nimrah's body against her.

As if acknowledging her thoughts, Nimrah dragged her thumb along the band of Malka's apron. "Is this alright?" she whispered.

"Yes," Malka gasped.

Nimrah's hand disappeared beneath her skirts, tracing the fold of Malka's undergarment.

Malka arched into her touch. She had never been this hot, like a fire had been lit inside her skin. Like she was about to set Tzvidi's library ablaze and didn't care if she burned.

Malka could tip over the edge just as swiftly, ruined by Nimrah's finger work. She was so vulnerable like this—Nimrah pressing between her legs, her fingers exploring in the way that only Malka had done before.

Malka wanted to beg for more. To rock against her. Anything to be free of this built-up tension.

Before she could, a cry racketed through the air, so high-pitched the wind carried it through the small alley.

Malka froze, turning to watch as commotion rang through the square. Her heart sank.

"What was that?" Nimrah asked, voice gruff.

Malka shook her head. Awkwardness settled between them as they stared at each other, chests heaving.

Malka ran from the alley, leaving Nimrah in the darkness.

⁂

A crowd had gathered around the platform at the square's center. The music had ceased, the people had grown quiet. A child's cry loosened the silence, and the comforting murmurs of a mother followed. Malka bumped her way through the crowd, looking for Chaia or Amnon among the ashen faces.

Malka's heart pounded as her anxiety grew. Finally, she managed to reach the platform where Chaia stood, her back to Malka. The skirts of her wedding dress billowed in the wind.

"Chaia?"

Chaia shifted to face her, revealing the tear marks staining her face. She was pale, so pale. So different from the Chaia who had danced with her minutes ago.

"Chaia, what's—" As soon as she noticed the woman behind Chaia, the question died on her lips.

Her curly, golden-brown hair was in disarray. Her green eyes almost black in the lantern light.

Danya.

She was here, hunched over like she could not spare the strength to stand, her hand wrapped around her waist. Surrounding her, a handful of people from their village.

As their eyes met, Danya let out a sob of relief.

Malka closed the distance between them, wrapping her in a firm hug. Her sister was here. Malka hadn't realized how homesick she had been.

Seeing Danya brought forward the emotions she had tried so hard to keep at bay.

Her sister trembled in her arms, and Malka's concern grew. She began to check her for injuries. "Danya, are you hurt?"

Danya sobbed again, and stared at the ground, breathing deeply until she could compose herself. "Only minorly. But Malka, there's something you must know—"

"It can wait until I attend to you," Malka responded, pressing her palms to Danya's cheeks.

Danya shook them off. "No, it can't."

"Is something wrong at home? With Imma? Did the Paja do something to her? I'll make it right."

"Malka." Danya said her name in a choke, the stoicism Malka had long associated with her sister crumbled to dust. "Eskravé has been destroyed."

CHAPTER 28

Malka stared at the sky as Danya recounted the events.

"We'd dealt with the Paja's extended stay as best we could. But last week, something festered in the air. I had woken earlier than I intended; the dawn had only just arrived. Even the moon's glow had not disappeared completely. I had barely begun to dress when someone yelled for help. Masheva had been beaten by an Ozmini knight who accused her of stealing the Order's sacrament, which had gone missing in the night.

"When Father Brożek came, he ordered that every house in Eskravé be raided to search for it. They were violent, trampling over people with their horses if we could not move quickly enough.

"But the worst were the Paja peasants, who assailed us in droves. Like they had been on the brink of violence the entire time they were there, and this was all they needed to justify their attacks.

"They beat the sick. Even grabbed Yael from her bed and kicked her until she bled from her mouth, nose, and ears.

"They destroyed everything. Throwing rocks against our synagogue windows, striking matches and tossing them on the ground until the weeds caught fire. They threw themselves on people fleeing their houses and dismembered them, cutting off their arms and legs and heads like flower petals.

"Even when the sun set, they did not stop. Nowhere was safe. You couldn't go anywhere without hearing the tearing of limbs or someone's dying pleas.

"When they finally decided to leave Eskravé, they took Imma with them. Once they complete their tour, they're going to bring her here to make a public display of her d—" Danya took a shaky breath. "Her death. To show what happens to disobedient Yahad. It took us longer to reach here without horses, they'll be here any day."

Hollowness dug inside Malka, shoveled her out. "Where's Hadar? Abba?" Her eyes roved over the familiar villagers, frantic and distressed.

"Abba fled with some others. But . . ." Danya kneeled over, another sob racking her body. "Hadar is gone, Malka."

She did not process the words. How could she? Language had ceased all meaning when Danya uttered them. Years later, she would recall the cadence of them with startling accuracy. Replaying in her mind in an endless loop. Something she would come to know as well as her own name.

No. No. No.

If she denied it enough, it wouldn't be true.

All the pain Malka had endured—Mavetéh's creatures, Brother Asak's stone feet, the Valonian guard's iron fists—dwindled at the strength of this.

In a few words, Danya had turned Malka's world upside down. All she could think of was Hadar's doe-like face, the vivid wonder behind her eyes, her contagious laugh. Gone forever.

The thought of Hadar in pain was a sharp dagger between her ribs. The thought of a world without her twisted the blade.

"I tried so hard to save her," Danya continued. "I ran back to our house as quickly as I could. So fast, I thought my legs would give out. But she wasn't there. She had run out during the commotion. She found someone dying in the street and was trying to help her when—"

Danya could not finish. Tears consumed her.

Malka crawled forward on her knees and wrapped Danya close. Danya cried into her shoulder, and Malka held on to her like a lifeline.

Malka had only ever wanted a peaceful life with her family, to wake each morning to the hum of the fire and work with Imma as a healer. She wanted to celebrate holidays with her family and watch Hadar grow up. To see Imma grow old and wise and watch as Danya constructed a life she loved. She wanted this life so much that she had stepped into Mavetéh. Stepped into her death for the chance of getting that life. She had made a bargain with a golem and deceived the archbishop for it.

And it was all for nothing.

Mavetéh had been her enemy. What stood between her and that peaceful life. But she was wrong. Mavetéh had not been the only threat.

The greatest threat to her and her people were those who wielded their beliefs like weapons. Who sought to eradicate those whose beliefs were different from theirs—beliefs that threatened their supremacy.

"Danya," Chaia said hesitantly. "Do you know what happened to my parents?"

Danya shook her head. "I'm not sure. They were part of the group that fled with Abba. While some of us escaped here, another group headed south toward the Balkisk Kingdom."

Something flickered across Chaia's face. Vilém wrapped an arm around her. She buried her face in his neck.

To her left, Amnon had gone deathly pale. "My family, Danya?" he asked, voice small.

"Your brothers escaped toward Vyš. Your father . . . I'm sorry, Amnon."

He nodded, but his hand shook around his cane.

Her people had become refugees. Her home had been destroyed. Hadar was gone.

Through blurry eyes, Malka sought Nimrah. She kept to the back of the crowd, burying herself into her cloak as if willing herself to disappear, her lips still swollen from what they had done. What Malka had taken for herself to satiate her own desires.

The Rayga, Malka had deemed her. But perhaps she and Nimrah were not so different, after all. Nimrah was created to protect the Yahad, and yet Eskravé was pillaged. Malka always did what was necessary to protect her family. And yet, Hadar was dead.

They had both failed.

↘

The lanterns had long grown cold by the time they returned to Chaia's house. Chaia had excused herself to shed her wedding gown for a simple blouse and trousers. When Malka saw past her own grief, she realized this day was ruined for Vilém and Chaia. Their wedding, a day of happiness and new beginnings, now rife with grief and sorrow.

Amnon heated some water and steeped tea in several mugs. Nimrah set a cup on the table for Malka. She lingered close, as if waiting to say something, but Malka did not move her gaze from the chipped groove of the mug in front of her. She did not want to acknowledge Nimrah. To confront what they had done—what they were about to do. She was wildly stupid for what had happened in the alleyway. She had let herself be distracted. Let herself take what she wanted. If there was any way she could've prevented . . . but that was foolish thinking. She was one person. Even Kefesh, the magic of *her people*, had abandoned her. Left her to feel even more powerless than she could've imagined.

What mattered now? Everything Malka had journeyed for was gone. The home she knew, the family she loved. Imma now sentenced to death; her only crime being a talented Yahadi healer. The Ozmins couldn't stand to think the Yahad could be as skilled as them, as talented.

"You're allowed to feel, you know," Chaia said. "However you want to feel. Angry, sad, hurt, afraid."

Malka hadn't heard her reenter the room. She sat next to her in a creaking chair. The room had emptied, and Malka hadn't noticed. All she saw was the crack in her mug.

"It doesn't matter how I feel. They're gone. Eskravé is gone." Malka traced her finger along the ridge of the chip. "I survived Mavetéh. I brought Amnon back from the brink of death. I stole a prisoner from a highly guarded dungeon. And yet, I couldn't stop this. I couldn't protect those I hold most dear. The people who needed me."

She had been willing to bend the earth to give Hadar the childhood Malka had once had.

But instead, Hadar had died alone. Died before life unfurled its wings to her.

"In the palace, I eavesdropped on a conversation between Sévren and Prince Evžen. Sévren spoke to the prince like a father, but the words he said . . . he whispered to him about maintaining control over Ordobav. To lead with an iron fist like his grandfather. He said something was his choice to decide."

Chaia's lips thinned. "Of course, they would do this as a power play. There was a similar attack on a Yahadi village equidistant from Valón up north. Eskravé was nothing but Sévren's next calculated move on his chessboard of control. He's destroyed the Yahadi villages who traded most with Valón, who traveled here most often. It's probably just the beginning, too."

"No one in Eskravé had their hand in powerful politics. They killed *children*."

"We will honor them, Malka," Chaia said fiercely, grabbing Malka's hand. "We will tell stories of them, like we do with the Shabhe Queen and her bravery during the Feast of Lots. We will tell stories about them until our throats run dry and our lips bleed."

Malka snubbed at this. "We'll waste away in such stories. What difference will it make? They are still dead."

Chaia frowned. "What are humans without stories, Malka? Do you think it won't take stories to shift the tide of war, to build nations up from the ground? Behind every tyrant is a story that justifies their means; behind every brutalized culture are stories that string generations together like emerald beads. Their stories will have meanings, and we will not forget them."

"Is that what you're thinking about? How their deaths can be weaponized against the Ozmini Church? Against Prince Evžen?"

"Malka, do you think I'm not also grieving? That when I snuck away from home in that cart I could've known that would be the last time I'd be able to see Eskravé? That their deaths do not eat at me? That I would not give *anything* to learn the fate of my parents, that there is a possibility they died thinking I was dead? You are not the only one who has lost. I am angry. I am hurt. But I find my strength in a higher purpose."

"You sound like him," Malka said. "The Maharal."

Chaia shrugged. "His teachings have inspired me."

Whatever Malka felt, it was worsened by Chaia's calmness, the way she never cried or was distressed by anything. It made her hot with anger, to see Chaia so composed while Malka's life fell apart, while her goals were torn to nothing.

She had failed. As a big sister, as a Yahad, as a person. She had never been brave, never *wanted* to be brave. But for Imma, she had tried bravery on as a mask. She had felt the curves of it along her jaw, and where it pressed around her nose. She had worn it for weeks until an unthinkable tragedy ripped it from her face.

There was nothing left for Malka.

She was not made for politics or revolution like Chaia. And Danya was so brave—braver than Malka could ever be. They were survivors and could handle anything.

And Nimrah? Nimrah was made of stone and would fall back on her knees at the Maharal's call.

Malka would never forgive herself for letting her family down. She would never forgive herself for robbing Danya of her mother and a sister.

⚶

Chaia fell asleep at the table, hand around her cold mug of tea. Vilém came in and wrapped her in his arms.

"Will you be alright?" he asked Malka.

Malka nodded, and Vilém smiled at her before carrying Chaia to bed.

Malka stood from her seat and wrapped herself in her cloak. Chaia had cleaned it and it smelled fresh as soap, though blood still stained the edge of her hood. Malka didn't mind anymore. She was not a stranger to blood.

She slipped soundlessly out the door. Without the lanterns lining the way, the walk was agonizingly cold. The breeze blew treacherously through Malka's unbound hair and tears stung the rims of her eyes.

She didn't know when she started to run, but tears blurred the trees and buildings around her. The rooting spell sent a warning bout of nausea as she moved farther away from Nimrah. She didn't care.

Malka was sorry for how the rooting spell would punish Nimrah for this distance between them. But Malka was also selfish. And if Nimrah could understand one thing, it was the desire to be punished for her failures. To let the pain consume.

The Yahadi Quarter was quiet; so still, that if Malka closed her eyes, she could picture herself back in her room in Eskravé, with the moon hanging low, and only Hadar's soft snores breaking the silent night.

A sound she would never hear again.

She kept running.

The nausea had begun to make her mouth water, her stomach twisting in cramping fits. Dizziness blurred her vision. She did not notice when the dirt paths outside of the city walls bled into the unruly trail leading into Mavetéh until the smell of pine tickled her nose. On the edge of the forest, the air was fresh. No longer did the city smells of Valón permeate the air—wheat and cooked oil, animal dung and incense. Instead, the ripe scent of balsam and figs, and the slight tang of dead leaves and branches. However, when she fell into the shadow of Mavetéh, the earth turned to rot. The scent of burning flesh clung in the air, like soiled fruit and moldy blood.

A lifetime had passed since she had been here, and no time at all. Returning to Mavetéh made her skin crawl. But it wasn't Mavetéh that had showed her violence first. It had been Father Brożek, giving the order to slice Minton's fingers from his hand.

Malka continued on.

She didn't know how long she walked or where she was going. The nausea and dizziness had only intensified; the unmooring making it hard to think. It was like Malka was hollowing herself out, insides shriveling with the absence of Nimrah. Soon, it would consume her entirely.

Wasn't that what she wanted, to be consumed?

She had once begged to make it through these woods alive, and now, she wanted it to claim her. Perhaps one of the monsters would bite her with its talon-like claws and end her suffering. Perhaps she'd greet the Tannin again, this time awake and hungry.

When Malka could not walk anymore, she began to crawl. Her palms and knees seeped into the wet earth, cold and slick from yesterday's snowfall. It soiled her skirts, and thorny branches dug into her skin, creating fresh wounds and staining the dirt beneath her like spilled wine.

The dark was unrelenting. Malka treaded forward blindly until a sharp pain shot up her arm. A piece of glass had stuck into her palm, jagged and unyielding.

She cursed, and yanked the glass, her skin tugging hard in resistance. It was embedded deep. With a yell, Malka managed to pull it free. She pressed her thumb into the wound to stop the bleeding.

She gasped when she noticed the looming structure ahead of her. Even in the shadow of the night, a pale slip of moonlight bounced off the ruins of the structure, revealing crumbling stone half consumed by the forest and swallowed arches and vines in the frames of the windows. Pillars made into trellises for the foliage, the greenery coiling around each one like a serpent's tail.

It was a synagogue. Even ruined, it stole Malka's breath.

Slowly she stood, wiping her bloody palm on her apron. Stepping closer, Malka could see the ark which had held the sacred scroll, and the platform where the rabbi had once stood. What broke her, though, were the remains of paper cuttings tacked to the ruined walls.

They were stunning, even touched by the elements and time.

"They are beautiful, aren't they?"

Malka froze. The Maharal's voice caught her unawares in the solace of the forest.

"One could say they are made more beautiful with age," he continued. "A true symbol that art lasts far after we are no longer there to appreciate it."

"How did you find me?" Malka pressed her forehead against the cool wall. Tears fell down her cheek, stinging against the scrapes the branches had left on her skin. She felt empty. So empty.

"In truth, Malka, I was not looking. But perhaps Yohev meant for me to find you here. You see, I was woken from a fitful sleep by the desire to walk and breathe in the rotted air of this forest."

"Are you not afraid of Mavetéh?"

The earth groaned at the use of the forest's name, the wind sending a whistle through the air. Malka suppressed a shiver.

"It was my magic that made this forest come alive. It seems to spare me. Out of pity or dishonor, I do not know."

A week ago, she would've shaken her head. Vehemently insisted his only fault was creating Nimrah. That Mavetéh was *her* doing, *her* liability. Now, she just sighed. "I have lost so much tonight. Will you let me grieve alone?"

Silence fogged the air for a stretch of time. Malka waited for the crunch of his footsteps to signal his leaving, but it never came.

"Humor me for a moment and I will leave you if you still wish it. Do you know the Orlon clock, Malka? Tell me you have seen it, for it is truly one of Valón's greatest beauties, even though it no longer works."

Malka recalled the astronomical clock, unlike anything she had ever seen before with layers upon layers of glass and metal that fit together to tell facts about the universe: the time, the day, and secrets of the zodiac. Malka also recalled the four figurines, which rendered the Yahad and the Fanavi people as outsiders. As people to be hated.

She nodded.

The Maharal climbed the creaking steps to the bimah. "Can I tell you the story of the Orlon and its maker?"

Malka was tired of stories but could not deny the Maharal. Instead, she focused on the cool press of stone on her forehead, dug her fingers into the ridges of the chipped rock, and listened.

"Many years ago, King Ordobav, from whom the kingdom gets its name, wanted Valón to be one of the most advanced cities in the world. A place to rival the river city of Lei, or the resource-rich Balkisk Kingdom. He had been told of this legendary creator, Hus. He was a master of clocks and mathematics who lived deep in the mountains, working on his trinkets, and perfecting his science. For many years scientists and mathematicians from universities across the world had come to him for his advice and mentorship. The king wanted no one else to create the clock, so the legendary clockmaker was summoned to Valón, where he met with King Ordobav in his personal meeting room.

"'I want you to build a clock,' he said to Hus. 'The grandest clock in all the world, one that will make all other kings red with jealousy.'

"Master Hus agreed and began working on the clock immediately. He would spend all day working on it and nothing else, until it was done. City folk would pass by and watch him work—from dawn until dusk, when it was so dark that not even the candlelight could help illuminate his work. People soon grew accustomed to the clockmaker, making it part of their routine to come and watch him work when their own chores had lulled. Finally, after weeks had elapsed, Master Hus finished his creation. When he presented it, King Ordobav was pleased.

"'I will be the envy of everyone with a clock as great as this,' he said, clapping his hands together. 'It is only a precaution, you see, that I cannot let you design a greater clock for anyone else.'

"With a flick of his hand, the knights grabbed Master Hus. He thrashed, but he was no match for the knights and their sturdy armor. The king stalked forward and clawed out Master Hus's eyes, leaving him with only bloody sockets.

"Angered by the king's deceit, the clockmaker threw himself into his masterpiece. The gears cut his flesh until he bled out and died. The great clock was ruined, and the king was devastated. He called forth clockmaker after clockmaker to fix the Orlon, but none were able to fix what Master Hus had created and destroyed."

Malka was breathing hard when the Maharal finished his recitation. Her life was filled with enough violence and grief without the knowledge of this tale.

"Why would you tell me this story?" she asked, voice cracking. More tears threatened to fall. She gritted her teeth and slammed her fist to the stone. She could never know peace again, only loss and grief and anguish.

The wall shuddered. So softly, Malka could have mistaken it for her own movement.

The ground crunched beneath the Maharal's footsteps as he approached. He traced his sleeve along the paper cuttings on the wall. "The king was greedy for Master Hus's talent. He wanted it for himself and no one else. He gouged out Hus's eyes so the power of the clockmaker would always be his. But power is not static. It flows like the Leirit river, winding and uncontrollable, easy to let slip through your fingers. The king did not expect Hus to give his life to destroy the clock. In that way, Hus took the power back."

He settled his arm gently on Malka's shoulder. She blinked away her tears.

"Sévren has your eyes now, Malka, and he thinks he has won. But he will not expect you and your strength. He will not expect your resilience. That is how you will win."

"He has taken my strength," Malka choked, thinking of Hadar, of Imma, sentenced to death.

"Look at me, Malka," he said, tilting her chin toward him.

Malka's body racked with tears, and the earth felt them, swaying with the force of her cries. The Maharal's eyes widened as if he, too, could feel the earth shift.

"There is a strength in you Sévren cannot take. It is the same strength I called forth to create Nimrah, the same force you wrapped around your heart to save your friend from the creatures in the forest."

"Kefesh."

The Maharal hummed. "That is the conduit, but what is Kefesh really? It is your relationship with Yohev—your belief in God. You nurture it every time you close your eyes to pray, when you kiss your hand and raise it to a mezuzah, when you strike a match and light candles for the Sabbath. We do not do these things to please Yohev as we would a king, or to meet certain expectations as we would a child looking to appease their parents. We do them to strengthen ourselves, to give order in the chaos. An explanation in a vague world."

"Why would Yohev allow this?" Malka asked, teeth gritted. "Why would this happen to Their people? I am not the only one who prays, who keeps the faith. Why are they dead? Hadar—"

Malka's voice cracked on her sister's name.

"It is true that Yohev is in those atrocities, in the hate and violence that our people experience. But They are also in our faith, in our ability to recover, and to take one step after the other in the face of unspeakable tragedy."

He leaned down, pressing the nub of his wrist to the ground, where moments earlier it had grumbled with her cries. "It responds to you still, even when you doubt your own strength."

"But I have not been able to use Kefesh since freeing you. It has abandoned me."

"Perhaps you have begun to doubt yourself in a way you did not when you conjured the magic in Mavetéh. The earth does not choose when we are or are not worthy of commanding it. Only we, as humans, doubt our abilities. When we forsake ourselves, that is when true failure happens."

Malka ruminated on that. She wasn't sure where she had begun to falter. When new doubt wormed its way in that had not already been burrowed deep.

"These paper cuttings," the Maharal began, "they mean something to you. That is easy to see."

"My sister was a master at the craft," Malka responded. "She would spend days on the same paper cutting, staying at it long after Danya and I had given up on our designs."

"How similar Kefesh is to a paper cutting."

The Maharal's eyes trailed the paper cuttings on the wall, and for a moment, the paper, previously dull and faded, began to glimmer. So lively these paper cuttings became, they sparked light into the space of the ruins until the synagogue appeared before her in all its former glory.

It was taller than the ruins suggested, sprawling as high as some of the oak trees. It was not out of place in the forest, but made for it: spires acting as branches, windows parting like gaps in the trees, seats like great tree logs. Candles were suspended in midair, floating like stars in the night. They flickered and shone, making the synagogue glow a soft orange light.

Malka stared in amazement. She knew the Maharal was powerful, that his magic was legendary. He had created Nimrah, someone who lived and breathed and thought, out of nothing but the earth. But Malka had never seen him use Kefesh. She had never seen Kefesh like this, a trickery of belief, a past and present pressed together as one. It did not seem possible that mere words in their sacred language could do this—could alter the universe and her mind.

"How are you doing this, Rav?" Malka asked hesitantly. "Without your . . ."

The Maharal chuckled and held up his nubs. "Ah, yes. They cut off my hands expecting to sever my ability to perform Kefesh. After all, how can one draw letters without one's fingers? But I have been studying this magic for many years, Malka. Longer than Sévren has been archbishop, and longer than Valski has been king. The letters of our ancient language are tied to the elements, to the shape of the world, yes. But our magic has never been exclusionary—many holy people have never been able to write. We speak and think prayers, but we rarely write them. Why can't Kefesh be the same?"

Even when writing the letters, Malka still could not command Kefesh. She could scarcely imagine the skill the Maharal must have to create with an unwritten word, especially the grand image before her.

"I have never heard of this synagogue. Surely people would speak about something as magical as this shul and not allow it to turn to ruins in Mavetéh."

"It was truly beautiful, wasn't it?"

The Maharal's eyes gleamed as he reveled in the wonder of the synagogue.

"We like to think the desire to preserve beautiful places would outweigh the desire for power," he responded sadly. "But places of worship are never safe. They are targets for violence, even though they are made for community and peace. The Ozmins want us to feel afraid in the places that strengthen us, to make us fear our desire to practice our faith. The name for this synagogue does not exist in the Kraž-Yadi language—it is as ancient as our sacred language, made when this forest was a young and wild thing. We refer to it now as the shul Amichati."

The synagogue for the life of our people.

"What happened to it?"

The Maharal tilted his chin up and breathed in deep. He smiled at the scent, probably smelling a memory, for this forest air held nothing but rot and death. Timidly, Malka closed her eyes and inhaled. It was subtle, but it was there—pine and rosemary, frankincense and myrrh. The scent of bread and honey, of fresh parchment and ink held close to the nose.

When she opened her eyes, the synagogue had changed again. It was filled with people. The chatter was like a buzz in the air, a song of its own accord. Musicians pressed their bows against string, twisting their pegs until the notes hummed together. Children chased each other down the aisles, some of the floating candles pressing low enough to worry their parents as they swung their hands in the air, trying to hit the candles from their hanging place. The people sang a hymn in unison, their voices melting into the music.

> *We remain*
> *An endless, undying flame*
> *Surviving by the strength of Yohev's name*
> *We remain, oh*
> *Still, we remain*

"To understand, we must start at the beginning," the Maharal said. But Malka's eyes were fixed on the scene before her, and she let the memory of it press into her skin, soul, and mind as the Maharal continued.

"When our people were small in numbers, and we had not grown beyond the borders of the ancient Anaya Sea, we gathered in this temple. Though it was not the first holy place where we practiced our religion, it was a symbol of our people and our determination to remain. The clay walls were built using Kefesh, and sunk so far into the earth, it did not rattle even during the largest quakes. It gave the Yahad strength. Strength enough to fight back against the Jalgani, the polytheists who ruled the empire, who determined what the Yahad could and could not do. When the Yahad revolted, the Jalgani burned the shul Amichati to the ground and massacred our people."

Like Eskravé. Like Hadar.

"They were in despair, having lost their loved ones and the place which grounded them. When they began to sort through the wreckage, they noticed the jut of clay from the earth—the same foundation which had survived deep below the ground. On it, an etrog shrub had grown, already bearing a green-yellow citrus.

"Life remained, and so the Yahad decided, so would they. They rebuilt the temple, over and over, as it was destroyed again and again. Each generation teaching the next how to pile the clay and sand the beams—how to save the sacred text from fire, and repair damage to the animal skin."

"But Rav . . . the ancient Anaya Sea is nowhere near here. How could the shul Amichati end up in Mavetéh?"

"Ah, that is my favorite part of the story, Malka. For as history came and went, and the Jalgani fell from power, so did the Yahad strengthen and grow in numbers. Soon, the temple could not contain all those who wished to pray there. So, more synagogues were built across all places where the Yahad lived. It was decided that the shul Amichati would be a reminder of our ability to remain. The etrog plant which had grown from the rooted clay was transported here for safekeeping. It is ready, should we need it, to grow the shul again."

The vibrant memories before them grew dull as the Maharal's story concluded, and the ruins once again materialized before her. But if the etrog plant was moved for safe keeping, how did the ruins appear?

"They are a memory of the shul's burning, and a reminder of history," the Maharal answered, seemingly knowing her thoughts. "But look close, Malka." He guided her to the decayed bimah. In its center, a stiff twig of an etrog plant spurted from the earth, its leaves beginning to unfurl.

"Still, it remains."

Malka's jaw slackened. It couldn't be. She fell to her knees, bending close to examine the plant. It looked new, yet she could tell it was not. Like the Great Oak tree at Mavetéh's center, she could feel the life it had lived, and the life it would live long after they were gone.

Her ancestors had persisted, despite the attempts to destroy them.

Still, we remain, they had sung, and the words flowed through Malka again. She heard Chaia, Amnon, and Danya in those voices. She heard Imma. And she heard Hadar sing to her the loudest.

Still, Malka would remain.

PART
Three

CHAPTER 29

Malka slipped back into Chaia's home before the sun rose. She leaned in the doorway of the room where everyone slept: Chaia and Vilém on the bed, Danya and Amnon wrapped in cocoons of blankets on the floor near the small secondary hearth. Nimrah was there also, her back hunched against the wall, arms crossed in her sleep. When Malka noticed the beads of sweat on Nimrah's brow, the hollowness of her cheek, she felt a twinge of guilt. No doubt it was from the distance Malka had forced upon them.

She was frowning, her face as guarded asleep as it was awake. Except for their shared moment in the alleyway when Nimrah's facade had broken. Malka had hungered for her vanished resolve; wanted to antagonize her until her mask was rubbed raw.

Maybe they would never speak of that alleyway again. Maybe they would let it die as plants shriveled in the winter, leaves blackening beneath layers of snow. Malka wanted that—to cover her shame and regret like packed snow on the earth. Bury it deep until it suffocated underneath the weight of the changing season.

She should have known not to take that moment in the alleyway for herself. She had a responsibility to her family, a responsibility to Imma. Responsibilities she had let herself get distracted from. But not anymore. She would not let her desire get in the way. She would not let herself swallow Nimrah's words, gorging until she was sick.

Shame prickled hot spikes along her neck. She tiptoed into the room and tugged Danya into her arms, finding peace in her even breaths as she had once done with Hadar. For so many she loved, dawn would never come. They were left with the memory of the night suffocating them. But Imma would have another dawn, Danya would have another dawn, and that was what she leaned into. That was what gave her hope.

※

The next morning, Malka drew herself from bed the same way she had the morning she ventured into Mavetéh: duty carrying her forward with two strong hands. Those hands guided her as she slipped into her clothes and shoveled a bowl of gruel into her mouth for breakfast.

Malka had kissed Danya's forehead as she left the room, careful not to wake her. Her sister had fidgeted through the night until she exhausted herself into sleep. Malka knew any rest after grief was a blessing, though. When Baba died, it had felt wrong to sleep without the telling of his stories tiring her eyes, sending her into a landscape of dreams. She would stare out the window each night instead, waiting for the sun to creep through the glass.

When Danya did wake, she walked hesitantly into the kitchen, hands hugged around herself.

"Come, Danya," Chaia said sweetly. "Have some hot food, you must be hungry."

There it was again. That even fortitude of her voice, even when despair curled in. But Malka had no fire left within her to be angry at the way Chaia grieved. She had laid it all out the night before, when Mavetéh's thorns pricked at her skin and the shul Amichati grew from its ruins and collapsed into memory once again.

"I still can't believe you're alive," Danya said. Whether the remark was aimed at Chaia or herself, Malka did not know, for Danya did not lift her gaze as she padded along the creaking floor.

More footsteps echoed and Malka tensed as Nimrah appeared. She dared not look at her.

"Malka," Chaia started, voice hesitant as she glanced between Nimrah and Malka, as if she, too, could feel the tension stretch between them. "Vilém sent word from the university. They brought your mother into the castle late last night. One of his colleagues was in the library when they transported her inside."

Malka's hand tightened around her spoon. "So, we break her out the same way we did the Maharal."

Chaia shook her head. "Our same tricks will not work this time."

Malka swallowed, remembering the guard whose skin had shaken loosely in the wind.

"Plus," Chaia sighed. "She is not in the dungeon as we knew it."

"What do you mean?" Nimrah asked.

Chaia bit her lip, eyes darting between Malka and Danya. "I don't know if I should say."

"Whatever it is, I have heard worse. *Seen* worse," Danya said determinedly.

Malka's heart ached. She *had* seen worse. She had seen her village—all that she knew—destroyed in front of her. Had seen Hadar die, and the Ozmini soldiers beat friends she had known all her life.

"Tell us," Malka agreed.

"She is in something worse than a prison—a cell below ground where a prisoner can only stand, neither move nor sit."

Something rang familiar about this prison Chaia described. It was where the prison guard had threatened to send Malka. And most likely would've, if his libido hadn't delayed him enough for Malka to write the prayer into the wall and pelt him with stone arrowheads.

You know what we do to betrayers? The guard had said. *We lower them into the ground, into a space so small, you can feel your own breath bounce off the walls.*

Malka tried to keep her breathing even, for Danya's sake if nothing else. She promised herself she wouldn't break.

"There is one trustworthy person who might know details about this prison. Eliška, the laundress who told you about the secret entrance through the chapel."

"So, we visit her again, as we did before, and find out where it is."

"Malka . . . she's ill," Chaia said. "Vilém keeps an eye on the infirmary patients. She has caught the Mázág sickness."

The woman had never been particularly welcoming, but Malka had seen how the sickness ravaged bodies. Amnon was only alive because of Malka's resolve to use Kefesh in the woods. He still slept in the next room, and she dared not wake him, either—not only did he need the sleep, but he was grieving, too. They all were.

"The Maharal . . . we can get him to use Kefesh to help heal her," Malka suggested.

Chaia shook her head. "You know Sévren is looking for any evidence to use during his trial to put him back in jail—this time permanently. He's legally required to stay in the Yahadi Quarter. He can't take the risk. That, and it's illegal to use any magic on the sick."

"Let me guess, another ordinance whispered into the king's ear by Sévren?"

"They believe we will anger Triorzay. That the sickness is a deserved punishment and any supernatural attempt to heal them would be to defy their God."

Malka rolled her eyes. If she could call the magic to her, she would try, anyway. As each day passed, she had less to lose. "Let me see her. You know I can't use Kefesh anymore, but I am still a healer's daughter," Malka added, words heavy on her tongue.

"You must be careful," Chaia warned. "Take Nimrah with you at least, since Vilém is working."

Malka swallowed her dissent but could not help the way her eyes flickered to Nimrah. She waited a moment too long to respond. "Fine," she said, voice dry. She could do without the nausea, anyway.

"Good," said Chaia. "Nimrah, will you show Danya the clothes I left out for her?"

Nimrah nodded, and escorted Danya from the room. Malka had not told her sister about Nimrah's rooting to the Great Oak. She didn't know what to make of anything anymore. Even without Mavetéh, her people suffered. Died. Only at the hands of men, not monsters.

"Did something happen between you two, Malka?" Chaia asked low, drawing Malka's attention.

Malka thought of Nimrah's hot breath on her neck, the heat of their bodies molded together.

"No," Malka said, too hurriedly. "What makes you say that?"

Chaia shrugged. "Something feels different between you two."

I'm a fool for wanting you, Nimrah had said. But Malka was the fool. She had always picked apart her desires with reason, the same way someone would pluck out pomegranate seeds with their thumb, until all that remained was an empty carcass. With Nimrah, she had placed a seed on her tongue, and the juice had dribbled in her mouth, sweet and sticky. She was the sweetest kind of poison—a craving that left her wanton and hungry.

"Nothing happened," Malka said, as if it were not a lie.

CHAPTER 30

The infirmary sat on the outskirts of Valón, as far as possible from the river bisecting the city. Many people feared the water could transport the sickness. Unlike the Yahadi Quarter, which sat at Valón's southern plains, the infirmary was so far north, the distant Orzegali mountains grew more imposing as they approached.

A nurse escorted them to a back room.

"Put these on," she said, offering them pieces of cloth which had been dipped in rose oil. "The smell is rather unpleasant."

Malka pressed the cloth to her nose. The rose oil was concentrated but could not drown out the putrid scent of dead bodies which came from a room they passed. She peered in. Stacks of the dead rotted away on top of one another.

"They are dying so fast we don't have the time to dispose of them all properly. At the end of each week, we roll them out and bury them together."

Malka's heart ached. For the Yahad, the dead should be buried as soon as possible, and she wondered if the Ozmins were the same. But there they were, decomposing without the earth to welcome them back. She wondered what became of Hadar's body; if the Yahad who remained had given her the burial she deserved. Tears pricked her eyes, and she blinked them away.

The room holding those with the Mázág sickness was the largest in the infirmary, with at least forty beds placed side by side. In each bed, a sick patient.

"Come," the nurse said. "Eliška is this way."

They must have passed a dozen beds before they arrived at Eliška's. The room was hot and stuffy, and they shed their cloaks. Imma's workroom always overheated, so Malka had planned accordingly, borrowing an elbow-length blouse from Chaia.

When Eliška shifted onto her back, Malka gasped. She was so pale, Malka barely recognized her. Her veins had blackened and bulged hard, blood struggling to flow through them. Her cheeks were a sallow green, eyelids thin as paper.

"I know," Eliška croaked. "I'm obviously the epitome of health." Not even the sickness could hide the sarcasm from her voice.

"You were fine only days ago, I can't believe it," Malka lamented.

Eliška shrugged. "Sévren will say I'm being punished for helping you commit treason. But I do not believe that. If anything, Triorzay, bless His name, is keeping me alive because of it."

Nimrah settled her hand on Eliška's knee. "Stay alive, Eliška, you must."

Eliška raised her brow. "Why, Nimrah, I did not think you cared so much about me."

"I don't," Nimrah said, though she did not move her hand. "Only I know you hide more secrets besides those under your floorboard, and we are in need of them once again."

Eliška huffed a laugh and spiraled into a coughing fit. When it subsided, Malka offered her the glass of water from her side table. Eliška accepted it and sipped. "Should have known you'd come here wanting something. Like Vilém and his damn surveys."

Nimrah cracked a smile. Malka was relieved to hear Eliška in good spirits. She certainly didn't look well, and years of helping Imma with her patients meant Malka had become familiar with the stages of sickness, and when someone was not long for this world.

"Eliška, I . . . please know that if I could, I would try and heal you as I did Amnon." Malka kept her wording vague, in case of prying ears. "But I brought some herbs, and if you'll let me, I'd like to try and help you."

"I know, Malka," Eliška responded with a yawn. "Tell me what you wish to know."

"Sévren has ordered Malka's mother to die for a crime she did not commit at the Léčrey celebration," Nimrah said. "They have taken her into a prison held deeper in the earth than the castle's main dungeon. They say she is in a cell underground, where she can only stand prostrate and do nothing else. Do you know of such a place?"

Eliška's face was incapable of growing any paler. "I know of it."

Nimrah dropped her voice low to guarantee they would not be overheard. "Do you know how we can break someone out? The same way you led us to the secret entrance to the prison in the confe—" The tip of Nimrah's flesh ear reddened. "The confessional."

"I'm sorry, my girl. That place is so hidden, I'm afraid they did not even put its location on the maps. The architect had it spoken to the construction workers, who spoke of its location to King Ordobav, who passed the location through the generations in whispers."

Malka's heart sank. "There has to be a way."

Eliška blinked sleepily. "Guards are always the most vulnerable when they are away from their usual posts. You say she will be taken to the Léčrey celebration? You'd have much more luck freeing her there than in that hell of a prison . . ."

Nimrah rubbed the nape of her neck, a physical emulation of Malka's distress.

What Eliška suggested sounded impossible. Though, so had the possibility of freeing the Maharal. Of holding Yahadi mysticism in her fingers. Only she no longer had magic to aid her. It was gone. Another thing to grieve, another thing to mourn.

Eliška drifted back to sleep. Nimrah went to shake her awake again, but Malka caught her wrist.

"Let her sleep. She needs it."

Nimrah's eyes fell to her arm, and Malka let go quickly, hardening her face.

One of the nurses entered the room, refilling a patient's glass of water and dampening their forehead cloth again. Nimrah waited until she left again to speak. "I'm not sure how wise it will be to wait until the Léčrey celebration to free your mother."

"Do we have another choice?" Malka questioned. "You heard Eliška. When we freed the Maharal, Sévren did not yet know you were back. He didn't know me. Now, he knows us both. He knows what we did, and he will be far more careful this time."

"There's something . . ."

"What is it?" Malka frowned. "You've obtained what you wanted out of this deal, now you no longer wish to help me, is that it?"

"Just . . ." Nimrah made a frustrated sound. "Let's go back and talk about this."

"I promised I'd try and help her," Malka deflected, unpacking her herbs, and settling them on Eliška's bedside. "You're free to go."

Nimrah lingered, as if she wanted to say something. Malka waited for a reproach, a curse, a denial. Instead, she stayed silent, and turned to leave.

Before she could, a familiar voice sent a phantom chill up Malka's spine.

"Ah, so it is the Yahadi girl and her monstrous golem, once again."

Two guards trailed behind Sévren as he approached, his red robes vibrant against the tempered steel of the guards' armor. He wore the same charismatic smile each time Malka saw him, the same disquieting slit of his eyes. Malka wanted to take away his mouth the same way he had taken the Maharal's fingers, painfully tearing through each nerve and tendon.

"I see your bruises are healing nicely, girl. Though I'm afraid that the cut on your cheekbone might scar."

"What are you doing here, *Your Grace*?" Nimrah asked, mocking his honorific, though her voice was sickly sweet.

"I am a connection to Triorzay. He speaks through me, and I convey His will. It would be a disservice to the people of Valón if I did not hear the laments of the sick, would it not?"

"Yes, of course. We all know how well you care for the ill," Nimrah responded, crossing her arms.

Sévren grinned. "Oh, golem. You doubt me but believe me when I say I want nothing but the best for Ordobav. I want nothing but the best for our retired laundress, Eliška." His eyes drifted to Eliška's sleeping figure and he frowned. "It is so sad to see her like this. How interesting that Triorzay has bestowed this punishment on her now, and it is you two I find here at her bedside."

Malka's insides tilted, unsure if Sévren had discovered who helped them locate the dungeon, or if he was slotting the pieces together now. If he knew Eliška had aided them, Malka wouldn't underestimate his ability to uncover Chaia's and Vilém's involvement. She felt sick.

"How curious," Sévren remarked, eyes glancing between them, "that you both share the same lettering carved into your arm."

Malka glimpsed her exposed skin, then Nimrah's, whose sleeves had ridden up her arms when she had crossed them. "I had wondered how you appeared again, after your beloved rabbi promised you would not return. If I recall correctly, he, too, has Yahadi lettering carved into his skin. It was hard to miss as our doctors sewed up his amputated hands."

Sévren grinned the same way Abba did when he held a winning hand in the card games he had played with the other men in Eskravé. They had bet jewelry and trinkets instead of money. Malka never forgot the rage that had flushed his cheeks when he lost his pocket watch.

"Two Yahadi villages were destroyed because of you. I know you convinced Evžen to order the raids."

Sévren shrugged, undisturbed that Malka had accused him in front of his guards. "You can blame me if it makes you feel better. Though I am not the one who threw stones at windows or stampeded my horse over those poor Yahadi children. I merely gave those Paja members permission to be angry. You understand why they're angry, don't you?" He motioned around the room. "It is the same reason why all of these people are here—the plague."

"And you've convinced them that the plague is the fault of the Yahad, have you?"

"I have not needed to convince them of anything. The Ozmins are not sheep, Malka. They have simply put the pieces together."

"And what pieces are those?" Nimrah asked.

Sévren scanned the room. "Funny, how so many Ozmins are dying in this infirmary, when yesterday you Yahad were out dancing in the streets celebrating. What else are people supposed to think, when more and more Yahad are coming into power, and more and more Ozmins are dying?"

Anger simmered Malka's cheeks. The infirmary was run by the Church, so it made sense the sick Yahad would choose to stay home and either recover or die there. The Ozmins, who saw their people sick and suffering, did not see this. Did not choose to see this.

"That's not true, and you know it."

"Is it not? Do you have proof?"

The condescending way he spoke the words made Malka shudder, his snide confidence stripping her of speech. She had commanded the earth, killed a soldier twice her size, but those few words on the archbishop's tongue made her faulter. Could she prove Imma's innocence? There was no way. Yahadi magic didn't work the way Archbishop Sévren and Father Brożek had described, but that didn't matter. It was a Yahad's word against the Ozmini Church. They were empowered by the crown, money, and fear.

Sévren had left the room, yet Malka didn't notice. She stared at the place he had stood, hands curled into fists.

"Malka," Nimrah said tenderly, placing her hand on her shoulder. She felt the gentle caress of the golem's thumb, the softness of her name in her breathy voice. It was too much.

Malka came back to herself and shrugged Nimrah's hand away. "Leave me!"

Nimrah's lips thinned and her eyes cooled. She walked away without another word.

CHAPTER 31

When Malka returned, Chaia and Danya were huddled on the floor playing a game of split tooth. She caught them in the middle of a round, the ball still high from its bounce, both of them cupping their hands to draw close the rabbit teeth.

"Who's winning?" Malka asked, settling a hand on her stomach. The nausea from the rooting spell had yet to cease; Nimrah was not here. Nonsensically, Malka's eyes still searched for her.

Danya counted the teeth she had collected before the ball hit the ground again. She stared defeatedly at Chaia's pile and sighed. "Chaia, of course."

"You won last round!" Chaia countered, pooling the teeth to the center again.

"Yes, but you won the three rounds before."

Malka couldn't hide her smile. Danya had seen what no one should have seen. Had witnessed a terror that would make even grown men crumble. Hadar's loss clung to her, but she was glad Danya was here, alive, playing a child's game with Chaia.

"Danya, can I have a word with Chaia?"

"Of course, Malka. Anyway, it would be an embarrassment to lose again." She lingered at the doorframe. "I am so glad you are both alive and well."

Malka smiled, eyes glazing. "Me too, *Achoti*."

It had been so long since Malka endeared her with that name as she did Hadar. The meaning of it so simple in their ancient holy language: *my sister*. As their personalities clashed and drove them apart in recent years, it had felt too intimate to use. Malka would not let that happen any longer. They were all each other had.

Danya smiled the way she always did—subtly and not touching her eyes, but Malka knew it was true. "I'm not upset that Abba ran. We are better without him."

He had been a good father once. But they had lost him to Mavetéh. Not his body, but his spirit. His kindness.

"We are," Malka agreed, though still she ached, betraying herself.

When Danya was gone, Malka settled herself on the floor next to Chaia. She was collecting the rabbit teeth and placing them back in their pouch.

"What do you think they have in store for her—Imma—at the Léčrey celebration?"

"Nothing good," Chaia responded. "They're on high alert since the Maharal's escape, especially now that they know Nimrah is back."

"I need her back, Chaia." Malka choked back tears.

Chaia cupped her cheek. "I know, *Yedid Nefesh*. We will free her."

Malka pressed her hand against Chaia's. "I want a part in this plan to kill Sévren. I thought I could take the cards the Church dealt me and play them cunningly. But it is a losing game. If you say this duke can open new doors for the people of Ordobav, I want to help."

A smile tugged at Chaia's lips. "You are different than when I left."

Malka *was* different. As an older sister in Eskravé, there were things she was not allowed to be. She could not be angry. Anger was for Danya, who always spoke her mind. She would fight with Imma, fight with Malka. But Malka could not be angry, too. Someone needed to be there to absorb her sister's heat.

She could not have been afraid, either. Afraid had been for Hadar when she awoke from nightmares, drenched with sweat and tears in her eyes. Malka had had to comfort her, holding her sister to her chest until her breath evened and her tears subsided.

But now, Malka was both angry and afraid. She would not cower from her emotions this time. She'd lean into them. Let them wrap around her like armor. She'd command them the way the Maharal had commanded the earth to create the golem. They would be hers to feel and use to her advantage.

The anger would drive her. The fear would remind her what was at stake.

But Malka felt a third emotion as fiercely as the others. It was one she had nurtured unknowingly, from the soft moments in Eskravé with her family. The nights under the stars with Chaia. When Amnon volunteered to come with Malka into Mavetéh, not sure whether they would come out alive. When she had danced with Nimrah at Chaia's wedding.

It was hope.

Hope that even in the darkest of moments, she could see the etrog plant poking through the earth, encouraging her to put one foot in front of the other.

And now, it was hope, fear, and anger that drove her to play a part in Ordobav's regime change. If change for her people would not come peacefully, she would take it violently.

Chaia began to play with her ring, her smile faltering. "Malka, there's something I must admit."

Dread crawled across her skin. "What?"

"When you left the Qehillah meeting room to speak with Amnon, Katarina and I proposed a plan to Nimrah. We asked . . . well, we asked if she would be willing to assassinate Sévren at the Léčrey celebration. Originally, we had planned to hire a Revaç. But while Sigmund's silence is guaranteed, the Revaç's was not. We knew we ran the risk of having him divulge his hiring to the highest bidder. Nimrah was a blessing for us. She could do it quietly. Quickly."

"But . . ." Malka's brow furrowed. "We weren't supposed to be here during the Léčrey celebration. We were supposed to be back in Eskravé." Malka's face blanched. "Before your wedding, this plan was made?"

Chaia nodded solemnly.

Betrayal stung like a slap across the face. It wasn't until the wedding that plans had changed. Before then, the bargain they had struck was still in motion. Nimrah coming back to Eskravé, pleading guilty to Father Brożek.

Chaia had known that. So had Nimrah. Yet they had agreed on the plan anyway. Chaia, her friend since birth. Nimrah, someone she . . .

"You proposed this knowing what Nimrah had agreed to do for Imma?"

"I'm sorry, Malka."

"Sorry?" Malka stood. She felt hot, dizzy. "What has happened to you in your year away? Or perhaps you have always been this selfish, and I had not seen it through my love for you. Maybe I was blind to how easily you could betray someone if it meant furthering your political goals."

"Malka—"

"That was my mistake."

Chaia stood, too, her face red. "You can't tell me you actually thought Father Brożek would keep his promise to you in the first place? If I thought there was the slightest chance Nimrah could save your mother through that deal, I wouldn't have suggested it to her. But I knew his promise was just a ploy. Just a *game*. The same kind that Sévren plays."

Malka wrapped her hands around herself, tears blurring the edges of her vision. "That wasn't for you to decide!"

Chaia drew her hands into fists. "I wouldn't have had to if you hadn't been so naive in the first place!"

Malka stepped back, shock slackening her jaw.

Chaia's hand flew to her mouth. "I'm sorry, Malka, I didn't mean—"

"Save it," Malka choked, and ran out the door.

The wind bit hard, pressing into her skin like the cut of a knife. She tugged the hood of her cloak more tightly around her face, blinking at the tears that had collected in her eyes.

Chaia was not the only one who had betrayed her.

What a fool Malka was for thinking Nimrah would so easily sacrifice herself. That she would pay for Mavetéh's crimes with her life.

You don't want this, Nimrah had said in the alley, breath tangling with hers. *You'll hate me.*

Perhaps Nimrah was warning her of her betrayal, and she had ignored it.

But Nimrah had kissed her all the same.

I will make it right, Nimrah had said to the Maharal. Only, Malka had thought she meant trading her life for Imma's. Now, she was not so naive.

She was the Foxwit again, believing the lies whispered into her ear as she searched the wrong hiding places.

Malka should have known she was bound to lose the game.

⚹

The doors of the shul Bachta glowed warm around their rims, inviting Malka inside from the torrential downpour. As she approached them, drenched and shaking with cold, a fervent sensation seized her. The rooting spell's nausea gave way to that maddening sense of awareness. Nimrah had to be close, perhaps inside the synagogue.

The realization pierced her with anger. She would not let Nimrah's presence stop her from seeking comfort in this place of worship. She refused.

She rolled her shoulders and stepped inside.

Malka reveled in the beauty of the synagogue as it was, no longer decorated for Chaia's wedding. Iron grills guarded the windows and chandeliers dripped from the ceiling, spilling their light across the room. Malka missed

Eskravé's shul. The one she had grown up in, where she had learned the shapes of the holy language and spoken them aloud for all to hear. It was all gone. Malka imagined it as ruined as the shul Amichati left hidden away in Mavetéh. It gave her comfort, knowing that one day her synagogue, too, would rise again. She would make sure of it.

"Malka?" The Maharal waved as he approached.

"Rav," Malka greeted, doing her best to keep her voice even. "Have I missed evening services?"

"You're in time," the Maharal replied. "Even a bit early, as you can see."

He motioned to the empty synagogue, where only a few people hovered, prepping for the service. They bent low, lighting the candles lining the pews.

The Maharal's gaze fell to the hem of Malka's cloak, which had dripped water into a puddle on the floor near her feet.

Malka resisted the urge to cower with embarrassment. "The rain caught me off guard."

"It's no problem, Malka. We keep a few spare towels in the attic if you'd like to dry off before the service. Though with the heavy rain, I doubt you will be the only one sporting damp attire tonight."

The Maharal's light tone eased Malka's shame. "Thank you, Rav."

"Be sure to take a candle, it's dark up there."

Malka collected her sopping cloak in her hand as she neared the spiral staircase, stopping first to grab a candle from the entrance table.

There was only one door at the top of the stairs, so Malka twisted the handle and slipped inside.

The room was stale. She wondered how often people ventured up here. As she closed the door behind her, dust motes flew around, illuminated by the flame.

She held the light out, running her eyes around the room to find the towels. It was a small space. Wooden beams protruded from the ceiling and pressed through the ground, creating a zigzag maze in the room. She ran her hand across the wall, her fingers pressing into tally marks in the wood.

Malka briefly remembered that Nimrah had once called the attic of the shul Bachta home. Peering around now, though, it seemed unlikely it was this exact space. She could not imagine anyone living up here in such conditions—not even the golem.

The awareness of *her* was incessant. Malka should not have come up here. She could no longer distinguish whether her mind clouded with thoughts of Nimrah because of the bond or if it was her own treacherous heart to blame.

Malka ambled over to another door in the attic, which she thought might be a storage room. She set down her candle and reached for the doorknob.

Before she could, the door swung open with a woosh, revealing Nimrah on the other side.

Malka's heart stuttered.

Nimrah's face had contorted in a slew of emotions before it settled on a pained expression as she stared at Malka.

Maybe Nimrah had also been unable to distinguish the signals of the rooting spell from her own feelings. She had nearly said as much when Malka had led her into that alley, not knowing if the strength of the spell was perpetuated by the feelings she admitted to having.

In the doorframe, they were only inches from each other. It would be so easy to kiss her again, to tangle her hands in Nimrah's hair and drag her fingers to the apex of her thighs, where they had left off. But she remembered what had followed. Knew now that even in that alley, Nimrah had known she would betray Malka. And still, she had kissed her mouth. Had buried herself beneath her skirts.

Malka was bruised by the memory of her.

Nimrah's low voice broke the weighted silence between them. "What are you doing here?"

"I was grabbing towels to dry off before the service," Malka pressed her palms into Nimrah's chest, pushing her away. "Why are *you* here?"

"The Maharal offered me my old room again now that . . ." she faded off, though Malka knew what she was going to say. Their deal was over now that Father Brożek had forsaken his promise, that Imma was doomed despite any true monster Malka could seize from the forest and plant at his feet. Her innocence did not matter.

"How convenient you had a place to welcome you back. Tell me, did it make it easier to betray me, knowing you could come crawling back to the Maharal?"

Nimrah swallowed. "Chaia told you."

Her distraught voice revealed the truth of her betrayal. Malka imagined it like a berry between her teeth, the lie popping and staining her chin red.

"I needed you to admit it."

"Malka, you must understand—"

Malka crossed her arms, fighting the warmth that spread from her name on Nimrah's tongue. It was wholly unfair, to feel betrayed by her body, as well. "I understand perfectly well. You meant to scorn our agreement regardless."

Nimrah sighed. She paced the small room. It was simple—devoid of personality and color. A bed sat shouldered against a wall, a small desk was littered with scrolls, a sheathed knife, and several guttered candles sighing ribbons of smoke with the last of their light. Malka could hardly imagine her room without Hadar's paper cuttings lining the wall and the glimmering wind chime hanging from her window.

Grief washed over her again, begriming like soot. All of that was gone. Hadar was gone. It suffocated her as if the grief were new again, but she could not be buried underneath its weight. Not now, when Imma's life still hung in the balance. So, Malka turned her grief into anger.

"Destruction truly does follow in your wake," Malka bit out, moving further into the room to lean against the edge of the desk, as if the wood itself could offer her strength. "Basám's son, the Mázág sickness, my village... Hadar."

Nimrah's face fell. She turned away. From this angle, Malka could only see the stone of her face, illuminated by the candlelight while shadows hid whatever human parts of her remained. "You don't understand."

"I understand why you forsook me. What is one Yahadi life when you have the opportunity to save Ordobav from the tyrannical hands of the Ozmini Church? You made an impossible choice, yet so did I—when I stepped into Mavetéh's arms and welcomed death's cool touch on the slight chance I might be able to save Imma."

Malka rolled up the sleeve of her blouse and traced the scabbed lettering on her arm. "The promise of our deal is mutilated into my skin. You have forced me to carry a lie forever."

"Then mutilate me in return." Nimrah stalked forward, caging Malka as she pressed her palms to the desk. "Scar me. Command me. Force me to remember my deceit by carving it into my stone. I'll allow it from you, only you."

When Nimrah pulled back, the knife that had been on the desk was now unsheathed in her grip. Measuredly, Nimrah sank to her knees. She ensnared Malka's wrist and pulled her closer. So close that if Malka bowed her back only slightly, Nimrah's lips would brush her chest. Her chin tilted up to meet Malka's gaze, eyes begging for absolution.

Nimrah began to wrap Malka's fingers around the hilt.

Malka tried to jerk her hand away, but Nimrah would not let it budge. Nimrah guided the blade to her neck.

"All I ever wanted was to protect the Yahad. How do you think I feel having let them down so many times? Having let *you* down?"

Malka hated the spark of compassion which seized her. She, too, knew what it was like to fail at protecting the people she loved most.

"When Chaia came to me with one last opportunity to show my worth as a golem—to protect the Yahad when I have failed in all other ways—I took it. You heard yourself what it would mean to bring religious freedom to Ordobav. What kind of place it could become if people are truly free to practice their religions, without a tithe, without a badge they must wear on their clothes. Without a church that seeps its way into commerce and politics."

The knife wavered in Malka's hand. Nimrah tightened her hand to steady her hold.

"I'm not doubting that, Nimrah."

It was the first time Malka had voiced her name, the shape of it in her mouth intoxicating, potent with meaning.

Nimrah's eyes darkened.

"Do you think I don't also long for that future?" Malka continued. "That I will not do all I can to help obtain it? I am angry. Angry I was betrayed by the people I care about. Tell me, how would you've cleared me out of your way when I demanded we begin our journey back to Eskravé? A kick to the head, like the Ordobav guard whose scar I will wear forever?"

"Don't say that." Nimrah leaned in, causing bright red blood to well from her neck as the blade pierced her.

Malka tried to pull away, but Nimrah held her tight. "What should I say? I wish I had never pulled you into that shadowed alley. I wish I had never kissed you."

Nimrah's face chilled, her eyes deep pools that swirled with hurt like the most poisonous colored waral fruit. "Punish me," she growled. The room shivered as she spoke. "Drive the blade into my skin for my betrayal, for the failure of my creation."

She had thought Nimrah angry at the words Malka spat as weapons. But she recognized it now as anger at herself. It was the same look that had crossed her face when she told the story of her exile—the same plummy glaze which meant she was deep in her thoughts, living in the failure of her actions.

Nimrah was a creature of Kefesh. She couldn't die without her murderer dying, too. But Nimrah didn't know that.

Whatever role she had played in Mavetéh's turn, Malka had never predicted this of Nimrah: a woman, on her knees, begging for punishment.

It didn't matter now. Malka had promised herself she would not be distracted again. Malka shoved Nimrah's hand away, which had gone slack around hers in waiting. The knife clattered on the floor.

"Whatever had bloomed between us is dead," Malka declared. "You will kill the archbishop, I will save my mother, and we will go our separate ways. I will forget about you, and you will forget about me."

Nimrah stared at the blade. Its sharp edge was swathed with her blood. "Is this how it shall be?"

"I want no memory of you," Malka said to drive in the point.

Nimrah pounded her fist on the floor. The wood creaked in anger, vines slithering through the cracks in the floorboard. She bent low to pick up the knife from the floor. She wiped her own blood from it on her tunic. She felt dangerous. Like the Rayga Malka had always imagined, pupils wide and anger flaring.

Then, it slipped away. Nimrah once again donned the mask she had so treasured, so strategically crafted.

"Fine," the golem said coolly.

Malka could not handle anymore. She slammed the door as she left, leaving Nimrah on her knees.

↘

"Do it," Malka said. "You owe me this much."

In the dark quiet later that night, Chaia settled the blade between her thumb and forefinger. "Are you sure?"

Sure? Malka wasn't sure of anything. She had been lied to, betrayed. Forsaken by multiple bargains. "I want no memory of her," Malka gritted, because it's what she had told Nimrah, because it was the truth. It was too painful, this constant reminder. This chain.

Pain seared as Chaia began to carve around the word, which had barely begun to scar. Around *shoresh,* the word which rooted them, she carved in the letters to make the word *rootless*. A new command made from an old one. The same she had used to free Nimrah from the Great Oak.

Their connection broke in a scouring wave, and Malka grimaced as her body adjusted. She shivered at the cold. Had it always been this cold without their connection?

"I think it's done," Chaia said, staring at the bloody mess of Malka's arm, face pale.

Malka was certain. All that remained was the haunting of what had once been. A sharp grief burying itself inside of her. The unwanted tang of memory.

She wondered if Nimrah felt it, too. If she knew what Malka had done.

"Good," Malka said, breathless.

CHAPTER 32

Bells rang from Valón's largest church on the day of the Léčrey celebration. So grand were they, the sound flooded into the Yahadi Quarter and through the window where Malka sat, combing Danya's hair. She tensed, hairbrush stilling. The bells rang the same as those in Eskravé to signal curfew.

"I'll never forget that sound," Danya said. "Do you remember the day they first rang? It was so hollow, like they would swallow all sounds of happiness."

Malka's chest tightened, but she resumed her brushing. "You were so young."

"And you were eighteen—my age now—still young, too."

Malka smirked. "Last you told me, you were an adult."

"I feel like I've aged so much these last few days, I will cling to all the youth I can."

Malka settled the hairbrush on Chaia's dresser.

"What was Mavetéh like?" asked Danya. "The first night you were gone, Hadar couldn't stop crying. I held her close, but she never felt comforted by me the way she did with you. There was something special between the two of you. Something I wish you and I had not lost as we aged."

Danya. Stubborn, independent Danya who didn't understand why Malka never stood up for herself. Why she swallowed her feelings. Danya didn't understand because she never *had* to. She was barely thirteen when Mavetéh began to hunt their girls. Of course, it was Malka who had to step up. But Danya was only defending her, in the way she did with the people she loved.

"We will find it again," Malka said, determined. "I love you, Danya. More than anything."

"I love you, Malka."

Malka tugged her sister close, resting her chin on Danya's boney shoulder. "There's one more thing, *Achoti*."

"What is it?"

Malka sat back. "Promise me you'll stay home during the Léčrey celebration with Amnon. You know we'll do everything in our power to save her. But ... to lose you would break me. He'll protect you."

Malka didn't know what the Léčrey celebration would bring, or how the events would unfold. It would give Malka peace to know Danya was safe.

Danya opened her mouth as if to argue, but resigned. "Alright, Malka. I'll stay here."

Malka's heart swelled, and tears gathered in her eyes.

A knock echoed on the door, and Chaia peeked inside. "Sorry for interrupting. We're preparing some last-minute things for tomorrow. Malka, could you join us?"

"Of course," Malka said, kissing Danya's cheek before following Chaia into the kitchen.

Amnon handed her a steaming mug of coffee which warmed her hands. "I'll go sit with Danya," he said in her ear.

"Thank you for doing this," Malka responded. "It means as much to me as any knightly deed."

She expected a retort, a sign of frustration about his circumstance, or his lack of role in freeing Imma. But instead, Amnon smiled. A true one, that touched the corners of his eyes. "Always, Malka. Always."

⚹

"There are two parts to the Léčrey celebration," Vilém began. "Shortly after it starts, Evžen will give a speech. It is usually a variation of the same speech he gives every year, about Saint Celine's blessing on him and thus, on Ordobav. Sévren and the king will stand beside him, but for the rest of the time they schmooze among the people."

"When will they bring Imma out?"

"At the end of the celebration. That is when, each year, well . . ."

"They sacrifice someone to Saint Celine," Chaia finished, but her voice was soft, comforting.

"Yes," Vilém cleared his throat. "The king, the prince, and Sévren will make their way to the balcony of the town hall to watch the burning. Katarina will delay Sévren by asking him to bless her rosary. He's all about face, so we think he'll do it. Especially if Katarina plays up her reverence of him, which she'll *surely* love. To avoid the guards on the balcony and by the town hall entrance, Nimrah will use her abilities to climb through the stairwell window. With everyone else already at the balcony, Sévren will be the only one left to head upstairs. That's when Nimrah will snap his neck. It'll look like he had a heart attack and fell down the steps. When they find him dead, the commotion that ensues will make it easier to divert attention away from freeing your mother."

They had explained that the transition would be slow after Sévren's death. The estate council in Lei, which the Maharal and a few of Vilém's fellow magisters had been collaborating with for years, would condemn King Valski's inaction on the worsening Mázág sickness and clergy corruption, and vote to replace him with the duke. Apparently, the estate council was already interested in the stability of the duke's rule after the lackluster reign of his older brother.

Chaia added, "Speaking of which, have you seen Nimrah?"

"No." She said the word too hotly, too fast.

Vilém and Chaia exchanged a look, and Chaia frowned.

Malka knew Chaia had regretted the words she had spat during their heated fight, that she felt remorse about her betrayal. She wore her regrets in the way she bit the skin from her lower lip, how she pulled at the split ends of her hair when Malka grew silent around her. For so much of their lives, Malka had hidden her feelings from Chaia the same way she had her family. It had never been intentional, only the side effect of a well-practiced muscle. But she wasn't hiding them now.

"I'll see if I can find her," said Vilém, pulling Chaia in to kiss her forehead and disappearing out the door. "I'll touch base with Katarina and the others while I'm out."

Malka and Chaia sat in silence. Malka bit from her bread, chewing the crust until her jaw ached.

"If you can't forgive me, I hope you'll eventually be able to forgive Nimrah. I pushed her. Told her it was the one way she could redeem herself."

Malka said nothing, resisting the urge to scratch the newly traced letters carved into her arm.

"She cares for you."

Malka bristled. "She cares for her duty."

"And you are so different?"

Malka glared at her. "We aren't the same."

"No," Chaia agreed. "You are more like the teal-taloned owl we would see in Kratzka Šujana's trees when we hid during the Game of the Foxwit, brooding over those you love so they have the chance to grow. Nimrah is more like the gray-faced lion, which roars as loud as its voice allows to scare off a threat. You both lead such different lives, but at the heart of it your goals are the same—to be protectors. Nimrah was made to protect the Yahad, yes. But from the time I met you, Malka, there hasn't been a second you haven't thought about protecting those you love. Even if it meant sacrificing yourself. Can you blame Nimrah for sacrificing her feelings for you to protect the Yahad in Ordobav?"

"I cannot help the betrayal I feel. How easily Nimrah was able to throw Imma's life to the wayside. How easily *you* could betray me. I think that hurts most. Knowing the one person I thought I could always trust has forsaken me."

"Of course, you can feel hurt and betrayed. Of course. You have every right to be mad at her. Mad at *me*. I will take your anger. All I ask is that you see how alike you and Nimrah are. That you give her a little grace with a tough decision she had to make. I can tell you she will never forgive herself for betraying you."

Chaia said the words about Nimrah, but Malka knew she meant them for herself, too. But it was harder to talk about Chaia's betrayal. Made her relive the pain over and over again. Anger at Nimrah was easy.

"She will fulfill her duty and I will fulfill mine. We will go our separate ways."

Chaia raised her brow. "And is that what you want?"

"It's what is best."

"Those are not always the same."

Malka gritted her teeth. "They will have to be this time."

"You are allowed to want something, Malka. Want *someone*."

Malka regarded her best friend. Her jaw ticked. "I wanted *you* to come home. I begged for it every day. And I lost you. Then I got you back, and you betrayed me. I wanted Hadar to have a future away from all this violence and look at what happened. I am not allowed to want. I *cannot* want."

"Malka, Hadar's death was not your fault. Neither was my disappearance. Leaving without any goodbyes will haunt me. Do you think I don't dream of it? That I don't wake up angry with myself knowing you thought I was dead? For letting my parents possibly go to their grave, thinking they had lost me first? You are not the only one who has lost people they love. Who regrets. Who feels they are letting everyone down. Who feels selfish for doing what feels right at the time, even if it means hurting the people I love. You do not own this grief, this heartache."

She wasn't just talking about her disappearance anymore, but the plan she had made with Nimrah that would have betrayed Malka.

"If this is the price you are always willing to pay for politics," Malka said, "you'll soon find yourself without anyone left to bargain."

"Everything I do is for the people I love! For you. For my parents. For Eskravé." Chaia drew her ring between her fingers, tracing the curve of the design. "When Vilém met me, I was so angry. My life had turned upside down all because I wanted justice for Eskravé. I had never felt more powerless. I had left everyone I cared about. I was so *angry*, Malka. Angry about the injustices forcing me to make this impossible choice. For feeling like I might have chosen wrong every day."

She took a deep, ragged breath before continuing.

"Vilém . . . he became the sand to my fire. He never tried to put it out, only made it more manageable for me to survive. When I felt homesick, he would take me in his arms and whisper silly songs in my ear until I laughed instead of cried. He has a terrible voice, you know."

Malka and Chaia both chuckled, and the tension in the room eased, like how a brush of rain can crack a simmering summer day. Malka struggled with the upkeep of her anger. She had lost so much; she could not lose Chaia, too.

"I forgive you for leaving me," Malka said. "I don't know if I can forgive you for betraying me."

Chaia's face fell. Her brows creased and her mouth drooped to cry. A tear fell from her cheek, and Malka wiped it away with her calloused thumb.

"I understand, *Yedid Nefesh*."

Malka would always feel hurt by Chaia's disappearance. The year Malka thought her dead would be etched into her heart. It would pull and ache. She'd never be rid of the feeling. But Malka understood Chaia, and why she had to stay in Valón.

She understood why Chaia had betrayed her, too. She had sacrificed what she loved for a greater cause, just as she said Nimrah had done. And sacrifice was something Malka knew well. Yet it did not ease the pain. Ease the loss of trust.

They stood, and Chaia wrapped Malka in her arms. Malka let herself be hugged. She pressed her chin to Chaia's shoulder, taking in her familiar rosewater scent. They stayed there until their muscles ached and the candles dimmed low, letting each other be the comfort they needed.

Malka had lost countless people already.

She hoped, eventually, she and Chaia could rebuild from this. Learn to trust again. It was the Yahadi way. The values Baba had instilled in her. She held them close.

For now, this moment was enough.

CHAPTER 33

The Léčrey celebration was an ostentatious revel that soured Malka's stomach. Strung flowers hung across the dais of Ordobav Square, constructing a sky of red and orange above them. Booths behind curtains revealed costumes, trinkets, and Ordobavian street food, from rolled pastries dusted with cinnamon sugar to hearty sausage dumplings and mulled wine. Festival goers traipsed from booth to booth in red and blue clothing and masks as a tribute to Saint Celine, who was clad in a red sash and blue vestment. Paintings and figurines of her and Prince Evžen moved around the square, carried by children who held them above their heads like flags.

It was hard to think that days ago, she had gone to the infirmary and seen how the sharp claws of sickness had dug its way through the city, leaving wounds of death and destitution. Yet, all signs of poverty-stricken citizens were costumed by this lavish affair.

Malka felt like a betrayer herself, tugging at the fabric of the same borrowed festive kroj Chaia had lent her for the wedding.

Nimrah's disappearance had put them all on edge, but Malka reassured them she would come. After the time they had spent together, Malka was sure about one thing: Nimrah would do anything to prove herself. And this was her greatest opportunity of all. However, it didn't stop Malka fidgeting with her necklace, pricking the pad of her thumb with the sharp points.

Any moment, Malka expected to feel the nausea and dizziness of the rooting spell because of Nimrah's absence. But it never came. Never *would* come now that she had severed the bond between them.

All that plagued her was the sense of unease at not knowing Nimrah's whereabouts. Malka hadn't realized how habituated she had become with the push and pull of their connection until the lack of it made her feel empty.

Her body stirred, as if the memory of the spell's effects livened something within her. A phantom craving of what had once become normal.

You're a fool, she thought to herself in reprimand. Betrayed by her own body.

She rolled her shoulders, drawing her mind back to the present and the revel unspooling around her.

Sévren would die today. It felt forbidden to know. And like Abayda as he held the book of knowledge in his hands for the first time, Malka held something dangerous. Something that would change Ordobav's course. Change everything she once knew. She thought of the Tannin in the Leirit river, warning of destruction. And oh, had it arrived.

Malka was no stranger to death. Nor was she a stranger to killing.

She recalled one of Imma's sick patients, many years ago. An infection had sunk into his bloodstream, worse than Imma could manage. In his strongest moments, he had asked for her to end his suffering.

Malka, small and naive, had asked if his request was forbidden.

"*There are many forbidden things,*" Imma had explained. "*But rarely does that mean we cannot make the choice to do them anyway. If the cause is right.*"

Malka had not understood what Imma had meant. She thought Imma was disobeying Yohev by controlling a fate that wasn't hers to control. But Malka respected Imma and watched anyway as she dropped the tincture into the man's mouth.

He had taken one more ragged breath and stilled. The tension that had held his face in a permanent scowl had ceased. His eyes, clamped so tight they watered, softened without pain.

Imma had lifted the sheet to cover his head and called for his family to collect him.

Malka had expected the family to be angry, but they only embraced Imma.

"*Thank you, for managing his pain, and for letting him be at peace.*"

"*May his memory be a blessing,*" Imma had responded, a tear glistening in her eye.

Lost in the memory, Malka didn't notice Vilém's approach.

"Peace and light, Malka," he greeted.

Around them, people stared at the Yahadi ring adorning his finger. To some, it was a mark of his betrayal. Yet they kept quiet, knowing his scholarly status. Even wearing his ring was an act of rebellion against the Church's strict societal requirements. Yet, Vilém had said he cared not for the blessing of the Church, only the blessing of Triorzay Himself.

"Chaia will be here soon," he said now, adjusting the clasps at his chest.

The clasps were beautiful gold pieces shaped into roses. While Vilém had expressed his interest in a kingdom where all religions held value, and the Church's influence fell to the wayside, Malka couldn't deny her suspicion. Especially when he wore gold clasps that would have fed her family for months.

"Vilém," Malka began. "Are you sure what's planned for today is what you want? You gain so much from this life already, why would you want things to change?"

Vilém didn't look hurt by her accusation, only interested that Malka had decided to ask him. "That's the same question Chaia drilled me with for the first few months I knew her. But I'm a scholar—knowledge is the bedrock of how I think about the world. As I do my work, as I engage with more and more colleagues, I wonder how many great minds have been disregarded due to prejudice. In what world is that fair to anyone? Knowledge has been lost throughout history because of those too afraid to let others have power. As a scholar, and as a man, I will not be responsible for making that same mistake."

"You and Chaia are meant for each other," Malka said, grinning. "I could've plucked your reasoning straight from her mouth."

Vilém's attention caught on someone behind Malka. His face brightened. "I am a lucky man, Malka."

Chaia had arrived, smiling. She, too, was dressed beautifully. The pieces of her kroj were beautifully embroidered. Her blouse was threaded with bright red flowers, stark against the cream linen. Her vest shimmered as she walked, beaded with crimson and gold in patterns that emphasized the shape of her waist and the billowing of her sleeves. The pattern matched the ribbons on her flowing apron, accentuated by the embroidered petticoats she wore beneath. The patch sewn into her robe was ugly, but Chaia embraced it as well as anyone could.

"Evžen's about to give his speech," she said. "Have you seen Nimrah?"

Malka scrutinized the crowd, hoping she might see Nimrah's black waves, or the gray stone which cut across her face. *I want no memory of you,* she had told her. Yet even without the rooting spell, Malka could not pry her from her mind, like the cloth drenched in rose oil she had pressed to her nose in the infirmary. Even when she disposed of the cloth, the scent had been embedded into her skin and lingered for days.

"No," Malka responded, a slight ache in the pit of her stomach.

Chaia huffed, but Malka knew she was nervous. "She better show."

"She will," Malka said, more to ease her own fears. If Nimrah didn't show, if Sévren didn't die, rescuing Imma would be impossible. "She must."

If she didn't, Malka would have no one to blame but herself. She had severed the connection between them; freed Nimrah of her chains. Malka had let her emotions get the better of her, not thinking of the consequences of the letters carved fresh around the rooting command. The possibility that, no longer bound, Nimrah might run.

She stared at the sky, at the glimmering flags flapping like bird wings in the wind. She had to have hope. Hope that the weeks spent with Nimrah meant something. That she knew the golem well enough to make that promise to Chaia.

They would soon find out.

CHAPTER 34

When the crowd circled around the stage began to drum with applause, Malka, Vilém, and Chaia found a good place to view the dais. It was decorated with pale snowdrops and bright mauve hellebores. A row of guards split a path and Prince Evžen and King Valski strolled toward the stage. Evžen had all of his father's features—sand-colored hair brushing to his ears in length, though most of it was covered by his jeweled crown, which glimmered under the festival lights. The king's gold crown was studded with rubies, the same red of Father Brożek's robes. It seemed impossible this was the Dull King, garbed in so much gold and velvet.

As they approached the dais, King Valski tapped his scepter onto the stone to settle the crowd, yet the sound only heightened. The king motioned to the guards, and they struck their swords together in a piercing clang, quieting the crowd at once. Evžen stood beside him, his arms clasped. Malka slit her eyes to see better, but she could not find Sévren anywhere.

Malka sent a worried glance to Chaia, who had grown pale at Sévren's absence. He was supposed to be here. At every Léčrey celebration, Vilém had told them, Sévren stood between the prince and the king.

"Citizens of Ordobav," the king began, and his voice was nothing like Malka expected. He slurred his words only barely. Anyone else would think it a result of the cold stiffening his jaw. But Malka recognized it from Abba's late-night returns, foul breathed and angry.

The king was drunk.

"Twenty-five years ago, Saint Celine gave her blessing to our rule and to the people of this great kingdom with the birth of my son. Today, we celebrate his miracle birth, and the blessing of the saints. Now, Prince Evžen has some words he would like to share with you all."

Vilém had said Imma would be secured in a tumbrel surrounded by guards near the square. Malka searched for any wooden cages, though it was unlikely she'd be where the revelers could spot her yet—her unveiling was part of the event. So close, yet still out of Malka's grasp.

Nimrah was nowhere to be seen. Sévren was absent. Everything was wrong.

Evžen stepped forward and began his speech. He was calm, voice even.

"It's an honor to celebrate my birthday with all of you. Though truly, it's a day for everyone. Saint Celine has blessed us. Each year, we grow stronger, greater. The most vital kingdom in Rhaška."

The crowd cheered, hands flailing in the air.

He opened his mouth to continue, but there was a barreling whoosh and the sound of metal thudding into a body. Evžen's face contorted, blood dripping from his mouth. He fell forward with a loud thump, a throwing axe embedded in his back.

The moment Evžen hit the dais, his blood seeping out from under him, time slowed. The clank of his crown as it fell from his head echoed. The crowd was silent as they processed the death of their saint-blessed prince until the horror struck them as real.

The crowd searched for the prince's murderer.

Malka's eyes were the first to catch on Nimrah, so instinctual that Malka would have blamed the bond between them had she not herself witnessed its severing.

Nimrah stood near a costume stall across from the dais. To anyone else, it would have been a difficult venture to aim a weapon so precisely that it hit its target without shaving off the heads of those in the crowd. But Nimrah was not just anyone.

Though, staring at her now, Malka did not know if she recognized this version of Nimrah: knuckles white around the handle of another axe, breathing hard as the wind whipped her hair around her like a shroud. Her eyes were like hot coals, dangerous and visceral.

Malka bit down on her tongue.

Screams filled the air as the crowd recognized Nimrah and took in her dark green veins, her half-stone body.

A knight yelled orders. Some rushed to the king, covering his body with theirs and pushing him away from the surging crowd. The others set their sights on Nimrah, unsheathing their weapons in pursuit. A priest ran to the dais and rested his hand on the prince's chest.

Malka couldn't move. She couldn't breathe. It was not supposed to happen like this. Evžen was not Nimrah's target, and no one was supposed to die on the dais.

She tracked Nimrah, who began her escape as she jostled past the festival goers. With the flick of her hand, vines unfurled from the earth and wrapped around the legs of a market stall, pulling it off balance and sending it clattering to the ground. Tapestries flew everywhere, masks decorating the floor. The knights stumbled over the stall.

Someone knocked into Malka, jolting her into someone else. Her jaw hit hard on a sharp shoulder as she lost sight of Nimrah and the knights chasing her. She tasted blood.

Children were sobbing, their celebration masks crooked and broken on their faces as parents tugged them to safety.

One of the knights who had escorted the king away returned to the dais and quieted the raucous crowd with his buisine.

"The king is offering a generous reward of one thousand Ordon coins to anyone who can bring the golem's head on a spike," he announced, though not even he could hide the slight waver of his voice. "She's an active threat to Valón and must be eradicated."

The crowd riled as a mob gathered, made mainly of Ozmini men, but some women had joined, as well. A few Yahad, distinguished by their rotas, drew away from them. The mob shouted threats. What they would do to Nimrah once they found her. *How* they would do it.

Malka's vision hazed as the commotion around her heightened.

In the crowd, she could faintly make out Chaia calling her name. Her eyes darted around frantically. When she finally spotted her, Malka's shoulders slumped in relief. They came together and Malka took Chaia's hand like it was a lifeline, like she would be swept away in the current if she were to ever let go. Together, they pushed their way out of the mass of people threatening to swallow them.

"We need to find Nimrah," Malka said, raising her voice to be heard over the roaring chatter. If Nimrah had killed Evžen and incited this mob, there must've been a reason. She and Nimrah had fought, and Malka knew Nimrah was angry with her, but she wouldn't do this. Did Nimrah know something they didn't? What did this mean for Imma?

"We will," Chaia responded. "But it's not safe here now."

Vilém grasped Chaia's other hand and beckoned them to follow, but Malka wouldn't budge.

"But Imma—"

Another person slammed into Malka, knocking the air from her. She doubled over, arm around her ribs.

"Malka, you'll be no help to anyone if we don't get to safety first. There's no telling what a mob would do to a Yahad right now if they noticed us."

Though leaving without finding Nimrah or Imma made Malka sick, Chaia was right. It was dangerous to stay here.

Reluctantly she nodded and let Vilém guide them away from the pit of the crowd which threw threats in the air like the children's saint figurines.

Malka did not let go of Chaia until they stumbled into the old Qehillah meeting room. Danya and Amnon raised their heads from where they played a game of split tooth at the table.

"What's happened?" Amnon asked. "Is it done?"

"Something's gone terribly wrong," Chaia said, and recounted the celebration's unforeseen events.

⚹

More and more people began to arrive, enough to fill every seat at the long table and then some. Katarina had been right when she said there were many different kinds of people involved in this plot; several of Vilém's fellow Ozmini magisters, as well as the duke's supporters, who ranged from cooks to shoemakers and merchants. Several Yahad and Fanavi were there, too. Katarina began to pace.

"She's betrayed us," one of the Ozmini men said, running his hand against his stubbled cheek. "We should've known better than to trust the golem with something so important."

"We don't know what happened," Chaia responded, crossing her arms.

Another magister raised his sparse eyebrows. "We know exactly what happened, Chaia. She disappeared and came back to send an axe straight into Evžen's back."

It didn't make sense. Nimrah had no reason to betray them. She wanted Sévren's death as much as they did.

The door opened, and the Maharal joined them. The rabbi was ragged—pale and disheveled, with creased robes and a crooked wool hat upon his head.

"Your golem's gone rogue," Katarina said to him, tapping her foot.

Malka shook her head. "No, it's something else. It *has* to be something else. She wouldn't do this. If there's one thing I know about Nimrah, it's that she'd never do anything to purposefully put the Yahad in danger. Certainly not kill Evžen when she knew what was at stake."

The man with the stubbled cheek cleared his throat. "Ignác is right," he said, motioning to the scholar who had spoken earlier. "Maybe she had good intent. That doesn't change the fact she chose to betray us instead."

Something wasn't right. Malka *knew* Nimrah. She had spent every day with her since Nimrah drew her from the river. She had heard her stories, gauged the truth in Nimrah's eyes. Nimrah wanted nothing more than to protect the Yahad. She wouldn't do something this careless. Even with Basám's son, it had been an accident—Nimrah's power slipping for a moment. This . . . this was different.

When Nimrah had shared the story of her exile, when she had begged for Malka's forgiveness for betraying her, Malka had seen her regret in the bob of her neck and the sullen look in her eyes. After she threw the axe into Evžen's back, Nimrah's face had been hardened—glazed over. Like she was a different person.

"Something must've happened to her," Malka said. "Between the time I saw her in the synagogue attic to when she showed up at the dais. No one knew where she was. Something could've happened within that time."

"You think someone forced her to kill Evžen?" Amnon asked.

Malka closed her eyes, tried to think. Where her connection with Nimrah had once been distracting, the absence of it somehow left her mind more askew.

Her arm began to itch again. The fresh wound tormented her nearly as much as the rooting spell itself had.

Her heart stopped, realization dawning as she stared down at the grotesquely scabbed sketch of letters on her skin. She had left Nimrah without a connection, something to tie her down. Exactly what had happened when the Maharal severed their shadows to make his trip to Lei. But that couldn't be all it was. Killing the Yahadi boy had been a mistake, but there was no denying the deliberateness with which Nimrah had killed the prince.

Nimrah still had the command on her skin, ready for the next person to control her.

Malka's breath hitched as she began to piece together a possibility. She recalled the infirmary, when Sévren had taken special notice of the command written into both Malka and Nimrah's skin, similar to the writing on the Maharal's. Could he have known Malka had severed her connection to Nimrah? Maybe he didn't know Nimrah had to be rootless for a new commander to seize her. She didn't want to believe her rash actions might have led to this foolish opening for Sévren to take advantage.

"What if it was Sévren?"

Chaia shook her head. "I thought only a Yahad could command Kefesh."

"It's not impossible, but the outcome is never good." The Maharal had that strange look on his face again, like he had drifted elsewhere, pulled to a time long past.

"We have a bigger problem than finding her now," Katarina said, scratching the back of her neck. "She's awakened a fury in the Valonian people. She has killed a saint-blessed prince. The Yahad will most likely take the fall for this."

Malka gritted her teeth. "And that's exactly what Sévren wants. He wanted to set off violence here just as he did in my village."

"What are we gonna do?" asked Danya, who bit the nail of her thumb.

"We reveal the truth," said Vilém. "We show Sévren is the one commanding Nimrah. That she is being used as a weapon and Sévren killed the prince. There's no other way. Even if we free Nimrah from his command, the damage is done. They need to see the Yahad are not to blame for this."

"And how exactly is that going to happen?" Amnon asked skeptically. "Do you even know where they went?"

The room fell silent.

Wherever Nimrah had gone, it had to be somewhere close. She had disappeared quickly after knocking down the market stall.

"It can't be far from the square," Malka said. "She was gone in an instant."

"Well, we weren't in the Yahadi Quarter," the man with sparse eyebrows said. "No Ozmin would let her inside of their house."

"Except for Eliška, of course," Chaia countered. "But she's still in the infirmary."

Vilém shook his head. "Even so, her house is far on the outskirts. Nimrah would've been noticed going there."

"The only other place around the square was the clocktower," Malka said.

Chaia's face lit up. "That's it! The construction on the clocktower. They would've had to open the inside of the clock in order to work on it. If it was Evžen's proposal, it's not a leap to think Sévren had his hand in it. It's hidden from view, but he could still see the happenings of the square below."

"You think he'd still be there?" Malka asked. "He did what he intended. Evžen is dead. He has no reason to linger."

"What if he's not done, Malka?" Danya said, her voice barely above a whisper. "What if this is just the beginning?"

"Danya's right," Chaia said. "Nimrah was made for violence. Sévren knows this. If he *has* taken command of her, he doesn't have to wait for the Ozmins to riot against their Yahadi neighbors. Nimrah would kill them all in half the time."

"One thing," Amnon interrupted. "If Sévren is commanding Nimrah, what chance do we have of stopping her? We've seen what she can do."

"Perhaps someone could get through to her," Chaia said, eyes darting to Malka. "If anyone could tear her from her commands and get her to stop, it would be you."

Malka shook her head. "You know it can't be me." She shut her eyes. "The rooting spell's been severed. We don't have that . . . connection, anymore."

The room was unbearably silent, but Malka couldn't get herself to open her eyes, until Chaia took her cheek in her palm.

"That's not what I meant, Malka," she said, hand cool against Malka's warm cheek. "She cares for you in a way that surpasses any spell."

"Not after the fight we had."

"Feelings don't disappear overnight. She knows why you were angry. She won't hold it against you."

"Chaia, the things I said to her . . ." she began, but Chaia cut her off with the shake of her head.

"She'll forgive you, Malka," she said softly, her thumb wiping at a tear Malka didn't realize she had shed.

"Chaia is right," the Maharal said. "Show her she can be something other than a weapon to control. Show her she is more than why I created her."

"If he is there, Malka, you must draw him out to the balcony wrapping around the clock," Vilém said. "It was built as a natural echo chamber for the kings to give their great speeches. If he confesses to killing Evžen there, the mob we draw below will hear him."

"Wouldn't he know of that already, and avoid it?"

Vilém considered, then shook his head. "It's unlikely. It was never used because the clock broke right after it was made. That knowledge is long forgotten to anyone but scholars and architects."

"And you're sure the villagers will listen to you and follow you back to the square?" Malka questioned.

Ignác waved his hand. "Yes, don't worry about that. The other magisters and I are well regarded by the Ozmins in the city. We have taught many of them, and many of our children play together. It's part of why we believe the duke will be successful here. Those who may be suspicious of his rule will find comfort in our support of him."

"And what if he isn't at the clocktower?" Amnon asked. "You'll have guided the mob for nothing, and we still wouldn't have any idea where they went."

The group silenced, thinking.

Another scholar cleared his throat. "There's an old bell in the clocktower. It was put there to manually signal the turn of the hour in case the automation broke. Before we lead the mob there, Malka could give us a sign. One bell if they aren't there, two if they are. Once we hear that, we can continue with our plan. If not, we reconvene."

"Good idea," Vilém said.

"And what about Imma?" Malka asked. "How will we get to her?"

One of the other Yahad responded. "We'll find her. With the chaos, I imagine more guards will be protecting the king and on the hunt for Nimrah. As much as we didn't prepare for what Nimrah did, neither did they."

"You're strong enough to get her out?" Malka asked.

The Yahadi man chuckled. "Hard work has strengthened our muscles. We are not Nimrah, but in numbers we will have a chance."

Chaia's palm returned to Malka's cheek. "Are you up for this, Malka?"

Malka nodded slowly, though she knew she didn't have a choice. She would do what she needed to do. She always did.

CHAPTER

35

As Malka separated from the group, the irony of the situation smothered her like midwinter's dense, blanketed snow. Every week, Abba and the other village men would take their weapons and hunt for the Rayga. Malka would hope each time they left they'd come back with the Rayga's head on the tip of their blades. If the Rayga was killed, the forest would stop taking girls. The plague on their village would end. It was so simple to her—an unquestionable fact, like the sun rising every morning. Now, there was a manhunt for Nimrah, the Rayga, not so different from the ones she had wanted to succeed. Yet Malka now found herself on the other side of the hunt, hoping they wouldn't find her. Hoping Malka could save her first.

Out of breath, Malka reached Ordobav Square again. It was empty, save for the discarded masks and decor which lay forgotten on the ground. Though his body had been removed, Evžen's blood still stained the dais.

She stared at the clocktower, searching for its entrance. Finding a narrow stone door carved into the side of the building, Malka hoisted it open. The door groaned, revealing a plain entryway to a spiraling staircase. It was narrow with uneven stone. She tripped once, barely catching herself before she got hurt.

By the time she neared the top, she was heaving, the layers of her skirts sticking to her with sweat. In front of her, the wooden door was already cracked open, candlelight spilling onto the stairs.

As she entered, she studied the room. It was about twice the size of Chaia's kitchen, which was bigger than she had expected. But it made sense; the workers would need a large area to comfortably tinker with the clock and carry their supplies. Metal tools and wooden beams littered the floor, abandoned by the workers for the holiday. Above her, a lattice of metal beams held up the clock construction. Along the back wall, which hid an alcove, were two rickety wooden chairs. Malka wondered how many men worked on the clock each day with an apparatus so intricate.

The clock was grander up close, spanning the entirety of the front wall. The colored glass washed the room in blue, green, and orange light.

The gear's inner workings stole Malka's breath. The hands shifted, gears grating rhythmically as the minutes pushed over the hour too fast to be accurate. The gears were hulking, rugged pieces, interlocking in more circular patterns than Malka could count. They ticked loud, in time with the racing of her heartbeat.

She noted the beams which led to the clock's balcony.

On the wall to the right of the clock was a small window. It brought a soft breeze into the already freezing room. Without a hearth, the tower was icy, and Malka's breath plumed in the air.

"Nimrah?" Malka called out while she searched for the bell. She scanned the walls and the ceiling until she caught sight of a dangling rope hanging through the roof near the window.

That was it.

She called out for Nimrah again.

"Malka?" Nimrah emerged from the shadow of the back alcove, her eyebrows tight with worry. The axe she had wielded earlier was now slung across her back. "What are you doing here?"

Malka relaxed as Nimrah approached, her breath slowing and heartbeat settling. "Trying to find you. Trying to find Sévren. Is he here?"

"Yes, Malka, but—"

At Nimrah's confirmation, Malka sprinted to the bell and pulled on the rope once. Then twice. Though the Yahadi man had said it was not a heavy bell, it had rusted from disuse and took all of Malka's weight to ring it. The clang of the bell echoed through the tower, shaking some of the rocks loose from the compact stone. She hoped it was loud enough for them to hear.

Nimrah's hand clamped around her wrist, yanking her away from the bell. "What the hell are you doing? You need to leave before he—"

"You always find yourself in places you don't belong, don't you, Yahadi girl?"

Nimrah's hand tightened around Malka's wrist. The cool, sharp stone of it tingled against her smooth skin.

Sévren appeared from the same alcove. Guile painted his face like holy water, his age lines pressing against his forehead with the raise of his eyebrows. But he was breathing heavily, like each inhale was a laborious and painful task.

"Though I'd be lying if I said I didn't expect you to come." He cocked his head at Nimrah. "Just as she came for you at my palace."

"Leave her out of this," Nimrah demanded, her hand trembling so slightly, Malka would not have noticed if not for Nimrah's iron grip.

"Oh, I can't do that, Nimrah. Not after you embarrassed me that day in the courtyard."

Sévren hiked up his sleeve, revealing the mangled skin of his forearm.

Malka's intuition had been right.

The skin was inflamed where he had carved, dried blood revealing the shape of Yahadi letters. He drew his pointed fingernail along an unscathed section. The pale scratch lines bloodied as the flesh peeled away, clotting deep purple under his nails.

Her scabbed shoulder began to itch where those same nails had been.

When he began to whisper under his breath, Malka pinched her brows together. What was he—

Next to her, Nimrah hissed. She jolted Malka forward with the hand on her wrist. Malka cried in pain as Nimrah twisted her arm, securing both of Malka's hands behind her back. Capturing her.

Nimrah's cloak shifted and Malka caught a glimpse of a new mangled word on her forearm—the only one etched onto her skin instead of stone. One, she imagined, Sévren had carved.

She stared at the archbishop's arm, swelled red from his lacerations.

He smiled sardonically. "Do you like what I can do? I must thank you for solving this little puzzle for me. I had always wondered how the Maharal had given orders to his golem. I thought, from reading his research, one had to be the master of the golem to command it. But no, it's as simple as carving into its skin."

So, he didn't know about the rooting. Didn't know how easy Malka had made it for him, leaving Nimrah rootless and vulnerable. She bit the inside of her mouth, attempted to even her breathing. Blaming herself wouldn't fix anything now. Luring Sévren to the balcony would. But Nimrah's grip on her was too tight, her wrists growing sore as the blood flow to them slowed. She had time, she reminded herself. Until she heard the blow of a ram's horn from the Yahad below, she had time.

"You commanded Nimrah to kill Evžen. Why?" she pushed. "I thought he was like a son to you."

Hurt crossed Sévren's face, which had grown exceptionally pale after his command, almost sick looking. Sweat now trickled above his lip. His eyes gaunt. "He was. And I will treasure his memory. But this was bigger than any of us. He wanted the life Saint Celine gave him to have meaning. If that meant his life had to be taken, so be it. We are not the arbiters of our own fate."

"How does it help you if he is dead? I heard you in his study. You said you needed him. That it was up to him to keep the future of Valón in the Valski line. Now, that line is over."

"Ah. That's always the problem with eavesdropping, isn't it? You hear pieces not meant for your ears and assume you understand the full picture."

Nimrah's warning brushed against her ear. Malka ignored it.

Sévren's sleeve fell back over his carvings. The blood seeped through, soiling the fabric. Something was not right about it—the way his skin rebelled against his commands. Why he had carved so many.

"Rulers and lineages come and go. They are overthrown, they die off. The one thing that has been constant over many years is the rule of the Ozmini Church. The strength the religion has had in guiding us into a new age. Valón is Valón *because* of the Church. Without Triorzay and the Church as His messenger, we would not be as prosperous. As revered."

Malka shook her head. "The Ozmini Church's control over politics is at its end. People no longer wish for the type of empire it has created. A stratified one, a corrupted one."

"They have gotten inside of your mind." His signature smile again, though it wavered at the corners. Beads of sweat gathered at the crown of his forehead. "Hajek. Sigmund. They've manipulated you with sweet words you wished to hear, but you're naive if you think they don't have their own interests."

Was this so new to her? Chaia had said herself the duke thought more of the empire's strength than the equality of its people. These reformers were not saviors, only politicians.

"Maybe," Malka conceded. "But people don't want—"

"They do not know what they want!" Sévren shouted, his face reddening. He collected himself, breathing deep before he continued. "They need to remember who has been keeping them safe, what has given them the life they have built."

Malka recalled Sévren's hands firm on Evžen's shoulders, how he held his fate above him as a constant reminder.

"You made Evžen a martyr. You wanted everyone to see his violent death. You wanted them to see it was Nimrah who killed him. She stared at Sévren's stained sleeve. "All the while you were carving commands into Nimrah's skin to do your dirty work."

"He made his own choices. When you are born from a miracle, it weighs on every decision you make." The archbishop's cheek ticked, his eyebrows furrowing in distress. "Sacrifice is the ultimate way to show commitment to your faith, to the life it has given you. It is how we all get into Vasicati. Saint Celine saved him from a death that would've taken him before his life even began. This was how he furthered that miracle, by giving up his life for the greater good of the Ozmini religion."

"So, you took a power that wasn't yours."

Sévren sneered. "You think you are the only people with mysticism? That only you can turn prayer into magic? No one owns magic or the way we extract it from the earth."

There were many faiths with magic, Malka didn't deny that. But he had not erected it from his faith. He had stolen it from hers. Even having read the Maharal's scrolls, he misunderstood Kefesh. It was not about sacrifice, not about the drawing of blood. He bled and bled, and all it made him was sick.

"It is sacred to us," Malka retorted. Despite the cuff of Nimrah's hands around her wrists, she drew her knuckles into fists.

"I am the archbishop. Sacred belongs to me, and the Ozmini Church," Sévren rebuked.

Malka attempted to hide her look of disgust. "So, you got what you wanted from her. Let Nimrah go."

Behind her, Nimrah shifted.

I want no memory of you, Malka had spat.

She wished she could take it back. She wished so many things.

Sévren brought a hand to his abdomen and hissed in pain. His sickness was worsening, the Kefesh rejecting him. When he recovered, he said, "Oh, Malka. That was only the beginning. It is not only important for the Ozmins to see how the Yahad pose a threat to the continuation of the Ozmini line, but for the Yahad to see they are truly better off—they will be safer and more prosperous—if they convert. How do you change a person's belief? You take what they worship and make it a lie."

"Belief is not meant to be wielded as a political weapon."

"Then why is it the most powerful sword, and the sharpest knife?"

She wanted to rip his fingers from his hand, pull vines from the walls and tangle his neck in their grip. But she could not command Kefesh, still. She hated him for manipulating her people's magic when she could not even use it. Hated him in a way she had hated no one before.

The archbishop coughed and blood splattered into his palm. It did not seem to faze him. "Do you know why I cut off the Maharal's hands?"

Sévren sauntered toward the gears and observed them. His eyes were soft, as if he were gazing at an altar and not the Orlon clock. "I'm not as naive as to think the Maharal would not find a way to command Kefesh again without the use of his hands. I did not do it to stop him. I did it because I knew what others would think. What they would say. They would lose hope. They'd see the Maharal, crippled, and think if not even the great Maharal gets the grace of your God, there's no hope for anyone else."

"You failed," Malka said. "Because people still have hope."

"Perhaps. But not for long."

"Not if I stop you."

Sévren guffawed. "I am not your enemy. Like you, my faith shapes me. It decides what I do, how I act, and the way I look at the world. It is my duty to protect that faith. You understand, don't you? The need to protect your faith?"

"Faith is not an excuse for violence, or a shield to justify yourself. Do not speak of faith like it is a means to an end."

He put a hand to his chest. Blood stained his robes right above his heart. "You are telling an archbishop what it means to have faith?"

"I am telling a *man* he cannot hide behind his faith. What is your goal, Sévren?" Malka asked plainly. "Even if you did destroy the Yahad's faith, it would not cease the papacy's failure to keep its hand in politics. You cannot stop a wave that is bigger than this city, than this kingdom."

"That is where you are wrong. The plague has rattled this kingdom, turning people away from our guiding hand. We used to be revered, a beacon of hope and direction for the Ozmini people. Until we could not stop them from dying."

"It is not the fault of the Ozmini people that you allowed your tithe funds to be spent on revelry and indulgence for your inner circle. You cannot blame your fall from grace on nature."

Sévren snarled, making him look more animal than human. "And you're sure it is nature that caused this plague? Because I do not think you nor I believe that."

Nimrah's hands had begun to shake again.

"With Evžen's death, there is room for a new ruler. The people want someone to save them, and it is meant to be me. I am the one who learned how to command the earth, *I* am the one who can shape the future of this kingdom."

Sévren dug his fingernail into his skin again and whispered. When he finished, blood dripped from his nose and the corner of his eye. He wiped at his face with his fist, but it only smeared the blood. He brushed his hands along his robes and sat in one of the wooden chairs. He settled into it like a throne, hands curling around the curved wood of the armrest.

Nimrah freed Malka from her grasp. Malka swiveled around, only to be met with Nimrah's face of anguish as she drew the axe from the sling on her back. It trembled in her hand.

Malka's eyes widened. She held out her newly unbound hands to protect herself, though she knew it was useless. Nimrah had been commanded.

If anyone could tear her from her commands . . . it would be you. Chaia had said it so certainly when they had made this plan. But she didn't see Nimrah's eyes now—black like the cavities of the teeth they used for their games of split tooth.

A horn echoed from outside, and Malka's stomach flipped. They were ready. Malka wasn't.

"This is not you—I know that," Malka said, though her voice wavered.

Nimrah swung the axe.

Malka sank to the floor to avoid the blow. Pain shot up her arms as she landed awkwardly. She had no time to recover before the axe swung at her again. Malka rolled out of the way, a few curls of hair falling to the floor where the axe had managed to cut.

The axe clattered to the floor and vines burst from the stone walls. Nimrah called them closer with the flick of her hands, and they slithered to Malka until they wrapped around her ankles and wrenched her quick and hard into the wall with a thud.

Malka blinked away the hazy spots covering her vision and put a hand to her head, which pulsed with pain. It came away red and sticky. She tried to stand but could not escape the grasp of the vines.

Nimrah put the heel of her shoe onto the blade of the axe and slid it closer to Malka, as if willing her to take it.

Malka didn't have time to question the move as Nimrah stalked toward her. She wrapped her hands around the axe's hilt. It was awkward to hold and reminded Malka of their sword fight in Mavetéh. How the length of the weapon made the weight unbalanced. The axe was lighter than the sword though, and Malka garnered the strength to send the blade through Nimrah's vine, freeing herself.

The room spun as Malka ran from Nimrah, though there was not much room to escape. If she fled to the balcony now, everyone would see Nimrah's attack.

Nimrah caught her, slamming her back against the wall. The axe was between them, blade held at Nimrah's neck.

"Do it, Malka," Nimrah said, her voice fierce. "I want you to. I will never be able to live with myself if I end your life. Plague me. Burn me. Strike me dead. But do not make me do this."

Malka was reminded of the attic. Nimrah's hands tight around hers as she pressed the dagger to her neck. Malka had spent so much time blaming Nimrah for the destruction she had caused. But Nimrah had been created to fight unjust violence—the type of violence Sévren held in his hands—with just violence. What were the other ways they could survive in their faith? They could not play into the hands of the Ozmini Church. Change had to be seized, torn from hands that held power tight.

If anything, Nimrah was a symbol of hope. A symbol of what it meant to keep a faith alive. To protect a people who held their beliefs close despite the violence. Who still had hope even when the world kicked them down. She was made to give the Yahadi people what they deserved—a try at peace, a try at life. Maybe Malka needed to let herself take part. Let Nimrah be a sign of hope for her, too. Maybe she could admit to herself Nimrah was important to her. She had to survive and let what they had mean something.

"You once told me the story of your creation—how the Maharal made you to be a monster. To be violent. I had called you a monster, too. But I was wrong. I didn't understand monstrosity then. You're more than the commands etched into your skin."

Something flashed in Nimrah's eyes, but it was gone as quickly as it came, and Nimrah tossed her to the ground.

Malka lost her grip on the axe and Nimrah seized it. She held the blunt end toward Malka, who dove before the handle could crush into her chest, pressing instead into the meat of her thigh. She grunted.

Nimrah rotated the axe blade-first and pressed it toward her, pinning Malka's injured leg with her knee. Malka held Nimrah's wrists, hands trembling violently from pushing against the weight of Nimrah's blow.

Malka was not strong though, and soon her skin gave way to the blade, unfurling like a flower. A gush of heat, a flash of red. The sharp pain seized her from head to toe. Nimrah's wrist moved with the axe, and Malka caught a glimpse of the words written into her arms. On the stone, the command which had once tied her to Malka. On the flesh, the command which allowed the archbishop control.

So many commands on Nimrah's body. Malka thought of Tzvidi's story, of the dangers of Kefesh's corruption. She thought of how the shalkat crawled into the Seefa Narach and changed the lettering of the prayers to become something different—something opposite to its intention.

With Nimrah pressing on top of her, Malka examined the sharp curves of the etching in her forehead: אמת. *Emet.* Meaning truth. Meaning life. Three letters the Maharal had carved and shaped with Kefesh, bringing her into this world to defend the Yahad against oppression, against violence. And like Tzvidi's prayer to light his candle that went awry, swallowing the library in flames, Nimrah was about to destroy the very person she was meant to protect.

Malka had doubted herself every step of her journey. Doubted herself when she took those first steps into Mavetéh, when no other woman had survived inside. She doubted herself when she made a deal with the golem to rescue the Maharal, when she first used Kefesh on the bruised waral fruit. When she stood in the prison waiting for the guards.

But when she saved Amnon from the bite of the creature, she didn't doubt herself. She didn't have the time. She had to believe in herself, her faith, her connection to Yohev, and the love that grounded her. She recalled the Maharal's words in the forest, in the hidden synagogue which held the etrog plant:

The earth does not choose when we are or are not worthy of commanding it. Only we, as humans, doubt our abilities. When we forsake ourselves, that is when true failure happens.

Malka would believe in herself now. Chaia had. Nimrah had. Danya,

Hadar, and Imma had. She deserved to believe in herself and the power she possessed.

Malka slowly released one of her hands from Nimrah's wrist and guided her fingers toward Nimrah's forehead. One-handed against Nimrah's strength, she would not last long. But she didn't *need* to last long. Only long enough to drag her finger across Nimrah's stone.

Malka needed to breathe and believe in what she could do. What she could be. What she *was*.

"What are you doing?" Nimrah asked through gritted teeth.

Malka pressed her thumb to the carving of the first letter on Nimrah's forehead—the *Alef*.

"Saving us both." She closed her eyes and steeled herself, thinking of her faith and how Kefesh had felt pressed between her fingertips. She scratched her nail through the letter as she muttered a prayer.

The power of Kefesh flowed through her, the strength of it in her bones codified as belief. She had missed this feeling, of holiness and power, of shimmering prayer in her blood. She could've cried at the strength she felt—not physical, but in her heart, in her mind.

The stone crumbled underneath her fingernail as she commanded the letter to disappear, transforming the word from אמת, *emet,* truth, into מת, *met,* death.

As soon as her prayer was done, Nimrah slumped over, the axe slipping from her grasp and clattering to the stone floor.

Malka trembled. Beside her, Nimrah was lifeless. Her eyes were open, yet no life gilded them. She did not breathe. Did not flinch. As still as those who died in Imma's workroom.

Malka had not killed her in the way a blade would. She had commanded eternal sleep, until she was woken again. Her religion was made of many interpretations, and she had found one that saved her, one that did not break the rule of killing a creature made from Kefesh.

Shakily, Malka got to her feet, grabbing the axe between her hands.

Sévren stood from his chair, anger simmering his cheeks. "You—"

Malka squinted at the archway to the balcony and hoped she was not too late. "I will tell everyone what you've done, Sévren."

"You think I have no power without her?" Sévren drew on his arm again, and one of the neglected wooden beams on the floor spiraled toward her. She had just reached the balcony archway when the wood hit her between the knees, tripping her. It had begun to rain, and freezing droplets pelted her face as her cheek slapped stone.

Still, he held Kefesh wrong. Drawing the commands into himself instead of the objects of the earth. Thinking his blood would pay some invisible cost.

"I am God-chosen, Malka," he said, joining her on the balcony. More blood flowed from his nose, his eyes, his ears. His burgundy cassock darkened where the blood stained, creating black streaks across his middle, like the scratches from a lion's claw. "I command your magic."

"It's killing you, Sévren." Malka crawled to her knees. "You'll be dead before you ever have the chance to rule."

"Do you think I am afraid of the ultimate sacrifice? I have dedicated my life to this cause. Spending decades at Evžen's side. Do you know how intentional I was to always be there? When tragedy struck, it was *me* at his side. Not his father. I made sure of it."

"What do you mean?"

"It was easy enough to replace the king's medicine with liquor every night. Until he could not go without. Until only the bottle could aid his pain. Until Evžen would have no father to turn to but me!"

He scraped his hand against his skin again. A vine flew through the archway and wrapped around Malka's neck. She tugged at it with both hands, gasping.

Sévren wheezed. His eyes were bloodshot. "I spent my life placating that boy to make him a martyr. Years planting the seeds to make the Valonian people *understand*. And I was rewarded by God for my commitment. The golem appeared again, after five years! Commanding her to kill Evžen was a sacrifice I had to make, so there would be no doubt left in their mind who was the true enemy." He pointed to the square.

"And they have seen," Malka choked out from the grip of the vine.

Sévren creased his brow. Cautiously, he turned, his face pale as stone when he noticed the crowd. Though Malka could not see them from her spot on the ground, Sévren's face was confirmation enough.

Maybe if he were well, Sévren would've tried to placate the crowd with his charisma. But the Kefesh was killing him, driving him mad with pain. He knew he did not have long.

When he faced Malka again, his eyes blazed with the desire for vengeance.

His distraction had allowed Malka to escape from the vines. But now, Sévren raised his fist, teeth sharp against his thin mouth.

Malka barely dodged the blow, rolling toward the balcony column. Her head hit the stone hard, mind slowing as she readjusted. The archbishop lifted her by the shoulders and pressed her over the railing.

The crowd gasped below. Chaia yelled her name.

She peered down, finally seeing the amassed crowd. Vilém, Chaia, and a few of the magisters were closest, surrounded by the distressed mob who watched the scene above.

She fought against Sévren, but he was much stronger than her and she tilted over the railing.

She shot out her hands, grasping the edge of the balcony. Fear struck her, arms shaking under her dangling dead weight.

Sévren shook as he carved more commands into his arms, pelting sharp rocks toward her. But he was weakening, his magic unstable. The rocks missed her and flooded into the crowd below.

Chaia.

Malka twisted her head, screaming as another rock flew past her, sharp as an arrow and headed straight toward Chaia's heart. In the space of a breath, Vilém stepped in front of her, the sharp rock sinking into his chest instead.

Malka's sweaty palms slipped on the railing, fingers straining.

Commotion below her. Sévren above her.

This couldn't be how it ended. Not after all she had been through.

Was she truly powerful enough to command Kefesh without tracing the words? Malka had taken the life the Maharal had given Nimrah with the etching of her nail. She had commanded vines and stone, had erupted a flame from nothing but the trace of her fingers in tallow.

Malka closed her eyes, letting her belief in herself and her magic flood her body. She thought of Hadar, imagined she was beside her, guiding her hand. It gave her strength, this memory of her sister.

Malka opened her eyes. She let go, falling only an inch before the vines she had commanded sprouted from the wall and wrapped around her hands, pulling her back onto the balcony, in front of the clock.

"No!" Sévren yelled.

He screamed as he charged toward her with his fists, but Malka jumped aside.

Sévren couldn't stop in time. His weight pushed him forward as he tripped toward the clock, his body breaking through its face and shattering the glass which covered the gears.

He screamed as the gears consumed him, metal crushing his skin piece by piece. He tried to move but couldn't free himself from the too-quick pace of the gears, which kept turning despite the obstacle of Sévren's body as they buried him further and further within its inner workings. The gears rustled and clanked together as they ate Sévren's skin and bones, until his screams grew silent, and the clock swallowed him whole.

CHAPTER 36

Back inside the clocktower, Malka kneeled close to Nimrah and ran her thumb across her stone cheek. *Soon,* she vowed, and hoped her promise would hold true.

The gears of the clock let out a ghastly rattle, drawing Malka's attention. Sévren had become unrecognizable. He was misshapen from the press of heavy metal, gears slicing through skin deep enough to free his organs. His intestines, his stomach, all bloated from his cooling body. So much blood. She swallowed bile and looked away for the last time before running down the spiral stairs.

In the square, Chaia cradled Vilém in her arms. Everyone was quiet around them. Even the knights had stilled, unsure of themselves after Sévren's outburst.

Chaia's hand was wet with Vilém's blood as she pressed it into his chest to slow the bleeding. He raised his hand delicately to Chaia's wrist and ran his thumb along her pulse point.

"How is he?" Malka dropped to her knees beside them.

Chaia's hands shook and tears stained her face. She pleaded, "Save him, Malka. I can't command Kefesh the way you do. Please save him."

Malka pressed her fingers to his pulse. It was so weak, struggling as so many hearts had once they ended up at Imma's workshop.

She closed her eyes and tried to call Kefesh forth as she had done with Amnon. The earth listened to her command but could not oblige it. It confirmed to her what she feared. Vilém's wound was fatal, and not even Kefesh could bring someone back from the dead. That power was for Yohev alone.

"I'm sorry, Chaia," Malka said, throat tight. "I'm so sorry, Vilém."

But Vilém didn't look surprised or disappointed. He was a scholar, an academic, and he knew he didn't have much time left.

Chaia sobbed. "Vilém, my love. You have to live. For me. Our life together has just begun."

He raised a shaking, blood-covered hand to Chaia's cheek and pressed the tip of his finger into the dimple at the side of her mouth. He cracked a smile. "It's an honor to give my heart so that yours keeps beating, Chaia."

Chaia covered his hand with her own. She bent forward and kissed his forehead, her tears staining his skin. "We have so much planned. Things are just beginning to change!"

Vilém gently consoled his wife, whispering to her things only she could hear. "We both know anything I could do, you will do with more grace."

"I love you, I love you, I love you," Chaia said between sobs, and wrapped him in her arms once again.

When his eyes finally dulled, Chaia stilled. Her hands trembled as she pressed her ear to Vilém's chest. When she heard nothing, she screamed his name until her throat was raw.

Tears clouded Malka's eyes once again. For Vilém, who had become a friend to her. And for Chaia, who had lost her love. They had been so close to victory. Yet loss had followed them again, like a wild dog one made the mistake of feeding. They would never be free of grief.

Malka traced her hand through Chaia's hair to soothe her.

A few moments later, Katarina approached. Her face was pale, eyes red rimmed as she stared at Vilém.

"Malka," she said, voice cracking before she cleared her throat.

Malka stared at her through blurry eyes.

"We found your mother. She's safe."

All the tension in her body dissipated. Every emotion she had buried during the last three weeks freed itself and Malka sobbed. She sobbed so hard her ribs hurt.

A light, she thought, *in all this darkness.*

⚹

Later that night, under Danya's watchful eye, Malka left Imma to rest in Chaia's kitchen, where they had set up a bed close to the oven. She held the cloak tight around, hiding herself underneath the glow from the wash of stars. Remnants of the Léčrey festival blew through the wind. Flower petals littered the cobblestone, frames of Saint Celine left abandoned against the walls.

She slipped into the doors of the shul Bachta and climbed the spiral staircase to the attic where Nimrah had been carried to rest. As she opened the door, Malka considered her, lying in her bed, still as death.

It didn't get easier to see her lifeless, like the stone she was made from. To know it was Malka's hands that had unmade her. Perhaps it was a glimpse into an alternate time, where the Ozmini Church had kept their word and Malka handed her over to Father Brożek. But Malka knew her death then would not have been as easy—it would've been bloody, reminiscent of how Mavetéh ate its girls. A Revaç would look at Nimrah's half-human, half-stone body as a challenge—creating new ways to make her suffer. Would he have died before or after he gained his golden tooth? She didn't know how Kefesh would kill the destroyer of holy magic, and she was glad she hadn't found out today.

Malka bent at Nimrah's bedside, brushing a thumb along her cheek. It was cool under her touch, the stone rough on the pad of her finger.

She could've left her like this. Eternal rest.

The Maharal said it was her choice. Perhaps it was better to leave Nimrah here. She had come to understand how true Baba's warnings about Kefesh could be—from Mavetéh sinking its teeth into Amnon's shoulder to Sévren's fraught attempt to control Nimrah. But Baba, like many, had learned his fear of it from stories spoken to him by his own grandparents. It was only natural. Malka had feared it, too.

But she didn't fear Kefesh now. Anything powerful held the potential to sour. The Ozmini Church, Sévren's desire to rule. Even Nimrah. But as power could overripen, it could also show strength. For Malka, Kefesh's power meant the strength of knowing Yohev's nearness, feeling her connection to Yahadism in her heart and the buzzing of her hands.

So, with a deep breath, Malka retrieved the chisel and rock she had stored in her pocket. She aligned the chisel on Nimrah's forehead, where she had once erased the letter that transformed Nimrah's truth into Nimrah's death.

She held up the rock, felt the grooves of it between her fingers. Something held her back, as if the moment she would press the tool into Nimrah's forehead, the golem would unfurl from sleep as someone different—a new creation unknown to Malka. She had to believe, had to hope. Had to lean into her strength.

She carved into the stone carefully, rock hitting the chisel in a rhythmic beat, prayer curling her lips. She let the strength of her magic comfort her as she brushed close to Yohev. Her faith wrapped around her, weightier than any woolen cloak in the cruelest Ordobavian winter.

She had questioned her faith when Hadar was murdered, when Eskravé was pillaged beyond repair. She had doubted her own strength as she tried to draw magic in the dungeon. But she did not question her faith or herself now. Her belief had given her so much. Strength, hope, and the love that warmed her when she saw Chaia, Danya, Amnon, and Imma.

When she finished carving the letter, she waited with bated breath, her eyes still closed. It was silent for one moment, two, three... so long that Malka thought she had failed. But Nimrah's fervent inhale split the quiet, raising the hairs on Malka's forearms.

Nimrah gripped Malka tight, crushing her wrist. For a moment, Malka feared she was not the same. That she had been changed from the golem Malka had known.

Timidly, Malka opened her eyes. Confusion crossed Nimrah's face, until the tension eased.

"Malka," Nimrah said, her voice groggy with disuse.

She looked as alive as the Maharal had made her.

"Do you feel like yourself?" Malka asked, heart pounding as she waited for the answer.

Nimrah nodded, but Malka feared she was not telling the truth.

"Prove it," Malka said, unable to curb her voice shaking. "Say something only the golem Nimrah would know."

"What should I say?"

Malka pondered this. "In Chaia's house, you told me what happened with the Yahadi boy and his death. I asked why you would tell me something so terrible."

Nimrah searched her eyes, her throat bobbing. "And I told you I would always be the monster you hate. And that was fine, as long as you knew the truth."

Malka's shoulders sank in relief. She fell into Nimrah's chest and let herself weep.

CHAPTER 37

Nights later, when the hazy, berry-dark sky turned the air frigid and the city of Valón curled near their ovens to sleep, Nimrah found a note from the Maharal, asking them to meet him in the shul Bachta, on the spiraling tower.

When they climbed the tower, Malka viewed the city around them. It stole her breath. Lanterns painted Valón like dew drops on fresh leaves, shining bright against the night. She could see the Orlon clock in the center square, its gears grinding Sévren's bones into dust.

To the south, she glimpsed Mavetéh's consuming darkness, the lattice of canopies absorbing the night in a blanket of obsidian. To think she had traveled through the woods weeks ago, yet all the terrors she had faced paled in comparison to those she witnessed in Valón. She tried to think of where the shul Amichati sat buried half beneath the earth, waiting for someone to raise it from the ground.

"Thank you both for coming here," the Maharal said. He wore his sapphire-colored robe, his silver beard glimmering in the moonlight. "I know how tough it has been, dealing with the aftermath of the Léčrey celebration. But this . . . this could not wait."

"What is it, Rav?" Nimrah asked. Already, she was far from Malka, putting space between them. Malka could barely see her face in the shadow where she stood.

"Nimrah, there is something I must tell you." The Maharal drew closer to his golem. "Something that has eaten at me for many years. Something I have already shared in pieces with Malka to save you from Sévren."

Though Nimrah was in shadow, it did not hide the rigid tense of her shoulders.

"It is no coincidence the forest began to grow teeth when I tied you to the

Great Oak tree. Only it is not as you think. It is not you who presses magic into the woods."

"What do you mean?"

The Maharal's chest rose and fell with a deep breath. He peered at the stars, letting the moonlight cover his face in a pale, milky glow. "In all my scholarship, I had read of a way one could use Kefesh to breathe life into this world. Much in the same way we plant a tree and watch it grow or birth a child who grows until they can have a child of their own. I began to practice my creation of you in the forest. Each day, I came back and logged the motions, the prayers, until I was sure they were right. But I had formed a pattern, and Sévren, ever keeping his eye on me, soon became interested in what I did inside the forest. He had the Qehillah raided and took all the scrolls detailing my attempts at creating you, learning the prayers I uttered, the instructions I followed. I wondered then if I should stop. But the next time I attempted to make you, Yohev let your existence be true. When you opened your eyes, I knew I had created something beautiful. Something holy.

"So, I kept a close eye on him in case he chose to pursue something with that knowledge. For years he did nothing. Each day that passed without incident eased my worry. Soon, three years had come and gone. I was comfortable that he had set aside his interests, until one day I saw him walk with a woman into the forest—the same Ozmini bride they would put me in jail for supposedly killing. I followed him. In the same spot near the creek where I had practiced all those years ago, as detailed in the scrolls, he handed the woman a few belladonna berries and she ate them without a second thought. After she died, Sévren carved into her skin the same word I had used to create you: *emet,* truth. While I had made you from stone, he chose to make a golem out of someone human already. Maybe he didn't think he could create a golem the same way I did, or maybe he was looking for a shortcut. Either way, once he had finished, the earth grumbled, and for one moment, I was in shock it had worked—that an Ozmin could command Yahadi prayer. But the woman began to mutate into something horrible. Her limbs morphed together, stone jutted from her skin, and she breathed again a ragged, wheezing breath.

"The earth wailed, wind howling through the trees, trunks groaning. Yahadi magic was not for Sévren to hold, much the same way that commanding you, Nimrah, made him sick."

Malka unconsciously traced the bruises on her arm from that night.

"The woman was in tremendous pain. It would've been a mercy to kill her. But I was too weak to do what needed to be done. I had not killed anyone, and I didn't want to. Even if her life was like this. So, I did what I thought was the next best thing. I transformed her into a different type of life. As I created life with you, Nimrah, I transformed that poor woman into the Great Oak tree. I did not expect what she would do in that form—how hungry for bodies she would become. The curse she as the Great Oak would cast over everyone. It took time, years, but she soon realized her tears could turn into poisonous fruit hanging from her branches, and each time she sobbed, they would spread throughout the forest."

Nimrah furrowed her brows. "But the waral fruit began to appear only after I was rooted there."

"When they sprouted, maybe. If you recall, it was an unusually long winter before the spring finally came. Already her work had begun, shifting the forest. Rotting it. The seeds had been planted, only waiting for the blooming season. I did not realize this when I tied you there on the first of spring. That you would blame yourself when they began to grow."

Each piece of the puzzle was slipping into place. Only, this realization did not come as much of a surprise to Malka as it did to Nimrah, who had grown pale across from her. Malka had tried so hard to blame her for everything, desperate to fit ill-shaped pieces together. Maybe she had not known exactly how Kratzka Šujana became Mavetéh, but it made increasingly less sense that Nimrah was its maker. How she was not safe from the creature attacks, the remorse she felt for those she harmed. The continuous haunting of the forest even after Nimrah had left it. Malka's evolving understanding of Kefesh.

The Maharal's confession only confirmed what part of her had already known. Nimrah was not the source of the curse.

The Maharal closed his eyes. "I knew my mistake immediately. By transforming that woman into the Great Oak tree, I had used Kefesh to create life. So, I knew I was no longer able to destroy it if I wished to live."

"What do you mean," Nimrah pushed, "if you wished to live?"

"Another secret I kept from you, so you did not have to bear its weight." His eyes met Malka's. "The price of destroying life made by Kefesh is the death of its murderer."

Shame filled Nimrah's face, and when she spoke, her voice was meek. "Why must you have created me? If this is all the trouble my creation has caused."

"Oh, Nimrah. You do not understand how desperate I was, how helpless I felt when the raids on the Yahadi Quarter began to increase in scale and frequency. I had long since studied the art of Kefesh, from the time I was small, when I was born knowing Yohev's true name. To hold such a great power in your hands, a power tied into the creation of the universe, and still have to stand by while your people were pillaged and killed . . . the same people who sought you to help guide their hopes and prayers. Imagine having all the power you could hold, and still having none at all. If I could not help my people and keep them safe, I wondered if I could create something that could." His eyes glinted with love. "*Someone* who could."

"It can't be a coincidence that the forest has been searching out girls?" Malka intoned the thought as a question, reworking what she knew through the lens of this woman-turned-Great-Oak.

The Maharal nodded. "I fear it's true. Kefesh is already a delicate thing. It is power, but power granted by Yohev. Creating life is one thing. Mothers bear children and bring life into the world. But death . . . to bring someone back from the dead, is only a power Yohev may hold. And this woman did not come back how she was. It threw off the balance of the earth. I believe the woman is searching for herself as she once was, in all the women her creatures take. Her tree form has only given her more strength, as the waral fruit germinates and creates more monsters."

"Is she the cause of the sickness, too?" The last piece of the puzzle, the last question.

The Maharal's expression wavered. "It's true the sickness comes from the poison of the waral fruit. Either through a rabid creature's bite, like Amnon, or consuming anything the waral fruit has touched. But I don't believe the woman is responsible for the worsening spread of the Mázág sickness. That, I'm afraid, is the work of greedy men."

"What do you mean?"

"As more and more orders were given to build and revive things from the golden age of King Manek's rule, the more Valski's men had to go into the forest to retrieve materials. The more trees had to be cut for wood to be shaped into frames for King Manek's portraits, more stone to be shaped into statues. More food for feasts that secured the court's faith in Ordobav's strong leadership. The more they attempted to hide the sickness with opulence, the worse the sickness became."

It made sense, then, why the increasing sickness in Eskravé juxtaposed the frequency of the Paja's tithe collections. The Paja did not only bring their brutality with them on their missions, but also their disease.

"Instead of letting me help, you tied me to the one who created this mess. You made me think Mavetéh was my fault alone," Nimrah said, rigid as a statue.

"Nimrah, you are my life's creation. You are . . ." he ran a hand through his beard, "the closest thing to family I have left. I could not kill you. Even though they wanted me to, I could not."

"I could have *helped*. You made me to protect the Yahad, yet you would not let me do that. All I have been created for . . ."

A tear pricked the Maharal's eye. It glimmered as it fell slowly down his cheek. He settled his hand on the back of Nimrah's neck in a fatherly caress, his thumb running circles in her hair. She turned her face away from him, but still leaned into his touch, like even her anger could not keep her from her master. "You know that would have not been fair. I am the tree's creator. I gave it life. I am the one who made her holy. I am the one who turned her into something worse. And it is about time I made things right. Now that you have someone," he said, eyes darting to Malka. "Ordobav will be in good hands under your watchful gaze and the support you will have to build a better future for the Yahad. I am not needed as I once was."

"What are you saying?" Nimrah's voice cracked on the question.

"No one has done what I have, Nimrah. No one has created holy life—life made by Kefesh. But that also means no one has to bear the consequences for taking that holy life away, except for me. If I destroy the Great Oak tree, I can end this. I have the power to end this, Nimrah."

An uncomfortable realization speared through Malka's chest. How many Eskraven lives could have been saved if the Maharal had made his sacrifice earlier? He had always known what needed to be done, yet he chose instead to live while Mavetéh feasted on the women of her village.

"I never could get myself to do it," the Maharal continued, "knowing the state of the kingdom and its tumultuous future for the Yahad. I could not abandon them. I knew I was a beacon of hope for people, and I could not let Sévren tear their hope away like he attempted by imprisoning me. For you see, either he would have to keep me alive or make me a martyr like Evžen. And either way, the Yahad would have hope."

"They need you now. They still need hope," Nimrah begged.

"Ah, but that's the thing about the Yahad and hope. We have always had to have it. I think we are more used to hanging on to it than many are led to believe. To be a Yahad and practice our religion is inherently hopeful, that one day, our people will be free. That one day, a sign from Yohev will come."

To Malka, he said, "I'll forever be sorry for the pain my selfishness has put you through. And I do not expect you to forgive me. I only ask that you forgive her."

Despite her frustration, Malka couldn't deny him this last request. She had placed the blame on Nimrah for too long. A blame she had never deserved.

"One more thing, Malka, if you'll allow me." His eyes gleamed. "Kefesh is a delicate thing, but I have seen no one command it with such hope as you do. With such a soul that you have. Even before you knew how to name it, the earth was bending for you. Come closer, child, for there is a secret I must share with you. A secret Yohev whispered to me. A secret you will carry with you until you find someone else who will carry on Their name in the hearts of our people."

Malka stood close to him, their cloaks brushing in the blowing wind, like every part of them shared the same secret. Malka closed her eyes, and tilted her head to the sky, as the name filled her ears and her soul. Her hands buzzed, and she let the wind press into her skin. Like Abayda the Mystic, she could've sworn she heard Yohev's voice as the wind blew through her hair, lapping at her ears like a prayer of its own.

The Maharal said something else, so low Malka could have missed it in the intensity of the moment.

"Take care of each other," he said. She pressed a smile into his cheek as he embraced her, and he understood her promise. When they pulled away from each other, Nimrah's back was turned, silhouetted by the moon as she watched the stars from beyond the roof.

"You have your duty and I have mine, Nimrah. Let me right my wrongs."

"What if it does not work?" Nimrah pressed. "What if you die for nothing?"

The Maharal sighed and breathed in the crisp air. He let his eyes remain closed for a minute, like a dying man reveling in the simplicity of living.

"When I created you, I felt a buzzing in my hands, a drumming in my ears. It felt right to me, like Yohev had whispered Their approval. And I feel it now, as I make this decision. I think it is what the world needs. What Yohev is granting me."

Malka stretched her own hands, wondering if that could be the reason for the tingling in her palms, which came to her before she performed Kefesh. And what she had felt again before she freed Nimrah with her magic after being dormant for so long.

In the end, they watched for hours from the tower of the synagogue as the Maharal of Valón, a myth that had become a man, became a myth again as he let his shadow disappear into Mavetéh. Mavetéh welcomed him, and Malka swore she saw two shadows like arms grasping at him, until his gray beard and blue robes were wrapped in their blackness.

↘

When it was done, the rustling of the trees calmed, and the murky blackness between the slits in the leaves faded into a sultry blue. Malka felt it instantly, the reprieve she had craved so desperately. When Mavetéh no longer needed to be named as a warning. She could not help but cry until her vision was blurred with tears. Until the sun rose from beyond the trees and the woods glistened with a hazy orange glow. Until at last, she recognized it again.

Kratzka Šujana.

CHAPTER 38

When she arrived at Chaia's house, Imma was sitting up in bed, a tonic pressed to her lips. Her pallor was sickly still, with sunken eyes and ghostly lips crusted with dried blood. The poultices at her chafed wrists had grown dry and cracked like scaly green skin.

"How are you feeling?" Malka asked.

Imma swallowed the medicine and ran the empty vial between her palms. "I'm fine, baby. A little tired, that's all."

Malka walked to her makeshift worktable, where she had been left the array of healing plants she requested. Eucalyptus clippings, sage, and chamomile leaves for Imma's wounds. Lemon balm to settle her sleep. Malka wrapped the eucalyptus in cloth and added it to the pot of boiling water already hung on the trammel hook above the hearth. She had done this so many times, it was almost easy for Malka to forget what had transpired—who she had lost. But Malka didn't want to forget. She wanted to hold their memory close, like the stain of herbs left on her skin after using them to heal.

When the poultice was ready, Malka dragged a chair next to Imma's bed. She peeled off the old poultice with a hot, wet cloth, and smoothed the fresh mixture on her reddened skin.

"This won't hurt," Malka promised, and muttered a prayer. The poultice glowed under her touch. Imma's breath hitched as the magic seeped into her skin.

Though Imma had tried to hide her pain, her relief was visible once the magical poultice began to take effect. Her jaw slacked, and a comforted sigh slid past her lips. Malka held back tears. It meant everything to her that she could ease Imma's pain, when once she could not.

"Come close." Imma stretched out her hand.

Malka wrapped their hands together and fell to her knees at Imma's bedside.

Imma squeezed her hand. It was weak, but Malka knew she would grow strong again.

"When you walked into Mavetéh, I did not think I'd see you again, Malka."

"Forgive me, Imma. It was the only way I could think to protect you. Protect the family."

She did not say she had failed. That Hadar's loss still followed her everywhere, like Nimrah's bond had once. *Lingering*, she had used to describe the ghost of the rooting spell's connection between them. The same word could describe her grief.

"You felt it was your job to protect the family."

Malka met Imma's eyes. In them was a sadness so deep, Malka wondered why she had never seen it before.

"Abba . . ." Imma continued, "I know he was not good to you. I know he wasn't good to your sisters. But you have to understand we had not married for love. We had married for duty. Eskravé had never been an easy place to live. And when you girls were born, I could not fathom leaving him. Not when I wanted you and your sisters to have a life much better than I knew I could give you alone. And when the forest—"

"Hush, Imma, please do not speak that way." Malka ran her thumb along Imma's knuckles. "It's not your fault. None of this is your fault."

"When I close my eyes, I see Hadar's face. And it eats at me that I could not keep her safe. That I couldn't be her mother when she needed me most." Imma caressed her cheek. "You have become more than I could ever have imagined. You hold magic in your palms like it is nothing. Like it was Yohev's gift just for you."

Malka shrugged. "Every Yahad could hold it if they wish."

Imma smiled softly. "Yes, but not in the way you do. Ah, my sweet girl. I fear I will dream of that prison for the rest of my life. I fear I will dream of losing you three every time sleep takes me. Will you forgive me, Malka, if I cannot be what I once was?"

"Always," Malka promised, eyes welling up with tears. "I love you, Imma."

"With the might of every star in the sky."

Malka cried, and Imma held her until her sobs subsided. They clung to each other in silence as Imma gently stroked Malka's curls.

After a while, Imma cupped Malka's face in her hands, and wiped her tears away with her thumb. "Nimrah, the golem who saved you from Mavetéh. You look at her with such love in your eyes. I think I should like to meet her properly."

Malka was glad her inflamed cheeks were hidden by Imma's hands. "It isn't like that."

Imma hummed. "You never could lie well."

Malka's throat felt suddenly tight.

Imma smiled, but it was a sad smile. A smile coming from a broken heart. "At a moment's notice, we can lose what we expect to have forever. Perhaps it's worth saying what our fear wants us to keep unsaid."

༄

Malka found Nimrah in the attic of the shul Bachta. She was leaned against one of the stone walls with her legs crossed, nose deep in a scroll. When Malka entered the room, she tensed.

"Some light reading?" Malka teased, desperate to break the tension between them. The last time they'd spoken had been days ago, when the Maharal called them both to the shul tower. Since, Nimrah had managed to be anywhere Malka wasn't.

Nimrah's gaze fell to her neck. The axe wound was still wrapped in thick gauze. She had used Kefesh to fend off infection from the dirty blade, but the wound was deep, and it would take time to heal. Nimrah had been commanded to kill her, but she still blamed herself.

"He left so much behind." Nimrah rolled up the scroll and tossed it onto the desk. "Projects he had yet to finish, unanswered correspondence with his friends across the empire. And it will never be done."

"You were the most important thing to him," Malka said, stepping close. "He knew what he decided to leave all this behind for."

Nimrah slammed her fist on the desk, but her eyes were cloudy. "It should have been me! It should not have been a choice, at all."

Malka had grown used to watching for cracks in Nimrah's restraint, like the tiny whiskers of weeds which grew from breaks in the cobblestone. She'd always wanted to wrap them around her finger and yank, exposing Nimrah's true feelings beneath.

Now she had her honesty. Her truth.

She thought of the words she had thrown at Nimrah days ago, with Nimrah on her knees and a dagger in Malka's hand.

"If I've learned anything about Kefesh, it's that it can be a powerful magic—one that makes you feel like you hold the power of the universe in your hand. But it also draws the line between creation and death in a way that can be dangerous. The Maharal gave everything to create you, but he made mistakes. This was him righting his wrongs."

"I would have died for him."

"And he would have lived a miserable existence afterward. Nimrah, don't forget that he racked himself to find ways to keep you alive when the people of Valón wanted you dead. A father doing everything for his daughter."

Malka wiped away thoughts of Abba. She had Imma and Danya, and that would be enough for her. The Maharal had been Nimrah's family, and he was gone.

Malka moved even closer, and waited a heartbeat for Nimrah to step back, like she had so many times. But Nimrah remained where she was, which Malka took as permission to reach out and curve her hand under Nimrah's elbow.

Nimrah's eyes met hers, and heat crawled up her neck and sullied her cheeks.

Malka smoothed her thumb along Nimrah's flesh forearm, where mangled cuts covered the archbishop's commands.

"What did you do to yourself?"

Nimrah tugged at her arm, but Malka held firm.

"I never want to look upon his commands again," she said fiercely, then eyed the word scarred into Malka's forearm. "I will leave soon, as promised. Chaia has asked me to stay until Sigmund arrives to speak with the court, and then I'll be gone."

Malka breathed, then murmured, "I don't want that."

Nimrah's jaw tightened. "I remember what you said you wanted."

Malka remembered, too. She felt ashamed. Ashamed of the visceral words she had thrown at Nimrah when she was scared. Scared of her joy. Scared of her affection.

"I didn't mean it."

"You must mean it now, after what I have done to you." Nimrah's eyes traveled to Malka's neck. She stared at the bandage, Malka knew, but the heat of her scrutiny still wakened the tendrils of desire in her belly, as Nimrah's eyes followed the cusp of her jaw.

"No."

"Tell me what you want, and I will do it."

She thought of Chaia and Vilém, how their lives together were cut short. She thought of Imma's words. She thought of the magic that lit her soul, which burned brightest when she was honest with herself.

"I want you to hear the truth from me. The truth I've been hiding from myself. The truth of what has grown between us. Out of a deal struck from desperation and a journey of grief and despair, we have made something beautiful. Something I don't want to let die."

Nimrah's blown pupils glittered, like candlelight in the endless dark.

"Something beautiful," Nimrah considered, cupping Malka's jaw. She ran her hand along her throat, careful of the bandage.

"Yes," Malka said, breathless.

Nimrah shook her head, defeated. "I cannot be beautiful for you, Malka."

"You are—"

"You said I was a monster. And you were right. There is nothing holy about the way I think of you. There are only wicked thoughts, which plague me night and day. I think they will plague me until I am dust again."

"Think them now," Malka said. She hardly recognized her own voice, deep and lecherous. "Think them always." She tilted her head and captured Nimrah's lips between hers.

She was warm, so warm. Malka needed her. She needed her like she needed the moonlight to fill her head with dreams, like she needed the crisp air to clear the sleep away from her eyes in the early morning. Like she needed fire in the brutal winter.

Their kiss in the alleyway had been desperate and sloppy with drink, fumbling hands and lips. This was different. They were not hiding now. *Malka* was not hiding now. They didn't need to rush. Not here, not again.

Malka fisted her hands in Nimrah's black doublet. It was warm against her skin. They kissed until it was not enough; until neither of them could bare so many layers of fabric between them.

With a hungry groan, Nimrah swiped her hand across the desk, sending the stationery that had once covered it clattering to the floor. She lifted Malka by her hips and pressed her onto the wood.

Above her, Nimrah's face was cast in sharp blades of light and pools of shadow. The contrast of them, brutal and severe, accentuated the carved stone which gave shape to her nose, chin, and cheekbone. In that moment—

and in all moments hence—it no longer mattered if she were woman or monster.

Malka was desirous for both.

Desperate to bring her closer, Malka wrapped her legs around Nimrah's hips. But Nimrah caught herself with her hands and put space between them.

"You don't have to do this . . . with me. *For me*," Nimrah said hesitantly.

Malka stared at the rawness of her lips, the darkness of the green veins which strained against her neck. She pressed her thumb to Nimrah's plump bottom lip.

"I know," she said. "But I want to, Nimrah. I think I've wanted to for some time."

"Since the alleyway?"

Malka considered. "Maybe before that."

"Since the confessional?"

"I think I have always wanted you. But this is different. Now, I want you the way the Shabhe King wanted his wife, even when he learned of her deceit."

Nimrah smiled devilishly, for it was the same thing she had said to Malka outside of Chaia's house, when she conjured black perphona from the ground.

When they laid themselves bare to each other, clothing strewn on the ground, the room had grown dim. The candles burned low, more wax melted into puddles than left burning. But it was enough. Enough for Nimrah to trace her stone hand down Malka's chest and between her legs, where she circled her finger around Malka's most sensitive part, making her hips buck. Once she was slick and wanting, Nimrah pressed inside.

Malka could not help the sound that escaped her, fervent and breathy, as Nimrah's finger curled.

"Tell me then, Shabhe Queen," Nimrah whispered, her mouth dangerously close to Malka's thigh. "What do you wish from your king?"

It is okay to want someone, Chaia had said to her. Malka hadn't believed her then. Perhaps she did now.

Malka wanted her inscrutable golem; her impossible companion with eyes darker than any night, with skin made from the wretched earth. In this moment, Malka seized what she wanted. She curled her fingers in Nimrah's hair and guided her to the ache between her legs.

The feeling of Nimrah's mouth sent her reeling. It was a kind of magic of its own, the way Malka's words lost to breath as the pressure built inside her. Her moans a prayer, a desperation. Nimrah's sighs against her skin. The cool stone of her chin hard against her softness. The two of them inexorably linked by something greater than them both, yet wholly intimate.

When Malka tipped over the edge, Nimrah's name fell from her lips, and magic sparked beneath her palms.

※

They lay together in Nimrah's small cot, covers tangled between their legs. Malka traced her finger over the stone curve of Nimrah's chin. Nimrah clutched her hand and pressed a kiss to her palm.

Malka smiled, then rolled onto her back, staring at the wooden beams which crisscrossed the curved attic ceiling.

"What are you thinking?" Nimrah asked.

"Do you remember when I told the story of Abayda the Mystic in the woods?" When Nimrah nodded, Malka continued. "All Yosef wanted was a wife, but he still betrayed Yohev for power, when love was at the cusp of his grasp."

A brief silence passed between them, Nimrah considering. "That's one way to interpret the story."

Malka propped herself up on her elbow. Nimrah's breath was hot on her cheek, and she pressed her lips into the curve of Nimrah's neck. "Your interpretation was different. What was it you said, that Abayda chose to take knowledge as his lover instead?"

"That is the tale the Maharal told me. I see why he viewed it that way, knowing how he let his knowledge cloud his judgment."

"I'm learning that stories are not merely stories at all. They are justifications. Ones we tell over and over to understand the decisions we make and those we *will* make."

Nimrah ran a hand through Malka's curls. "Let us tell our own story."

"And what would this story be about?"

"The maiden and her monster," Nimrah declared. "Whose story began in a flesh-eating forest and ended between the sheets of my bed."

"That does not sound like the type of story we should tell," Malka teased.

"We will keep it just for us." Nimrah grasped Malka's hip and drew her closer. "A story left to time."

Malka hummed. What was a myth to her so many weeks ago was now more real than anything she had ever known. The stories of Tzvidi and Yosef painted in a new light now that she herself had commanded the holy magic. Stories she once thought meant to deter her from holding holy magic between her fingers. But perhaps stories did not always have one meaning. Like Nimrah and the Maharal.

Malka wondered what other myths were real. What other stories were given for others to hold close when the world pressed in around them.

But for now, Malka would hold close to her own story, and the myths that were real to her.

"Yes," Malka agreed. "A story left to time."

EPILOGUE

SIX MONTHS LATER

Malka leaned out of her bedroom window and observed the unfurling fingers of dawn, the sun's rays greeting her skin in a warm, tender caress. She cherished the sun's heat after the long, brutal winter.

The gentle warmth made Malka recall Baba's lively disposition. How his stories of the sun would keep her company in the early mornings when she rose before the rest of her family and greeted the cusping brightness. As Imma's apprentice, she had delighted in the opportunity to pluck herbs from the garden before Eskravé awoke and cherished the solitude. The sun was again her company as it splayed across her face and danced along the walls of her bedroom.

"This one is my favorite of hers."

Malka relinquished her spot in the sun. Danya leaned against the doorframe, holding one of Hadar's paper cuttings.

Malka's heart clenched.

Hadar had crafted that paper cutting for Danya's sixteenth birthday. It had hung on the wall of their bedroom since, and the sunlight had paled the colors. But it was still beautiful—blue, white, and gold painted along the border in swirls. Hadar's cuts were messy, her small hands had barely been able to wrap around the knife. Imma had helped her trace Danya's name and portion of the holy scrolls she was to recite at services in messy block letters at the top and bottom of the paper.

Malka remembered how much Danya had stumbled while chanting her portion, unwilling to learn the annotations written into the script. She had been angry at Danya for not caring how she read from the holy scrolls. Not caring if she chanted right, or dipped the consonants deep in her throat, the holy language on her tongue. The holy scrolls were so sacred to her people, and it was a blessing to read from it.

Now, Malka understood it differently. Danya did not follow the rules as closely as Malka or Imma, but she held Yohev close in the way she worried over her family, in the quiet songs she would sing to Hadar when Malka stayed late in Imma's workshop to heal an ailing patient.

How closed-minded Malka had been, to think there was only one way to show faith.

"I want to keep all of her paper cuttings," Malka said, fighting a lump in her throat. "The ones we still have, anyway."

In Evžen's raid, he had ordered all Yahadi treasures worth something to be melted and sold, and the rest destroyed. So many of Hadar's paper cuttings had been torn or burned, ripped where the Yahadi block letters filled the page. Most of them were nothing more than decoration, and a way to celebrate birthdays and holidays, but it did not matter if the holy language of Yohev was traced into the cutting.

Danya buried her face into the crook of Malka's neck. Hot tears fell on her skin. Malka ran her hand through her sister's hair, which she left loose around her shoulders.

"Do you remember when Hadar was just old enough to speak, the one story she always wanted to tell?"

Danya smiled into her neck. "Yes, I do. The Wizard and the Hare. She used to take the broom off its handle and wear it like a wig!"

Malka smiled, immersing herself into the memory. "Imma used to get so upset with her. But she'd take one look at Hadar's round face and her sweet, innocent eyes, and she could hardly stay mad."

Danya pulled back. "Imma sends word by the way." She rustled inside her pocket, pulling out a crumpled piece of parchment, handing it to Malka. "I had Nimrah read it. She should be back in a month's time. It seems like those still infected by the sickness are beginning to heal well."

"That's good," Malka responded, tracing her fingers over the swirling handwriting.

The six months after Sévren's death had been a whirlwind. The duke had arrived in the city with a retinue of his lords while the council voted for the king's dismissal. Prosperity had slowly crept back into the city, Mavetéh no longer draining it of life. The council had determined Valski unfit to rule. Without his son, Valski had no inspiration to stay on the throne and hadn't fought the decision. He had moved from the New Royal Palace to his land in the Orzegali mountains, where he brought a handful of mistresses, servants, and palace staff to run his estate. Sigmund took over as they had planned.

When Malka and Danya journeyed back to Eskravé to finally assess the damage and rebuild, Imma, ever the healer, stayed to treat those recovering from the Mázág sickness. It was the hardest thing Malka could do, leaving Imma again. But she knew any argument would be futile. Imma would not abandon those who needed her most.

Danya continued. "She says the markets are doing better. They are even offering imported spices again now that the economy is improving, and people are no longer hoarding. Eliška is healing well. Even Amnon seems to be doing better in her care, though he still cannot walk for long periods of time."

Imma had diagnosed Amnon with a bone disease. Mavetéh's bite had seeped into his bones and joints, making them brittle and weak.

Malka remembered her last conversation with Amnon before she departed for Eskravé. She had held his hands in hers and declared she could not marry him. That she didn't know what the future held for her and Nimrah, but she couldn't doubt there was something there. *A fire,* she had described to him, *unquenchable by any Kefesh magic.*

"I know, Malka," he admitted. "I saw you sneak away with her the night of Chaia's wedding. I should have known it before. You never did look at me the way you looked at her." He wore a dainty smile on his lips.

"I still love you, Amnon. Very much."

"I know, Malka."

"You are not upset with me?"

"I could never be upset with you," he said. "Just as well." He tapped his cane to the ground. "I need to get used to this new way of living, before I can be a good husband to anyone. I need to learn to be at peace with my body again, the way it is."

Malka studied his cane. "Do you miss who you were, before your sickness?"

Amnon rubbed the stubble at his jaw, considering. "No," he said finally. "Because this is who I have become. This is what it means to stay alive. *To live.* I will learn to live in a different way."

Learning to live in a different way. It wasn't so dissimilar from what they all had to do. To take their heartbreak, their loss, their grief, and learn to live again.

"Things won't ever be the same, will they?" Danya asked, pulling Malka from her memory. Her sister's mind had drifted to the same place.

"No," Malka agreed. "Things will move forward. And we can only choose to ride the wave or be buried under it, lost in a past no longer there, and not as good as we made it out to be."

Danya peered at her, and said affectionately, "You sound like Imma."

Malka tucked a piece of hair behind Danya's ear. "And you look like her."

Someone cleared their throat. Nimrah was standing awkwardly in the doorway.

"Chaia is looking for you both," she said. "She's at the shektal."

Malka squeezed Danya's hand. "Go, I'll be right there."

Danya nodded, raising her eyebrow in warning to Nimrah before she left.

Though months had passed, Malka understood her sister's reluctance toward Nimrah. She had seen only the golem's wreckage.

Malka traced the scar at her neck, like she had many times since it healed. Its curves were familiar now, like any other part of her body. She thought of how many scars Nimrah had left her with—her neck, the carving on her forearm, and perhaps worst of all, on her heart. Each time she looked at Nimrah, she could feel the scar pulse, a dangerous wreck of a thing. And Malka wanted nothing but her.

"Is it bothering you?" Nimrah asked, worriedly gazing at Malka's throat.

"No," Malka said, dropping her hand. "Not any more than the last time you asked."

The wind hummed through the window, blowing at Nimrah's thick mane of hair.

Slowly, carefully, Nimrah settled her fingers on Malka's scar, dragging her thumb over the sharp curve of Malka's jaw. "I will spend eternity wishing away that scar. And I'll spend another eternity repenting for what I did to you."

Malka wrapped her hand around Nimrah's. "I won't. This scar is a reminder of what you overcame. What we overcame together. It shows your strength. Even when the magic that created you was forced into undeserving hands, it did not win. This scar is a reminder of what I've lost, and what gives me hope. I wear it with pride, and I won't have you brooding over it."

"Fine." Nimrah pressed their foreheads together.

"You don't have to go, you know."

Nimrah sighed and pressed a brief kiss to Malka's lips.

Malka groaned in frustration, curling her hands in Nimrah's doublet, and pulling her close.

Nimrah chuckled, but did not give in. Instead, she wove her hand into Malka's hair and pressed her lips to the top of her curls where the kerchief did not cover.

"I want to do this," she said. "The Maharal made me to protect the Yahad, and it is a duty I want to uphold. In his honor, I will go."

Nimrah would be a watchful eye as Ordobav seeped into reformation and prosperity grasped hold of the city. As the remains of the Mázág sickness dredged from its citizens and life began once again under Sigmund's rule. Though the duke had promised safety for the Yahad under his reign, they knew it was far easier to speak pretty words than create swift and lasting action. After all, there was much to gain from forgoing promises. Already, Sigmund had received letters from the aristocracy, who were all too eager to collect on the duke's past promises.

To stop the aristocrats from holding the debts over his head, Sigmund had offered them property in western Ordobav, available to them only when the current residing Yahad had moved or passed on. The landlords had interpreted his promise in a way that most pleased them and used the king's words as permission to forcibly throw out the Yahad currently living in the houses.

Upon hearing this, Nimrah had gone out west, and twisted the landlords' fingers until they could no longer hold a key to unlock their doors. Unused to Nimrah's magic, they had cowered, and spun themselves mad as they screeched to their courtiers to write their objections to the king now that they could not. Nimrah had appeared back in Valón with a vengeance, demanding answers from Sigmund. He had pleaded ignorance, saying he knew not what the lords would do. Unsatisfied, Nimrah had demanded to travel alongside him to make sure the Yahad were not abandoned during his rule.

"A group of Vilém's university advisors are traveling to Lei tomorrow to begin talks about a university exchange, where ideas could be shared across kingdoms. It was, apparently, a project the Maharal and Vilém had begun in the years I was tied to Mavetéh."

Nimrah's voice was sorrowful, but Malka could also see the pride that lingered at the corners of her mouth at the project her master had begun—a seed that would bloom into something beautiful.

"It will bring Valón into a new age," Malka said, rubbing her thumb along Nimrah's arm. "A better age."

"Chaia is coming with me. I think she plans to stay awhile in Lei to get the project on its feet. To honor Vilém."

Malka smiled, swallowing the lump in her throat. She would have to say goodbye to both of them. But Chaia would return to Valón and visit Eskravé often as they rebuilt.

And Nimrah... She would see Nimrah as often as time would allow. With the curse of Mavetéh lifted, it would now only be two days' ride through the forest to get between Valón and Eskravé.

And, maybe, if Malka allowed herself to dream, Nimrah could come home to Malka when the Yahad were no longer in need of their golem.

Valón had slowly welcomed Nimrah back. They began to understand her, and the reason for her creation. She was made to be powerful, as the Maharal intended. But power was hard to contain. And too much of it could turn anyone monstrous. The Maharal, before he died, sent a liturgical poem to the post. It hung all around Valón and was sung in the shul Bachta during services. It told the story of him—the Maharal and his golem; a story of creation and destruction, of the necessity of violence against oppression, and how the golem should be seen as a symbol of hope, not fear. A symbol of what was possible when the Yahad fought back.

Now, to the Ordobavian Yahad, she was more myth than woman. Malka dreamed of the story they would tell once Nimrah could return to her. Stories of the golem of Valón, who swore to protect the Yahad from harm. Duty done, mission finished, she would retire to the attic of the synagogue, where they would say she rested until the Yahad needed her again.

But Malka would know the truth. She would know the golem didn't rest in the synagogue attic, but in her arms, in the home Malka would rebuild for them.

Malka leaned in to capture Nimrah's lips in her own, but Nimrah tilted her head.

"Why won't you kiss me?"

"It will make it harder to leave you."

Malka pressed her leg between Nimrah's thighs, leaning close to her ear to whisper, "What if your Shabhe Queen demands it of you?"

"You know how weak the king is for his wife's requests." Nimrah ran her finger along Malka's lower lip. "Especially when the requests come from such a pretty mouth."

"Let me press it to every part of you, and we'll see how weak you can get."

And Malka did. She kissed her way down Nimrah's neck, across her collarbone and down her arms, where the letters once rooting them to each other protruded, to the slope of her hips.

She pressed her lips between Nimrah's thighs, through the thick fabric of her trousers, but it wasn't enough. She undressed her slowly, as the sun shone on them, and pressed her lips to Nimrah's slick warmth, where she needed to find no other words to speak her affection.

⊻

Malka's heart clenched as she approached the shektal, the memory of the Paja and their threats embedded deep. She stared at the crumbled cobblestone, where Václav had amputated Minton's fingers. Both of them dead now. The shektal had once been a joyous place, the market a vibrant part of Eskravé's livelihood. She hoped it could be again, one day.

Chaia waved her over, where a structure rose from the ground, half built but sturdy. It was not too tall, and not too wide, but enough to cover them when the sun relented to the night's plummy grip.

Malka walked into the structure and pressed her hand to the wood. Vines sprouted from the cracks, and traveled through the planks of their temporary structure, zigzagging to create a shaded reprieve from the elements.

Danya, who had already been inside the structure, dropped to her knees. She ran her hand across one of Hadar's crumpled paper cuttings and pinned it to the wall next to the others. They blew in the wind, the slits of sun falling through the roof casting a warm glow across the art.

There were many times, still, when self-doubt twisted Malka's spells into dust, when the tingling in her palms subsided and she wondered if her faith stretched far enough, if she could hold the prayers tightly in her mouth without feeling imposturous. Being a Yahad could mean so many things. And with that came strength, but also the fear one's kind of faith was not correct, in whatever that way might be. But those moments would pass, and Malka would press her hand to the earth and breathe deep, until the magic filled her lungs, and prayer shaped the words that would bring the world alive.

The Maharal's words drifted back to her, about Kefesh having the power to breathe life into the earth. An idea sparked. Carefully, she pressed the palm of her hand to one of Hadar's paper cuttings. It was the last paper cutting they had made together before the Paja came, with stars and moons and vines wrapped around the Yahadi block letters of *Bayit Ohr*.

She said a soft prayer and watched as vibrant colors washed through the faded paper cutting and the tears mended themselves. Malka gasped as the letters and symbols on the paper livened before her.

Danya's eyes gleamed as she followed the dancing letters of their language. A hand pressed to the small of her back, and Nimrah brushed her lips against the shell of Malka's ear.

The Ozmins had pillaged a great deal. They had converted the gravestones from Yahadi cemeteries into stairs for their churches and melted down Yahadi gold to sell. So much was lost, destroyed, or taken. But Malka still had some of Hadar's paper cuttings, and now they shone in the hut they had built. It was enough. It would always be enough.

She stared at the art before her, glimmering with Yahadi magic. She decided—this was how she'd hold the memory of her people. The memory of her sister. In the palm of her hand, with the power of her religion's prayer in her mouth, surrounded by the people she loved most.

When she fell asleep under the stars, she dreamed of ancient letters dancing through the night sky, stringing together a universe where she could speak to the earth, and the earth would speak back.

AUTHOR'S NOTE

Dear Reader,

Like Malka, I am always thinking about stories. Their formation, how we consume, digest, and regurgitate them. How they are sustenance for hope, while also brandished as weapons. My interest in stories—particularly folklore and fairy tales—began young. I have vivid childhood memories of gathering around a storyteller at synagogue and listening to Jewish folktales told in vibrant recantation, often accompanied with props or song. At the conclusion of each story, the teller would ask us questions and ask for questions in return, a spirited call and response. There was no decisiveness of story, only edifying dissection and curiosity.

This interest in stories stayed with me into adulthood, shaping the course of my postgraduate studies. I became obsessed with the ebb and flow of literature—its revival, its desecration—as befitting the political motivations of the time. Stories shaping narratives shaping stories, repeated indefinitely. My academic focus on history and conflict allowed me to uncover the darker, more sinister underbelly of stories, and how they become tools of identity politics and nationalism. It's this malleability of stories that led me to the Middle Ages, and to the rediscovery of the legend of the golem.

The Middle Ages in Europe was a time rife with antisemitic narratives—from the myth of blood libel to accusations that Jews worked with the devil to carry out the Black Death. Yet, emerging in this period was another story, too: The Golem of Prague.

Birthed from Jewish mythology, the golem's story has seen many variations and interpretations dating back to the Babylonian Talmud. But I grew increasingly interested in this sixteenth-century rendition. The Golem of Prague tells of a rabbi—the Maharal of Prague—creating a lifelike creature from clay (or stone) to protect the Jews from antisemitic attacks. Yet as time passes, this creature, a golem, grows increasingly violent (or in some renditions, they worry the golem *will* grow violent) and the rabbi's forced to lay him to rest in the attic of the Old-New Synagogue in Prague, ready to be awakened again to protect the Jews if needed.

The listener of the story is forced to think: Man or monster? Good or evil? Is violence necessary for peace? Was the rabbi right to create the golem, or did he step too close to divinity's domain? The creation of this legend fashioned a new narrative I wanted to explore in my own way.

While the legend of the Golem of Prague served as great inspiration for *The Maiden and Her Monster,* I have taken many liberties with this tale and its historical context. My hope is that it will exist like many other golemic tales: adhering to the locality of where the story is told. In the case of *The Maiden and Her Monster,* that is a fictional world, with fictional locations, cultures, and characters. While inspired by the history of Jews in medieval Prague, this novel is not an accurate depiction of the time period nor its people. This is also true of the magic system. Kefesh is not meant to be a direct or adequate representation of any method, discipline, or school of thought within Jewish mysticism. Instead, it is drawn from ideas across many forms of early Jewish mysticism, entangling understandings of the earth, creation, and faith. It is one perspective, and it's meant to be vague, because I think it's very Jewish to leave things up for interpretation.

The Maiden and Her Monster was my attempt to preserve a hidden history and explore the danger and resiliency of stories and faith. To tell a story about the Jewish experience that feels both timeless and lost to time. The golem, in the attic of the synagogue, waking once again. Thank you, dear reader, for opening its pages.

ACKNOWLEDGMENTS

Memory, thus storytelling, is a rich part of the Jewish tradition. It's the pleasure of a lifetime to tell this story, inspired by the lush tapestry of Medieval Jewish history in Europe. But I did not get here alone.

I'm so grateful to have a steadfast advocate in my agent, Victoria Marini, and the rest of the team at High Line Literary Collective. Thank you for taking a chance on me and my girls! To my wonderful editors Stephanie Stein and Grace Barber, who both saw straight to the heart of this book and challenged me to make it the best it could be, while showing their love for it at every stage. I could not have asked for a better team. Truly. I pinch myself every day that I get to work with you both.

Thank-you to the rest of the Tor teams for bringing this book to life and getting it into the hands of readers. On the US side: Sanaa Ali-Virani, Greg Collins, Jeff LaSala, Bailey Harrington, Susan Cummins, Rafal Gibek, Steven Bucsok, Jordan Hanley, Khadija Lokhandwala, Saraciea J. Fennell, Michelle Foytek, Erin Robinson, Claire Eddy, Will Hinton, Lucille Rettino, Devi Pillai. On the UK side: Michael Beale, Sian Chilvers, Rebecca Needes, Neil Lang, Natasha Tulett, Lucy Doncaster, Poppy Morris, Mia Lioni.

To Lesley Worrell, for designing, and Christin Engelberth, for illustrating, what is quite literally the cover of my dreams. I'll never get over how beautiful it is!

Much gratitude to Heather Shapiro at Baror International and the foreign rights teams for bringing *The Maiden and Her Monster* around the world. It's beyond my wildest dreams to see this book translated and made more accessible for non-English speaking readers.

I owe so much to my industry friends, who gave constant encouragement, brainstorming, and love when I needed it most. Ysabelle Suarez, Chelsea Abdullah, Melissa Karibian, and Kamilah Cole—I think about the confluence of fate that brought us together and know there must be magic in this world. There are no other words for it. Wen-yi Lee, Tiffany Liu, Sophia Hannan, Birdie Shae, Nadia Noor—thank you for the laughs and laments despite the distance. If we are ever all in the same time zone, it will be a miracle. Bri, Elise, Bailey, El, and the rest of the Reading Space discord, thank you for the company and comradery as I spent many late nights revising, revising, and . . . revising. Laura R. Samotin, Taylor Grothe, K.M. Enright, Betty Hawk and Christina Li, thank you for the lovely, warm welcome to the city (and for the coffee dates and happy hours).

To the authors who took the time to read and blurb this book, I'm forever grateful. I remain constantly in awe of your work and am honored to call you all my colleagues.

It would be remise of me not to thank my public school English teachers, particularly Mr. Breneman and Mrs. Pulido. You both let my creativity roam and flourish during such formative years. Thank you for all you do.

To my friends outside of the publishing world, thank you for being a bright place to go when the tumultuous world of publishing dimmed my light. Sorry I never stop talking about books. Thank you for loving me anyway.

To my small but mighty family—Auntie Faith, Cousin Alice, Ivy, Mom. Mama, I owe everything to you, from my love of reading to my resiliency and determination. You raised me to believe I could do anything, and supported me down whatever path I chose. It's because of you I achieved this dream. I love you so much.

And lastly, to my grandparents. Over the course of working on this book, I lost both of you eight months apart. The grief in these pages is very real to me. But so is the love.

ABOUT THE AUTHOR

Maddie Martinez was born and raised in Albuquerque, New Mexico. She has a BA in political science from Northeastern University in Boston, Massachusetts, and an MA in international peace and conflict resolution from American University in Washington, D.C. You can now find Martinez in New York City, filling her tiny apartment with an unwieldy number of books. *The Maiden and Her Monster* is her first novel.